Delores Fossen, a *USA TODAY* bestselling author, has written over one hundred novels, with millions of copies of her books in print worldwide. She's received a Booksellers' Best Award and an RT Reviewers' Choice Best Book Award. She was also a finalist for a prestigious RITA® Award. You can contact the author through her website at www.deloresfossen.com

Elle James, a *New York Times* bestselling author, started writing when her sister challenged her to write a romance novel. She has managed a full-time job and raised three wonderful children, and she and her husband even tried ranching exotic birds (ostriches, emus and rheas). Ask her, and she'll tell you what it's like to go toe-to-toe with an angry 350-pound bird! Elle loves to hear from fans at ellejames@earthlink.net or ellejames.com

Also by Delores Fossen

Also by Elle James

Discover more at millsandboon.co.uk

A THREAT TO HIS FAMILY

DELORES FOSSEN

TACTICAL FORCE

ELLE JAMES

MILLS & BOON

First Published in Great Britain 2020
by Mills & Boon, an imprint of HarperCollins*Publishers*
1 London Bridge Street, London, SE1 9GF

A Threat to His Family © 2019 Delores Fossen
Tactical Force © 2019 Mary Jernigan

ISBN: 978-0-263-28013-5

0120

MIX
Paper from
responsible sources
FSC™ C007454

This book is produced from independently certified FSC™
paper to ensure responsible forest management.

For more information visit: www.harpercollins.co.uk/green

Printed and bound in Spain
by CPI, Barcelona

A THREAT TO
HIS FAMILY

DELORES FOSSEN

Chapter One

Deputy Owen Slater knew something was wrong the moment he stopped his truck in front of his house.

There were no lights on, not even the ones on the porch or in the upstairs window of the nursery. It was just a little past eight and that meant it was his daughter Addie's bedtime, but she always slept with the lamp on.

If the electricity had gone off, the nanny, Francine Landry, would have almost certainly texted Owen to let him know. Besides, Owen had already spotted a light in the barn. That wasn't unusual since the light was often left on there, but it meant the power definitely wasn't out.

Because he was both a father and a cop, the bad thoughts came and his pulse kicked up hard and fast. Something had maybe gone wrong. Over the years, he'd made plenty of arrests, and it could be that someone wanted to get back at him. A surefire way to do that was to come here to his home, to a place where he thought he and his child were safe.

The panic came, shooting through him when he thought of his daughter being in danger. Addie was only eighteen months old, just a baby. He'd already lost her mother in childbirth and he couldn't lose Addie, too.

That got Owen drawing his gun as he started running. He fired glances all around him in case this was an ambush, but no one came at him as he barreled up the porch steps.

Hell.

The front door was slightly ajar. That was another indication that something wasn't right. Francine always kept things locked up tight now that Addie was walking and had developed some escape skills.

Owen didn't call out to Francine, something he desperately wanted to do with the hope he'd hear her say that everything was okay. But if he called out, it could alert someone other than the nanny. Still, he prayed that she would come rushing in to give him some account for what was happening. But no good explanation came to mind.

Owen tried to rein in his heartbeat and breathing. Hard to do, though, when the stakes were this high, but he forced himself to remember his training and experience. That meant requesting backup before he started a search of the area. He quickly texted his brother Kellan to get there ASAP so he'd have some help if needed.

The tight knot in Owen's gut told him it would be needed.

And Kellan was the best backup Owen could ask for. Not only was he the sheriff of their hometown of Longview Ridge, he lived just two miles away. Kellan could be there in no time.

Using his elbow, Owen nudged the door open all the way and glanced around. His house had an open floor plan, so with a single sweeping glance, he could take in the living room, kitchen and dining area. Or at least he could have done that had it not been so blasted dark.

There were way too many shadows. Too many places for someone to hide.

Owen flipped the light switch. Nothing. That snowballed the wildfire concerns because it meant someone could have cut off the power to the house. He doubted this was some kind of electric malfunction because if it had been, Francine would have gotten out the candles and flashlights since she was well aware of Addie's fear of the dark.

Even though his brother would be here in minutes, Owen didn't want to wait for him. The thought of his baby hurt and scared got him moving. With a two-handed grip on his gun, he checked behind the sofa, making sure he continued to keep watch. No one was there, so he moved to the dining room. Still no one.

But he heard something.

There were footsteps upstairs. Not Addie's toddling feet, either. These were heavy and slow, probably the way his own steps would sound if he were up there looking around. Owen turned to head in that direction in case it was Francine, but that was when he noticed the back door was open, too. And there were sounds coming from the yard.

"Shh," someone whispered. "We need to play the quiet game."

Because the voice was so ragged, it took Owen a moment to realize it was Laney Martin, his ranch manager. That sent him hurrying straight to the door, and he saw Laney running toward the barn. She had Addie clutched to her chest, her hand cupping the back of the baby's head.

Owen didn't call out to them, but he did catch a glimpse of Laney's face as they ducked into the barn.

She was terrified. He hadn't needed anything to up his own level of fear, but that did it. He ran across the yard and went straight into the barn. He heard another sound. Laney's sharp gasp.

"It's me," Owen whispered just in case she thought it was someone else who'd followed them in there.

Laney had already moved to the far corner of the barn next to a stack of hay bales. When she shifted her position, Owen could see his baby's face. Addie was smiling as if this were indeed a fun game. It was good that she was too young to realize the danger they were in.

"Where's Francine?" he asked. "Is she in the house?"

Laney shook her head. "The nursing home called about her mom a half hour ago." While her voice was level enough for him to understand her, each word had come through her panting breaths. "Francine asked me to watch Addie while she went over there to check on her."

Francine's mom had dementia so it wasn't unusual for the nanny to get calls about her. However, this was the first time she'd left Addie with Laney. Maybe, though, Francine had done that because she'd known Owen would soon be home.

An intruder who'd been watching the place would have known that, too.

"Who's in the house?" he asked.

Another head shake from Laney. "A man."

Not that he needed it, but Owen had more confirmation of the danger. He saw that Laney had a gun, a small snub-nosed .38. It didn't belong to him, nor was it one that he'd ever seen in the guesthouse where Laney was staying. Later, he'd ask her about it, about why she hadn't mentioned that she had a weapon, but for now they obviously had a much bigger problem.

Owen texted this brother again, to warn him about the intruder so that Kellan didn't walk into a situation that could turn deadly. He also asked Kellan to call in more backup. If the person upstairs started shooting, Owen wanted all the help he could get.

"What happened?" Owen whispered to Laney.

She opened her mouth, paused and then closed it as if she'd changed her mind about what to say. "About ten minutes ago, I was in the kitchen with Addie when the power went off. A few seconds later, a man came in through the front door and I hid in the pantry with her until he went upstairs."

Smart thinking on Laney's part to hide instead of panicking or confronting the guy. But it gave Owen an uneasy feeling that Laney could think that fast under such pressure. And then there was the gun again. Where had she gotten it? The guesthouse was on the other side of the backyard, much farther away than the barn. If she'd gone to the guesthouse to get the gun, why hadn't she just stayed there with Addie? It would have been safer than running across the yard with the baby.

"Did you get a good look at the man?" Owen prompted.

Laney again shook her head. "But I heard him. When he stepped into the house, I knew it wasn't you, so I guessed it must be trouble."

Again, quick thinking on her part. He wasn't sure why, though, that gave him a very uneasy feeling.

"I didn't hear or see a vehicle," Laney added.

Owen hadn't seen one, either, which meant the guy must have come on foot. Not impossible, but Owen's ranch was a good half mile from the main road. If this was a thief, he wasn't going to get away with much. Plus, it would be damn brazen of some idiot to break into a cop's home just to commit a robbery.

So what was really going on?

Owen glanced around the barn, also keeping watch on the yard in case the intruder followed them out here. Part of him wanted that to happen so he could make the piece of dirt pay for putting Addie and Laney through this.

There were no ranch hands around that he could see. Not a surprise. He ran a small operation and only had three full-time hands and Laney, who managed the place. Other than Laney, none of the others lived on the grounds. Not even Francine, since she had her own house only a couple of miles away.

He glanced at the light switch and considered turning it off, but that might only make things worse. If the intruder saw it, he would know they were in the barn, and he might come out there with guns blazing.

Owen's phone dinged with a text message from Kellan.

I'm here, parked just up the road from your truck. Where is he?

Owen texted back.

Still in the house, I think.

But the moment he fired off the message, Owen saw something in the back doorway of the house. The moonlight glinted off metal and he caught a glimpse of the gun. That confirmed his worst fears, though he couldn't actually see the person holding the weapon. That was because he was likely dressed in all black and staying in the shadows.

Owen ducked back to avoid the barn light. That light probably helped Addie since she wasn't fretting as she usually did in the dark, but it might seem like a beacon to some thug looking to start trouble.

"Stay down," Owen instructed Laney. "I'll see if I can draw this guy out into the open—"

"You could be shot," she said before he even finished, her voice shaking.

Yeah, he could be, but if anyone was going to become a target, Owen wanted it to be him. He didn't want any shots fired into the barn or anywhere near Addie.

He texted Kellan to let him know that he was about to head out the back of the barn. He could then use the corral fence and nearby shrubs for cover to circle around the house.

Keep watch of the front, Owen added to the text.

He didn't intend to let this joker get away. He wanted to know who he was and why he'd broken in.

Owen eased the barn door shut and moved a saddle in front of it to block it. It wouldn't stop anyone for long, which was why he had to hurry. He ran to the back of the barn and climbed out through the opening sometimes used to push hay into the corral. When his feet hit the ground, he took a quick look around him.

No one.

No sounds, either. If the intruder was coming their way, he was being quiet about it. Owen tried to do the same as he made his way to the front side of the barn to take a look at the back porch.

Owen cursed.

The guy with the gun was no longer in sight, but the door was still open. Maybe he'd stepped back into the shadows to look for them. But that didn't make sense, either. By now, the intruder must have spotted Owen's truck, which was rigged with a police siren, and would have known that he had called for backup. That meant he possibly could have already fled the scene.

His phone dinged again with a text message. Owen was about to look down at the screen when he heard a sound he didn't want to hear.

A gunshot cracked through the air.

It didn't go into the part of the barn where Laney and Addie were, thank God, but it did slam into the wood right next to where Owen was standing. That forced him to move back. And to wait. He didn't have to wait long. However, this time it wasn't another shot. It was a man's voice.

"Elaine?" a man yelled. "I know you're out there."

Owen had no idea who this Elaine was, so maybe this was a case of the thug showing up at the wrong place.

Except, wasn't Laney a nickname for Elaine?

Was this man someone from Laney's past? Maybe an old boyfriend who'd come to settle a score?

If so, she'd never mentioned it and nothing had shown up about relationship issues in the background check he'd run on her, and he'd been pretty darn thorough since Laney would be living so close to Addie and him. While he continued to volley glances all around him, Owen checked his phone screen and saw the text from Kellan.

I'm moving to the right side of your house.

Good. There was a door there, just off the playroom. Maybe Kellan would be able to slip into the house and get a look at this guy. Or, better yet, arrest him.

"I'm Deputy Owen Slater," Owen called out. "Put down your weapon and come out with your hands up."

It was something that, as a cop, Owen needed to say. He had to identify himself in the hope it would cause the idiot to surrender. Of course, it was just as likely to cause him to fire more shots. If he did, Owen would be justified in using deadly force.

But no other shots. Just another shout.

"Elaine?" the man yelled again.

Owen used the sound of the man's voice to try to pinpoint his location. He was definitely no longer by the back door. Nowhere near it. This guy was in the guesthouse, where Laney lived. How he'd gotten there, Owen didn't know, but it was possible that he'd climbed through a window.

Since the intruder was now on the same side of the yard as Owen, it made him an easy target, and that was why he hurried back into the barn. He glanced at Laney. Or rather, where he'd last seen Addie and her, but Laney had moved a few feet. She had positioned herself behind the hay bales and was using one as support for her shooting hand.

"Where's the baby?" Owen immediately asked.

"On the floor behind me. She's playing with my necklace. I wanted to be between the door and her in case… Well, just in case," Laney added.

Just in case wasn't looking very good right now. But at least they were all still safe. He heard Addie then, and she wasn't fussing. It was more of a cooing babble, so the necklace must have been holding her attention.

"Elaine?" the man called out. He had moved since his last shout, but Owen wasn't sure to where. He also wasn't sure of Laney's reaction.

The color had blanched from her face and he didn't think it was because of the danger. Owen didn't have to be a cop to figure out what that meant.

"You know this guy," he said.

She didn't deny it, causing Owen to curse under his breath.

"What does he want with you?" Owen demanded.

She didn't get a chance to answer him because the man shouted again. "Elaine, let's do this the easy way. Come out now and leave with me, and no one will get hurt."

Hell. There was a good bit of anger now mixed with fear for his daughter. Anger that this thug would try to bargain like this. No way was Owen going to let Laney leave with a man who'd just fired a shot at him.

"Watch out!" someone yelled. Not the thug this time. It was Kellan. "He's coming right at you."

That wasn't the only thing that came, either. There was a gunshot, quickly followed by another one. From the sound of it, the second shot had come from a different weapon.

Maybe Kellan's.

Owen hoped it had anyway. Because he didn't like the odds if this intruder had brought his own version of backup with him.

He debated opening the barn door so he could help his brother, but since this guy was likely coming for them, Owen's top priority was to make sure that Addie was protected. He hurried to Laney and Addie, standing guard in front of them and waiting for whatever was about to happen.

Owen didn't have to wait long. Someone kicked the barn door hard, and bits of wood went flying. The saddle shifted, too, and Owen steeled himself to fire. He was about to do that when he got a glimpse of the person who'd just broken down the door. The man, dressed in black, took aim at them. However, before Owen could pull the trigger, shots blasted through the barn.

Laney had fired.

And she hadn't missed.

The bullets, first one and then the other, slammed into the man's chest and he dropped to the ground like a stone. If he wasn't dead, he soon would be, because he was already bleeding out.

Addie started to cry so Owen hurried to her. The relief came flooding through him because his baby was okay. She hadn't been hurt.

He didn't scoop her up into his arms, something he desperately wanted to do. First, he had to wait for the all clear from Kellan, and that might take a couple of minutes. In the meantime, Owen would need to hold his position. However, that didn't stop him from asking one critical question.

Owen's eyes narrowed when he looked at Laney. "Start talking. Who the heck are you?"

Chapter Two

From the moment this nightmare had started, Laney had known that question—and many more—would come from Owen.

Who the heck are you?

No way would Owen Slater just let something like this go. Of course, he probably thought her answer would help him understand this mess. It wouldn't. In fact, it was going to make things even worse.

At least he and Addie hadn't been hurt. And the toddler was so young that she hopefully wouldn't remember anything about this attack. However, the assault would stay with Owen for the rest of his life, and Laney was never going to be able to forgive herself for allowing things to come to this.

Sweet heaven. She could have gotten them killed.

With his scalpel-sharp glare, Owen reminded her that he was well aware of that, too. In fact, the only reason he likely didn't take Addie from Laney when she picked up the baby was that he needed to keep his shooting hand free in case someone else fired at them.

She glanced at the man she'd just shot. Who the heck was he? How had he known who she was? And why had he done this? He hadn't given her any choice, but it still twisted away at her. A man was dying or already dead because of her. And worse, this wasn't over. If she'd managed to somehow keep him alive, he might have been coerced into telling her who'd put him up to this, but she'd had no choice but to take that shot.

"Who are you?" Owen repeated.

Judging from the tone and his intense glare, he no longer trusted her. Good. Because Laney didn't trust herself.

It crushed her to have it all come to this. She'd thought she was safe, that Addie and Owen would be safe, too. Obviously she'd brought her fight right to their doorstep.

"I was Elaine Pearce," she said, speaking around the lump in her throat, "but I changed my name to Laney Martin."

Of course, that explanation was just the tip of the iceberg. Owen would demand to know about not only the name change, but also how it connected to the dead man. And how it connected to this attack.

Owen sent a text to someone. Probably to one of his fellow deputies to do a quick background check on Elaine Pearce. It was what Laney would have done had their positions been reversed.

"I want you to put your gun on the hay bale," he instructed. He sounded like a cop now, and he looked at her as if she were a criminal.

Laney did exactly as he said, knowing the gun would be taken as part as of the evidence in what was now a crime scene. An investigation would quickly follow, which meant she'd be questioned and requestioned. Soon, everyone in town would know who she was, and she'd be in more danger than she already was. That was why she had to figure a way out of here—fast.

"Elaine Pearce," he repeated. "And you didn't think that was something I should know?" Owen grumbled. "You didn't bother to mention that you weren't who you were claiming to be?"

"No." Laney took another deep breath. "I thought I'd find the info that I needed and be out of here before anything could happen."

"You were obviously wrong about that." He gave a disapproving grunt and went to the man, kicking his gun farther away from where it had fallen from the shooter's hand. Owen then touched his fingers to the guy's neck.

"Dead," Owen relayed as he did a quick search of the guy's pockets. Nothing. Of course, he hadn't expected a hired gun to bring an actual ID with him.

"You recognize him?" Owen asked.

Laney somehow managed to stand upright, though every part of her was trembling. She also moved closer to Owen and then made another quick check on Addie. The little girl's cries were already starting to taper off, but she'd obviously been frightened by the noise of the gunshots.

A muscle tightened in Owen's jaw and, though Laney hadn't thought it possible, his steel-gray eyes narrowed even more when he glared at her. He made a circling motion with his index finger for her to continue, but before Laney even had the chance to do that, his phone rang. She saw his brother's name on the screen. In the months that she'd been working for Owen, she'd met Kellan several times and knew he lived close by. She had figured Owen had called him or their other brothers for backup.

"This conversation isn't over," Owen assured her as he hit the answer button on his phone. He didn't put the call on speaker, but Laney was close enough to hear Kellan's voice.

"There's a second intruder," Kellan blurted out, causing a chill to ripple through her.

Laney hurried back to Addie and pulled the little girl into her arms. Because of her position, she could no longer hear what Kellan was saying. But judging from the way Owen's gaze fired around, he, too, was bracing himself for another attack. He didn't stay on the phone long and, once he was finished with his conversation, maneuvered himself in front of them.

"The second guy was in the guesthouse," Owen told her. "He ran into the woods across the road. Kellan and Gunnar are searching for him now and they've called Dispatch for more backup."

Gunnar was Deputy Gunnar Pullam, someone else that Laney had seen around town. Like Owen, he was an experienced lawman. Something they needed right now. Maybe they'd find the second man and stop him from circling back to try to kill them again. The thought didn't help with her heartbeat, which was already thudding out of control. Addie must have picked up on that, too, because she started to whimper again. Laney began to rock her.

"Kellan said the second man had something with him when he ran out of the guesthouse," Owen went on. "A bag, maybe." His back was to her now, but she didn't need to see his face to know he was still glaring. "Any idea what he took?"

Laney's thoughts were all over the place as she tried to fight off the panic, but it didn't take her long to come up with an answer. "Maybe my toothbrush or something else with my DNA on it. Something to prove who I am."

Other than changing her hair and wearing colored contacts, she hadn't altered her appearance that much. If they'd looked closely enough, whoever was after her could have recognized her from old photos she was certain were still out there on the web. But a hired gun would have wanted some kind of proof to give to his boss and DNA would have done it.

That didn't feel right, though.

She fought through the whirlwind of thoughts and spiked adrenaline, and remembered that one of the intruders had called her by her real name. Elaine. And the one she'd killed had come into the barn to either take her with him or gun her down. So maybe they hadn't been looking for someone to prove who she was. Maybe they'd been after something else in the guesthouse and the man she'd shot had been just a distraction for his partner.

"My laptop," she added on a rise of breath. Though everything on it was password protected or stored on a cloud with several layers of security, a good hacker would be able to find what she had there.

"Keep talking," Owen ordered her while he continued volleying glances between the front door and the window at the back. "Why'd you lie to me about who you were?"

Again, this would only lead to more questions, but she doubted that she could stall Owen, especially since the sense of danger was still so thick around them.

"I lied because I didn't want anyone, including you,

to know my real identity." Laney paused when her breath suddenly became very thin. "I'm working on an investigation, and the clues led me here to Longview Ridge."

Owen pulled back his shoulders. "Are you a cop?"

"A private investigator."

Owen growled out some profanity under his breath and looked as if he wanted to do more than growl it. He'd kept it quiet, no doubt because his daughter was right there, but thankfully Addie was falling asleep, her head now resting on Laney's shoulder.

"So, you're a PI and a liar," Owen rumbled. Obviously he didn't think much of either. "I obviously missed way too much about you when I did your background check. And now you've put my little girl, me and now Gunner and my brother in danger."

Yes. She'd done all of those things and more. "I'm investigating Emerson Keaton."

She saw the brief moment of surprise, followed by a new round of silent profanity that went through his eyes. "My brother-in-law. Addie's uncle."

Laney could add another mental *yes* to that. Emerson was indeed both of those things, along with being the town's district attorney. She was also convinced that he had a fourth label.

Killer.

Of course, there was no way Owen would believe that, and she wasn't going to be able to convince him of it now. Laney couldn't blame him for his doubts. Nearly everything she'd told him had been a lie, including the résumé and references she'd manufactured to get this job.

Owen's intense stare demanded that she continue even though they obviously still had to keep watch.

"Seven months ago, my half sister was murdered. Hadley Odom." Laney had said Hadley's name around the thick lump in her throat. "We were close."

Not a lie. They had been, despite the different ways they'd chosen to live their lives.

"What the heck does your half sister's murder have to do with Emerson?" Owen snapped.

"Everything," Laney managed to say, and she repeated it to give herself some extra time to gather her words and her breath. "Hadley and Emerson had an affair."

"Emerson?" Owen challenged when she paused. There was a bucket of skepticism in his tone. With good reason. Emerson was the golden boy of Longview Ridge. He had a beautiful wife, two young kids and a spotless reputation. "I've known Emerson my whole life, and there's never been a hint of him having an affair."

"He and Hadley kept it secret. Not just for Emerson's sake but for Hadley's. Hadley and I had the same mother, but her father, my stepfather, wouldn't have approved." Actually, Laney hadn't approved, either, but it was impossible to sway Hadley once she'd had her mind set on something.

Owen stayed quiet for a moment, his expression hard, ice-cold. "You have proof of this?"

"I heard Hadley talking to him on the phone, and I saw them together once when they were at a restaurant."

Of course, that wasn't proof she thought Owen was just going to accept. And she was right. Owen's scowl only worsened.

"Hadley told me they were having an affair." She spelled it out for him. "She also told me that she got very upset when he broke things off with her. In anger, Hadley threatened to tell his wife and, less than twelve hours later, she was dead."

"And you think Emerson killed her." It wasn't a question.

Owen wasn't believing any of this. Neither had anyone else she'd told, but Laney had plenty of proof that she was pushing the wrong buttons with her investigation.

She tipped her head to the dead man. "He came here after me. Why else would he do that if I weren't getting close to proving what Emerson did?"

Owen didn't roll his eyes, but it was close. Then he huffed, "If you're really a PI as you say you are, then I suspect you've riled some people. You've certainly done that to me."

"Yes, but you don't want me dead. Emerson does."

However, she had to mentally shake her head. Someone wanted to kill her and the most obvious suspect was the one she was investigating. But there was someone else and her expression must have let Owen know that.

"Remembering something else?" Owen snapped.

No way did she want to lie to him again, but before Laney could even begin to answer him, she heard footsteps outside the barn. That gave her another shot of adrenaline and she crouched again with Addie.

"It's me," someone said.

Kellan.

Not the threat her body had been geared up to face. However, like Owen, Kellan was scowling when he came into the barn. He glanced at his brother and niece.

Then at the dead man. Then at Laney. She didn't think it was her imagination that she got the brunt of the scowl he was doling out.

"We got the second intruder," Kellan explained. "He's alive."

Laney released the breath she hadn't even known she'd been holding. "Who is he?" she blurted. "Has he said anything?"

"Oh, he's talking a lot," Kellan grumbled. "He's demanding to see you. He says he's a friend of yours, that you're the one who hired him."

"No." Laney couldn't deny that fast enough. "He's lying."

Judging from the flat look Kellan gave her, he wasn't buying it. Apparently, neither was Owen because he walked closer and took Addie from her. He immediately moved next to his brother.

"There's more," Kellan added a moment later. "The intruder says that you hired him to kill Owen."

Chapter Three

Owen hadn't wanted to spend half the night in the sheriff's office, where he spent most of his days, but he hadn't had a choice. This was not just a simple B and E, and with the shooting death of one of the intruders, it was a tangled mess.

One not likely to be resolved before morning.

That was because Laney had denied hiring the intruder, and the intruder was insisting he was telling the truth. That put them at a temporary stalemate. Or at least it would have if Owen had any faith in the intruder. Hard to trust someone who'd come to his home and broken in while his baby daughter had been there. Of course, the reason the intruder had come was Laney.

That meant this was another stalemate.

One that he hoped to break soon.

There was an entire CSI team going through his place, which meant he wouldn't be going home tonight. The only silver lining was that Francine had taken Addie to her place. Not alone, either. Owen had sent Gunnar with them just case this "mess" got another layer to it with a second attack.

In the meantime, Owen had been in the mind-set of collecting as much information as he could through phone conversations and emails. He hadn't done all of that under Laney's watchful eyes and alert ears, either. He'd left her in his office for some of those calls and was now trying to process everything he'd learned.

Laney hadn't been idle, either. She'd made a call, too. With a cheap, disposable cell phone, he'd noticed. And Owen had made sure he kept his ears alert during her conversation. She'd spoken to someone she called Joe and told him to be careful.

That was it.

The chat had lasted less than five seconds and then Laney had immediately surrendered the phone to Owen. Not that it had been of any use to him since Joe hadn't answered when Owen had tried to call him. Laney had briefly—*very briefly*—explained that Joe Henshaw was her assistant, and that she didn't know where he was. Neither did Owen or the San Antonio cops helping him look for the guy.

"I didn't hire that man to kill you," Laney repeated when Owen finished his latest call, this one to the medical examiner.

Declaring and redeclaring her innocence was something Laney had been going on about during the entire five hours they'd been there. He suspected she would continue to go on about it until the intruder either recanted or Kellan and he were indeed able to prove that he was lying.

Owen figured proving it wouldn't be that hard.

However, they couldn't even start doing that because the guy had lawyered up and they now had to wait for the attorney to arrive from San Antonio. Until then, they were holding not only the intruder but also Laney. Owen had not yet decided if she was a suspect, but he was pretty sure Laney—or rather Elaine—was going to be the key to them figuring out what the hell was going on.

"The guy you shot and killed was Harvey Dayton," Owen told her. He'd just gotten the ID during his call with the ME. "Ring any bells?"

"No," she answered without hesitation. "And I'm sure I've never seen him before, either. His prints were in the system," Laney added in a mutter. "That's how you got the ID this fast?"

He nodded. "Dayton had a record," Owen settled for saying.

What he didn't spell out for her was that the rap sheet was a mile long, and yeah, it included a couple of assault charges with a pattern of escalating violence. Along with a history of drug use, which made him a prime candidate for becoming a hired gun for people who wanted cheap help.

"Did Dayton say what he took from the guesthouse?" Laney asked.

Good question because, other than a gun, Dayton hadn't had anything on him when Kellan and Gunnar had found him. The CSIs would search the area, but Dayton had been captured by the road, a good quarter mile from Owen's ranch. There was no telling where he'd put whatever it was he'd taken.

"Your laptop is missing," Owen added, and he instantly saw the frustration and anger in her eyes.

"I keep copies of my files in online storage," she said with a heavy sigh. "But everything was also on my hard drive. It means whoever took it won't have trouble accessing everything."

Later, he'd want to know more about exactly what was on it. For now, Owen went with giving her more info that would then lead to more questions. Hopefully, more answers, too. "Your toothbrush was there, so that axes your DNA theory. Your purse was open, and your wallet and cell phone were gone. No jewelry around, either, so if you had any—"

"The only jewelry I have is this." Laney touched her fingers to the gold dragonfly necklace that she'd gotten back from Addie. There was also a small key on the chain. "It was a gift from my sister." She paused. "You really think the motive for this was robbery?"

"No." Owen didn't have to think about that.

The gunman had called her by name and come to the barn. Plus, nothing was missing from his house. If this had been a robbery, they would have taken his wallet and anything else of value. They also would have had a vehicle stashed nearby, and so far, one hadn't turned up.

"And the second man, the one who's lying about me, any ID on him yet?" she queried.

"Rohan Gilley." Owen watched for any signs of recognition.

She repeated the name several times, the way a person would when they were trying to jog their memory. But then Laney shook her head. "He had a record, too?"

Owen settled for a nod. Gilley's rap sheet was almost identical to Dayton's, just slightly shorter. They'd even served time together.

"Gilley's lying to save his hide," Laney grumbled. "Or because someone put him up to it." She added some muttered profanity to go along with that.

The last five hours hadn't improved her mood much. She was just as wired as she had been during the attack. At least, though, she wasn't trembling now. For reasons he didn't want to explore, the trembling got to

Owen, and right now the only thing he wanted to feel for this woman was the cool indifference he felt toward anyone who'd been involved in any way with a crime.

But indifference was impossible.

If she was telling the truth about not hiring Gilley—and he believed that she was—then that meant she was a victim, one who'd saved his daughter by getting her out of harm's way. Hard for something that big not to be on the proverbial table.

Laney's tough exterior, or rather the front she'd tried to put on for him, cracked a little. She didn't go back to trembling, but it was close, and before she could gather her composure, he caught another glimpse of nerves.

Big ones.

She was a PI—he'd confirmed that—but this could have been the first time she'd actually been in the middle of an attack. Maybe the first time she had been a target, too.

Along with having a good aim, she had an athletic build and was on the petite side, only about five-three.

And attractive.

Something he hated that he noticed, but it was impossible to miss. Being a widower hadn't made him blind. However, he still had plenty of common sense that reminded him that Laney had way too many secrets behind those cool blue eyes.

"The CSIs found a jammer," Owen went on a moment later. "That's how Dayton and or Gilley cut off the electricity."

She stayed quiet for a moment. "That proves I'm innocent. I wouldn't have needed to jam the power since I was already in the house." Her eyes widened. "Did you check to make sure Francine really had an emergency? Those men wanted me there, and they could have tricked Francine into leaving."

At least Laney wasn't accusing the nanny of any wrongdoing, but it was a clever observation. An accurate one, too. "The call from the nursing home was bogus." Of course, Francine hadn't learned that until she'd gotten there to check on her mom. By then, the attack at the ranch had already been in progress.

"More proof," Laney said under her breath. She looked up, her eyes meeting his. "If I wanted you dead, I wouldn't have kept Addie there. I would have told Francine I couldn't watch the girl so that Francine would have had to take Addie with her."

That was the way Owen had it figured, too, which was why he was leaning toward the conclusion that Laney was innocent. Of the attack anyway. But there was a boatload of other troubling concerns here. Not just the lies that she'd told him about her identity and work résumé, but there was also the problem with the accusation about Emerson.

"Go back over what you told me in the barn," Owen insisted. "Tell me about your half sister's murder."

This would be a third round of Laney doing that, but thanks to an emailed report he'd gotten from the San Antonio PD in the past hour, Owen knew that Hadley's death had indeed been ruled a murder. She'd died from blunt-force trauma to the head. No eyewitnesses, no suspects. Well, no official suspects for SAPD. Laney clearly felt differently about that.

"Hadley and Emerson had an affair." Laney stared at him. "I'm not going to change my story, no matter how many times you have me repeat it."

That was what he figured, but this was another

square filler, like calling out his identity to the intruder. It was especially necessary because she'd lied to him about who she was.

Something that still riled him to the core.

Hell, here he was a cop, and he hadn't known one of his employees was living under an alias. Of course, there was no way he would have hired her had he known who she was and what she was after. That got Owen thinking—exactly what was she after anyway?

"Did you think I was covering up about my brother-in-law?" he asked.

"Yes." Her answer came quickly, causing him to huff. If she truly believed Emerson had murdered her sister, then she'd just accused Owen of assorted felonies by not reporting the crime and obstructing justice. An accusation she must have realized because her gaze darted away. "I know you're close to him."

Yeah, he was. Emerson had helped him get through Naomi's death. Those days had been so dark, Owen would have slid right down into the deepest, darkest hole if it hadn't been for Addie and Emerson.

Of course, Emerson had been grieving, too, since he'd lost his only sister that day. Naomi and Emerson had been close, and while Owen didn't have the deep connection with Emerson that Naomi had, Owen respected the man, especially after Naomi's death when Emerson and he had been drawn together in grief. Maybe "misery loves company" had worked for both of them. Though there were times when Owen wondered if anything had actually worked. The grief could still slice through him.

"Tell me why you think Emerson killed Hadley,"

Owen demanded. "And stick to only what you can prove. Gut feelings don't count here."

Her mouth tightened a little. "Hadley told me it got ugly when her relationship with Emerson was over. Like I said, she threatened to tell his wife, and then Emerson threatened her. He said he'd hurt her if she didn't keep her mouth shut."

Emerson could have a hot head. Owen had even been on the receiving end of one of his punches in high school when they'd disagreed over the score in a pick-up basketball game. But it was a big stretch to go from a punch to hurting a woman, much less killing her.

"That isn't proof," Owen quickly pointed out. "It's hearsay."

Laney didn't dodge his gaze this time. "I have pictures."

That got his attention. There'd been nothing about that in the police report. "Pictures?" he challenged.

She nodded. "Of Emerson and Hadley together." Another pause, then she mumbled something he didn't catch. "Hadley told me about them and said she kept them in a safe-deposit box."

Owen wasn't sure what to react to first. That there could be pictures or that this was the first he was hearing about it. "And you didn't bother to tell the cops that?" he snarled.

"I did tell them, but I didn't know where they were. Hadley hadn't given me the name of the bank where she had the box." Her forehead bunched up. "I didn't ask, either, because I didn't know how important those pictures were going to become."

"They still might not be important. If the photos exist, they could possibly be proof of an affair and nothing more." Though it twisted at his insides to think Emerson could have cheated on his wife.

Laney made a sound of disagreement. "They're important. Because they're the first step in proving that Emerson carried through on his threat to hurt her."

Owen glanced at the key on the chain around her neck and groaned. "That's for the safe-deposit box?"

Her response wasn't so quick this time. "Yes, I believe it is. And I'll give it to the cops when I find out which bank has the photos. By cops, I mean the San Antonio Police, not anyone who has a personal connection to Emerson."

Of course. Laney wouldn't trust him with the key because she believed he would tip off Emerson. Or destroy the pictures.

He wouldn't.

If Owen did find something like that, he would do his job. But he doubted he could convince Laney of that. Doubted, too, that he could convince her of anything else right now.

"If there are photos and a safe-deposit box, they could be anywhere," he pointed out. "You need help finding them... Joe Henshaw's helping you with that."

She nodded. "He's a PI, too, and we became friends in a grief support group. He lost both his parents when they were murdered. Sorry," Laney added.

The apology was no doubt because his father had been murdered, too, about a year ago, not long after Owen had lost his wife. His father had been gunned down by an unknown perp who was still out there. Owen had hope, though, that the case would be solved since they had an eyewitness. Too bad the witness had received a head injury and couldn't remember squat about what had happened. But maybe one day she would remember.

One day.

Even though it had nearly killed Owen to lose Naomi, it was a deeper cut to lose his father. Naomi's death had been a medical problem. A blood clot that had formed during delivery. But his dad's life had been purposely taken. Murdered. And all of Owen's skills learned in training as a cop hadn't been able to stop it. Or bring the killer to justice.

Owen pushed that all aside, as he usually did when it came to his father, and went to the next item he needed to discuss with Laney.

"Tell me about Terrance McCoy."

She raked her finger over her eyebrow and shifted her posture a little. "SAPD told you about the restraining order." That was all she said for several moments. But yes, they had. "Then you also know that Terrance was a former client who wasn't happy with the outcome of an investigation I did for him."

That was a lukewarm explanation of a situation that had gotten pretty intense. Apparently, Terrance had hired Laney to do a thorough background check on a woman he'd met on an online dating site. When Laney hadn't turned up any red flags, Terrance had continued to see the woman, who ultimately swindled him out of a sizable chunk of his trust fund. He blamed Laney for that and had even accused her of being in cahoots with the swindler. No proof of that, though.

"Terrance assaulted you," Owen reminded her, letting her know what info he'd been given about the restraining order. "And he's been out of jail for weeks now. He could have hired those men who came after you tonight."

She looked him in the eyes again when she agreed with him. "Yes, and Joe is looking for Terrance now."

Apparently that had come up in the short conversation she'd had with Joe. Or maybe Joe agreed that Terrance was definitely a person of interest here.

"The San Antonio cops are looking for Terrance, too," Owen added.

After what had just happened, Terrance was at the top of their list of suspects. Ditto for anyone else Laney might have rubbed the wrong way. There were maybe other former clients out there. Dangerous ones. And because of the danger to Laney, Owen wasn't going to forget that Addie had been put in danger, too.

"I hate to ask, because I know it's just going to rile you even more than you already are," Laney said, "but could this be about your father?"

Yes, he'd considered it. Briefly. And then he'd dismissed it, and Owen was pretty sure the dismissal had been objective. Hard to be completely objective when it came to that kind of raw grief, but he thought he'd managed it.

"I'll be investigating all angles," Owen assured her. But he'd be looking especially hard at any of those directly connected to Laney.

Laney and Owen both glanced up when there was movement in the doorway of his office. She practically jumped to her feet when she saw their visitor.

Emerson.

The man was wearing a rumpled suit, sporting some dark stubble and equally dark circles beneath his eyes. Emerson looked about as happy to be there as Owen was.

It probably wasn't a surprise to Laney that Owen had called his brother-in-law. Nor was it a surprise that Emerson had come. It'd taken him a couple of hours to get there because he'd had to drive in from Austin where he'd been away on a business trip.

Emerson frowned at Laney after sparing her only a glance, and then he looked at Owen. "Please tell me you have her accusations cleared up by now so I can go home and get some sleep."

"He hasn't cleared it up." Laney jumped in to answer before Owen could respond.

Emerson gave a weary sigh and rubbed his hand over his face. "Has she given you any proof whatsoever?" he asked.

Owen went still. It was a simple enough question, but it didn't feel like the right thing to say. He would have preferred to hear Emerson belt out a denial, tacking on some outrage that anyone was accusing him of cheating on his wife. There was something else that bothered him, too.

"You know Laney?" Owen asked him. "Elaine," he corrected. He waited because he had already seen the recognition in Emerson's eyes.

"I know her," Emerson stormed. "She's the PI who pestered me with calls about her sister. I told her to back off or I'd get a restraining order."

Arching his eyebrow, Owen shifted his attention to Laney and she acknowledged that with a nod. So, before tonight, Emerson had known about Laney's accusations, but he hadn't said a word about it to Owen. Something he should have done. Then again, maybe

Emerson hadn't considered Laney enough of a credible threat.

"Emerson?" a woman called out, causing the man to groan.

Owen wasn't pleased, either, or especially surprised when Emerson's wife, Nettie, came hurrying through the front door, heading straight for them. "When you didn't answer your cell, I called the house, looking for you," Owen explained to Emerson. "Nettie answered, but I didn't tell her about Laney or the attack."

Emerson nodded and gave a resigned sigh. "Something like this won't stay quiet for long."

No. It wouldn't. And Nettie's expression was sporting a lot of concern. Ditto for the rest of her. Nettie was usually dressed to the nines, but tonight she was in yoga pants and a T-shirt. Her blond hair hadn't been combed and her eyes were red, as if she'd been crying.

"God, you're all right." Nettie threw herself into Emerson's arms. "I was so worried."

Owen glanced at Laney, and as expected, she was studying the couple. There was a different kind of worry and concern on her face. She was looking at them the way a cop would. No doubt to see if there were any signs that this was a marriage on the rocks because of a cheating husband. No signs, though. Emerson brushed a loving kiss on Nettie's forehead before he eased her away from him.

"Could you give Owen and me a minute alone?" Emerson asked his wife. "I won't be long. It's business."

Nettie studied him a moment and nodded before her attention went to Owen. Then Laney. There was no recognition in Nettie's icy gray eyes.

"I'll wait by the reception desk," Nettie said. She

whispered something to Emerson, kissed him and then walked out of the office.

Emerson didn't do or say anything until his wife was out of earshot and then he tipped his head to Laney. "Anything she tells you about me is a lie, and I've wasted enough of my time dealing with her. Are you okay?" Emerson added to Owen. "Is Addie okay?"

Again, that bothered Owen. As Addie's uncle, it should have been the first thing for Emerson to ask. Of course, Owen had verified the okay status when he'd had a quick chat with Emerson earlier, so maybe Emerson thought that was enough.

But it wasn't. At least it didn't feel like it was.

Owen silently cursed. He hated that Laney had given him any doubts about Emerson. Especially since there was no proof.

"Addie's fine," Owen answered. "Francine said she would text me if Addie has any nightmares or such." Owen cursed that, too, but this time it wasn't silent. Because there could indeed be nightmares.

"I'll check on her first thing in the morning," Emerson volunteered. "Anything else you need or want me to do?"

Owen muttered his thanks and then nodded. "You'll have to make a statement about Laney's accusations."

Emerson gave another of those weary sighs. "I'll come by in the morning to do that, too."

Owen was about to ask him to go ahead and do it now. That way, Laney couldn't say that he'd given Emerson preferential treatment. Of course, she'd likely say that anyway. However, he didn't even get a chance to bring it up because Kellan appeared in the doorway.

One look at his brother's face and Owen knew that something else was wrong.

"I just got off the phone with San Antonio PD," Kellan said, looking not at Emerson or Owen but at Laney. "They found your assistant, Joe Henshaw." Kellan paused. "He's dead."

Chapter Four

The shock felt to Laney like arctic ice covering her body. She blinked repeatedly—hoping she had misunderstood Kellan, that this was some kind of cop trick to unnerve her. But she knew from the look in his eyes that it was the truth.

"Oh, God." That was all she managed to say. There wasn't enough breath for her to add more, but the questions came immediately and started fighting their way through the veil of grief.

"How?" she mouthed.

Kellan's forehead bunched up, but he spoke the words fast. "He was murdered. Two gunshot wounds to the chest. That's all we know at this point because the ME has just started his examination."

Murdered. Joe had been murdered. The grief came, washing over her and going bone-deep.

"Joe's apartment had been ransacked," Kellan added a moment later. "Someone was obviously looking for something."

"Terrance," Laney rasped, though first, she had to swallow hard. "Joe was looking for him, and Terrance could have done this."

Since neither Owen or Kellan seemed surprised by

that, she guessed they'd already come to the same conclusion. Good. If that snake was responsible, she wanted him to pay. But then if Terrance had killed Joe, he'd done it to get back at her.

She was responsible.

This time she wasn't able to choke back the sob and Laney clamped onto her bottom lip to make sure there wasn't another one. Sobs and tears wouldn't help now. Not when she needed answers. Later, when Owen and Kellan weren't around, she could fall apart.

"The San Antonio cops found him in his apartment," Kellan went on. "It appears someone broke in and killed him when he stepped from the shower. No defensive wounds, so it happened fast."

That last part was probably meant to comfort her. To let her know that Joe hadn't suffered. But in that instant, he would have seen his attacker and known he was about to die.

And all because of her.

Joe had not only been looking for Terrance, he'd also been looking for the safe-deposit box with those pictures. Someone had killed him because he'd been following her orders.

Laney groped around behind her to locate the chair because she was afraid her legs were about to give way. Owen helped with that by taking hold of her arm to help her sit. He was studying her, maybe to gauge her reaction. That was when she glanced at Emerson, who was doing the same thing.

"I suppose you'll say I had something to do with this, too?" Emerson snapped, his words ripe with anger.

Laney didn't have a comeback. Couldn't even manage a glare for taking a swipe at her when she'd been dealt such a hard blow. But then the swipe only confirmed for her exactly what kind of person Emerson was. Not the sterling, upstanding DA of Longview Ridge. A man who was capable of striking out like that could be capable of doing other things, too. Like cheating on his wife. Of course, it was a huge leap to go from that to murder, but Laney wasn't taking him off her very short suspect list.

"Emerson," Owen said, no anger in his voice, though there seemed to be a low warning, "come back tomorrow and I'll take your statement."

Owen got a slight jab, too, when Emerson flicked him an annoyed glance. However, the man finally turned and walked out. Kellan looked at Emerson. Then at Owen. Finally at her.

She had no idea what Kellan was thinking, but something passed between him and Owen. One of those unspoken conversations that siblings could have. Or rather, she supposed that was what it was. She'd never quite managed to have a relationship like that with Hadley.

"SAPD will want to talk to Laney tomorrow," Kellan said to Owen. He checked his watch. "But it's late. Why don't you go ahead and take Laney to the ranch so you two can try to get some rest?"

Laney practically jumped to her feet. "No. I can't go there. It could put Addie in danger."

"We're taking precautions," Kellan assured her. "And I didn't say to take you to Owen's but rather the ranch. You can't go back to Owen's place because the CSIs are there processing the scene, but our grandparents' house is in the center of the property. No one lives there on a regular basis, so it's been kept up for company, seasonal ranch hands and such. Plus, it has a good security system. Addie, Francine, Gunnar and Jack are headed there now."

Jack was Kellan and Owen's brother. And he was also a marshal. Another lawman. But that didn't mean Laney could trust him.

"What about your fiancée?" she asked Kellan. Laney knew her name was Gemma, and she'd met her several times. "She shouldn't be alone at your place."

"She won't be. She'll be going to my grandparents' house, too. Eli's taking her there."

Eli was yet another brother and a Texas Ranger. So, she would be surrounded by Slater lawmen. Not exactly a comforting thought, but it could be worse. As Addie's uncles, they'd do whatever it took to protect the baby.

"I'll have two reserve deputies drive Owen and you, and once Eli and Jack are in place at the ranch, I can have them come back here to help with the investigation," Kellan told them. "With Owen at our grandparents' house, Addie won't have to be away from her dad."

Until he'd added that last part, Laney had been ready to outright refuse. She hadn't wanted to do anything to put the child in more danger, or to separate father from child. Still, this was dangerous.

"There's a gunman at large," she reminded him. "If he comes after me again, I shouldn't be anywhere near Addie, Gemma or Francine."

Owen stared at her a moment. "Whoever sent that gunman could try to use Addie to get to you. They would have seen the way you reacted, the way you tried to protect her. They would know she's your weak spot."

Addie was indeed that. It had crushed Laney to think of the baby being hurt.

Owen dragged in a weary breath before he continued, "It'll be easier to protect you both at the same time, and it'll tie up fewer resources for Kellan. He needs all the help he can get here in the office to work the investigation and try to get a confession out of Rohan Gilley."

She mentally went through what he was saying and hated that it made sense. Hated even more that she didn't have a reasonable counterargument. She was exhausted, and it felt as if someone had clamped a fist around her heart. Still, Laney didn't want to do anything else to hurt Owen's precious little girl.

"I'm a PI," Laney reminded Owen. Reminded herself, too. "I can arrange for my own security. I'll be okay."

She saw the anger flash in Owen's eyes, which were the color of a fierce storm cloud. "I don't need to remind you that your assistant is dead. Or that you're in danger. So I'd rather you not add to this miserable night by lying to yourself. Or to me—*again*. When it comes to me, you've already met your quota of lies."

This was more than a swipe like the one Emerson had given her. Much more. Not just because it was true but especially because it was coming from Owen. It drained what little fight she had left in her and that was why Laney didn't argue any more when Owen gathered up his things and led her out the front door to a waiting cruiser.

Obviously, Kellan and Owen had been certain they could talk her into this. Which they had.

"This is Manuel Garcia and Amos Turner, the reserve deputies," Owen said when he hurried Laney into the back seat with him. The deputies were in the front.

Laney recognized both of them. That was because whenever she was in town or dealing with the other ranchers, she'd kept her eyes and ears open. For all the good it'd done. Owen's ranch had been attacked, Joe was dead and she was no closer to the truth than she had been when she'd lied her way into getting a job with Owen.

It would have been so easy to slip right into the grief, fear and regret. The trifecta of raw emotions was like a perfect storm closing in on her. But giving in to it would only lead to tears and a pity party, neither of which would help.

"I'm sorry," she said to Owen. That might not help, either, but she had to start somewhere. "Believe me when I say I didn't mean for any of this to happen."

The interior of the cruiser was dimly lit, yet she could clearly see Owen's eyes when he looked at her. Still storm gray. It was a different kind of intensity than what was usually there. When he'd looked at her before—before he'd known who she was and the lies she'd told him—there'd been…well, heat. Though he might not admit it, she'd certainly seen it.

And felt it.

Laney had dismissed it. Or rather she had just accepted it. After all, Owen was from the superior Slater gene pool, and the DNA had given him a face that hadn't skimped on the good looks. The thick black hair, those piercing eyes, that mouth that looked capable of doing many pleasurable things.

She dismissed those looks again now and silently cursed herself for allowing them to even play into this. She had no right to see him as anything but a former boss who had zero trust in her. Maybe if she mentally repeated that enough, her body would start to accept it.

"Believe me when I say I'm sorry," she repeated in

a whisper, forcing her attention away from him and to the window.

Some long moments crawled by before he said anything. "You were close to your assistant, Joe Henshaw?"

The question threw her. Of course, she hadn't forgotten about Joe, but she'd figured that learning more about the man hadn't been on the top of Owen's to-do list. Plus, he hadn't even mentioned whether or not he would start to accept her apology.

"We were close enough, I suppose," she answered. "He worked for me about a year, and I trusted him to do the jobs I assigned him to do."

"Did he ever come to my ranch?" Owen fired back as soon as she'd answered.

Oh, she got it then. Laney knew the reason he'd brought up the subject. He wanted to measure the depth of her lies. "No. I only had phone contact with Joe when I worked for you. I didn't bring anyone to the ranch," she added.

From his reflection in the mirror, she could see that he was staring at her as if waiting for her to say more. Exactly what, she didn't know. When she turned back to him, Laney still didn't have a clue.

"I just want to know who and what I'm dealing with," Owen clarified. "Joe was your lover?"

"No." She couldn't say that fast enough and shook her head, not able to connect the dots on this one. "He worked for me, *period*."

Now it was Owen who looked away. "Just wanted to make sure I wasn't dealing with something more personal here."

"You mean like a lover's spat gone wrong," she muttered. The fact he had even considered that twisted away at her almost as much as the regret over lying to him.

"No. Like Terrance McCoy killing your assistant as a way of getting back at you."

Everything inside Laney stilled. Only for a moment, though. Before the chill came again. Mercy. She hadn't even considered that. But she should have. She was so tied up in knots over Emerson having killed Hadley that she hadn't looked at this through a cop's eyes. Something she'd always prided herself on being able to do. She'd never quite managed it with Hadley, though.

"Hadley's my blind spot." Laney groaned softly and pushed her hair away from her face.

She steeled herself to have Owen jump down her throat about that, to give her a lecture about loss of objectivity and such. But he didn't say anything. Laney waited, staring at him. Or rather, staring at the back of his head because his attention was on the window.

"Addie's my blind spot," he said several long moments later. "I didn't want her in the middle of whatever this hell this is, but she's there."

Laney had to speak around the lump in her throat. "Because of me."

"No. Because of whoever hired those men to come to my house and go after you." He paused, turning so they were facing each other. Their gazes met. Held. "Don't ever lie to me again."

Not trusting her voice, Laney nodded and felt something settle between them. A truce. Not a complete one, but it was a start. If she was going to get to the bottom of what was going on, she needed Owen's help and, until a few seconds ago, she hadn't been sure she would get it.

The deputy took the turn off the main road to the

Slater Ranch, which sprawled through a good chunk of the county. Kellan ran the main operation, just as six generations of his family had done, but Owen and his brothers Jack and Eli helped as well, along with running their own smaller ranches.

Separate but still family, all the way to the core.

It occurred to her that she might have to go up against all those Slater lawmen if it did indeed come down to pinning this on Emerson. But Laney was too exhausted to think about that particular battle right now.

"For the record," she said, "I told you the truth about most things. I grew up with horses, so I know how to train them. And every minute I spent with Addie—that was genuine. I enjoyed being with her. Francine, too," she added because the part about Addie sounded...personal.

A muscle flickered in Owen's jaw. "What about the day in the barn?" He immediately cursed and waved that off.

When he turned back to the window, she knew the subject was off-limits, but it wasn't out of mind. Not out of her mind anyway. And she did not need him to clarify which barn, which day. It'd been about a month earlier after he'd just finished riding his favorite gelding, Alamo. Owen had been tired and sweaty, and he'd peeled off his shirt to wash off with the hose. She'd walked in on him just as the water had been sluicing down his bare chest.

Laney had frozen. Then her mouth had gone dry.

Owen had looked at her and it had seemed as if time had stopped. It had been the only thing that had stopped, though. Laney had always known her boss was a hot cowboy, but she'd gotten a full dose of it that day. A kicked-up pulse. That slide of heat through her body.

The physical need she felt for him.

She hadn't done a good job of hiding it, either. Laney had seen it on his face and, for just a second—before he'd been able to rein it in—she had seen the same thing in Owen's eyes.

Neither had said anything. Laney had calmly dropped off the saddle she'd been carrying and walked out. But she'd known that if she hadn't been lying to him, that if they'd been sitting here now, with no secrets between them, she would have gone to him. She would have welcomed the body-to-body contact when he pulled her into his arms. And she would have let Owen have her.

Owen knew that, too.

Just as they had done that day in the barn, their gazes connected now. They didn't speak, and his attention shifted away from her just as his phone dinged with a text message.

"Jack's got Francine and Addie all settled in," Owen relayed. He showed her the picture that his brother had included with the text. It was of Addie, who was sound asleep.

Laney smiled. Addie looked so peaceful and, while it didn't lessen her guilt over the attack, at least the little girl didn't seem to be showing any signs of stress.

Laney was still smiling when she looked up at Owen and realized he had noticed her reaction. And perhaps didn't approve.

Despite that shared "barn memory" moment, he probably didn't want her feeling close to his daughter. Laney certainly couldn't blame her. She was about to bring up the subject again about her making other arrangements for a place to stay, but Owen's phone rang.

It was Kellan and, while Owen didn't put the call on speaker, it was easy for Laney to hear the sheriff's voice in an otherwise quiet cruiser.

"Just got a call from the CSI out at your place," Kellan said. "They found something."

Chapter Five

A listening device.

That was what the CSIs had found in the bedroom of the guesthouse where Laney had been living. Owen figured the thug who'd broken in had planted it there, but that didn't tell him why. What had those men been after? What had been so important for them to hear that they'd been willing to risk not only a break-in but also a shoot-out with a cop?

It was those questions and more that had raced through his mind half the night.

The other half he'd spent worrying if he'd done the right thing by bringing Laney here to his grandparents' old house. He needed to talk to Kellan about other options, but he figured his brother was getting some much-needed sleep right now. Owen hoped he was anyway, since Kellan had opted to stay the night at the sheriff's office.

Owen got out of the bed he'd positioned right next to Addie's crib—one they had borrowed from Francine's friend. Addie was still sacked out, thank goodness, and since it was only 5:00 a.m., she should stay that way for a while. Just in case she woke up, though, he took the baby monitor with him into the adjoining bathroom.

Francine had a monitor, too, and she was right across the hall, bunking with Laney in the master bedroom. Gemma was in the only other bedroom upstairs.

Owen grabbed a quick shower, dressed and headed downstairs to make coffee, but someone had already beat him to it. Someone had obviously beat him to getting up, too, because Eli and Jack were at the kitchen table, drinking coffee. They looked as if they'd been at it for a while.

"Get your beauty sleep?" Eli asked. His voice was like a grumbling drawl, and Owen figured the comment was just his way of showing brotherly "affection." Eli showed it a lot.

Owen had never been able to tell if Eli was truly just a badass or if he'd just been in a sour mood for the past decade. Either way, he appreciated him being here. The nice thing was, he didn't even have to say it. This was the sort of thing that family did for each other.

"The question should be—did our little brother get his beauty sleep *alone*?" Jack smiled as he gulped down more coffee.

Owen shot him a scowl, not completely made up of brotherly affection because he didn't like even joking about this. "I'm not having sex with Laney."

Both Eli and Jack raised eyebrows, causing Owen to curse and repeat the denial.

"Maybe you didn't last night…" Jack took his life into his own hands by continuing to smile.

"Never," Owen insisted, pouring himself some coffee as if he'd gone to battle with it. "Laney works for me— *worked* for me," he corrected. "And I shouldn't have to remind you that she lied to me about who she was."

"Yeah, but you didn't know about the lie until last

night." Jack again. "There were plenty of nights before that when sex could have happened. Laney's a looker."

She was, and before he could rein it in, Owen got a flash of that look she'd had on her face when she'd seen him in the barn. There'd been a whole lot of lust in the air in that moment.

"Hard to believe you wouldn't go after her," Jack commented.

Owen's scowl got a whole lot worse. "Are you looking to get your butt busted before the sun even comes up?"

Of course, Jack smiled.

Eli shrugged and kept his attention on his coffee. "Well, then, if you're not interested in Laney, then maybe I'll ask her out."

Owen hadn't thought his scowl could get worse, but he'd been wrong. "Laney lied to me," Owen emphasized in case they'd both gone stupid and had forgotten. "And because she lied, I didn't know there was a possibility that thugs could come to my house."

Eli lifted his shoulder again. "Bet she didn't know it, either. Plus, she lied because she wants justice for her sister. A good cause even if she didn't go about it the right way." He paused. "She's taken some hard hits, and she's still standing. Sounds like my kind of woman." He gave a satisfied nod. "Yeah, I'll ask her out."

Owen felt the snap of anger as he caught Eli's arm, ready to drag him out of the chair. The fact that Jack kept smiling and Eli didn't punch him for the grab clued Owen into the fact that this had been some kind of test. A bad one.

"Told you Owen was attracted to her," Jack said with a smirk.

Yeah, a test, all right.

Eli shook off Owen's grip the same easy way he shrugged, took out his wallet and handed Jack a twenty. So, not just a test but also a bet. One involving his sex life.

Owen was about to return verbal fire, but the sound of footsteps stopped him, and a moment later Laney appeared in the doorway. She immediately froze, her gaze sliding over his brothers before it settled on him.

"Did something else happen? Is something wrong?" The words rushed out and alarm went through her eyes.

"No," Owen assured her. Nothing wrong other than him wanting to throttle his brothers.

Laney released the breath she'd obviously been holding and put the laptop she'd tucked beneath her arm on the table. "Good. That's good." She fluttered her fingers to the stairs. "Addie's still asleep, but Francine and Gemma are in there. Gemma wants to hold her when she wakes up."

Owen had suspected as much. His little girl would get lots of attention today. Too bad it was because of the attack. Addie had been in danger, and it was going to be a very long time before he or anyone else in his family got past that.

Laney looked at his brothers again, probably thinking she'd interrupted a sensitive conversation about the investigation. She hadn't, and there was no way in hell he'd tell her about the bet. But it was time for him to get his focus back where it belonged. Better to deal with the investigation than to notice the fit of the jeans Laney had borrowed from Gemma.

"The Ranger lab has the eavesdropping device," Owen said, turning to get her a mug from the cupboard. "They might be able to find where the info was being sent."

That eased some the alarm on her face, and she poured herself some coffee. "The audio was being sent to a receiver or computer?"

"It looks that way." And since he'd started this briefing, Owen added, "Terrance is coming in this morning."

"Terrance," she repeated, her voice strained. "I want to be there when you question him."

Owen shook his head. "I can't allow you in the interview room—"

"I can watch from the observation room." She paused, met his gaze. "I just want to hear what he has to say."

He didn't have to think too hard on this. Owen had to take Laney in to make a statement, so she'd already be in the building when Terrance arrived. Since there was no harm in her observing, he nodded and then tipped his head to the laptop. It, too, was a loaner from Gemma.

"Have you been able to access copies of the info you had stored on your computer?" he asked.

"Not yet. But I will. I've been going through Joe's files on our storage cloud."

Owen immediately saw the shimmer in her eyes. Not alarm this time. She was fighting back tears.

"I need to find Joe's killer." Her voice was just above a whisper. "I need to put an end to this so your life can get back to normal."

He nearly laughed. It'd been so long since he'd had normal, Owen wasn't sure that he'd recognize it. First, losing Naomi and becoming a single dad, and then losing his father. Yes, it had been a while.

"I emailed both Kellan and you the link and password to the files," Laney said a moment later. "Joe was more tech savvy than I am, so I'm hoping he has hidden files. It's a long shot, but something might turn up."

"Gemma could maybe help you with that," Jack said. "Or I know someone else who might be willing to take a look. She's in WITSEC, but she's got good computer skills."

"Caroline Moser," Laney provided.

Owen hadn't been sure that Laney would know who Jack was talking about, but Longview Ridge was a small town with lots of gossip. Plenty of people knew that Caroline and Jack had been lovers. In love, Owen mentally corrected. But Caroline had been injured in an attack and couldn't remember any of that. Ditto for not remembering the crime she'd witnessed.

His father's murder.

When Caroline got her memory back, they'd know the truth. Well, maybe. It was possible that she hadn't even seen the killer. Obviously she had recalled how to work a computer, so that was a good sign. What they needed, though, were a lot of good signs, not just for his dad's killer but also for the attack at his place.

"Don't involve Caroline in this just yet," Owen advised Jack. He wanted Caroline to concentrate on recovering so they could get those answers about his father even sooner.

Jack nodded in a suit-yourself gesture. "What about the gunman you have in custody? Rohan Gilley. He couldn't have killed Laney's assistant because he was in jail at the time, but maybe we can use the murder to twist him up a little? Maybe let him believe his boss is tying up loose ends and he could be next?"

It was a good angle, and Owen would definitely try it

and others. It riled him that he might have to offer Gilley some kind of plea deal, but that might be the fastest way to put an end to whatever this was.

And that brought Owen to the next part of this conversation. A part that neither of his brothers was going to like. Neither did he, but it was something they needed to know.

"About a week ago, I asked a PI out of Austin to take a look at the file on Dad's murder," Owen started. "I just wanted someone with a fresh eye."

That definitely got Eli and Jack's attention. Laney's, too. "I'm guessing the PI didn't find anything or you would have told us," Jack remarked.

"You're right. But I have to consider that Dad's killer might have found out and decided a *fresh look* wasn't a good idea, that it would lead us to him or her."

Since his brothers didn't seem the least bit surprised by that, Owen knew they had already considered it.

"I do new runs on the info all the time," Eli commented. "Calls, going out to the crime scene, and I'm not quiet about it. It seems to me that if the killer was keeping tabs on us, he would have come after me. I'd be the easiest one to get to."

He would be. Unlike Jack, Kellan and him, Eli didn't have any full-time help on his place, only a couple of part-time hands who checked on his horses when he was working.

"I do runs, too," Jack interjected, "and if the killer came after one of us, I figure it'd be me. Because I'm the smartest," he added, no doubt to lighten the mood.

It didn't work, but then nothing could when it came to the hell they'd been through for the past year.

Owen finished off his coffee and put the cup in the

dishwasher. "I'll go up and check on Addie." He looked at Laney. "Then I'll call the reserve deputies to escort us to the sheriff's office so I can get ready for Terrance's interview. You can give your statement while we're waiting for him."

Owen headed for the stairs, but he only made it a few steps before his phone rang, and he saw Kellan's name on the screen. The call got his brothers and Laney's attention, because they all looked at him. Waiting.

Since this could be an update on the investigation, he went ahead and put it on speaker.

"Eli, Jack and Laney are here," Owen said in greeting to let Kellan know their conversation wouldn't be private.

Kellan didn't hesitate. "The lab just called and they found where the info from the eavesdropping device was being sent." Kellan paused and cursed softly. "You should come on in so we can discuss how to handle this."

Owen silently groaned. If Terrance was behind this, then Kellan would have quickly volunteered that information. "Did Emerson set the bug?" Owen came out and asked.

"No." Kellan paused again. "But according to the crime lab, his wife did."

NETTIE KEATON.

The woman's name just kept going through Laney's head while she drove with Owen and the reserve deputies to the sheriff's office. And there were questions that kept repeating, too.

Why had Nettie done something like this? Had the woman also been responsible for the attack?

Not only was Nettie the DA's wife, she was also Owen's sister-in-law. Family. From all accounts, Nettie had been there for Owen after he'd lost his wife and had even taken care of Addie until Owen had been able to find a nanny. It was an understatement that their tight relationship wouldn't make the interview with her pleasant. But Laney hoped that it would be objective, that Owen would dig hard to get to the truth.

"The CSIs didn't find dust on the listening device," Owen said, reading from the report that Kellan had messaged him just as they were leaving the house. "But since it'd been planted beneath the center drawer of your desk, it's possible dust wouldn't have had time to accumulate on it."

In other words, there was no way to pinpoint how long it had been there. It turned Laney's stomach to think that maybe it had possibly been there for weeks. Or maybe even the entire time she'd worked for Owen. Of course, that only led to another question—had Nettie known who she was when she'd come to Longview Ridge?

Laney had already searched back through her memory to try to figure out if her sister had ever mentioned meeting Nettie. She didn't think so, but Hadley hadn't told her everything.

"The audio feed from the listening device was going to a computer registered to Nettie," Owen noted.

Yes, she'd already come to that conclusion from what Kellan had said earlier. "I'm assuming Kellan will get a search warrant for it?" she asked.

Owen looked up from the report and his eyes narrowed for just a moment. Then he glanced away as if frustrated. "Kellan and I aren't wearing blinders when it comes to Nettie. If she's done something wrong, we'll get to the bottom of it."

After just seeing his reaction, Laney didn't doubt that part, but there was another layer there. Some more fallout. Because this could add another family scar on top of plenty of other wounds.

"Emerson knew who you were," Owen said a moment later. "If Nettie did, too, then this could have been her way of keeping tabs on you. It doesn't make it right," he quickly added. "But if she was worried about you coming after Emerson, that could be her justification for doing it."

True, and Nettie wouldn't have had trouble getting into the guesthouse. Heck, she probably had a key. There'd been plenty of times when Laney had been in the pasture working with a horse and wouldn't have been near the guesthouse. Nettie could have easily gotten in without anyone noticing.

Owen's gaze came back to her. "Of course, you know I don't believe Nettie would put me or Addie in danger by sending those thugs to the ranch. And I just can't see her hiring a hitman to go after your assistant."

Laney gave that some thought and considered something else that Owen wasn't going to like. "Maybe she didn't think things would go that far. You were still at work, and she might have thought Francine would take Addie with her to the nursing home. She might have *justified* what she did by believing her niece wouldn't be in harm's way."

A muscle flickered in his jaw, but his eyes didn't narrow again. Nor did he dismiss what she was saying. That meant he'd likely already considered it. *Was considering it*, she amended. It wouldn't be easy for him, but he would do what was right. So would she. And maybe what they found wouldn't hurt him even more than he already had been.

The reserve deputy pulled to a stop in front of the sheriff's office. When they went inside, Laney steeled herself to face Nettie and Emerson, who would almost certainly be there with his wife. But they weren't in the waiting area.

However, Terrance was.

When he looked at her and smiled, Laney forced herself not to take a step back and kept her shoulders squared. That was hard to do. Even though she hated feeling it, Laney remembered the way he'd attacked her, that look in his eyes clearly letting her know he'd wanted to kill her.

Terrance was masking that look today. Maybe because he no longer hated her, or perhaps he'd just managed to rein it in. If so, Laney needed to do some restraining of her own. It was best not to show any signs of fear or weakness around a man like Terrance.

It was the first time she'd seen Terrance since she'd testified against him at his trial for assaulting her. That'd been six months ago and his short stint in jail hadn't changed him much. With his acne-scarred face and beaked nose, he was still a very unattractive man in an expensive suit.

Next to Terrance was another suit and someone else she recognized. The bald guy reading something on his phone was Terrance's lawyer. He, too, had been at the trial and had tried every dirty trick in the book to have his client declared not guilty. It hadn't worked, which was probably why the man gave her an unmistakable sneer.

"Laney," Terrance greeted her, getting to his feet. "Did I scare you?" That oily smile still bent his mouth a little.

"No." Laney made sure she looked him straight in the eyes. "Why should I be afraid of you? We both know if you touch me again, you'll spend a lot longer than six months in a cage."

Terrance's washed-out blue eyes dismissed her with a glance before he turned to Owen. "I'm guessing you must be Deputy Slater, the local yokel who ordered me here for an interview?"

"Deputy Slater," Owen confirmed, ignoring the insult as Terrance had ignored Laney's comment. Instead he looked at Kellan, who was stepping into the doorway of his office. "I was about to send our guests to an interview room where they can wait until you're ready to talk to them."

"We've already waited long enough," Terrance snapped.

"And you'll wait some more. Interview room." Owen pointed up the hall, his voice and body language an order for them to go there. "Since you're on probation, it probably wouldn't be a good idea for you not to co-operate with the cops. Even when they're local yokels," he added a heartbeat later.

Apparently, Owen hadn't ignored the insult after all, and it caused Laney to smile. Not for long, though. She spotted Nettie sitting in Kellan's office. Terrance, who looked in at the woman, too, as his lawyer and he walked past Kellan, cast a glance at Laney over his shoulder. She wasn't quite sure what to make of that look, but she dismissed it when Nettie jumped to her feet.

"You planted that bug so that I'd get blamed for it," Nettie immediately blurted. "Well, you won't get away with it. I won't have you telling lies about me."

Laney had already considered that Nettie might try to blame her for this, but it was odd that the woman was the one making the denial. Laney had thought it would come from Emerson first.

As she'd done with Terrance, Laney faced Nettie head-on. "I didn't plant a bug, didn't tell lies about you and I certainly didn't have men fire shots at Addie, Owen and me."

There was a bright fire of anger in Nettie's eyes as she glared at Laney before snapping at Owen. "Please tell me you don't believe her."

Owen dragged in a breath and put his hands on his hips. "I believe her. Laney could have been killed in that attack, so she's not the one who set this up."

Nettie opened her mouth, closed it and then made a sound of frustration that might or might not have been genuine.

"I have no motive to plant a bug and link it to you," Laney reminded the woman.

"But you're wrong about that. You do have a motive. This could be your way of getting back at Emerson."

That got Laney's attention and she stared at Nettie.

Nettie practically froze, but Laney could see the woman quickly gathering her composure. "I don't know exactly what grudge you have against my husband," Nettie amended, "but I believe that's why you're here. Why you came to Longview Ridge. Whatever it is you think about him, you're wrong. Emerson's a good man."

"Is he?" Laney challenged.

Nettie made a sound of outrage and turned to Kellan this time. "Can't you see that I'm being set up?" She flung a perfectly manicured finger at Laney. "And that she's the one who's trying to make me look guilty of something I didn't do."

Kellan dragged in his own long breath. "The eavesdropping device was linked to a computer registered to you. Before Owen and Laney came in, I told you that I needed to have the CSIs do a search of your house to find that computer—"

"No." Nettie practically shouted that and then, on a groan, sank down into the chair next to Kellan's desk. "If you do that, then Emerson will know about these ridiculous allegations."

Owen and Laney exchanged glances. "Emerson doesn't know?" Owen asked, looking first at Nettie and then Kellan.

Kellan shook his head. "Nettie asked me to hold off telling him until she had a chance to clear this up."

"I don't want Emerson bothered by this nonsense," Nettie piped in.

"There's no way around that," Kellan assured her. "I have probable cause to get a search warrant, and I'll get it. The lab will go through all the computers in your home and, from the preliminary info gathered, there'll be a program to link to the eavesdropping device found in the guesthouse where Laney lives."

Laney braced herself for another onslaught of Nettie's temper, but the woman stayed quiet for a moment. "Someone must have broken into my house and added the program," Nettie finally said and then her gaze slashed back to Laney. "You did it. You broke in when I wasn't there so you could set me up."

Laney sighed and was about to repeat that she had no

motive, but Owen spoke first. "Just let the CSIs look at the computers and we'll go from there. The techs will be able to tell when the program was installed, and if someone did that while you weren't there, then you might have an alibi."

Nettie didn't jump to agree to that and nibbled on her bottom lip for a few seconds. "Would Emerson have to know?"

Kellan groaned, scrubbed his hand over his face. "Yes. He's the DA, and even if he wasn't, this sort of thing would still get around."

Yes, it would get around, and then Emerson would likely hit the roof when he found out that CSIs were in his house looking for evidence against his wife. Laney was betting he'd accuse her just as Nettie had done.

"You're right," Nettie said several long moments later. Instead of nibbling on her bottom lip, it trembled. "Someone will tell him, but he'll know I don't have any reason to plant a bug. Emerson will be on my side. He won't believe I could do anything like this because I just wouldn't."

Laney didn't know Nettie that well, but it seemed as if the woman was trying to convince herself of Emerson's blind support. She decided to press that to see if it led to anything.

"Emerson's never mentioned me to you?" Laney asked.

Nettie's head whipped up. "What do you mean?" The anger had returned and had multiplied.

Laney decided to just stare at the woman and wait for her to answer. Kellan and Owen obviously decided to do the same, and their reaction brought Nettie back to her feet. However, the fiery eyes stayed firmly planted on Laney.

"I know you've told lies about my husband," Nettie said, her tone sharp, edgy. "I don't know the details, but I've heard talk. It's lies. All lies."

So, Emerson hadn't told his wife about his affair with Hadley. Of course, that probably wasn't something he'd wanted to discuss with her, especially since Emerson was claiming he was innocent.

Nettie hiked up her chin. "I suppose you want some kind of statement from me about that bug?" she asked Kellan.

He nodded. "And permission to search your house for the computers. If I don't get permission, then I'll have no choice but to get the warrant. Then plenty of people will know about this."

She squeezed her eyes shut, her mouth tightening as she took out her phone. "Let me call Emerson first." Nettie didn't wait for permission to do that. She walked out of the office, through the squad room and to the reception desk before she made her call.

Laney turned to Owen to get his take, but before she could say anything, she spotted Terrance again. He was outside the door of the interview room—where he could have heard the conversation they'd just had with Nettie.

"I don't owe you any favors," Terrance said to Laney, "but I'm going to do one for you anyway."

"What favor?" Laney didn't bother to tone down her very skeptical attitude.

Terrance gave her another of those slick smiles. "A couple of months before my trial, my legal team started gathering information that they thought would help with my defense. They hired PIs to follow you and people connected to you."

Laney's heart sped up. Hadley had been murdered just a month before Terrance's trial. Terrance had an airtight alibi for the murder—he'd been at a party and there were dozens of witnesses. But his PIs could have seen something.

"Did you know you were being followed?" Owen asked her.

Laney shook her head, her attention still fixed on Terrance. "You know who killed my sister?" She heard the quiver in her voice, felt the shudder slide through her body.

"No. But my lawyers were having Hadley followed. Not full-time but on and off to see if there was something they could use to prove my innocence."

"Cut to the chase," Owen demanded. "What the hell do you know about Laney's sister?"

Terrance smiled again when he tipped his head to Nettie. "Why don't you ask her?" He continued before any of them could attempt to answer, "The DA's wife was with Hadley the night she was murdered."

Chapter Six

Owen stared at Terrance, trying to figure out the angle as to why the man had just tossed them that lie. But there was nothing in Terrance's expression or body language to indicate that he was telling them anything but the truth.

Hell.

Was it actually true? Had Nettie not only known Hadley but also met with her?

Owen shifted his attention to Laney and noted that hers was a different kind of body language. A highly skeptical one. She huffed, folded her arms over her chest and stared at Terrance.

"Why would you volunteer that information to me?" Laney demanded.

It was a good starting point as questions went, but Owen had plenty of others for the man. And then he would need to confront Nettie if he felt there was any shred of truth to what Terrance had just said.

Terrance flashed the same smile he'd been doling out since Laney and Owen had first laid eyes on the man in the sheriff's office. He was a slick snake, the type of man who assaulted a woman, and Owen had to rein in his temper because he wanted to punch that self-righteous smile off Terrance's smug face. That wasn't going to solve anything, though, and would make things a whole lot worse.

"I volunteered the info because I'm doing my civic duty," Terrance answered, and there was nothing sincere in his tone. "As Deputy Slater pointed out, I'm on probation. Withholding potential evidence could be interpreted as obstruction of justice. I wouldn't want that, because it could violate the terms of my parole."

Owen stepped closer and met Terrance eye to eye. "Yet if this so-called evidence is true, you withheld it for months."

Terrance lifted his hands palms up. "I've been in jail and I've been focusing my time and energy on... rehabilitation."

"My client didn't know the information was important," the lawyer added. When he took a step closer, as if he might come into Kellan's office, both Kellan and Owen gave him a warning glance that worked because he stayed put.

"It's true," Terrance agreed. "Until I overheard the conversation just a few minutes ago, I didn't make the connection between the DA's wife and Laney's dead sister." He turned to Laney then. "Here all this time, you thought your sister's killer was Emerson, and now I've put a cog in your wheel by handing you another suspect."

Laney continued to stare at him. "Two other suspects," she corrected. "You're high on my list of people who could have murdered Hadley."

She'd sounded strong when she said that, but Owen knew that, beneath the surface, this was eating away at her. After all, she was facing down the man who'd assaulted her and put her in the hospital.

"Do you have any proof whatsoever of what you're saying?" Owen demanded.

Terrance lifted his shoulder. "Reports from my PIs. It's possible they took photos, but if so, I don't remember seeing them."

Reports could be doctored. Photos could be, too. Still, Owen would need to treat this as any other potential evidence that fell into his lap. Because if Nettie was indeed connected to Hadley's murder, then she could have had something to do with the attack at his ranch.

That put a hard knot in his gut.

"I'll want everything from your PIs ASAP," Owen insisted.

Terrance nodded. "I'll get right on that. Wouldn't want it said that I didn't cooperate with the law." He glanced at Nettie, whose back was to them. She was pacing across the reception area while still on her phone. "And what about her? You think she'll cooperate?"

"She's not your concern," Kellan assured him, sounding very much like a sheriff who'd just given an order. "Come with me." He led Terrance and the lawyer into the interview room and shut the door before he came back to them.

"I didn't know Terrance was having me followed," Laney immediately volunteered. "I'm a PI, and I should have noticed something like that."

No way was Owen going to let her take the blame for this. "If Terrance didn't lie about the timing of this alleged meeting, you would have been in the hospital and then recovering from the injuries he gave you. A broken arm, three broken ribs and a concussion. That's a lot to distract you."

Laney quickly dodged his gaze while the muscles in her jaw tensed. Maybe she hadn't wanted him to dig into her medical records, but Owen considered it connected to the investigation of last night's attack. At least, that was what he'd told himself. After reading the police report of Terrance's assault, Owen now had to admit that it had become personal for him.

And that was definitely something he didn't want.

"I have no idea if Terrance is telling the truth about Hadley and Nettie," Laney went on a moment later. "Hadley never mentioned meeting Emerson's wife."

Owen had to consider that was because Hadley had never gotten a chance to tell Laney. After all, Terrance had claimed his PIs saw the two women the same night Hadley had been murdered. That still didn't mean Nettie had killed her. Didn't mean that anything Terrance had told them was the truth.

Before Owen could talk to Kellan about how they should handle this, Nettie finished her call and came back toward them. "Emerson just left for a business meeting in Austin and will be gone most of the day," she said and then paused. "I didn't tell him about the eavesdropping device."

Owen only lifted an eyebrow, causing Nettie to huff, "You should have told him."

Nettie shook her head. "I know it's all some misunderstanding, that I had nothing to do with the eavesdropping device, so there's no reason to worry him." She turned to Kellan. "Go ahead and get someone in the house to take whatever you need. Just try to be finished with the search before Emerson comes home.

Test the computers and have them in place so that he doesn't know."

No raised eyebrow for Kellan. Instead he gave Nettie a flat look. "I can't guarantee that. In fact, I'm pretty sure it'll take a couple of days to go through the computers once I get everything to the lab. You'll need to tell Emerson," he quickly added. "He'll hear it sooner or later, and I'll give you the chance to have him learn about it from you."

Nettie volleyed some glances between Kellan and him as if she expected them to budge on their insistence that she tell her husband what was going on. They wouldn't. And Owen made certain that his expression let her know it. It didn't matter if this was all some kind of "misunderstanding." It still had to be investigated.

As did Terrance's accusations.

"If you want to interview Terrance, I can get a statement from Nettie," Owen offered his brother.

Nettie blinked, pulled back her shoulders. "A statement?" Her voice was sharp and stinging. "I've already told you I had nothing to do with that stupid bug."

"Why don't we take this to the second interview room?" Owen suggested, hoping this wouldn't escalate.

But it did.

Nettie didn't budge when Owen put his hand on her arm to get her moving. "A statement?" she repeated. Not a shout but close. She slung off Owen's grip and snapped at Laney. "You're responsible for this. You've somehow convinced them that I'm a criminal. I'm not. You're a liar, and now you're dragging me into those lies."

"Nettie," Kellan said, "you need to calm down and listen."

The woman ignored him and charged toward Laney.

Nettie had already raised her hand as if to slap Laney, but both Laney and Owen snagged the woman by the wrist. The rage was all over Nettie's face now and she bucked against the restraint.

"I don't only need a statement about the bug," Owen snapped. "But also about your meeting with Hadley Odom."

Nettie's rage vanished. In its place came the shock. Only for a second, though. "I have no idea what you're talking about."

Because Owen was watching her so carefully, he saw something he didn't want to see. Nettie touched her hand to her mouth, then trailed it down to her throat. She did that while staring at him, her eyes hardly blinking. All signs that she was lying.

"You've never met Hadley Odom?" he pressed.

Her hand fluttered to the side of her face and she shook her head. "No. Why would I have met her? I don't even know who she is."

Kellan and Owen exchanged glances as Kellan stepped in front of Nettie. "What if I told you there could be proof that you not only knew this woman but that you met with her?"

Nettie huffed, "Then I'd say someone lied. Or that you're mistaken. I have to go," she added, tucking her purse beneath her arm. "Make those arrangements for the computers to be picked up. I need to go to Austin and talk to my husband."

Owen didn't stop Nettie when she walked out. She wasn't exactly a flight risk and, once they had more info on the computers—or from Terrance—they could bring her back in for questioning. It'd be necessary because

Owen was certain that Nettie knew a lot more about this than she was saying.

Nettie paused when she reached the door and glanced at them from over her shoulder. "Emerson's going to ruin both of you when he finds out how you've treated me," she declared just seconds before she made her exit.

Owen kept his eyes on Nettie until she was out of sight, then turned to get Kellan's take on what had just happened. But he noticed Laney first. She was pale and looking a little shaky.

"Nettie could have killed my sister," Laney said, sinking down into the nearest chair.

Owen wanted to curse. He'd been all cop when he'd been listening to Nettie and hadn't remembered that this was more than a murder investigation to Laney. She'd lost a member of her family, and he knew what that was like. Knew that it could cut to the core. It would continue to cut until Laney learned the truth and found justice for her.

He knew plenty about that, as well.

"I'll take the interview with Terrance," Kellan advised.

Still looking shaky, Laney got up. "I want to listen to what he has to say."

Judging from the way Kellan's forehead bunched up, he was likely debating if that was a good idea. But he finally nodded. "Take her to the observation room," he told Owen.

Owen did, but that was only because he knew he wouldn't be able to talk Laney out of it. Besides, she knew Terrance, and she might have some insight into whatever he said. Owen was betting, though, that Terrance wouldn't reveal anything incriminating. No way would he risk going back to jail, unless he was stupid.

And he definitely didn't strike Owen as stupid.

Just the opposite. Terrance could have told them about Nettie and Hadley's meeting as a way of covering himself. By casting doubt on Nettie, Terrance might believe it would take the spotlight off him when it came to Hadley's murder. It didn't. He had motive and means. As for opportunity... Yes, he had an alibi, but he could have hired someone to do the job.

Laney's top suspect in her sister's murder was Emerson. Or at least it had been before Terrance had just thrown Nettie into the mix. But Owen was going to take a hard look at Terrance himself.

"Are you all right?" Owen asked Laney when they stepped into the observation room. It was a small space, not much bigger than a closet, and it put them elbow to elbow.

"I will be," she answered after a long pause. That meant she wasn't all right at the moment. Of course, he hadn't expected her to absorb it all and look at this through a PI's eyes. Not when there was this much emotion at stake.

She kept her attention on the two-way glass window where Kellan, Terrance and his lawyer were filing into interview room. "I'll be better if I can figure out a way to put him back in a cage."

Owen made a sound of agreement and because he could feel the tight muscles in her arms, he put his hand on her back and gave her a gentle pat. That took her gaze off Terrance. She looked at him. Then she groaned.

"You're feeling sorry for me." She said it like an accusation. There was some anger in her eyes and her voice. "You're thinking about the way Terrance beat me up and how that's weighing on me—"

Owen didn't let her finish. He snapped Laney to him and kissed her. What she'd said was true, but for some reason, her anger riled him. It had obviously made him stupid, too, because his go-to response had been a hard kiss. That didn't stay hard. The moment his mouth landed on hers, everything changed.

Everything.

The anger melted away from him, along with the rest of his common sense, and in its place came the heat. Of course, the heat had been stirring for a while now between them, but the temperature inside him soared to scalding temps when he tasted her.

Oh, man.

He was toast. That taste and the feel of her in his arms worked against him when she moved right into the kiss. Apparently she'd gotten rid of her anger, too, because she certainly wasn't fighting him. In fact, he was reasonably sure Laney was also feeling plenty of the heat.

The memories of that look in the barn slammed into him, mixing with this fresh fire and making this so much more than just a mere kiss. That, of course, only made him even more stupid. He shouldn't be lusting after her. Not with the chaos that was in their lives. And he darn sure shouldn't be wondering if he could take this kiss and let it lead them straight to bed.

She slid her arms around him, first one and then the other. Not some tight grip that would anchor him in place, which made it all the more dangerous. Because he suddenly wanted the anchor. He *ached* for it. Owen wanted to feel every inch of her against him. He silently cursed himself. And he cursed her, too.

When Owen heard Kellan's voice, he automatically tore himself away from Laney. It took him a moment to realize his brother wasn't in the observation room with them but that his voice was coming from the intercom. Kellan wasn't speaking to Laney and him, either. He was reading Terrance his rights.

Great. He'd gotten so tied up in that kiss and in the thoughts of bedding Laney, he'd forgotten there was something very important going on just one room over. They were there to hear what Terrance had to say, to try to look for any flaws or inconsistencies in his statement. Not for a make-out session. Even if that session had been damn good.

"Don't you dare apologize to me for that," Laney warned him. She ran her tongue over her bottom lip, causing his body to clench and then beg him to go back for more.

Owen stayed firmly planted where he was, though it was still plenty close to Laney. "I'm sorry that I lost focus," he settled for saying. "Not as sorry as I should be about the kiss."

It was the truth, but it was also true that it would happen again. That was why Owen groaned and cursed. He didn't need this kind of distraction, not with so much at stake, but his body didn't seem to be giving him a choice.

"We should have done something about this in the barn that day," he grumbled. "Then we would have burned it out of our systems by now."

At best, that was wishful thinking, but Laney didn't dismiss it. That told him she believed this was just lust, nothing more. But maybe that, too, was wishful thinking.

She smiled, but then quickly tightened her mouth to stop it. "I still have dreams about that day in the barn," she said.

Great. Now that was in his head. Dreaming about him having sex with her. Or rather, him wanting to have sex with her. The urge to do just that had been plenty strong that day. Still was. And Owen figured he'd be having his own dreams about not only that but the scalding kiss they'd just shared.

Thankfully, Kellan got their minds back on track when he sat across from Terrance at the table and opened with his first question.

"Where were you last night?"

The lawyer immediately took a piece of paper from his briefcase and handed it to Kellan. "We anticipated that you'd want to know that, so there's my client's alibi. As you can see, he was having dinner with several friends. I've included their names and contact information should you want to verify."

Slick move, Owen thought, and he had no doubts that the alibi would check out. That didn't mean Terrance hadn't been involved, though. Nope. He could have hired those men to break in. Heck, he could have hired them to plant the bug and set up Nettie.

Kellan looked over the paper the lawyer had given him. "Did you have a PI tail on Joe Henshaw, too?" he asked Terrance.

"Not recently, but yes, before my trial I did," Terrance admitted. "I've already told you that I had Laney and anyone connected to her under watchful eyes in case something turned up that I could use in my defense."

"You do know that Joe was murdered last night?" Kellan threw it out there.

Terrance nodded. "But I didn't see him, if that's what you're about to ask next." He tipped his head to the paper. "And that proves I was elsewhere when he died."

Kellan didn't even pause. "You'd be willing to turn over your finances so I can verify that you didn't hire someone to kill him and hire others to attack Laney and kill Joe?"

Terrance smiled, definitely not from humor, though. It was more of amusement, and then he waved off whatever his lawyer had been about to say. "I'll turn them over to you if and when you get a warrant. I'm guessing, though, you don't have enough probable cause to do that, or you would have already gotten it."

"You're right. I don't have probable cause, not yet, but it's still early," Kellan answered. "A lot of hours left in the day, and I don't think it'd take much to convince a judge that I need a look at your financials. Not with your criminal record. Judges are a lot more apt to help when a convicted felon's name comes up in a murder investigation."

The anger flared in Terrance's eyes. Heck, his nostrils did, too, and that caused Owen to smile. It was nice to see Terrance get a little comeuppance, but it wasn't enough. They needed to get into his bank account, and despite what Kellan had just threatened, it might not happen. Terrance's lawyer would almost certainly stonewall any attempts at a warrant.

"How much did the woman he met online steal from Terrance?" Owen asked Laney.

"According to Terrance and the lawsuit he filed against me, it was about three million."

Owen's mouth fell open for a moment. "Damn."

Laney made a sound of agreement and glanced up at him. "A judge threw out his lawsuit, but from what I could gather, that three million was about two-thirds of Terrance's entire inheritance. His family wasn't happy about that."

No one other than the swindler would be happy about that. And with Terrance blaming Laney, it gave him three million motives to get back at her. Maybe even enough to kill or hire killers.

However, if Terrance had indeed paid someone to do his dirty work, his old-money background might have given him the skills to hide transactions like that. There could be offshore accounts. Heck, the funds could have come from a safe with lots of cash. Still, Owen would press to get that warrant. Right now, it was one of the few strings they had to tug on Terrance. If they tugged hard enough, things were bound to unravel and get them the proof they needed for an arrest.

"I've heard you have one of the so-called gunmen in custody," Terrance went on a moment later. "I gather he hasn't said anything about me hiring him, or you would have used that to arrest me."

There was enough snark in Terrance's tone to let them know it was a challenge of sorts. No, the gunman hadn't pointed the finger at Terrance. Maybe he never would. But the longer they held the gunman, the higher the chance he might start to get desperate. The guy could ask for a plea deal in exchange for giving up his boss. Owen figured it would make plenty of people happy if it turned out to be Terrance.

Kellan stared at Terrance for several snail-crawling moments. "A lot of hours left in the day," he repeated.

"Who knows what kind of dirt we'll be able to turn up on you."

This time Terrance flashed one of those cocky smiles, and Owen thought he saw some honest-to-goodness frustration slide into the man's eyes.

Terrance leaned forward, resting his forearms on the metal table. "Let me make your job easy for you, Sheriff Slater, because I want you to get off my back. I didn't hire any gunmen. I also didn't kill anyone, but I might have some more information that can put you on the right track."

Owen didn't miss the *more* and he found himself moving even closer to the glass. However, he also reminded himself that anything that came out of Terrance's mouth could be a lie or something meant to throw them off his track.

"I'm listening," Kellan said to the man.

Terrance opened a bottle of water first and had a long drink. "I've already told you that I hired PIs to follow people connected to my trial. That's how one of the PIs saw Nettie with Hadley." He paused. "But that wasn't the only time they saw Hadley."

That grabbed Owen's attention. Laney's, too, because she moved in closer, as well.

"I'll give you the reports from the PIs, of course," Terrance went on, "but I can tell you that about two days before Hadley was murdered, one of my men followed her to Austin."

Austin was a city only about an hour from Longview Ridge. Owen glanced at Laney to see if that rang any bells as to why her sister would go there, but she just shook her head.

"Hadley had a package with her," Terrance continued a moment later. "She went into the First National Bank on St. Mary's Street, stayed inside about a half hour, and when she came out, she didn't have the package with her. I know I'm not a cop, but I figure what she left there is worth you checking out."

"The photos of Emerson and Hadley," Laney said, snapping her eyes toward him. "Owen, we have to go get them now."

Chapter Seven

Now didn't happen. Despite Laney's insistence, she and Owen still did not have the photos even after Terrance had given them the name and street address of the bank where his PIs had seen Hadley.

Laney tried not to be frustrated and impatient about that, but it was impossible not to feel those things. And more. The urgency clawed away at her. She was so close to the evidence she needed to nail down Hadley's killer. She knew that in her gut. But she was going to have to tamp down that urgency because of one simple fact.

There was no safe-deposit box in Hadley's name at the First National Bank in Austin.

That meant either Terrance had lied about it or Hadley had used an alias. Laney was betting it was the latter. Hadley had wanted to make sure Emerson couldn't get to those pictures because she'd seen them as some kind of insurance policy. Proof of an affair with a married man.

Hadley had likely believed that as a DA, Emerson could have used his contacts to do searches of banks. And maybe he had indeed managed to do just that. But Laney wasn't giving up hope yet.

She would *never* give up hope, even if her patience was wearing thin.

Laney was pacing across the living room floor of Owen's grandparents' house—something she'd been doing a lot since they're returned an hour earlier from the sheriff's office. She stopped when Owen came in. One look at his face and she knew he didn't have good news for her.

"We're having trouble getting the search warrant for the bank." He sounded as frustrated as she felt. "The judge wants more verification that Hadley actually had a box there, and we just don't have it."

She touched her hand to the chain around her neck. It now only had the dragonfly pendant. "The bank manager has the key."

"A key that may or may not belong to one of the boxes," Owen reminded her. It wasn't his first reminder, either.

She wanted to argue with him. But she couldn't. She'd found the key in Hadley's apartment shortly after she'd been murdered. Laney had no proof that it was the one for the safe-deposit box Hadley had told her about. But Laney believed that it was. She believed it with all her heart. Too bad the judge wouldn't take her gut feeling as more verification for the search warrant.

"Even if it is the right key," Owen went on, "the manager says the bank employees can't just test that key on the boxes to find the right one."

"So, we need either the name Hadley used to get the box or the box number," she said, talking more to herself than to Owen. Laney forced herself to think, to try to figure out where Hadley might have left information like that.

Owen nodded, but it wasn't a nod of total agreement. "If the bank gets the right box and opens it, the manager says he can't release the contents without proper authorization."

Laney knew that, of course. Kellan had already told her that when she'd given him the key. The key that he'd then passed along to the bank manager. It still didn't make it easier to swallow. Plus, there was the hope that if and when the box was opened, there might be enough inside to spur the manager to help them get that warrant. After all, the photos could confirm motive for Hadley's murder.

Could.

Again, it would take some convincing with a judge, but at least they'd have tangible evidence. Emerson might fall apart and confess everything when confronted with pictures of him and his lover. At a minimum, it might cause Owen to start doubting him so that he and Kellan would take a much harder look.

"What about the PI report from Terrance?" Laney asked, but then she immediately waved that off.

That wasn't *proof.* Far from it. Terrance was a convicted felon and probably still held a grudge against her. He could have given them this info to send them on some wild-goose chase. One that would take the spotlight off him. One that would put her in an extra frazzled frame of mind. If so, it was working because that was where she was right now.

"Kellan's bringing in the PI who claims he saw Hadley go into the bank," Owen told her. "If the PI will sign a sworn statement as to what he saw, we can go back to the judge."

It was a long shot, but Laney refused to believe it wouldn't work. They had to find that box and get into it.

Owen walked closer to her, but still kept some distance between them. Something he'd been doing since that kiss in the observation room. Despite Laney telling him not to apologize for it, she could tell he was sorry. And that he regretted it.

"The bank manager did agree to go through all the names to see if there were any red flags," Owen said several moments later. "Is there any alias you can think of that Hadley might have used?"

It was something Kellan had already asked her, and Laney had come up with zilch. However, she had given Kellan the full names of Hadley and her parents, their pets and even childhood friends in case her sister had used any one of those.

"What about the PI report of the meeting between Nettie and Hadley?" she asked. "Has Terrance sent that to Kellan yet?"

"He emailed it, and Kellan sent me a copy."

Laney huffed. She wasn't frustrated that Terrance had sent it but because she'd wanted to see it as soon as it arrived.

"You read the report," Owen said, obviously picking up on her frustration. "It's on my computer."

Upstairs and in his bedroom. Or, at least, that was where his laptop had been the last time she'd seen it. Upstairs was also where his brother Eli and Gemma were. Addie and Francine, too. And while Laney liked all of them, she'd wanted to give Owen some space to be with his daughter and the rest of his family.

Owen motioned for her to follow him as he headed for the stairs. She did. "The reason I wasn't jumping through hoops to tell you about the report Terrance sent is that there's nothing in it other than what he told us at the sheriff's office."

That wasn't a surprise, but it was an annoying disappointment that only added to her frustration. Still, there was no way Terrance would give them anything they could use against him, and the PI likely wouldn't have realized the importance of a meeting between the two women. Still, Laney wanted to read it, study it, because it could possibly have something they could use.

"There are probably other reports," she said as they walked up the stairs. "Ones that maybe Terrance is holding on to. He can maybe use them as bargaining chips if it comes down to that."

His quick nod let her know that Owen had already considered it. "Kellan will try to get a search warrant on Terrance, too."

It would be easier to get that than it would be to get one for the bank, but Laney was betting Terrance had covered his tracks and there'd be nothing to find. There would definitely be nothing on his personal computer since he wouldn't risk going back to jail.

When they made it to Owen's bedroom, she was surprised that it was empty, but she could hear the chatter next door in the master bedroom. Chatter that she was betting wouldn't stop Eli from keeping watch. He was just doing it from the upstairs window now instead of the downstairs one. Laney had thankfully seen no lapse in security, which would need to continue until they found the person responsible for the attack.

Too bad they weren't any closer to doing that.

Owen's laptop was on a small folding table in the corner and he pulled out the chair for her to sit. The report was already on the screen. She noted the date and time.

"Lee Kissner," Laney said, reading the PI's name aloud. "I don't know him personally, but he has a good reputation."

"A good rep, but he was working for Terrance," Owen pointed out.

She nodded. Shrugged. "I sometimes took on slimeball clients who were trying to clear their names." Laney could see this from that side of things, but it didn't make her feel better that Terrance had had her sister and her followed.

Laney read through the report, noting the description of the clothes Hadley was wearing. Red dress with silver trim and silver heels. Her sister did indeed have an outfit like that. In fact, the details matched all the way to the purse.

"According to the notes, Hadley didn't talk to anyone before going into the bank," Laney pointed out. "But someone—an employee—inside would have spoken with her. I'm assuming they've all been questioned?"

Owen nodded again. "One of the clerks thinks she might have remembered her when Kellan showed Hadley's photo. That's not enough to get a warrant," he quickly added. "The clerk isn't positive and doesn't remember why Hadley was there."

Laney groaned softly. She'd never been to that particular bank, but she'd checked the facts about it online, and it was huge. In addition, this visit would have happened months ago. That wasn't going to help, not with the steady stream of customers who would have gone in and out of there during that time.

As she continued reading, Laney could feel her

frown deepening with each sentence. Her sister had spent a half hour inside the bank. That was plenty of time to not only open an account for a safe-deposit box but also enough time to lock the pictures inside and then come out.

Hadley hadn't spoken to anyone as she'd walked back to her car. She had simply driven away. The PI hadn't followed her since he was waiting on further instructions from Terrance. According to Lee Kissner, those instructions had been to suspend, at least temporarily, following Hadley. Too bad he hadn't stuck with her because it might have given them more clues about her killer.

Laney finished reading the report, stood and started to pace again, hoping that she could come up with an angle they could use to sway a judge. But nothing came to mind. Given the way Owen's forehead was furrowed, he was drawing a blank, too.

"I shouldn't have kissed you," he said. So, no blank after all. His mind hadn't been on the report, though she was certain he'd already given it plenty of thought.

"Yes," she agreed. "Loss of focus, blurred lines, bad timing." She'd hoped her light tone and dry smile would ease the tension on his face, but it didn't.

"Heat," he added to the list. But Owen didn't just say it. There was also some heat in his voice, along with a hefty dose of something Laney had been feeling all morning. Irritation and annoyance.

Owen looked at her the same moment she looked at him, and their gazes collided. Oh, mercy. Yes, there it was. So much fire. Way too much need. Way too much *everything*.

With all the memories going through her head, she

wanted to smack herself as the image of Owen in the barn jumped right to the front of her mind. Followed by the more recent image of their kiss. Her body reacted and she felt that heat trickle through her.

"It's too dangerous for me not to be able to see all of this clearly," Owen added.

Until he'd said that, Laney had been about to go to him and kiss him. Nothing hard and deep like the one in the observation room. Just a peck to assure him that the heat could wait. It would have maybe sated her body a little, as well.

No assuring and sating now, though. They were just standing there, much too close, their gazes connected, the weight of the attraction and their situation bearing down on them.

It stunned her when Owen leaned in and brushed his mouth over hers. Stunned her even more that just a peck from him could dole out that kind of wallop. It was a reminder that any kind of contact between them was only going to complicate things.

"Sorry to interrupt," someone said from the doorway. Jack.

The man moved like a cat. And, despite the fact that he'd no doubt just witnessed that lip-lock, he didn't give his brother a ribbing smile.

"Just got a call from one of the hands," Jack told them. "Emerson's at your house, and he's demanding to see you."

Emerson had likely heard about Kellan taking the computers from his home. Or maybe Nettie had finally filled her husband in on everything.

"Emerson's already spoken to Kellan," Jack went on. "Guess he didn't get the answers he wanted, so he drove out to the ranch. I'm thinking it's not a good idea to have Emerson brought here."

"No, it's not," Owen agreed. He paused, his forehead bunching up even more. "Tell the hand to keep Emerson at my place. I'll drive over there to see him."

"Not without me—" Jack immediately said just as Laney piped in, "I want to see him, too—"

She knew Owen wasn't going to argue with his brother about going, but considered he would nix her request. He surprised her when he didn't. He gave her a nod.

"Just let me check on Addie first," Owen muttered.

Jack stepped to the side so that Owen could head there.

"No one in the room will bite," Jack added under his breath to her. "And if anyone can lighten the mood around here, it's Addie."

Jack was right. The little girl had a way of making everything better. Laney thanked him for the reminder and followed Owen, intending to stay in the hall and just get a glimpse of Addie. She didn't want to interfere with Owen's time with her. But Gemma remedied that as she took hold of Laney's arm and led her into the room.

Eli was in the exact spot that Laney thought he would be. Keeping watch at the window. Francine, seated near him, was sipping coffee. Laney smiled when she saw Addie on the bed, playing with a stash of stuffed animals, blocks and books. Addie smiled when she spotted her dad and put aside a toy horse to scoot toward him. Owen picked her up and kissed her cheek.

"Da-da," she said and dropped her head in the crook of his neck. The loving moment didn't last, though, when Addie's attention landed on Laney. "Aney," she attempted to say.

Laney didn't know who was more surprised when the little girl reached for her, but she felt a lot of relief. She'd been so afraid that Addie would associate her with the loud blasts from the gunfire and the terrifying run to the barn, but apparently she hadn't remembered that as well as she had Laney's name.

Owen passed Addie over to her, and when Laney had her in her arms, she had another surprise when Addie kissed her. The little girl babbled something that Laney didn't understand, but she caught the word *horsey*, so maybe she was talking about her toy stash.

Jack stepped up to Eli, probably to tell him about Emerson's arrival. When Jack went back into the hall, clearly waiting, that was Owen's cue to get moving.

Owen took Addie from Laney, giving his daughter another kiss before putting her back on the bed.

"My advice?" Eli said. "Put on a flak jacket because Emerson won't be a happy camper."

No, he wouldn't be, Laney thought. And it was possible that Nettie hadn't even told him the whole truth. The woman certainly would have put her own slant on things, and that, in turn, could cause Emerson to aim even more venom at Owen and her.

With Eli following them, Jack, Owen and Laney went back downstairs, and she heard Eli reset the security system as soon as they were out the door. They hurried into the cruiser so they wouldn't be out in the open too long. Of course, even a minute was probably too long as far as Owen as concerned.

Laney waited for Owen to remind her that it was an unnecessary risk for her to insist on going to this meeting. But he didn't. Maybe because he knew it wouldn't do any good. Besides, just seeing her might trigger Emerson into a fit of temper that could get him to spill the secret he'd been keeping about Hadley.

When Owen's house came into view, she immediately saw the crime scene tape fluttering in the breeze. Laney also noticed the sleek black car parked in front just a split second before she spotted Emerson. He was talking on his phone while he paced the front porch. And yes, he was riled. Every muscle in his body and face showed that. She had even more proof of the man's anger when they got out of the cruiser.

"What the hell do you think you're doing?" Emerson barked. The question wasn't aimed at Owen but rather at her.

"I'm trying to find out who nearly killed me and Owen," Laney answered. She didn't dodge Emerson's fiery gaze and definitely didn't back down. That was one of the few advantages of being just as riled as he was.

Despite the thick tension in the air, Owen somehow managed to stay calm as he unlocked the door. "There's a hired killer still at large, so we'll take this inside."

Emerson looked ready to argue, but he probably would have argued about anything at this point. He was spoiling for a fight.

Owen ushered her in first and Laney immediately saw that some of the items had been moved. Likely the CSIs' doing. She was betting the entire place had been checked for prints and trace evidence. An attack on a police officer's home would have caused everyone involved to be on the top of their game.

"You convinced Kellan to have a CSI go into my

home," Emerson ranted at Laney as he came inside. He was still aiming his rage at her, too. "You upset my wife."

Owen didn't say anything until he had the door shut, and then he eased around to face his brother-in-law. "Nettie gave us permission to get the computers and have them analyzed. Did she tell you why?"

"Yes," Emerson snapped while Jack went to the living room window to keep watch. "It's because someone set her up so that it looks as if she planted a bug in your guesthouse." His narrowed eyes cut to Laney. "*You* set her up."

"I have no reason to do that." Laney tried to restrain her temper enough to keep her voice calm as well, but she wasn't quite as successful as Owen.

"Yes, you do, because you have some kind of vendetta against me." Emerson opened his mouth as if to say more, but then he closed it.

"What else did Nettie tell you?" Owen asked.

Silence. For a very long time. Emerson finally cursed under his breath and leaned against the wall. "Nettie said she met with her—" he tipped his head toward Laney to indicate the *her* "—sister." While there was still some anger in his voice, she thought she heard disgust, too.

"Hadley," Laney provided, though she was certain he knew her sister's name. "Hadley Odom," she said, spelling it out because she wanted to try to gauge his reaction.

Emerson dismissed her with a glance before his attention went back to Owen. "Nettie heard rumors that I was having an affair with *Hadley*." He said the name as if it were venom. "I'm guessing your sister started those rumors. So, Nettie confronted her. Apparently some private investigator witnessed the meeting and told Kellan about it."

"Did Nettie also confront *you* about the affair?" Owen asked.

Another long pause. "No. I didn't know that Nettie had heard those rumors until about two hours ago when she told me what's been going on."

"Rumors?" Owen questioned.

Since it sounded like the accusation that it was, Emerson cursed again. Then he groaned when Owen continued to stare at him. "I knew Hadley."

For only three words, they packed a huge punch. Finally, Laney had heard the man admit the truth. Truth about knowing her sister anyway. But she figured Owen was experiencing a gut punch of a different kind. As a cop, he wouldn't have wanted to hear his brother-in-law just confess to a relationship that was now a motive for murder.

Owen dragged his hand over his face and did some cursing of his own. "I need to read you your rights."

"I know my damn rights." Emerson pushed away from the wall. "I'm the damn DA!"

Owen went closer until they were toe-to-toe. "Then act like it and tell me what happened between Hadley and you. *Everything that happened*," Owen emphasized.

Emerson's glare went on for so long that Laney thought he was going to clam up or demand that she leave. Maybe even ask for a lawyer. He didn't. He stepped back, shook his head. When his gaze returned to Owen, some of the anger was gone.

"I didn't kill her…" Emerson started. "I swear, I didn't kill her." He looked at Laney when he repeated that. "And I don't care what she told you. There was no affair. I barely knew her."

She studied his eyes, looking for any signs that was a lie, and Laney thought she detected one. However, she didn't know Emerson well enough to use his body language to try to convince Owen that the man wasn't being honest with them.

"How'd you meet Hadley?" Owen persisted when Emerson didn't continue.

"At a party that I attended in San Antonio. She came onto me, and I brushed her off. Told her I was a married man, that I didn't play around on my wife." Emerson glared at Laney as if challenging her to prove him otherwise.

She couldn't.

She'd never personally seen the two of them together, but she'd believed her sister when Hadley had told her about the affair. And, just as important, she didn't believe Emerson. Yes, she could see Hadley coming onto him, but Hadley was a very attractive woman. She could have likely had her pick of the men at that party and wouldn't have come onto Emerson had he not been sending off the right signals. Or in this case, the wrong ones, since he was a married man.

"I never saw Hadley again after that night," Emerson went on. "But she called me and claimed I'd given her some kind of date rape drug at the party. I denied it, but she didn't believe me. She cried and carried on and told me that I'd be sorry."

Owen jumped right on that. "She threatened you?"

Emerson shook his head. "Not then, not with actual words anyway, but I knew she was very upset and believed I'd actually drugged her. So upset that when I first heard she was dead, I wondered if she'd killed herself to set me up, to make it look as if I'd murdered her. The woman was crazy," he added in a mumble.

"Hadley didn't commit suicide," Laney insisted. But she would give him a pass on the crazy part. Hadley could be overly emotional. Still, Laney didn't believe she'd lied about having an affair with Emerson.

That meant Emerson was lying now.

"I agree about her not killing herself," Emerson said when Laney just kept glaring at him. "I realized that when I read the police report about her murder. The angle of the blunt-force trauma wound was all wrong for her to have done that to herself."

For just a moment Laney saw something more than anger. Maybe regret? Or it could be that Emerson had once had feelings for Hadley. That didn't mean, though, that he hadn't murdered her.

"There's more," Emerson continued, his gaze firing to Laney again. "And if you're responsible, so help me God, I'll make sure you're put behind bars."

Laney raised her hands. "What the heck are you talking about?"

"Blackmail." Emerson let that hang in the air.

Owen didn't even glance at her to see if she knew what Emerson meant, and that helped ease a little of the tension in her chest. Twenty-four hours earlier, if Emerson had accused her of something, Owen would have considered it a strong possibility. Or even the truth. But he now knew she wouldn't do anything like that.

"A couple of days ago, I got a phone call," Emerson explained. "The person used one of those voice scramblers, so I didn't know who it was. Still don't. But the person claimed to know about the so-called affair I had with Hadley and threatened to tell Nettie if I didn't pay up. He said he had some kind of proof, but that's impossible. There's no proof because there was no affair."

Owen kept his attention nailed to Emerson. "You paid the blackmailer?" he snapped.

"No. Of course not. I'm not going to pay for something I didn't do. I put the person off, said that I needed time to get some money together. I've been using that time to try to figure out who's behind this."

Owen huffed and Laney knew why. Emerson's first response should have been to go to the cops. To his brother-in-law, Owen. Of course, that was the last thing a guilty man would have wanted to do.

"And did you find out who's behind this?" Owen challenged, the annoyance dripping off his tone.

Emerson shook his head, took out his phone. "I got another call yesterday. I recorded it and had a private lab analyze it. They were unable to get a voice match because of the scrambling device the person used, but the tech thought the caller was male. You can listen to the recording if you want."

Owen nodded.

Both Laney and Owen moved closer to Emerson's phone before the man hit the play button on his phone.

"I made it clear that I want thirty grand to keep your dirty little secret," the caller said. "Since I don't have it yet, it's gonna cost you a whole lot more." The person rattled off a bank account number. "Fifty grand should do it. If I don't have the money in forty-eight hours, the amount doubles and then I go to your wife. I'll go to the press, too. Think of all the damage to your reputation when this comes out. You'll never be able to get the mud off your name."

Emerson clicked off the recording. "Don't bother tracing the bank," he said. "It's an offshore account."

That would indeed make it almost impossible to trace. But a conversation with the blackmailer might have given them plenty of clues. Laney so badly wanted to say that Emerson should have gone to Kellan and Owen with this, but she figured the man had already realized that.

"I won't send money," Emerson insisted. *"Can't,"* he amended. "Even if I had done something wrong, you know I don't have those kinds of funds. You know how little a DA makes in a small town. And I won't go to my wife's trust fund to pay a blackmailer to keep a secret that I don't even have."

Laney had known about Nettie's trust fund and that she was from a prominent family. It had come up when she'd run a background check on the woman. But Laney had assumed that Emerson had money of his own. Apparently not.

Emerson closed his eyes for a moment before he continued, "I don't want Nettie to know anything about this supposed affair. It'll upset her, and there's no reason for it."

Owen dragged in a breath. "Upsetting Nettie is only one part of this, and right now it's a small part. You withheld potential evidence in a murder investigation. That's obstruction of justice and you, of all people, should know that."

Laney figured that would bring on another wave of Emerson's rage, but it didn't come. The man merely nodded, as if surrendering. "I intend to talk to Kellan about that. In the meantime, I'll send you a copy of the recording from the blackmailer and will cooperate in any way the sheriff's office needs."

"Even financials?" Owen quickly asked.

Emerson didn't nod that time. He stared at Owen, and Laney wished she could see what was going on in his head. Obviously there was hesitation, but there seemed to be something more.

"Nettie and I don't have shared accounts," Emerson finally said. "That's the way it's written in her trust fund, that it can't become a joint account. I can give you access to mine but not hers."

"That'll do for now," Owen assured him.

Laney figured either Kellan or Owen would soon press Nettie to do the same.

Emerson made a sound to indicate that he would. "Just keep Nettie out of this, and I'll cooperate in any way that I can." He started for the door but then stopped when he reached Laney. "I didn't have an affair with your sister," he repeated.

She stood there and watched Emerson walk out. He drove away as soon as he got in his car, leaving Laney to try to sort through everything he'd just told them. That sorting, however, was getting some interference from her own emotions.

Emerson had stayed insistent about not having the affair, but he'd admitted to the obstruction of justice. Admitting to the first might cost him his marriage, but the second could put him behind bars. Why admit to one and not the other?

"You believe him?" Owen asked.

"If I do, it means my sister lied." She groaned softly, pushed her hair from her face. "Hadley could be irresponsible about some things, but lying about this wouldn't be like her." And Laney hated the words that were about to come out of her mouth. "Still, it's possible she did."

Owen nodded, not giving her his take on what he thought about all of it. But he was probably leaning in Emerson's direction. Specifically, leaning toward believing Emerson hadn't killed Hadley. After all, Owen didn't know Hadley, and it would make his personal life much easier if he didn't have to haul in his brother-in-law for murder.

He shut the door, took out his phone, and she saw him press Kellan's number. "I want to get that recording analyzed by the crime lab," he said. "And Kellan will need access to Emerson's phone records. We might be able to find out who made the two calls."

Maybe, but she figured a blackmailer would use a burner cell, one that couldn't be traced. Especially if Terrance had been the one to make the calls. He was too smart to get caught doing something that stupid.

"Terrance knew about the meeting between Nettie and Hadley," she said while they waited for Kellan to answer. "The blackmail could be a way of his recouping some money he lost from his trust fund. It'll barely put a dent in what he lost, but he could be planning on going back to Emerson for more."

Owen made eye contact with her to let her know he was considering that, but he didn't get a chance to say anything because Kellan came on the line.

"I was just about to call you," Kellan volunteered. "We got a lucky break. The banker in Austin found the box. It's under an alias, Sandy Martell."

"How did they find out it belongs to Hadley?" Owen wanted to know.

"Because Hadley put Laney's name on it. There's a condition, though. Laney can only get into the box if she has the key. How convinced is Laney that the key she gave me is the one to the box?"

Good question, one that Owen had already asked Laney.

"I believe it is," Laney said. "I'm not positive, though."

Kellan stayed quiet for a moment. "All right. Then I'll meet you at the bank so I can give you back the key. Owen needs to get you there ASAP because the manager's going to let you have access."

Chapter Eight

A lot of thoughts went through Owen's mind, and not all of them were of relief.

Having Laney's name on the safe-deposit box meant it would eliminate hours and maybe days of red tape to not only locate the box but to gain them access to it. It also meant they might finally have those photos Hadley had claimed would prove her affair with Emerson.

However, for them to get the photos—or whatever was in the box—meant taking Laney off the ranch and all the way to Austin. That wasn't his first choice of things to do when someone had already attacked her. She'd be out in the open where hired guns could come at her.

"Talk to the bank manager again," Owen told Kellan. Laney moved closer to him, no doubt so she could listen to the phone conversation Owen was having with his brother. He considered putting the call on speaker, but the truth was, he didn't mind her being this close to him. It eased his suddenly frayed nerves more than it should. "See if there's a way for us to get access to the box without Laney actually being there."

From the other end of the line Owen heard his brother sigh. "I already asked. Or rather, I demanded, and he said Laney had to come in person with a picture ID. Either that, or we have to go the search-warrant route."

Owen had expected that to be the manager's response, but he still cursed. "Try again." He dragged in a long breath. "Emerson just left here, and I don't like the way things are starting to play out. He claims someone's trying to blackmail him."

"Blackmail? Did Emerson admit to the affair with Hadley?" Kellan quickly asked.

"No. He denied it. He's got a recording of the blackmailer's demand. This might not have anything to do with Laney, but I don't like the timing."

"Neither do I," Kellan agreed. "I'll call the bank manager one more time and see what I can do." His brother paused. "How deep do you think Emerson is involved in this?"

Judging from Laney's expression, she wanted to say "very," but Owen still wasn't sure. "Emerson gave us permission to look into his financials," Owen settled for saying. "I'd like to get that started."

"You think Emerson could have paid for those hired guns?" Kellan pressed.

"I just want to be able to rule it out, and this is a start." Maybe not a good start, though, because someone as smart as Emerson could have a hidden account. No way would he have paid for hired killers out of his checking account and then offered to let Owen take a look at it.

"Yeah," Kellan said a moment later, both agreement and concern in his tone. "I'll let you know what the bank manager says."

When Owen ended the call, he turned back to Laney and saw exactly what he figured would be there. Hope with a hefty layering of fear. "I'll have to go to the bank," she insisted before he could say anything. "I need to see what's in that safe-deposit box, and me being there is the fastest way to do this."

She did need to see the contents of the box. So did he, but Owen was still hoping the bank manager would come through and Laney could then view the box through a video feed. *Safely* view it. Owen stared at her, trying to come up with some argument that would convince her of that, but he drew a blank on anything he could say to change her mind.

A blank about the argument anyway.

Unfortunately his mind came up with all sorts of other possibilities. None good. But plenty of them were pretty bad. Because they involved kissing her again. Heck, they involved taking her to bed.

Silently cursing himself, Owen slipped his arm around her waist and pulled her to him. Since Jack was only a few yards away and still at the window, his brother would no doubt see the embrace and give him grief about it later. But this was like the close contact he'd gotten from Laney when she'd been listening to Kellan's call. Owen needed this, too.

Apparently, Laney needed it as well, because she sighed and moved in closer.

Owen didn't dare pull back and look at her since that would have absolutely led to a kiss, but he pressed her against him and let the now-familiar feel of her settle him. Ironic that Laney would be able to do that.

The settling didn't last, though. That was because the other thoughts came. The guilt. The feeling that he was somehow cheating on his wife. Again, ironic. Naomi wouldn't have wanted him to go even this long without seeking out someone else. He'd been the one not willing to jump back into those waters.

Until now.

Owen might have considered that progress if it hadn't been stupid to get involved with someone in his protective custody.

His phone rang, thankfully putting a stop to any other thoughts about kissing Laney. He frowned when he saw the caller. Not Kellan. But rather Terrance. Laney frowned, too, and that expression only deepened when Owen answered.

"Ask Laney what the hell she thinks she's doing," Terrance snarled the moment he was on the line.

"Anything specific, or is this just a general rant?" Owen countered.

"Yes, it's specific. Someone's following me, and I figure she's responsible. The Longview Ridge Sheriff's Office doesn't have probable cause to put a tail on me."

"You're wrong about that. You're on probation, and you're a person of interest in an attack. We have a right to tail you."

But that was just a reminder, not something that'd actually happened. Kellan hadn't put a deputy on Terrance. He glanced at Laney just to make sure she hadn't hired someone to do that, and she shook her head. Not that Owen had thought for one second that she would without talking to him.

"Who's following you?" Owen asked Terrance.

"How the hell should I know? Someone who's driving a dark blue sedan. I figure it's either your man or Laney's. Maybe one of her PI friends."

"Well, it's not. I would say it's your imagination, but since you've got a lot of experience putting tails on people, you should know the real thing when you see it. Where are you?" Owen asked, not waiting for Terrance to gripe about the comment he'd just made.

"My lawyer and I are on the interstate, and the car's been following us for about ten miles now. You're sure it's not someone you know?"

"No," Laney and Owen answered in unison.

He would have pushed Terrance for more info than just the vague response "on the interstate," but Terrance hung up.

"It could be a ruse," Laney immediately said. "Terrance might think he'll be less of a person of interest if he makes us believe someone's after him."

Owen couldn't agree more, but he had to look at this from both sides. They had two other persons of interest: Emerson and Nettie. If one of them was guilty, then Terrance would make a fine patsy, and they could pin all of this on him.

He was about to put his phone away, but it rang again. This time it was Kellan so he answered immediately. Owen put the call on speaker so that Jack would be able to hear.

"It's a no-go from the bank manager," Kellan told them right away. "He needs Laney there with her ID. If not, then we have to wait for the warrant."

Owen didn't even bother to groan since it was the answer he'd expected. "How close are we to getting the warrant?"

"It could come through later today now that we've got the box narrowed down. Still, the bank manager is saying if the key doesn't match, then he'll fight the warrant. Apparently, Hadley emphasized that condition in writing when she set up the safe-deposit box."

Hadley had likely done that as a precaution, to make sure no one got into it by posing as Laney or her.

"There should be two keys," Kellan noted. "The second one wasn't found on Hadley's body or in her apartment or vehicle. Any idea who she would have given the other key to?"

Since that question was obviously aimed at Laney, Owen just looked at her.

"No," Laney admitted. "She didn't actually give one to me. I found this one when I was going through her things." She paused. "But it's possible she had the key with her when she died, and if so, the killer could have taken it."

Kellan didn't disagree. Neither did Owen.

"But her killer might not have known the location of the bank," Laney added. "He or she might have been looking for it all this time."

Again, that was true, and Owen only hoped the killer had managed to get to it before they did.

"Jack and I will drive Laney to the bank," Owen explained to Kellan. "You're still planning on meeting us there?"

"Yeah. I'll have one of the deputies with me," Kellan assured him, and he ended the call.

Four lawmen. Maybe that would be enough.

Jack went to the front door, opened it and glanced around. He still had his gun drawn. Owen did the same, waiting until Jack gave the nod before he took hold of Laney's arm to hurry her to the cruiser. It wasn't far, only about fifteen feet away, but it still meant being out in the open.

Jack went ahead of them but stayed close, and Owen positioned Laney in between them. The bad feeling in the pit of his stomach hit him hard just as they reached the bottom step. It wasn't enough of a warning, though, for him to do anything about it.

Because the shot blasted through the air.

THE SOUND OF the shot barely had time to register in Laney's mind when Owen hooked his arm around her and dragged her to the ground.

Her pulse jumped, racing like the adrenaline that surged through her. Sweet heaven. Someone was trying to kill them again.

Just ahead of them, Jack dropped, too, and both Owen and he fired glances around, no doubt looking for the shooter. Laney forced herself to do the same, though it was hard for her to see much of anything because Owen had positioned his body over hers.

Another shot came, slamming into the ground between Jack and them. Laney couldn't be sure, but she thought the gunshots had come from her left, where there was a pasture.

And trees.

Some of the oaks were wide enough to conceal a gunman. If so, he was in a bad position. Well, bad for them. Because he would have a clear shot if they tried to get to the cruiser. He'd have just as clear a shot if they tried to scramble back onto the porch. They were trapped and with very little cover.

"There," Jack said, tipping his head toward one of the oaks.

Owen nodded and turned his attention in that direction. Not Jack, though. He kept watch around them. Something that caused Laney's heart to jump to her throat. It meant Jack was watching to make sure there wasn't a second gunman.

Or even a third.

The hired guns could be closing in on them and there was nowhere for them to go. But even with the terrifying realization, Laney had to wonder who was behind this. Who wanted her dead?

A sickening thought twisted at her. Terrance's call could have been meant to pinpoint their location. For that matter, so could Emerson's visit. Word about the safe-deposit box could have leaked, and now someone was going to try to kill her rather than give her a chance to reach Austin and get her hands on those pictures or whatever else was in the box. Unfortunately, Jack or Owen could be collateral damage.

Another bullet rang out, then another. These two shots blasted into the side of the porch, which confirmed to her that the shooter was definitely behind the tree. Maybe now that they knew his location, either Jack or Owen could stop him when he leaned out to fire again.

"Can you keep him busy while I get Laney to the cruiser?" Owen asked his brother.

Her gaze zoomed across the yard to the cruiser. It was closer than the porch but not by much. And the cruiser doors were closed. Jack would be able to open it with the remote on his keys, but to get the door open, he would have to leave what little cover he had.

"Yeah," Jack verified. "Move fast in case we get company."

That certainly did nothing to slow down her thudding heart. Laney shook her head. "It's too dangerous."

"So is staying put," Owen pointed out just as quickly.

"Stay as low as possible, hurry and get underneath the cruiser. I'll be right behind you."

At least they weren't going to try to open the doors, and the cruiser itself would indeed give them some protection. Still, getting there wasn't going to be easy.

While there was another round of gunfire, Owen sent a text. Probably to Kellan to let him know they needed backup. The hands from Kellan's place would be able to get there faster than he would. Maybe in only a couple of minutes. And that gave her some hope that they might actually survive this.

Owen glanced back at her again. "Go as fast as you can," he told her.

That was the only warning she got before he moved. Not forward. He pulled her to his side so that he'd be between the gunman and her, and then he gave Jack a nod. Jack immediately levered up just enough to send some bullets in the direction of the tree.

And Jack started firing.

Owen started moving, and Laney scurried along beside him, digging her elbows and knees into the ground to get some traction. Each inch seemed to take an eternity, and there were more shots. Wild ones that she suspected the gunman was just blindly firing off with the hope of hitting them.

Along with a fresh hit of adrenaline, the raw fear came roaring through her. Fear not just for her safety but for Jack and Owen. Once again, she'd put him and a member of his family in danger. Once again, she was the reason he might die, that by helping her, Owen might never see his little girl again.

Owen, though, had obviously figured out a way to get past the fear and focus on getting to the cruiser. The moment they reached it, he practically shoved her beneath it. Laney moved over far enough for him to get under there with her.

He didn't.

"Move," Owen called out to his brother. With his body only partially beneath the cruiser, he started firing, sending a series of shots in the direction of the gunman.

Jack turned and, staying low, crawled toward them. When he got closer, Laney took hold of him to pull him in next to her. Owen sent another round toward the shooter and then joined them.

The gunman was still firing so there was no way Laney could relax, but because they were no longer in the direct line of the shots, she did feel some relief.

It didn't last.

When the gunshots abruptly stopped, Laney heard another sound. Someone revving up a car engine. She hoped it wasn't one of the hands who would come charging in. If so, he or she could be shot, too.

"Hell," Jack swore.

Since she was between the two men again, Laney couldn't see what had caused him to curse. But she heard the car engine again. Closer this time.

"Hold on," Jack warned them.

Owen threw himself over her, gathering her beneath him just seconds before the crash. There was the deafening sound of metal colliding with metal, and from the corner of her eye, she saw the tires of the other vehicle. It had rammed into the cruiser, bashing in the side enough so that the tires were nearly right on Jack. He scrambled back, bumping into Owen and her.

The engine revved up for a third time and she could see the vehicle reverse, readying to bash into them.

Owen moved fast, rolling her until they were out from beneath the cruiser and into the yard. Jack was right behind them. And not a second too soon. The cruiser was no doubt reinforced, but there was the horrific sound of metal being crunched.

"Keep an eye on Laney," Owen told his brother, rising as he passed her off to Jack.

She wanted to yell for Owen to get back down, but Laney realized what he was doing. With the cruiser between him and the vehicle that'd been ramming them, Owen started firing, almost certainly aiming his shots at the driver.

Laney sucked in her breath, so hard that she felt the pain in her chest. Mercy. Owen right there, putting his life on the line. He could be killed.

There was another squeal of brakes and Laney braced herself for another jolt. It didn't come. Instead of coming toward them, she heard the vehicle speed away.

Owen took off running after it.

Chapter Nine

Owen stood in the observation room of the sheriff's office and watched Laney as she gave Kellan her statement about the attack. Owen had already done his report, but each word he'd written had only fueled his rage. It didn't soothe his temper one bit hearing and seeing Laney replay the ordeal.

He wanted to curse himself, but he didn't even know where to start. He'd screwed up way too many things today—things that could have gotten people killed.

Here, he'd ignored his gut instinct and allowed Laney to be put in yet another dangerous situation. One that had not only involved his brother but also his daughter. All those shots had been fired way too close to the house and Addie.

Owen had known it hadn't been a good idea to take Laney to the bank, had known her being out in the open was just asking for trouble. And trouble was exactly what they'd gotten.

However, that was only the start of things that he'd botched. The driver of the SUV that had nearly killed them had also gotten away. Now the ranch was yet another crime scene, and he had nothing to show for it. No shooter and no safe way to get Laney to Austin. Whoever was after her would just use that trip to make another attempt on her life.

When he saw Laney push back from the table and stand, Owen went back into the hall so he could see her. She wasn't crying, wasn't shaking. That was something at least, and she looked less on edge than he felt.

"Still beating yourself up?" she asked, sliding a hand down his arm.

Kellan came out of the room, his glance at Owen connecting long enough for them to have one of those silent brotherly conversations. At the end of it, Kellan only lifted an eyebrow.

"Laney held up just fine," his brother told him before he headed back to his office.

Owen was glad about the "holding up" part, but it didn't let him off the hook. "I deserve some beating up," he told her.

Laney made eye contact, too, but it was more than a long glance with those baby blues. "You saved my life" was all she said before she leaned in and brushed a kiss on his mouth.

He didn't know what stunned him more, the kiss or the fact that she seemed sincerely grateful even though he'd nearly gotten her and others killed by not listening to that bad feeling he'd had in his gut.

"I can see you don't want my thanks," she whispered. "You want to beat yourself up for something that was out of your control. Should I beat myself up, too? After all, I'm the reason for the danger."

Owen cursed. "I knew it was a mistake to try to take you to the bank."

"I pushed you into it," Laney insisted and then paused. "Maybe we can beat ourselves up together?"

Laney added what might have been a smile to that, but he didn't want any attempt at being lighthearted right now. He was angry…and scared. Because no matter what he did, he might not be able to keep Addie, Laney and the others safe.

She stayed close, right against him, while she looked up at him. She seemed to be holding her breath as if waiting for something.

Behind them, he could hear the chatter in the squad room. Could also hear Kellan talking to someone on the phone. There was so much to do with this new investigation, but he didn't budge. Owen just stood there. Until he gave up on the notion of common sense.

And he kissed her.

He instantly felt the relief, the tension, draining from his body. Of course, he got a tension of a different kind. The heat from the attraction. But he didn't care. Right now, he just needed this, and he was pretty sure Laney needed it, too.

She moved against him, slipping right into his arms. Moving into the kiss, too. He took in her taste, her scent, and likely would've have taken a lot more than he should have if he hadn't heard the footsteps.

Owen pulled away from her and turned to see Gunnar coming toward them. If his fellow deputy had seen the kiss, then he wisely didn't say anything about it.

"I just had another go at questioning Gilley," Gunnar explained.

Owen certainly hadn't forgotten about the hired gun they had in a holding cell, but he'd moved the man to the back burner. He was glad, though, that Gunnar hadn't because right now Gilley was the one person who might be able to give them answers.

"Please tell me that Gilley's talking," Owen said.

Gunnar shook his head, but then he shrugged. "He's not talking about the attack, but when I mentioned that someone had tried to kill Laney and you again, he didn't exactly seem pleased about that. He got nervous and then demanded to speak to Emerson."

"Emerson?" Laney and Owen repeated at the same time.

"Did Gilley say why he wanted to see him?" Owen asked.

"No, but I figure Gilley's still wanting a plea deal, and he wants to go straight to the source."

Maybe. But with everything that had gone on, Owen had to wonder if Gilley wanted to talk to his boss, the man who'd hired him. And that man could be Emerson.

"I called Emerson to let him know about the *request*," Gunnar went on, "but he didn't answer, so I left him a voice mail." Gunnar stared at him. "You don't think it's a good idea for Emerson to see Gilley?"

Kellan had almost certainly filled Gunnar in on the investigation. All aspects of it. But it was possible that Gunnar didn't know that Owen now considered the DA a suspect in Hadley's murder.

"No, it could be a very good idea." Owen thought about it for a second. "But if Emerson shows for that talk, I'd like to be here to listen."

Gunnar nodded, started to walk away and then turned back. "Jack checked out the car that Terrance said was following him, but when he didn't get any hits, he went ahead to the ranch. He said he figured you'd want him to be there with Addie and the others."

Good. He did indeed want his brother at the ranch to make sure Addie stayed safe. Maybe the same at-large gunman was the one who'd attacked them, but it was just as possible there were several of the hired thugs. Either that or the shooter had manager to get away from the tree and into that SUV darn fast.

"I need to get some paperwork done," Owen told Laney after Gunnar had left. "You should try to get some rest in the break room."

She shook her head. "I can work, too, if I can borrow a computer. I need to touch base with the San Antonio cops to see if they're making progress on Joe's murder. I also want to contact some people who knew him and try to come up with a lead." She paused, met his gaze. "It's very likely that his killer and our attackers are one and the same."

Owen couldn't dispute that. He hated that her mind would be on murder when she was clearly exhausted, but if their positions had been reversed, he'd be doing the same thing. Any thread they could latch onto right now could lead them to an arrest and put an end to the danger.

"You can use my desk," he offered as they headed for the squad room. "I'll work in Kellan's office with him. Just stay away from the windows."

And Owen hated that he had to add a reminder like that. Not while the memories of the most recent nightmare were so fresh. Still, they had to take precautions even in the sheriff's office since one of their suspects was the district attorney who could easily gain access to the building.

"You do the same." Laney stopped as if she might say something else. Or kiss him again. But then she managed a thin smile before she went to his desk.

Kellan was on the phone when Owen walked into his

office. Owen didn't know who he was talking to but, judging from his brother's tight jaw, it wasn't a pleasant conversation. Kellan wrote something down on a notepad, finished the call and stared at the phone for a few seconds before he put it away and looked at Owen.

"The link for the eavesdropping device was on one of the computers we took from Nettie and Emerson's house," Kellan finally said. "Specifically, it was on Nettie's laptop."

Owen understood his brother's tight jaw. Oh, man. This wasn't going to be pretty.

"The techs got not only a date but the exact time of installation." Kellan passed him the notepad and Owen saw that the software had been put on the computer less than a week earlier at four thirty in the afternoon. "Obviously, I'll need to get both Emerson and Nettie in here to see if they have alibis."

"They do," Owen immediately said. "That's when they had a big birthday barbecue for Nettie. I even dropped by with Addie." Owen cursed. "And that means Emerson and Nettie will claim one of the guests or someone from the catering company could have slipped inside and done this."

"Yeah," Kellan grumbled profanely. "I don't have to ask if you saw anyone suspicious."

Owen dragged a hand through his hair and tried to pull up the memories of the party. "No, but there were a lot of people that I didn't know. Some of Nettie's old college friends and some of Emerson's business associates. Addie was fussy—teething," he added, "so I didn't stay long. Only about half an hour."

Still, Owen would go back through what he could remember of the day to see if there was anything to recall. One thing was for sure, he hadn't remembered anyone who'd looked like a hired thug. That would have certainly snagged his attention.

Kellan put his hands on his hips. "Let's go with the theory that Nettie knew about her husband's affair. An affair that her husband claims never happened. But maybe she wants to know for sure, and the best way for her to do that is to listen in on what Laney is saying."

"And have a look at her computer files," Owen piped in, agreeing with his brother's theory.

Kellan nodded. "Nettie could have hired someone to put the program on her computer, and the party would have been a good cover. Her hired man could just pose as part of the catering crew or a guest. Or Nettie could have even slipped away and installed the software herself."

Both were possible. Ditto for Emerson being able to do it, as well. No one would have thought anything about the host disappearing for the handful of minutes it would have taken to plant the device.

So they were right back to square one. Not a good place to be with the possibility of another attack looming over them.

"The next question is how Joe Henshaw fits into this," Owen noted, still going with Kellan's train of thought.

Maybe Laney had heard him say her assistant's name because she hurried to the doorway and volleyed glances at both of them. "What happened?"

Owen and Kellan looked at each other and Kellan gave him the go-ahead nod to answer her question.

"The eavesdropping software was on Nettie's computer," Owen explained. Then he filled her in on the time of the installation and the party that either Nettie or Emerson could have used as an alibi.

When he finished, Laney's only reaction was a long exhale of breath. Obviously the news wasn't a surprise to her, so the frustration he was seeing on her face was for him. Because she knew it wasn't easy for a member of his family to be a murder suspect.

"I don't know if Joe found something to link Nettie or Emerson to Hadley's murder," she said after she'd taken a moment to absorb everything. "I've been going through his files, and I haven't found anything like that. Maybe Nettie or Emerson didn't want to risk him, or me, learning something."

Owen tried to wrap his mind around Nettie and Emerson committing cold-blooded murder. He couldn't, but they likely hadn't been the ones to put the bullets in Joe. Maybe hadn't even been the ones who'd personally murdered Hadley. However, they could have hired someone to do their dirty work.

"Emerson gave us permission to review his financials," Owen reminded Kellan.

Kellan nodded again. "I got them just a couple of minutes ago. Nothing pops, but I haven't had time to take a close look."

"I can do that for you," Owen offered. But Emerson's bank accounts were only half of the picture. "Is the eavesdropping software enough for us to get into Nettie's accounts?"

The sound Kellan made let Owen know even with that kind of connection, it wasn't going to be easy, but he took out his phone anyway. It rang before Kellan could make a call.

"It's Austin PD," Kellan relayed to them. He didn't

put it on speaker, but whatever the caller said to him had Kellan blowing out what sounded to be a breath of relief. Relief that didn't last long, though. "No. That's not a good idea. There's been another attack, and it's not safe." He paused, obviously listening, and ended the call with "Good. I'll get right on that."

"What happened?" Owen immediately asked.

Kellan typed something on his laptop keyboard. "The search warrant on the bank came through, *finally*, and since it's not safe for Laney to go there, I convinced the Austin cops to do a video feed for us when they open the box."

Owen didn't exactly cheer, but that was what he felt like doing. He'd wanted to know what was in that box without putting Laney in harm's way, and this was the best way to do it.

"I'm setting up the feed now," Kellan explained. He continued to work on the laptop while he turned the screen so that all three of them could see it.

Laney automatically moved in closer and, while she didn't say anything, Owen knew this had to feel like a victory for her. She'd been looking for this safe-deposit box for months because she believed it held the photos that would confirm her theory that Emerson had killed Hadley.

And maybe it would.

Owen certainly wasn't feeling victorious about that. Yes, if Emerson had indeed murdered Laney's sister, he wanted the man brought to justice. But that wasn't going to be easy when the photos might only prove an affair and nothing else. Of course, it was possible Hadley had something else in there.

As they waited, Laney took hold of his hand just

as the images and sounds popped up on the computer screen. The audio feed crackled with static, but Owen had no trouble seeing the two uniformed cops go into the vault area. Owen didn't know who was operating the camera, but it didn't pan around much. The focus stayed on the box that a guy in a suit—probably the bank manager—pulled from one of the slots in the wall.

The suit set the box on a plain table that reminded Owen of the ones they used in the interview rooms, and he took out a key.

"Is that the key we got from Laney Martin?" Kellan asked the cop.

The uniform nodded and, several moments later, they had confirmation that it was when the manager used it to open it the box.

The person holding the camera immediately moved closer, zooming in on the interior.

Owen immediately cursed when he saw what was inside.

Chapter Ten

Empty.

That definitely hadn't been what Laney had expected when the bank manager opened the box. Nothing. Not even a scrap of paper.

Her thoughts immediately started to run wild.

"Maybe it's not the right box." Laney threw the possibility out there.

Owen made a sound of agreement. Kellan wasn't paying attention because he was already on the phone with the bank manager.

The cops cut the video feed, leaving her to stare at the blank screen. Mercy. Why couldn't there just have been pictures inside? Or something that would have confirmed what Hadley had told her about the affair with Emerson? Now they had nothing, no reason to go after Emerson so they could stop another attack.

If Emerson was to blame, that was.

"My name was on the box," she added, talking more to herself than Owen. Still, he answered her, along with sliding a soothing hand down her back.

"It was the right key," he pointed out, "but Hadley could have moved the contents."

That was possible, but it didn't answer why her sister

would have done that, especially without telling Laney. After all, Hadley had volunteered the info about the pictures, but maybe she'd been murdered before she could let Laney know they'd been moved.

Kellan was cursing when he finished his call. "The bank manager said someone—a woman—accessed the box yesterday."

That got her attention and Laney's gaze shifted from the laptop to him. *Yesterday.* So, Hadley hadn't been the one to empty the box. But that left them with a huge question of who exactly had done that.

"Any reason the bank manager didn't tell us this sooner?" Laney demanded.

"He claims that he couldn't release any info about it until he had the search warrant." Kellan glanced down at the notes he'd taken during the call. "The person had a picture ID with Hadley's name, and she must have also had a key."

"The missing second key," Laney said under her breath. She wanted to blurt out some of that same profanity Kellan was using. "And she must have used a fake ID or one that she stole from Hadley when the key was taken."

Kellan stared at her. "Could Hadley have given the second key to someone else?"

Her mind was whirling so it was hard to think, but Laney forced herself to focus. "She could have perhaps given it to Joe." But almost immediately she had to wave that off. "He would have told me if she'd done that—especially after she was murdered. He would have known it could be critical to finding her killer."

So, not Joe, but maybe a friend. Still, a friend should have come forward by now, which led Laney to consider that Hadley's killer might have taken the key. The only problem with that was why the killer had waited all this time to access the box.

"Hadley might have left it at Joe's place without him knowing," Owen suggested several moments later. Obviously they were all trying to work this out.

That was possible, but another thought flashed into her mind. Not a good thought, either. "Joe had...feelings for Hadley. Actually, I think he was in love with her. So, if she gave him the key and asked him to keep it a secret, he might have, especially since he knew I had found a key in her apartment."

Still, she was going with the theory that Joe hadn't known. And that the person who'd murdered him had searched his place, maybe found the key and then used it. That would explain why the killer had taken so long to get into the box. Maybe a female killer.

Maybe Nettie.

Of course, it was just as likely that Terrance or Emerson had hired a woman to pose as Hadley.

"The timing works," Owen said as if reading her thoughts. "Whoever broke into Joe's could have gotten the key and used it to go to the bank."

She shook her head. "But how would the person have known which bank?" Laney stopped, her eyes widening. "Terrance. He had the PI report, so he knew the location."

Owen was taking out his phone to call Terrance before she'd even finished. Because she was right next to him, she heard the unanswered rings and, a few seconds later, the voice mail message. Owen left a message for Terrance to call him back ASAP. Whether the man would actually do that was anyone's guess. If he was guilty, Terrance might even go on the run rather than answer any questions that could lead to his arrest.

"I'll get the footage on the security cameras from the bank, and that way we can see who went in there. I also want Terrance's financials," Kellan grumbled. "And on any other PI reports he might not have shared with us." He looked at Laney. "Do you still have any PI contacts?"

"I do. You want me to make some calls to see if Terrance hired anyone else that he hasn't told us about?"

Kellan nodded. "I'm especially interested if he had a female investigator who could have passed for your sister. Of course, he wouldn't need a PI for that because he could have hired anyone, but we might get lucky."

It was a long shot, but at this point, it was all they had. Laney went back to Owen's desk where she'd left the loaner laptop and got to work, finding contact numbers for every PI she could think of. Too bad her cell phone had been taken in the break-in because she'd had plenty of the numbers in it.

Laney had just finished a list when the front door flew open. Owen came rushing out of Kellan's office and he automatically stepped in front of her and drew his weapon. But it wasn't a hired gun who'd come there to attack them.

It was Emerson.

Along with being out of breath, the DA looked disheveled. His suit was wrinkled, his hair messed up, and there was a fine layer of sweat on his forehead. He opened his mouth and then glanced around at the two other deputies and the dispatcher before he motioned toward Kellan's office.

"We need to talk," Emerson said, his voice a little shaky. Owen studied him for a couple of seconds before he got moving, staying between Emerson and Laney as they entered Kellan's office. Emerson immediately shut the door.

"The blackmailer called me again." Emerson took out his phone, put it on Kellan's desk in front of him and hit the play button.

"Time's run out, DA," the caller said. It was the same mechanical voice they'd heard before. "You've got an hour to get me that fifty thousand or I tell your sweet wife what's going on. No routing number this time. I want cash, and I'll be in touch as to where you can leave the money."

Kellan listened to it again and checked the time on the call. "It's already been nearly an hour."

Emerson nodded. "I figure he'll call me back any minute now. I don't have the money," he quickly added.

"You shouldn't be paying him anyway," Owen insisted. He moved so that Emerson and he were eye to eye. "You need to tell Nettie. That won't give this snake anything to hold over you. It'd be a lot better for her to hear it from you than him."

Obviously that wasn't the solution Emerson wanted because he huffed. Then he groaned and squeezed his eyes shut for a moment. "Nettie could believe the lie about the affair. She could leave me because of it."

"Maybe," Owen said. "But she's going to find out one way or another." He paused. "Besides, Nettie might have her own secrets."

"What do you mean?" Emerson snapped, his attention slicing to Owen.

Owen dragged in a long breath. "Go home, Emerson, and talk to your wife."

Emerson's stare turned into a glare. He held it for so long that Owen figured the man was about to have a burst of temper. But Emerson finally just shook his head. "I want to clear up this mess with the blackmailer first." His gaze shifted to Kellan and now there was some temper in his eyes. "If you can't or won't help me, then I'll have to handle it myself."

"I wouldn't advise that," Kellan told him.

Emerson's glare intensified as he snatched up his phone, obviously ready to storm out.

But Owen stopped him. "Rohan Gilley wants to talk to you."

Laney studied Emerson's expression, and she figured Owen and Kellan were doing the same. Something went through his eyes, something she couldn't quite peg. Frustration maybe? Or maybe something more. Fear? Of course, she could just be projecting that.

"I don't have time for Gilley right now," Emerson snapped. "Tell him that. Tell him I'll get back here when I have some things settled."

Emerson walked out, leaving Laney to wonder if that had been some kind of assurance or even a veiled threat for the gunman.

Kellan sighed. "I need to get both Nettie and him in here, *together*, for a face-to-face interview. An official one where I ask some hard questions. I think a good air clearing might help all the way around since both of them have motives for the attacks."

Owen shook his head when Gunnar stepped in the office doorway. "Emerson won't be talking to Gilley for a while," he told his fellow deputy.

"I'll let him know, but that's not why I'm here." Gunnar paused. "It's bad news. We have a dead body."

Owen STARED AT the photo the Austin PD had just sent them and felt the punch of dread when he saw the dead woman's face. A face he'd seen on the surveillance footage that the bank had sent over earlier. He had no doubts that she'd been the same person who'd gotten into the safe-deposit box with Hadley's fake ID.

And now she wouldn't be able to tell them what she'd taken or where it was.

Laney touched her fingers to her mouth as she studied the photo, and Owen saw her blink hard. No doubt fighting tears. "She doesn't look like my sister. Not really."

No. The hair color was the same, but that was about all. It was something the woman could have easily dyed to come closer to a physical match for the person she'd been impersonating.

"What happened to her?" Laney asked, glancing at Gunnar before her gaze went back to the photo.

"Two gunshot wounds to the chest," Gunnar explained. "Point-blank range. She had two IDs on her. One in your sister's name and the other was her own driver's license. Her prints were in the system, so they were able to confirm her identity as Nancy Flanery."

Laney's forehead creased, and she repeated the name as if trying to recall where she'd heard it before. "It sounds familiar, but I don't recognize her."

"Austin PD's running a background check now. I'm doing the same," Gunnar added a moment later. "She's from San Antonio and is a criminal informant."

That got Owen's attention. "A CI?" he said under his breath. "For Austin PD?"

"San Antonio," Gunnar clarified. "She has a record for drug possession, but her latest arrest was three years ago. She seems to have stayed clean since then. Or maybe she just hadn't gotten caught."

Either was possible. Obviously she had crossed paths with someone who'd either paid her to impersonate Hadley or had forced or coerced her into doing it.

"Someone must have hired her to go to that bank," Laney said.

That was Owen's top theory, too. Hired her, used her to get their hands on the photos and then murdered her so that she wouldn't be able to tell the cops who'd paid her to get into that safe-deposit box.

"Oh, and I thought this was interesting..." Gunnar continued, reading from his notes. "According to the preliminary report, Nancy Flanery had gunshot residue on her hands, but there was no weapon found on her."

Owen thought about that for a second. "Maybe because her killer took it. But she could have gotten off a shot first."

With luck, perhaps she could have even wounded her attacker. If so, Austin PD might find blood other than the victim's at the crime scene.

Laney went into the squad room and brought back the laptop she'd been working on. "Let me do a search of my files to see if anything pops up. Like I said, her name sounds familiar, so it's possible she was connected to one of my investigations."

She put the laptop on Kellan's desk and, leaning over, typed in "Nancy Flanery." She frowned when nothing came up. "Let me switch to Joe's files." Laney repeated the process.

Then she froze.

"She's here." Laney turned the screen so that Kellan, Gunnar and Owen would better be able to see it. "A week ago Joe talked to her after he'd gotten a tip that she knew something about Hadley's killer. Nancy claimed she didn't, but Joe apparently didn't believe her." She tapped the screen to show the triple question marks Joe had added at the end of the short report.

"Did you ever meet this woman?" Kellan asked.

"No. I'm almost positive I didn't. According to these notes, this was the first time Joe had met with her. Since it was only a week ago, I was already at Owen's. I didn't do any interviews after I moved there."

She looked at Owen and once again he saw the apology in her eyes. He definitely didn't like that she'd lied to him, but with the attacks, he knew why she had been so cautious.

"Do you think she's the one who killed Joe?" Laney asked. "If she's working for the person who attacked us, then she could have gone after Joe." But she waved that off. "I know it's a long shot."

It was, but it could still be a connection. Joe might not have had his guard up if someone he'd known had approached him, and it was possible Nancy had murdered Joe and then gone to the bank in Austin. The timing would work. If she had indeed committed murder and then fraud, the woman would have been a bad loose end.

And it had likely gotten her killed.

"I'll try to put a rush on that background check,"

Gunnar offered. He headed back into the squad room just as Kellan's phone rang.

Kellan scrubbed his hand over his face and showed them the name on the screen. Nettie. After blowing out a huff of frustration, he answered the call and put it on speaker.

"Emerson's missing," Nettie blurted out before Kellan could even issue a greeting. Her voice was practically a shout. "You've got to find him now."

"Nettie, he's not missing," Kellan assured her. "He was just here in my office."

She made a hoarse sob. "He's there? I need to talk to him."

"He left already." Kellan huffed again. "I was hoping he'd go home to you."

"He hasn't been here. What did he say?" Nettie demanded, her words running together.

Owen could tell from his brother's expression that Kellan was trying to figure out how to answer that. He took several moments and the woman continued to cry. "What's this about, Nettie?"

Nettie took a couple of moments, as well. "His assistant said Emerson was very upset, that he grabbed some things from his desk and practically ran out. She'd never seen him like that, and was worried about him, so she let me know about it. But when I tried to call him, he didn't answer. Something's wrong, and you need to find him now."

That didn't help ease the frustration on Kellan's face. "I'll see what I can do. If I find out anything, I'll let you know."

"Emerson could be meeting with the blackmailer," Laney said the moment Kellan ended the call with Nettie.

Kellan made a sound of agreement and stepped out into the squad room. "Raylene," he said, speaking to one of the deputies, Raylene McNeal. "I need you to find Emerson. Make some calls, ask around, see what you can come up with."

Since Raylene had witnessed Emerson storming out earlier, she didn't seem especially surprised by the request. She just nodded and took out her phone.

Owen was about to volunteer to help, but he saw their visitor walking toward the front door. Terrance. The moment he was inside, he flicked Laney a glance before his attention zoomed to Owen.

"I couldn't take your call, but your voice mail sounded...urgent," Terrance said. "What can I do to help?" As usual, there was a chilly layer of indifference in his tone and expression.

"It is urgent," Owen assured him. "A woman was murdered, and I want to know if one of your PI tails happened to see her."

Terrance shrugged his shoulders. "I can ask them, but why would they have done that? Does this dead woman have a connection to Laney?"

Owen held off on answering. Instead he turned the computer screen toward Terrance so he could see the photo Austin PD had sent them. "Her name is Nancy Flanery."

The indifference vanished and Terrance whirled toward Laney. This time, there was fiery anger in his eyes. "What kind of sick game are you playing?" he demanded.

That rage was in his voice, too. So much rage that Owen actually stepped between Laney and him. Laney didn't let that last long, though. She moved to Owen's side and faced Terrance head-on.

"I'm not playing a game," Laney insisted. "Do you know that woman?"

Terrance had to get his jaw unclenched before he spoke. "Are you trying to set me up?"

Owen figured Laney looked as surprised as he did. "Why would you think that?" Owen demanded.

Terrance jabbed his index finger at the picture on the screen. "Because Nancy works for me."

Chapter Eleven

Laney wasn't sure what she'd expected Terrance to say, but that wasn't it. She shook her head. "Nancy was a criminal informant."

Terrance groaned and, with his gaze back on Nancy's picture, sank into the chair next to Kellan's desk. Laney couldn't tell if he was genuinely upset or if this was all some kind of act.

"Nancy sold info to the cops every now and then," Terrance admitted. "But I'd also hired her to keep an ear out for any information about Hadley's murder." He looked at Laney again and some of his anger rekindled. "I figured eventually you'd try to pin your sister's death on me. Just to get back at me. If you ended up doing that, I wanted some ammunition I could use to defend myself."

Laney didn't take her gaze from his. "I want to find her actual killer, not simply *pin* it on someone."

"Right," he said as if he didn't believe her. He tipped his head to the photo. "Who did that to her? Who killed her?"

Owen stepped closer, standing directly in front of Terrance. "That's what we're trying to find out. Start talking. When's the last time you saw her?"

It was a simple enough question, but it only seemed to bring Terrance's rage. "I didn't kill her, and I refuse to stay here and be accused of it." He sprang to his feet, obviously ready to bolt, but Owen took hold of his arm to stop him.

"You can either answer that here, or I'll arrest you for obstruction of justice and withholding evidence," Owen warned him. "Then you'll wait in a holding cell until Austin PD can come and pick you up."

Terrance slung off his grip with far more force than was necessary before he got right in Owen's face. "Are you doing Laney's bidding now? Her witch hunt?" Terrance practically spit the words out.

"I'm asking a question." Owen definitely didn't back down. "One that it sounds like you're evading. When's the last time you saw Nancy?"

They continued to glare at each other for several long seconds before Terrance ground out some raw profanity and dropped back a step. "Three days ago. She called to say she needed some cash and wondered if I had any jobs for her. I told her I didn't, but that if I found something, I'd get back to her." He paused. "Did she do something stupid to get the money she needed?"

"It looks that way," Owen conceded. "Posing as Hadley, she went into the very bank where your PI had followed Hadley shortly before she was killed."

Terrance cursed again, but this time when he spoke, his voice was much softer. "Someone obviously hired Nancy to do that and then killed her after she'd finished the job. And no, it wasn't me," he quickly added. He shook his head. "I wouldn't have had a PI on her or the bank so I can't tell you who did this."

Laney considered not just what he'd said but also his

body language. Terrance looked and sounded sincere, but this could definitely be an act. If so, then why had he used one of his own employees to get into the bank? Maybe it was some sort of reverse psychology. By putting himself in the center of this, he perhaps thought it would make him appear innocent.

Laney had no intentions, though, of taking him off her suspect list.

"I'll speak with my PIs," Terrance said, glancing over at Kellan before staring at Owen. "Do you plan to arrest me?"

Owen took his time answering. "Not yet, but we'll need an official statement."

"I'll take it," Kellan volunteered.

Terrance's mouth tightened again. "I'll want my lawyer here."

"Then call him and tell him to get over here ASAP. Until he arrives, you can stay in the interview room." Kellan led him in that direction.

Laney waited until they were out of earshot before she turned to Owen. "I just don't know if what he said was true," he commented before she could ask. "But even if it was, I still don't trust him."

So they were on the same page and, while it was comforting to have him on her side, they were in a very frustrating position. Someone else was dead and they still didn't have the photos or whatever else her sister had left in the safe-deposit box. Worse, they couldn't arrest anyone to make sure no one else got killed. Or that there were no more attacks on Laney and him.

Owen stared at her a moment, slipped his arm around her and eased her to him. "I'd like to be able to get you out of here, to take you back to my grandparents' house."

She filled in the blanks. Yes, he wanted to do that, but it wasn't safe. "We can stay here as long as necessary." Laney paused. "Maybe we should put out the word that we're here. It could put off someone sending hired guns to the ranch."

He pulled back, met her gaze. "And make ourselves targets. Especially you." Owen cursed softly. "You're thinking of Addie. Thank you for that."

"You don't have to thank me. Of course, I'm thinking about her. I'd rather thugs come after me here than there. In fact, maybe it's time to use me as bait."

This time his profanity wasn't so soft and he jerked away. "No," he snapped. "No." When he repeated it, his voice was a little softer, but filled with just as much emotion. "And that doesn't have a damn thing to do with that kiss. Or this one."

She didn't even see it coming, but his mouth was suddenly on hers. Taking. And his right hand went to the back of her neck, holding her in place. There was no gentleness here, only the raw emotion of the moment. It was rough, punishing, but even then she could feel the heat in it. Could feel the need that it stirred in her.

"No," he repeated for a third time. His hand was still on her neck, his fingers thrust into her hair, and he stayed that way for several moments before he finally backed away from her.

"I just want Addie safe," she managed to say when she gathered enough breath to speak. "I want *you* safe."

The corner of his mouth lifted, but the amusement vanished as quickly as it had come. "Now, that's the kiss talking."

No, it wasn't. It was what she felt for him, but rather than say that, Laney kept things light. "Well, it was a good kiss. Memorable," she added, trying out one of those partial smiles. Like his, hers was short-lived. Because it hadn't been just memorable.

The kiss had been unforgettable.

Owen was unforgettable.

And when this was over and they'd caught the person trying to kill them, she was going to have to deal with not only the aftermath of the violence but also something else. Having her heart broken into a million little pieces.

The thought of having sex with him flashed into her head, and she nearly blurted out that they should go for it at least once so they could burn off some of this fire that was flowing through them. Thankfully, she didn't get the chance to spill all—something she would have no doubt regretted—because someone came in through the front door of the squad room.

Nettie.

Great. Laney didn't have the mental energy to deal with the woman, and she figured Owen didn't, either. But Nettie stopped the moment her attention landed on them. Laney was no longer in Owen's arms, but she realized that he hadn't taken his hand from her hair. He eased his grip away as he turned toward Nettie.

"I'm glad you have time for that sort of thing," Nettie said, irony and bitterness in her voice.

Laney was a little surprised when Owen didn't move away from her. He stayed shoulder to shoulder with her, still touching her as they faced the woman.

"You're supposed to be looking for Emerson," Nettie added. She marched toward them. "But I find you here with your hands on the very person who's responsible for the mess we're in."

"Excuse me?" Laney said at the same moment Owen snarled, "What the hell does that mean?"

"We didn't have trouble until she came here. She lied to you, turned you against Emerson and me, and now Emerson is missing." Each of Nettie's words snapped like a bullwhip, but the fit of temper must have drained her because on a hoarse sob, she sagged against the door frame. "I need to find my husband. Please." She looked at Laney when she added the *please*.

Laney wasn't immune to the woman's pain. That seemed like the real deal. But she didn't trust Nettie any more than she did Terrance or Emerson.

"I take it that Emerson didn't return your call?" Owen asked as he helped Nettie to a chair. He also turned the computer where the photo of the dead woman was still on the screen.

"No. I called him six times. Maybe more. And he hasn't answered." A fresh round of tears came, but Nettie quickly brushed them away. She looked up at him. "Tell me what happened to him. I have to know what's going on." Nettie added another whispered *please*.

Owen stared at her a moment then dragged in a long breath. "Just know that Emerson isn't going to thank me for telling you this." He paused several long moments. "Someone's been trying to blackmail Emerson."

Nettie looked up at him, blinked. Judging from her stunned reaction, she hadn't been expecting that. "Wh-what?"

"A blackmailer who's called him several times to try to extort money from him."

Nettie shook her head and volleyed wide-eyed

glances at Laney and him as if looking for any signs this was a joke. "Blackmail him for what?"

Owen just stared at her.

The woman did another round of glancing before she shook her head. "No. My husband didn't have an affair with her sister." She flung an accusing finger at Laney.

Laney figured she was the one who looked surprised now. "What do you know about my sister?" she prompted. Of course, Terrance had said there'd been a meeting between Hadley and Nettie, but Laney hadn't known if he was telling the truth or not.

"I know my husband didn't have an affair with her." Nettie seemed adamant about that, too, and when she got to her feet, she seemed a lot stronger than she had just seconds earlier. "Yes, I've heard talk, but I know it's not true. Emerson wouldn't cheat on me."

Laney didn't argue with her, but she would mention something else. "Why else would someone try to blackmail your husband?"

Nettie's chin came up. "There are plenty of reasons. Emerson's an important man, and he's prosecuted a lot of bad people. One of them could be trying to get some revenge."

"This doesn't seem to be about revenge," Owen quickly pointed out. "Blackmailers usually want money to keep a secret. Of course, they usually end up wanting more and more money."

Nettie stared at him again and Laney thought she was maybe trying to find a reasonable comeback. But Nettie only huffed, "I don't know why someone would demand money. But it's not because he cheated." She started to pace across Kellan's office. "It probably has something to do with that mix-up about the eavesdropping program being on my computer."

It wasn't a mix-up. The program had been there, but obviously Nettie wasn't going to accept responsibility for that.

"Was Emerson upset about that?" Owen asked, sounding very much like a cop who was fishing for information from a potential suspect.

"Of course, he was. But he knows I was set up, that there's no way I would do something like that." Nettie stopped the pacing so she could glare at Laney. "Why would I care about eavesdropping on you anyway?"

Laney didn't even have to think about the answer to that. "Because you're worried that your husband did indeed have an affair with my sister and you wanted to know if I'd found any proof of it."

"No!" Nettie's glare got worse. "I didn't do that because there's no proof to find. I know you want to find your sister's killer, but you'd better keep my husband and me out of your lies."

Owen took Nettie by the shoulders. "What if she's not lying?" he asked. "What if Laney's telling the truth?"

Laney steeled herself for another lash from Nettie's temper, but the woman stilled and shook her head. There was nothing adamant about that head shake, though, and the tears shimmered in Nettie's eyes again.

Owen turned at the sound of footsteps. When Kellan stepped into the doorway, he looked at the three of them, obviously piecing together what had been going on. He motioned for Owen to join him in the squad room and extended the gesture to Laney. They stepped out, but Kellan didn't say anything until he was back in the hall and out of Nettie's earshot.

"Terrance called his PIs," Kellan told them. "All of them claim they hadn't seen Nancy in days and that they don't know who hired her to go into the safe-deposit box."

"You believe them?" Owen asked.

Kellan lifted his shoulder. "Terrance put the calls on speaker so I could hear, and the PIs seemed to be telling the truth. Of course, Terrance could have coached them to say that. After all, we would have found the connection between Nancy and him, and he would have known that would eventually lead to us talking to his PIs."

Yes, it would have, and coaching was something Terrance would have done. He would cover any and all bases rather than go back to jail.

Laney glanced in the direction of his office just to make sure Nettie hadn't come out. She hadn't. "As far as we know, Terrance is the only one of our suspects who knew Nancy."

Kellan nodded. "So, I ask myself, why would he use her? But maybe he did that because he might not be the only one of our suspects with links to Nancy. I want to take a look at Nancy's phone logs and financials that Austin PD will be getting. There might be something there to help us with our investigation."

Laney agreed, and her gaze drifted back to Nettie. "And her financials?"

"I'm working on it," Kellan said with a sigh. He opened his mouth to say more but a loud shout stopped him. It had come from the squad room, and it had both Owen and Kellan drawing their weapons.

"Get out here now!" someone yelled.

Emerson.

Kellan and Owen both moved in front of Laney and

rushed into the squad room. From over their shoulders, she immediately saw Emerson. And he wasn't alone. He had a man with him.

Emerson was also armed.

He had a gun pointed at a man he was dragging in by his collar. When Emerson slung the man onto the floor, Laney could see that his hands were tied behind his back.

"I had him meet me," Emerson huffed, his breath gusting. His clothes were torn, too, and there was a bruise forming on his right cheek. "And then I bashed him on the head so I could bring him here."

"Who is he?" Kellan asked.

"The blackmailer." Emerson spit the word out like a profanity. "Arrest him now."

OWEN HAD ALREADY had too many surprises today, but obviously they weren't finished when it came to that.

"Give me the gun," Owen ordered Emerson.

Owen intended to get to the bottom of...well, whatever the heck this was, but he didn't want to start until he got that weapon out of Emerson's hand. That wild look in his brother-in-law's eyes let Owen know this was still a very volatile situation.

"Arrest him now," Emerson repeated.

"I'll start doing that when you give me your weapon," Owen countered. He made a quick check to see if Kellan was still in front of Laney. He was. Kellan also had his arm hooked around Nettie, no doubt to prevent the woman from rushing to her husband.

The fire in Emerson's eyes heated up even more, and it didn't look as if he had any intentions of surrendering the weapon. Not until Nettie spoke.

"Emerson, you're hurt," she said, her voice cracking. "He needs an ambulance," she snarled to Kellan.

Emerson glanced at his wife, at the man on the floor, and seemed to realize what he'd just done. He passed the gun to Owen, and Owen handed it off to Gunnar.

"What happened?" Owen asked Emerson.

But he didn't get a chance to answer. Nettie broke away from Kellan and ran to her husband. She landed right in his arms. Owen considered pulling them apart so he could pat down Emerson for other weapons, but Kellan came forward to do that. Judging from both his and Nettie's glares, neither cared much for that.

"He needs an ambulance," Nettie repeated. She was crying now, but they all ignored her. Even Emerson. Though she did gently touch her fingers to that bruise on his face.

"I did what I needed to do," Emerson snapped. "What you wouldn't do." He glanced at both Owen and Kellan when he added that. "He was blackmailing me, and I put a stop to it."

"I wasn't blackmailing him," the man insisted. There was a bruise on his cheek as well, and the anger radiated over every inch of his face. "I told this nutjob he has it all wrong."

"He met me to take the money that he'd demanded," Emerson insisted. "I didn't have the cash, but I'd stuffed some newspapers in a big envelope to make him think I had it. That's how I got him close enough to hit him."

"I didn't know it was blackmail," the man snapped. "I was just doing somebody a favor."

A bagman. Or else he was claiming to be one.

"Who are you?" Owen demanded. He hauled the man

to his feet so he could pat him down. No weapons, and his hands had been secured with a pair of plastic cuffs.

"Norman Perry." The sour tone matched his expression.

"Running him now," Gunnar volunteered.

While Owen waited for Gunnar to do that, Nettie looked up at her husband. "What happened? Why would this man be trying to blackmail you?"

It wasn't a question Owen had intended to ask—because he already knew the answer—so he paused to give Emerson a chance to tell his wife. Emerson certainly didn't jump to do that. He took his time while he looked at everyone in the room but Nettie.

"Someone lied and said I did something I didn't do," Emerson finally said. He tipped his head to Perry. "He had a gun, but I took it from him. It's in my car, and it's unlocked out front."

"I'll get it." Gunnar volunteered. He had his phone pressed to his ear as he went out.

With a firm hold on Perry's arm, Owen led him to the chair next to Gunnar's desk and had him sit. He hadn't done that for Perry's comfort but rather so he could get Laney away from the front windows. When she followed him, Owen motioned for her to go back toward the doorway to Kellan's office. She'd still be able to see and hear everything, but it might keep her out of harm's way.

"What you did was stupid," Kellan said, and he wasn't talking to Perry but rather to Emerson. "You confronted an armed man who could have killed you."

"I wasn't gonna kill anybody," Perry snapped.

Emerson came closer, practically toe-to-toe with Kellan. "You wouldn't stop him, so I did."

Nettie shook her head. "What's going on here? Why wouldn't you stop someone who was trying to blackmail my husband?"

"I didn't get a chance to stop him," Kellan assured her. "I only recently found out about the blackmail, and Emerson stormed out of here before giving me a chance to do anything about it."

They all looked at Gunnar when he came back in. He'd bagged a gun and was off his phone. "His name is Norman Perry. Age forty-three. He lives in San Antonio. No police record."

Now, that was another surprise. Owen would have thought the guy had a rap sheet. "Is the gun legal?" Owen asked Gunnar.

"I'll run it, but he's got a permit to carry concealed."

Another surprise, though Owen figured that people with permits could and did commit serious crimes. And this was indeed serious. Well, it was if Emerson had told the truth about the man.

"I took the classes for carrying concealed," Perry grumbled. "You've got no cause to hold me."

"He does," Emerson practically yelled. "He tried to blackmail me."

"No, I didn't." Not quite a shout from Perry, but it was close to one. "My girlfriend works for a company, Reliable Courier. She's sick, and her boss was swamped, so I said I'd make the delivery and do the pickup. That's all. Call Rick at Reliable Courier if you don't believe me."

This time, it was Kellan who made the call. While he did that, Owen continued with Perry, "Who hired Reliable Courier to meet with Emerson?"

"Wouldn't have a clue," Perry answered. "You'd have to ask Rick."

Owen was certain Kellan would do just that. "What were you supposed to pick up and deliver?"

Perry huffed, "Don't know that, either, but you can see for yourself on the delivery. The card is in a small envelope in my wallet. I put it there because it was little and I didn't want to lose it. My wallet's in the back pocket of my jeans."

Owen put on a pair of plastic gloves that Gunnar handed him. Without cutting off the restraints, Owen retrieved the wallet and pulled out a small envelope, the size that would be on a gift bouquet of flowers. There was a card inside, and someone had written what appeared to be the URL for a website. Beneath it was more writing labeled as a password.

"What is this?" Owen asked Perry.

"Hell if I know. Like I said, I'm just the deliveryman."

"He is," Kellan verified a moment later. He was still on his phone. "I'll check it all out, of course, but according to the owner, Perry was indeed just doing him a favor. He's getting me the client info now on the person who wanted this pickup and delivery."

Good. That might clear things up. Owen bagged the card and envelope, and Gunnar took it, first putting the official info on the bag and then taking it to the computer.

"Can I go now?" Perry complained.

"Not yet." Owen went to the computer to watch as Gunnar typed in the website, and Laney joined him. Nettie was still fussing over Emerson's injuries, but Emerson's attention was nailed to the monitor.

Gunnar entered the password, waited, and the images loaded on the screen. Photos.

"That's a photo of the safe-deposit box at the bank," Laney said, studying the image.

It was. Whoever had taken the picture had made sure the number was clearly visible.

Gunnar went to the next shot. A photo of the box open to show the manila envelope inside. Owen couldn't be sure, but it could have been the one from the photograph Terrance's PI had taken of Hadley the day she'd visited the bank.

"This is a hoax," Emerson said, and he hurried to Gunnar. Owen stepped in front of Emerson to stop him from doing whatever he'd been about to do. "Obviously this is just part of the blackmail scheme," Emerson insisted. "It'll be lies. All lies."

Owen wasn't sure about the lies part, but yeah, it was likely part of the blackmail. He held off Emerson while Gunnar loaded the next picture. It was a shot of photographs that appeared to have been removed from the manila envelope.

Photos of Emerson and Hadley.

"What is that?" Nettie asked. She moved closer, too, her gaze slashing from one image to the next.

"They're fake," Emerson growled, but the color had drained from his face, making that god-awful bruise stand out even more.

Owen didn't think so. There were two rows of photographs. The ones on the top row were semiselfies with Hadley awake and in bed, next to a sleeping Emerson. Since Emerson was on his back, it wasn't hard to miss that he was naked, and he certainly wasn't being restrained. His arms were stretched out like a sated man getting some rest.

The shots on the bottom row were ones that looked as if Hadley had taken them on the sly. Emerson in a glass shower and then while dressing. Owen couldn't tell if Emerson had been aware of the shots beings taken.

"They're fake," Emerson repeated, his voice wavering now.

Nettie didn't seem to hear him. She continued to study the photos.

"Rick at Reliable Courier got the name of the person who arranged for pickup and delivery," Kellan said. "He claimed his name was James Smith. The guy paid in cash, so I'm betting it's an alias."

Yeah. Owen figured that would prove to be true. He was also betting this James Smith was yet another hired gun. But why had the person who'd hired him left the blackmail to a courier company? That was something Owen needed to dig into.

Nettie shook her head. When she finally looked up at Emerson, there were tears in her eyes. She didn't have the distraught expression she'd had when she'd entered the sheriff's office. Now there was only hurt.

"You had sex with her," Nettie muttered. "Admit it. I want to hear you say it." Emerson reached for her, but she batted his hands away. "Say it!" This time her voice was a lot louder.

Emerson stared at her. And stared. "I had sex with her," he finally admitted. His gaze immediately flashed to Kellan. "But I didn't kill her."

The silence came, and it felt as if the entire room was holding its breath, waiting for whatever was about to happen.

Nettie finally broke that silence. "You lied," she said and, without even looking at Emerson, she headed for the door.

The first word that came to Owen's mind was *broken*. Nettie was broken.

"Wait!" Emerson called out as he rushed after her.

Nettie didn't stop. She just kept on walking, Emerson trailing along behind her.

"I'll go check on them," Gunnar said. "Should I bring them back inside?" he added to Kellan.

Kellan shook his head. "Not yet. Just make sure they aren't going to attack each other or anything. Then, once they've cooled off, I want Emerson back in here for questioning."

About a possible murder.

Hell. Owen groaned. Emerson had been denying this affair, but those pictures proved otherwise, which meant the man had been lying through his teeth.

But what else had he lied about?

Had Emerson actually been the one to kill Hadley?

Owen glanced at Laney, expecting to see some "I told you so" on her face, but there was none. There was only grief. No doubt because all of this had brought back the nightmarish memories of her sister's murder. She'd been right about Emerson lying about the affair, but sometimes being right didn't fix things.

"Emerson's not a flight risk," Kellan noted, "but I'll feel a lot better after Gunnar's brought him back in and I have him in the interview room."

Owen felt the same way.

"Can I go now?" Perry snapped.

Dragging in a frustrated breath, Kellan went to him and cut the restraints. "I'll need a statement first and then you can go." He tipped his head toward his office. "In there."

Only then did Owen remember they still had Terrance in the interview room, which was why Kellan hadn't sent Perry there.

"Let me get this website to the lab guys, and I'll talk to Terrance," Owen offered.

Owen started to do just that when his phone rang and he saw Eli's name on the screen. Since his brother was still at their grandparents' house with Addie and the others, Owen answered it right away.

"We got a problem," Eli immediately said. "One of the hands just spotted a gunman on the ranch."

Chapter Twelve

Everything inside Laney was racing. Her heart, her breath and the adrenaline. Just seconds before Eli's call, so many thoughts had been going through her head, but now there was only one.

Keep Addie safe.

Sweet heaven. The little girl had to be okay.

"Drive faster," Owen ordered his fellow deputy Raylene McNeal.

The deputy was behind the wheel of the cruiser with Owen and Laney in back. It had taken a stern, direct order from Kellan to stop Owen from driving, and Laney had been thankful for it. She figured his thoughts had to be racing even more than hers were.

Raylene mumbled something about already going too fast, but she sped up anyway. With the siren howling and the blue lights flashing, she raced down the road that led out of town and toward the ranch. At this speed, it wouldn't take long to get there, but every mile and every minute would feel like an eternity.

Owen had his gun drawn and had his phone gripped in his left hand. He no doubt wanted to be ready if Eli called him back with an update. And Eli would. But he obviously wouldn't be able to call if the ranch was under attack.

"You shouldn't have come," Owen said to her.

He'd already told her variations of that since they'd rushed out of the sheriff's office. Kellan hadn't issued her one of those stern orders but instead had given her a gun. It made sense. After all, she was a PI, knew how to shoot and Owen might need more backup than Kellan could provide. Still, Owen would see this as her being in danger again.

And he could be right.

But there was no chance she was going to stay back. Kellan had had no choice about that since someone needed to man the office, but Laney had had a choice. One she'd made despite Owen's objections.

Owen's phone dinged with a text, the sound piercing through the silence. "Gunnar's on his way to the ranch," he relayed when he read the message. "Kellan called him and pulled him off Emerson and Nettie."

Good. They might need all the help they could get. Plus, Emerson and Nettie might welcome the time to figure out how they were going to handle the bombshell of the affair. And then maybe Kellan could just go ahead and arrest him. Of course, Kellan would need some kind of evidence.

The photos were proof of an affair but not of murder.

Laney kept watch around them, knowing full well that the gunman at the ranch could be a ruse to get them on the road for another attack. But Laney didn't see anything, not even another vehicle.

The silence gave her mind a chance to stop racing, and maybe it was that temporary calm that allowed a fresh thought to creep into her head.

"Why would Hadley have taken those pictures?" Laney hadn't meant to say that aloud, but she had, and Owen had clearly heard it. Since he had, she continued, "She said he threatened her when he broke things off, but those photos were obviously taken when they were still together."

He glanced at her before he returned to keeping watch. "You think she was going to try to blackmail him?"

She shook her head. "Not for money. But maybe for emotional blackmail." Laney paused, forced herself to give that more thought. "Maybe Hadley thought she could use the pictures to force Emerson to stay with her."

Before Owen could respond, he got another text from Eli.

Gunman spotted just off the road leading to the ranch. Approach with caution. I'm in pursuit. Jack and one of the hands are in the house with Addie.

The road leading to the ranch was less than a mile away so Laney moved to the edge of her seat to try to spot him if and when he came into view.

"This had better not be a trap to lure Eli away from the house," Owen said under his breath.

And that sent her pulse into a full gallop. A gallop that was almost impossible for Laney to tamp down. "We're almost there," she reminded Owen, and in doing so, she reminded herself, so she could try to stay calm. "We need to keep an eye out for both the gunman and Eli."

Taking her own advice, Laney did just that while

she kept a firm grip on her gun. Unfortunately, this stretch of the road was lined with fences, ditches and trees. Too many places for someone to hide. There was also another possibility: that the gunman had already driven off. It was possible he'd left a vehicle on the road, sneaked onto the ranch and, when he'd been spotted, could have run back to whatever transportation he'd used to get there.

"Kill the sirens," Owen told Raylene, and the deputy shut them off. No doubt so they'd be able to hear whatever was going on outside. Going in hot might drown out sounds that could lead them to the gunman's exact location.

Raylene slowed as she approached the turn for the ranch, and again Laney tried to pick through all the possible hiding places to spot or hear him. Nothing. No sign of Eli, either, though she was certain he had to be somewhere in the area.

"There," Owen said, pointing toward the fence.

Laney immediately shifted her gaze in that direction, but she still didn't see anyone. Not at first anyway. And then she saw the blur of movement as someone darted between two trees.

"That's not Eli," Owen added.

No, it wasn't. Eli was tall and lanky, and this guy had bulky shoulders and a squat build. From the quick glimpse she'd gotten of him, Laney had thought he was armed with a rifle. That made sense because he could use it to fire from a distance. Heck, he could fire from this spot, depending on how good a scope he had. He likely wouldn't be able to fire into the grandparents' house, but the idiot could shoot at Eli.

Or at them.

And that was exactly what happened. Laney had no sooner had the thought when the bullet slammed into the window right where she was sitting. The safety glass shattered, but it held in place.

Cursing, Owen dragged her down onto the seat. Not a second too soon because three other shots blasted straight toward them, all hitting the glass. This time, it didn't hold, and the shards fell down onto them.

The sounds of the shots were still ringing in her ears, but Laney heard something else. Other rounds of gunfire, and these didn't seem to be coming from the shooter.

"Eli," Owen said. He kept her pushed down on the seat, but he levered up. Now that the glass had been knocked out, he took aim through the gaping hole.

He fired, too.

It was just a single shot, but it seemed to be enough because almost immediately she felt him relax just a little.

"The gunman's down," Raylene relayed.

Good. Laney didn't want the snake in any position to hurt Addie or anyone else. Maybe, though, he was still alive so he could give them answers.

"Pull up closer to Eli," Owen instructed Raylene. When the deputy did that, Owen moved off Laney. "Raylene, wait here with Laney," he said just seconds before he threw open the door.

Laney didn't get out with him, but she levered herself up so she could look out the window. She saw Owen running toward the man on the ground. Eli was also approaching him from the direction of the ranch. Owen reached the guy first and, after he kicked away the rifle, he reached down and touched his fingers to his neck.

She didn't need to hear what the brothers said to each other to know that the shooter was indeed dead.

She heard the sounds of sirens. Gunnar. The cruiser was speeding up behind them, but as Raylene had done, Gunnar turned off the sirens as he came to a stop. The deputy barreled out of the car and ran toward Owen and Eli. Again, she couldn't hear what they said, but it didn't take long before Owen started quickly making his way back to Raylene and her.

When Owen got into the cruiser, he looked at Laney. Not just a glance, but more of an examination to make sure she hadn't been injured. She did the same to him. Thank goodness they hadn't been hurt. Not physically anyway. But this had put more shadows in his already dark eyes.

"Take us to my grandparents' house," Owen told Raylene.

Owen took hold of Laney, sliding her against him. Away from the glass and into his arms. For such a simple gesture, it did wonders. It steadied her heart enough that it no longer felt as if it might beat out of her chest. He didn't say anything but instead brushed his mouth on the top of her head. Another gesture that was anything but simple. It soothed her, aroused her and made her realize something.

She was falling in love with him.

Great. Just what she didn't need—and what Owen wouldn't want.

When Raylene pulled to a stop in front of his grandparents' house, she spotted two ranch hands, one on each side of the house. Jack opened the front door and, with his gun ready, stepped out onto the porch. No doubt to give them cover in case there were any snipers still around.

Owen didn't remind her that they'd have to move quickly. They did. Raylene, Owen and she all rushed out of the cruiser and into the house. The moment they were inside, Jack shut the door and rearmed the security system.

"I would ask if you're all okay," Jack said, "but I figure the answer to that is no. How about Eli?"

"He's with the dead gunman," Owen answered.

Jack gave an approving nod and tipped his head to the stairs. "Addie, Francine and Gemma are in the master bathroom. I told them to get into the bathtub and stay down."

Now it was Owen who gave a nod as he started up the stairs. Laney headed in that direction, too, but she stopped next to Jack. "I'm sorry."

He cocked an eyebrow. "I only want one apology and it's from the SOB who put all of this together. It took plenty of bucks to hire this many thugs to do these attacks and kill at least two people."

Yes, it did. "Both Terrance and Nettie have money like that."

"And Emerson," Jack quickly added. "No trust fund, but you can bet he could figure out a way to tap into his wife's money. Heck, Nettie's so much in love with him that she might have given him the cash with no questions asked."

All of that was true, and it was yet another reason for them to take a look at their financials.

Jack gave her a friendly, almost brotherly nudge on the arm before she tucked her loaner gun into the back waistband of her jeans and went up the stairs. She fol-

lowed the sounds of the voices and found them still in
the bath. Addie was in the giant tub, playing with a stash
of toys, and Gemma, Francine and Owen were all sitting on the floor next to her.

The moment Laney stepped in, Addie looked at her
and smiled. Like the way Owen had held her in the
cruiser, that smile worked some magic.

"Horsey," Addie said, holding up one of her toys. It
seemed to be an invitation for Laney to come closer. So
she did, kneeling down beside the tub. Thankfully, the
little girl didn't seem to be aware that she was in this
room because there had been another attack.

"You think it's okay for me to go to the kitchen?"
Francine asked Owen.

He nodded. "Just stay away from the windows."

Francine thanked him as she got to her feet. "I think
I need a cup of tea."

"I need a drink," Gemma added, getting up, as well.
"A strong one with lots of booze, and then I'm going
to call Kellan."

Laney nearly told the women there was no reason to
leave on her account, but she realized she wanted this
time with Owen and Addie. Even if it was for only a
few seconds.

Gemma gave her arm a gentle squeeze, a show of
support, which Laney greatly appreciated.

After the women were gone, Laney brushed her hand
over the tips of Addie's curly hair and got another smile
from the little girl. Laney found herself smiling, too.
Yes, this was definitely magic.

"I'll go into the other bedroom so you can be with
her," Laney told him, but when she started to stand,
Owen took hold of her hand and kept her in place. He

didn't say anything. He just kept his grip on her while he continued to watch his daughter.

"I've been thinking about setting up a safe house and moving Addie there," Owen finally told her long moments later.

That didn't surprise her, not with the repeated attacks, but Laney thought she knew why that had put such an unsettled look on Owen's already troubled face. "You wouldn't be able to go with her."

"No. I'd need to be here, to see this investigation through to an arrest. Plus, it might be a good idea to put some distance between her and me."

"Distance between Addie and *me*," Laney corrected. She sighed, groaned. "I'm the target."

Owen quickly shook his head and caught her chin to force eye contact. "Maybe you were the sole target in the beginning, but those shots have been fired at me, too."

"They wouldn't be if you weren't with me," she pointed out just as fast.

Now he was the one to sigh, and he stared at her a long time before he said anything else. "So far, the attacks have happened when we were outside, and the hired thugs haven't managed to get close enough to this house to fire any shots inside."

That was true, but she was about to argue that it could change, that this latest gunman might be the first in a string of others to come. But she could see the risk of taking the baby out on the road—even in a cruiser. Yes, a cruiser was bullet-resistant, but shots could get through. They'd just had proof of that.

"The ranch hands are willing to keep guarding the place?" she asked.

Owen nodded. "I suspect Jack will have to leave. Raylene, too. But Eli and I can stay here. And we have you for backup."

That was more than just a little vote of confidence. It actually caused some of the tightness in Laney's chest to go away. Owen trusted her to be part of this.

"Thanks," she managed to say, half expecting him to ask why she'd said that.

He didn't. Owen reached out, sliding his fingers over her jaw. To her cheek. And then to the back of her neck. He leaned in slowly. So slowly. Until his mouth brushed over hers. Almost immediately, he pulled back, their gazes connecting. A dozen things passed between them. Unspoken words but they still understood.

The need.

The ache.

The impossibility of it all.

Laney felt every one of those things, in every inch of her, and she was certain Owen did, too.

"Kissy," Addie said, clapping.

The moment between Laney and Owen was gone, replaced by another one that seemed even more important. And possible. Using the side of the tub, Addie got to her feet and dropped a kiss on Owen's cheek before doing the same to Laney.

"Kissy," Addie repeated, beaming with that incredible smile.

Yes, this was more important.

Owen scooped Addie out of the tub and into his lap and showered her with loud kisses that had the little girl giggling. Addie leaned over and spread some of those giggles and kisses to Laney, including her in a moment that she didn't deserve to share. But it was a moment that she'd never forget.

It didn't last, though. Owen's phone rang and even though Addie was only a toddler, she seemed to understand the importance of it because she moved into Laney's lap when Owen took out his phone. Laney saw Kellan's name on the screen, which was probably why Owen didn't put the call on speaker. Not with Addie right there. He wouldn't want to risk her hearing anything about the dead gunman.

To make sure Addie was spared that, Laney got up and shifted the little girl onto her hip so they could go out into the adjoining bedroom. Keeping hold of her hands, she let Addie jump on the bed, something that Francine had let her do. Of course, that seemed like a lifetime ago.

Everything did.

She'd come here, lying, looking for Hadley's killer. That had seemed the most important thing in the world. In some ways, it still was. But now it wasn't just about finding justice, it was about putting an end to the danger so that this precious little girl, Owen and his family would be safe.

Laney pulled Addie back into her arms when Owen entered the room, and she could tell from his expression that he'd just gotten more bad news.

"Rohan Gilley's lawyer just visited him at the sheriff's office, and after he left, Gilley told Kellan that he was finally ready to talk," Owen explained.

She shook her head, not understanding his somber tone, because it was good that the hired gun had broken his silence. "And?" Laney prompted when Owen didn't add anything.

Owen dragged in a breath through his mouth. "Gilley said that Emerson is the one who hired him."

Chapter Thirteen

Emerson.

Owen had already cursed his brother-in-law, but he kept cursing under his breath every time his calls to Emerson went to voice mail. Where the hell was he? Since Nettie wasn't answering her phone, either, Owen could only guess that Emerson had gotten wind of Gilley's "confession" and had gone on the run.

To avoid being arrested for murder.

That only caused Owen to silently swear even more, and the profanity wasn't just aimed at Emerson. He aimed plenty at himself. All the signs had been there, and Laney had said right from the get-go that Emerson had killed her sister. He hadn't listened and now they were in this mess.

"No one in Emerson's office has seen him," Eli relayed when he finished his latest round of calls.

Eli and Owen were only two of the people looking for Emerson. Gunnar and Raylene were back at the sheriff's office. Kellan was no doubt doing it, too, though he likely had his hands full with Gilley and getting the warrant not just for Emerson but for his financials. Because he'd been swamped and since there'd been no evidence to hold him, Kellan had cut Terrance loose. Temporarily anyway. Terrance would be making a return trip to the sheriff's office for further questioning. That might not even be necessary, though. If they could arrest Emerson and get him in the box for questioning, he might confess all.

Might.

And he might deny it, just as he'd denied the affair with Hadley. At least, he'd denied it until he'd had to face those pictures.

"I'm sure it's occurred to you that Gilley could be lying through his teeth," Eli pointed out.

Owen nodded. Yeah. In fact, that had been his first thought. After all, Gilley wasn't exactly a responsible, law-abiding citizen. He could have simply grown tired of being in a cell, waiting for a plea deal, and had decided to strike out.

"If there'd been no circumstantial evidence against Emerson, Kellan probably wouldn't have even told me what Gilley had said," Owen answered. "But there is evidence."

Eli made a sound of agreement. "And it doesn't help that he's gone AWOL. If that's what happened."

Owen looked at his brother, who was at the living room window. "You think something could have happened to him?"

"Depends on if he's really a killer or not. If it's Nettie or Terrance, then Emerson could be the next victim. They might try to make it look like a suicide."

Owen could definitely see that happening, but maybe before anyone else died, Emerson would come in and give a statement.

"You should get some rest," Eli added when Owen

groaned and rubbed his eyes. "I'll be fine to keep first watch. Better yet, why don't you make sure Laney is okay?"

Eli took something from his pocket and tossed it to Owen. Only after Owen caught it did he realize what it was. A foil-wrapped condom.

Owen scowled at him.

"You think you'll need two of them?" Eli asked in his best smart-mouthed tone.

Owen scowled some more. But he slipped the condom into his pocket, causing Eli to smile. It made Owen want to punch him. Or thank him. Before he could decide which, he turned and made his way up the stairs.

He checked on Addie first and saw that she was sacked out in her crib. Francine and Gemma had taken the bed and were asleep, too. Only then did he remember he'd told them that he'd likely be getting up in the middle of the night for watch duty. Obviously the women had decided to make that easy for him by switching around the sleeping arrangements.

Owen checked on Laney next because he hadn't had a chance to talk to her since the Gilley bombshell about Emerson. And no, "checking on" her didn't have anything to do with the condom.

Probably not anyway.

Her door was open, but his heart dropped to his knees when he didn't see her inside. A few seconds later, she came out of the hall bathroom. She was wearing a robe several sizes too big for her and was toweling her wet hair.

"Emerson?" she immediately asked, and her whispered voice hardly had any sound.

He shook his head, saw the mixture of disappointment and frustration go over her face, but she didn't say anything else until they were in the bedroom. "Emerson might not be guilty."

Since that was the same conversation he'd just had with Eli and then with himself, Owen nodded and shut the door so they wouldn't wake Addie, Francine or Gemma.

"Gut feeling?" he asked.

"Just trying to give him the benefit of the doubt. I want the attacks to stop, but I want to make sure the right person pays for that." She paused. "Even if Emerson killed Hadley, it doesn't mean he hired those thugs."

Owen believed that, too. That, of course, put them right back to not having a clear suspect.

He stayed by the door while she continued to dry her hair and pace. Owen figured she wouldn't be getting a lot of sleep tonight, either. However, when the towel shifted a little, that was when he saw the cut on her right temple.

"You're hurt?" he asked, going to her.

"No. It's only a little cut."

He didn't have to ask how she'd gotten it. It'd been when the gunman had shot through the glass. He hadn't seen it earlier because her hair had covered her.

No, she wouldn't be getting any sleep tonight.

She looked at him, forced a smile. "You do know it's not a good idea for you to be in here, right?" she asked.

"I know." He didn't hesitate, either, and had no doubts about that. It was a *very bad* idea.

But he didn't budge.

There was a storm stirring inside him, and it spread until he thought there wasn't any part of him not affected by it. All fire, and it was edged with danger. He thought maybe if he'd been facing down gunmen, it wouldn't have felt as strong as this.

Laney must have sensed that storm because her breath kicked up a notch. It was heavy, causing her chest to rise and fall as if she'd just run a long distance. He saw the pulse on her throat. Took in her scent, something beneath the soap she'd used in the shower.

Her scent.

It roared through him even faster than the storm.

He had a dozen arguments with himself as to why he should turn around and leave. And, one by one, he lost every one of those debates. Because right now there was only one thing that mattered. One thing that he knew he had to have.

Laney.

Owen went to her, pulled her into arms and started what he was certain he would regret soon enough. He kissed her.

FROM THE MOMENT she'd stepped from her shower and had seen Owen, Laney had figured it would lead to this kiss. She hadn't seen any way around it. That didn't make it right.

No. Owen would almost certainly feel guilty about this. Once the heat had cooled down, he would consider it a lapse in judgment. But she wouldn't. She would see it as her one chance to be with him.

And she would take it.

Even if Owen wasn't hers to take.

Laney melted into his arms, into the kiss. It wasn't hard to do. She wanted him more than she wanted her next breath, and with that clever kiss, he was giving her everything she needed. The taste of him. The fit of her body in his arms. The feel of his mouth on hers. And she got even more of that when he deepened the kiss.

Both his mouth and hands were rough. Rushed. Maybe from the same fiery need she was feeling or because he didn't want to pause long enough to change his mind. But Laney made him pause. She pulled back, met his gaze, looked straight into those storm-gray eyes. She didn't say a word. Didn't have to. She just gave him those seconds to reconsider.

Their gazes held. So deep. So long. And it wasn't necessary for them to have a conversation. He told her all she needed to know when his mouth came back to hers. Owen snapped her against him, his hand slipping into her robe and pushing open the sides.

She was naked beneath, something he soon discovered when his fingers brushed over her nipple. He still didn't stop. Didn't even hesitate when he lowered his head and took her nipple into his mouth.

The fire shot through her, flooding the heat to the center of her body. Oh, she wanted him.

Owen didn't stop with the breast kiss. He trailed his mouth, and tongue, lower to her stomach. He might have gone even lower if she hadn't stopped him and pulled him back up.

"You're wearing too many clothes," she protested and immediately tried to do something about that.

She fumbled with the buttons on his shirt and then cursed his shoulder harness when she couldn't get it off him. Owen helped with that, kissing her and backing her across the room. At first, she couldn't figure out why he wasn't taking her to the bed, but then Laney realized he'd locked the door.

Good grief. Anyone could have walked in on them,

and his daughter was just across the hall. That reminder gave her a moment's pause that might have lasted longer if Owen's next kiss hadn't sent her back into the melting mode. Mercy. The man could kiss.

And touch.

Yes, she soon learned he was very clever at that, too. With his hands skimming along her body, he moved her toward the bed, easing her back on the mattress while his fingers found their way between her legs.

The touch took her breath away and caused the pleasure to spear through her. But soon, very soon, it wasn't nearly enough. She wanted him, all of him, and that started with getting him naked.

"Still too many clothes," she complained. "Get them off now."

That finally spurred him to a different kind of action and, while still kissing her, he shucked off his shirt. Laney finally got her chance to touch him. His chest was toned and perfect like the rest of him. She ran her hand down to his jeans to get his belt undone.

And she unzipped him.

She gave in to the heat from the kisses and touched him, sliding her hand into his boxers. Touching him. A sound came deep from his throat. Part groan, part pleasure. She saw urgency come to his eyes. Felt it when he shoved his hand in his jeans pocket and took out a condom.

Laney pushed off his jeans and boots as he put on the condom. Both ate up seconds and caused the pressure to soar. *Now*, she kept repeating in her mind. *Now*.

Owen gave her now.

With the fire and need consuming them, he pushed into her and she closed around him. Owen stilled for a moment, his eyes coming back to hers. More long moments. But these seemed…necessary. As if they both had to know that this wasn't ordinary. That it wasn't just the heat. No. It was a lot more than that, whether they wanted it to be or not.

He was breathing through his mouth now. Heavy, sharp gusts. But still, his eyes—dark and heavy—moved over her, taking her into his mind just as she'd taken him into her body.

When he started to move, he did it slowly. Long, easy strokes. Stretching out the pleasure. That didn't last, either.

Couldn't.

The urgency returned with a vengeance. Something primal that was bone-deep. His need to finish this. The strokes came faster. Deepened. Kept pace with her quick, throbbing pulse. The need came faster, too. Demanding that now, now, now.

Owen gave her that, too.

He pushed into her until the climax slammed through her. Her vision pinpointed just him before it blurred. Before the only thing she could do was hold on. And take him with her.

Chapter Fourteen

When Owen came back from the bathroom, he'd expected to find Laney already dressed and either pacing or working on the laptop. But she was still naked and apparently asleep. She was on her stomach, her hand tucked like a pillow beneath her face. She looked... well, peaceful.

And beautiful.

No way would he convince his body otherwise. Not a chance of convincing it—or rather, certain parts of him anyway—that he didn't want her all over again. That wouldn't have been such a bad thing if one of those parts hadn't been his heart.

Hell.

He hadn't just had sex with her. He'd made love to her. Big difference, and he was honest enough with himself to not try to downplay it. Sex was easy, often with no strings or ones that didn't matter. But there'd be important strings with Laney. Not from her. He was guessing she'd give him an out and say that it didn't matter. She wouldn't be doing that for herself but rather for him.

Owen wouldn't take an out. He'd never been the sort to dismiss his feelings, which meant he was going to have to somehow work out this guilt going through him about Naomi. In a way, it felt as if he'd cheated on her. Or worse, it felt as if he'd finally gotten past her death. And that was worse than the guilt.

Pulling in a long breath, he eased down next to Laney on the bed. She automatically moved closer to him, draping her arm over his chest, and he felt the muscles tense in her arm. She opened one eye, looked at him and frowned.

"You're dressed." She started to scramble away from him, probably to put on her clothes, but he dragged her against him, holding her.

She didn't move away, but she did look up at him. He recognized suspicion in a person's eyes when he saw it. Suspicion. Then lust. She glanced at the door, probably to see if he'd shut it. He had.

"I'm naked," she said. "You're not. I think this would probably work better if you were naked, too."

That made him smile, and Owen brushed a kiss on the top of her head. He just wanted a moment, with her like this in his arms. It didn't settle the guilt trip in his mind, but it sure as heck settled the rest of him.

She levered herself up, touched her fingers to the bunched-up part of his forehead. "What is it?" she asked.

Owen wasn't sure he would have told her, but he didn't get the chance to decide because his phone buzzed. He'd turned off the ringer so that it wouldn't wake Addie, Francine or Gemma, but the buzz came through loud and clear.

Emerson's name was on the screen.

"Put it on speaker," Laney insisted as she got to her feet and began to dress.

Owen did, but he turned down the volume. "Where are you?" Owen immediately asked.

"I'm driving to the ranch. We need to talk."

Yeah, they definitely needed to talk, but Owen didn't want Emerson within a mile of the ranch. "Go to the sheriff's office. Kellan's there and he'll talk to you."

Emerson made a sound of outrage. "You're my brother-in-law, not Kellan. I want to talk to you."

"The hands have orders not to let anyone on the ranch." Owen spelled it out for him. "They won't let you on."

Emerson cursed. "Didn't you hear what I said? We need to talk. I can't find Nettie, and I think someone's trying to kill me."

Owen didn't say "Welcome to the club," but that was what he was thinking. Laney, too, because she rolled her eyes. "What makes you think someone's trying to kill you?" Owen prompted.

"Because a car's been following me. I've got a gun, but if these are hired killers, they'll be a lot better shot than I am."

"Funny you should mention that. Rohan Gilley, the gun we have in custody, said you were his boss."

That brought on a whole new round of cursing from Emerson. "He's a lying SOB. I didn't hire him. I haven't done anything wrong."

"Nothing other than lying to keep your affair with Hadley a secret," Owen reminded him.

"I didn't kill her!" Emerson shouted. "I didn't kill anyone, and I sure as hell didn't hire Rohan Gilley."

Owen had no idea if that were true, but even if he believed him, he wouldn't let Emerson on the ranch.

They were on lockdown, and it was going to stay that way until they were no longer in danger.

"Go to the sheriff's office," Owen repeated. "Give your statement to Kellan. If there's someone following you, someone who intends to do you harm, then Kellan can also put you in protective custody."

"Is that where Nettie went?" Emerson snapped.

Owen didn't have a clue, but since that might urge Emerson to go there, he settled for saying, "Could be. You should check and see. And do it soon, Emerson," Owen added just as the man ended the call.

He had no idea if his brother-in-law would actually do that, but maybe he would so they could begin to start putting together the pieces of this puzzle.

By the time Owen put his phone away, Laney was completely dressed. Something that didn't please the nonheart part of him. He considered getting her out of those clothes again and going for another round, but he didn't have a second condom and wouldn't ask Eli for one.

Well, maybe he wouldn't.

Owen was pretty sure the moment Eli saw his face, his brother would be able to figure out what had gone on. Heck, Eli might even volunteer another condom then—even though the timing sucked. Owen mentally repeated that part about the timing, got up and faced Laney.

"I'm going down to relieve Eli for a while," he said.

"I'll go with you and grab something to eat."

Until she'd added that last part, Owen had been about to tell her to get some rest, but since she hadn't eaten anything all day, he didn't want to nix a good idea. He might even be able to grab a bite, as well.

Apparently, good sex spurred the appetite.

Owen peeked in again on Addie before Laney and he made their way down the stairs. And yep, Eli did figure it out. The corner of Eli's mouth lifted in a smile, but he thankfully dropped the expression when Laney came in. She greeted Eli and went straight into the adjoining kitchen.

"Don't say a word," Owen warned Eli.

Eli didn't, but he did chuckle. If it was loud enough for Laney to hear, she didn't react. She started making sandwiches from some cold cuts that she took from the fridge.

"Why don't you get some sleep?" Owen suggested.

"Will do after I fix me one of those sandwiches." Eli traded places with him, and Owen moved to the window as his brother went into the kitchen with Laney.

It was dark outside. No moon. But there were security lights on the road leading to the house. Owen had debated as to whether or not to turn them off. Debated keeping off all the lights inside, too, so that no one would easily be able to see they were there. However, he'd nixed the idea since the security lights would make it easier for the hands to see if someone tried to get onto the ranch.

Owen was less than a minute into his watch duties when his phone buzzed again. He silently cursed, figuring it was Emerson. But no, it was Terrance. Owen answered, putting the call on speaker because both Laney and Eli had entered the room, no doubt to listen.

"Are you at the sheriff's office?" Terrance asked, continuing before he gave Owen a chance to answer. "Because I need to see you."

"I'm a popular man tonight," Owen grumbled. "What do you want?"

Considering Terrance had blurted the first part of his conversation, it surprised Owen when the man went silent. Owen was about to repeat his "what do you want" demand when Terrance finally spoke.

"Look, I need to explain some things, that's all." Terrance definitely didn't sound like his usual cocky self. "Your brother, the sheriff, made it clear that he's looking at me for Nancy's murder."

"Yeah, because she worked for you," Owen was quick to remind him.

"She did, but I swear I didn't have anything to do with her murder."

That was the second time tonight that someone had denied being a killer. Owen wasn't any more inclined to believe him than he was Emerson.

"I didn't kill Nancy," Terrance went on. And he paused again. "But she did get into that bank box to get the pictures."

Laney dropped the bag of chips she'd taken from the cabinet and hurried closer to Owen. Eli moved closer, too, eating his sandwich. While he wasn't hurrying, it was obvious his attention was nailed to the conversation.

"I'm listening," Owen told Terrance.

"Once I made the connection between Hadley and a safe-deposit box, I wanted to know what was inside," Terrance admitted.

Owen's jaw tightened. "Why? Because you thought there was some kind of evidence in there that would get your conviction overturned?" And yes, that question was loaded with sarcasm.

"No. I was guilty of assaulting Laney, and I served my time," he quickly added. "I just thought there might be something that would…punish Laney. Something to give her a dose of the same pain she gave me when she didn't do her job and vet the gold digger who drained me dry."

Owen was about to point out that Terrance had been the one stupid enough to fall for a con artist, but Laney spoke before Owen could.

"Punish me?" Laney repeated. "How?"

Terrance muttered some profanity. "I thought it would bring back bad memories for you. Something that would make you feel guilty for not finding your sister's killer." He paused. "When I told Nancy this, she took it upon herself to get into the bank. I never hired her to do that, never encouraged her."

Owen doubted that. There'd likely been plenty of *encouragement*. Payment, too.

"How'd Nancy get the key to the box?" Owen queried.

"I'm not sure. She didn't tell me."

Owen doubted that, as well. There was a slim chance that Nancy could have bribed someone at the bank to get her a duplicate key. Also a slim chance that Nancy had killed Joe and got the key from him. But all of this pointed straight back to Terrance.

"Nancy acted of her own accord," Terrance declared. "Because she thought it would be a favor to me."

"A favor?" Owen challenged. "She committed a felony. This is more than just a favor."

Terrance made a sound of agreement. "She had a thing for me and probably thought I'd be so grateful that it'd start up something personal between us. It didn't."

Owen would give that some more thought later, but for now he wanted to keep pressing for details. Then he could sort out what were lies and what were truths.

"What happened when Nancy went to the bank?" Owen asked.

"She called and said the only thing in the box was a bunch of pictures. Pictures of Hadley and the married DA. I wasn't sure how I could use those, but I told her to copy them, put them in online storage and then put the originals in a safe place."

"And then you killed Nancy?" Owen finished for him.

"No! Of course not." There was plenty of emotion in his voice now and some of it sounded like regret. "Nancy asked if she could make some money off the pictures, maybe by getting the DA to buy them. I told her no, that I didn't want her to do that." Another pause. "But I think she tried. I think that's what got her killed."

Yeah, maybe killed by Terrance himself because the woman had disobeyed his order. "Who murdered Nancy?" Owen demanded.

"I don't know, but I refuse to be blamed for her death. I won't let your brother come after me and try to stick me behind bars." The anger was back with a vengeance, and his voice started to rise. "I won't go back to jail."

"You won't have a choice about that. If there's any proof whatsoever that you paid Nancy to go to the bank—"

"There isn't," Terrance interrupted. "Because I'm innocent, and as far as I'm concerned, this will be the last conversation I have with Laney, your brother or you." With that, Terrance ended the call.

Owen wasn't so sure about this being the last, but

he hoped that Terrance would truly stay out of Laney's life. That would definitely happen if Terrance was arrested for murder.

"If Terrance was telling the truth about Nancy," Laney said, "maybe the woman used the courier so she'd be one step removed from the blackmail. In fact, she could have paid someone to contact the courier service."

As theories went, it wasn't a bad one, and if that was what happened, then Terrance could indeed be innocent. But that left them with the same question he'd just presented to Terrance. Who killed Nancy?

Eli was still chowing down on his sandwich when his phone buzzed. "It's Jeremy," he relayed to them. Jeremy Cranston, one of the ranch hands. Eli took the call on speaker.

"I just spotted someone in the back pasture," Jeremy said. "A man. And he's got a rifle."

LANEY'S STOMACH TIGHTENED into a cold, hard knot, and she realized this was something she had been expecting. Something she'd prayed wouldn't happen.

But here it was.

"The armed guy isn't close to the house," Jeremy added a moment later. "I saw him through the binoculars as he came over the fence. Should I leave Bennie here and head out to that part of the pasture?" Laney knew that Bennie Deavers was the other ranch hand helping them guard the immediate area around the house.

"No," Owen answered. "Just keep an eye on the intruder. He could be a lure to get us to go after him."

Oh, God. She hadn't even considered that. She should

have, though. Laney should have anticipated that whoever was behind this would do anything to get to her.

But why?

She still didn't know, and that tore away at her as much as the fear for Owen, his family and the hands.

"Have you seen anyone else?" Owen asked Jeremy. "Maybe somebody on the road?"

"Nobody. Don't have to tell you, though, that there are a lot of acres. A lot of ways for someone to get here if they're hell-bent on it."

No, Jeremy didn't have to tell them. And yes, the person after her was definitely hell-bent.

She thought of all the old trails that coiled around the ranch and fed out into the roads. Once they'd been used to move cattle and equipment before the roads had been built. Now they could provide access to someone who wanted to get close without being seen.

"Keep an eye on all sides of the house," Owen instructed as he turned off the lights. Eli went into the living room and did the same. "Just keep an eye on the gunman and text Eli or me when he gets closer to the house."

Eli had already moved to the front window to keep watch when he ended the call. Owen moved to the kitchen window, but he looked at Laney.

"Have Francine and Gemma move Addie into the tub," he said. "You go in the bathroom with them."

"Yes to the first. No to the second," Laney argued. "You need backup, and I not only have a gun, I know how to use it."

Laney didn't give him a chance to answer. She ran up the stairs to get Addie to safety. Gemma must have heard her coming because the woman stepped out into the hall.

"There's an armed man in the pasture" was all Laney said, and Gemma hurried back into the room to scoop up Addie.

"Francine, get up," Gemma insisted, already heading to the adjoining bathroom. Thankfully, Addie didn't wake up, and Laney hoped it stayed that way.

The nanny sprang off the bed, her eyes wide with fear. Fear that Laney couldn't soothe because the danger had returned. "I'll come back up when the threat is over," Laney assured her. She prayed that wouldn't be too long.

Of course, after this threat was over, Owen would no doubt make the decision to move Addie. This was the second intruder in only a handful of hours, and he had to get his daughter out of harm's way. That meant taking the little girl to a safe house—away from Owen. And Owen would almost certainly insist that Laney go into a safe house, as well. Not with Addie, though. No. The best way to protect Addie was to get her away from Laney.

Once Francine and Gemma had Addie in the bathroom, Laney made sure all the upstairs lights were off and then hurried downstairs. Since Owen was still in the kitchen and Eli at the front of the living room, Laney went to the side window positioned between the two areas. They could cover three sides of the house in case this armed thug got past the ranch hands.

And the wait began.

It was impossible for Laney to tamp down all the fear that was rising inside her. Impossible to keep her breathing and heartbeat level. But she forced herself to remember her training. She didn't have nearly the level of expertise that Owen and Eli did, but she'd taken self-defense and firearms classes. Maybe, though, it wouldn't come down to any of them using those skills.

The room was so quiet that Laney nearly gasped when she heard the sound. Not an intruder. It was Eli's phone that dinged with a text message.

Volleying glances between the window and his phone, Eli read it. Then he cursed. "Jeremy said he lost sight of the armed idiot and thinks the guy went behind the trees."

Laney wanted to curse, too. That definitely hadn't been what she'd wanted to hear. Now the guy could be anywhere, including much too close to the house.

"Keep watch," Eli reminded them as he slipped his phone back into his pocket.

She did. Laney's gaze went from one side of her area to the other. Trees, yes. A white rail fence. And she could see the edge of the barn behind the house. What she couldn't see were any signs of a hired gun. Since Owen had a much better view of the barn, she glanced at him just as he glanced at her. And he shook his head.

"Nothing that I can see," he said.

"How's the security system rigged?" she asked. She was certain that Owen had already mentioned it, but she wanted to make sure.

"There are alarms on all windows and doors, including the windows on the top floor. If anyone tries to get in, we'll know about it."

Good. It was especially good about the alarms being on the second story of the house. Laney doubted the intruder could get a ladder past the ranch hands, but even if by some miracle that happened, he wouldn't be able to just break in without alerting them.

Her heart skipped a couple of beats when she saw something move by the barn, and Laney automatically pivoted in that direction. It got Eli and Owen's attention, and she heard them shift their positions, too. Then she saw the yellow tabby cat skirt out from the barn and dart across the yard.

"It was just the cat," Laney said. Even though she couldn't actually hear Eli and Owen take breaths of relief, she figured that was what they were doing. She certainly was.

Eli's phone dinged again, putting her heart in her throat as she waited for him to relay the text. "Jeremy caught sight of him by the left side of the barn."

The barn. Much too close. And possibly the reason the cat had run.

She couldn't see the left side of the barn from her position, so she shifted, moving to the other side of the window. She still didn't have a clear view, but she could see more of the barn.

As she'd done earlier, Laney took aim in that direction. Just as she heard another sound. One she didn't want to hear.

A gunshot.

Owen saw the rifle a split second before the bullet crashed through the kitchen window right next to where he was standing.

Almost immediately the security alarm went off, the shrill, clanging sounds pulsing through the house. The bullet had been loud, deafening even, but the alarms were drowning out sounds that he wanted to hear.

Like any kind of movement in the yard.

If this armed thug was coming closer to the house, Owen darn sure wanted to know about it. Plus, he needed to make sure Francine and Gemma weren't calling out for help.

"Kill the alarm," Owen shouted to Eli.

His brother was closer to the keypad by the door, and besides, the shooter was obviously at the back of the house, where Owen was.

Using the wall as cover, Owen glanced around the window frame at the barn. He didn't see anything, but he knew the guy was there, hiding in the shadows. Waiting to do some more damage. He got proof of that when he saw the rifle again.

Owen immediately fired, but the shooter must not have been hit because he managed to get off a shot. A second bullet came crashing through what was left of the window. The guy fired a third shot, then a fourth, but Owen couldn't tell where the last two had landed.

He prayed they hadn't gone upstairs.

Just the thought sent his heart and fear into overdrive. He knew that Francine would have Addie in the tub where she'd be relatively safe, but he didn't want *relatively* when it came to his daughter. He wanted this idiot gunman dead so he couldn't send any more lethal shots anywhere near the house.

The house went silent when Eli turned off the alarm, and Owen immediately listened for Francine. Nothing, thank God. And he added another thanks when he didn't hear Addie crying.

"I've reset the security system," his brother said. "But I had to turn off the sensors on the windows. *All* the windows," Eli emphasized. "It was the only way to shut off the alarms."

That wasn't ideal, but at least the doors would still be armed, and if the gunman came through a window, he'd have to break the glass since they were all locked. Owen knew that because he'd checked them all himself.

With his attention still on the barn, Owen heard the dinging sound of a text message from Eli's phone.

"Jeremy's been hit in the leg," Eli relayed, tacking on some raw curse words. "Bennie says it's not bad, and he's tying off the wound."

Good. Owen definitely didn't want the hand dying, but the injury basically took out both men who'd been guarding the house. It pinned them down so they might not be able to shoot the gunman even if they caught sight of him.

"Should I call for backup?" Laney asked.

Owen purposely hadn't looked at her—because he hadn't wanted to remember that she, too, was in danger, but he glanced at her now and shook his head. "I don't want anyone else coming into an ambush."

In fact, he wanted her away from the window, but the truth was, with the hands out of commission, Owen needed her eyes and gun right now. Laney seemed ready to give them both. She certainly didn't look as if she might fall apart. Just the opposite. She had a firm grip on her weapon and had it aimed in the direction of the barn.

"I'll call Kellan and an ambulance," Eli volunteered. "But I will tell them to hold off, to keep some distance from the house. I agree. I don't want anyone else gunned down tonight."

Owen listened while his brother made the quick call.

That would put Kellan and the EMTs on standby at least, and he hoped like the devil that no one else got hurt. Well, no one other than the idiot who'd shot Jeremy.

He dragged in a hard breath and held it while he continued to take glances out at the barn. He couldn't wait long, though. Despite having Bennie there to help, Jeremy would soon need medical attention. Besides, Owen couldn't have any more shots being fired into the house.

"I see him," Laney blurted. Before Owen could even respond, she fired, her shot blasting through the window. The glass practically exploded from the impact.

Laney ducked back. Barely in the nick of time because the gunman returned fire, sending a shot right at her. This one didn't just take out more glass but also a chunk of wood from the window frame. A reminder that those bullets could go through the walls.

Owen saw the blood on Laney's face. No doubt a cut from the flying glass or wood. And it turned his stomach. She was hurt, and even though it was probably minor, he hated that this snake had been able to get to her. Hated even more that the injury could have been much worse.

Laney didn't even react to the cut. She adjusted her position again, still staying by the window, and Owen quit glancing at her so that he could keep his attention nailed to the barn.

The seconds crawled by as he waited, his finger on the trigger. He knew that Eli and Laney were doing the same thing, but Owen didn't hear or see anything.

When the seconds turned to minutes, Owen knew he had to do something. Jeremy needed help, and they couldn't just stand there. He was going to have to do something to draw out the gunman.

"Eli, keep low but come back here," Owen instructed. "I'm going to duck out from cover. When he takes aim at me, shoot him."

"No," Laney insisted. "You could be shot."

Yeah. But so could everybody else in the house. Owen didn't say that to her, though. He just waited until Eli was in position on the other side of the window. Owen gave him the nod and leaned out from cover.

Nothing.

No rifle barrel. No gunman.

Where the hell was he? Owen was about to ask Eli to text Jeremy to see if he had eyes on the gunman, but before he could do that, Owen heard something that shot fresh adrenaline through him.

The alarm from the security system.

Someone had tripped it, and that someone was in the house.

Chapter Fifteen

Laney tried to tamp down the jolt of fear she got from the alarm, but it was impossible not to react.

The gunman was almost certainly inside.

She forced her mind to clear so she could do a quick review of the house. Eli had said the windows were no longer armed so the intruder must have come in through a door.

Laney could see both the front door in the foyer and the back door in the kitchen. They were closed, so that left two other points of entry. The one at the side of the house off the family room. Or the one that led from carport area and into the house. Either one of those could give him access to the kitchen.

Or the back stairs that led to the second floor.

"Addie," Owen said over the clamor of the alarm.

Eli nodded. "I'll go up and guard the door." She saw the same fear and concern in his eyes that was no doubt in hers.

Eli had likely volunteered because he was closer, right at the base of the front stairs. Without waiting for Owen's response, he disengaged the security system, silencing the alarms again, then barreled up the steps, taking them two at a time.

Owen hurried into the living room with her, positioning them so they were back to back. He didn't have to tell her to keep watch of the foyer in case the gunman came that way. He did the same to the back of the house.

Even with the silenced alarm, it was still hard for Laney to hear, but she picked her way through her throbbing pulse so she could listen. Nothing. Not at first. And then she heard what she was sure was someone moving around.

Owen must have heard it, too, because the muscles in his body stiffened even more than they already were. "It came from the family room," he whispered, automatically switching places with her so that he faced that direction.

Laney didn't like that he'd done that to take her out of the line of fire, but she knew that was an argument she wouldn't win. No way would Owen just stand there and let her face danger when he could do something about it.

Owen cursed softly when something or someone bumped against the wall. Not in the family room. Laney was almost positive this sound had come from the carport area. That caused the sickening dread to flood through her.

Because it meant there were likely two killers.

Her gun was already raised and ready, but she tried to steady her grip. A shaky hand wasn't going to help them now. Especially since it was possible the two thugs had coordinated an attack. They could come after them at the same time, trapping them in the crossfire.

That put a crushing feeling around her heart to go with the dread that was already there. Owen could be killed. And all because of her. Then these monsters could go upstairs and finish off everyone in the house.

That meant she and Owen had to stop them before they got a chance to do that.

Owen's phone dinged, the sound she recognized as a text from Kellan. But Owen didn't take his phone from his pocket. She was thankful for that. Laney didn't want anything to be a distraction right now even though the message could be important.

Laney kept watching. Kept waiting. With her breath so thin, she felt starved for air, and her shoulders so tense, the muscles started to cramp.

She heard another sound. Not footsteps this time but rather a car engine. She didn't risk looking at Owen, but she saw the slash of headlights coming straight for the house.

Kellan.

Maybe.

Eli had told him to stay back to avoid being ambushed. Maybe Kellan had decided against that, which would explain the text to Owen's phone that he hadn't been able to check. If Kellan had indeed decided to come forward, she hoped he wouldn't be shot.

She glanced over her shoulder when the sound and lights got closer. In the distance, Laney could hear the sirens. Too far away to be the vehicle approaching the house.

And it was coming too fast.

There was a loud crash, and it felt as if it shook the entire house. The impact sent the front door flying open, and that was when she realized the car had collided with the front porch.

Maybe this was a third gunman. Or some kind of ruse to distract them from the two who were already in the house. If so, it worked, because the person who staggered through the front door got their attention.

Emerson.

"What the hell is going on?" he grumbled. "The ranch hands wouldn't let me in, and I had to bash through the gate."

The headlights on the car were out now, maybe damaged in the collision, making it was hard to see Emerson in the dark foyer. However, she could tell that he wasn't armed, or rather that he didn't have a gun in his hand, which was probably the only reason Owen hadn't shot him on sight.

Even in the darkness, she noticed that Emerson's eyes widened when he looked at them, and he shook his head as if dazed. Maybe drugged or drunk. Something was definitely wrong.

"What the hell is going on?" Emerson repeated, his words slurred.

"Why are you here?" Owen asked. He had his gun aimed at his brother-in-law while his gaze fired all around the area.

Emerson opened his mouth, closed it and scrubbed his hand over his face. "Something happened to me. I'm not sure what."

Laney had no idea if he was telling the truth, but even if he was, she had no intention of trusting the man. This could all be some trick to make them believe he was innocent when he could be the one pulling the strings on the hired guns. He could have already given them orders to attack.

"Get facedown on the floor," Owen told Emerson. "Put your hands behind your back."

Good. That way, they could maybe restrain him until they could take care of the intruders.

"You're arresting me?" Emerson howled. Now the anger tightened the muscles in his face. "Who the hell do you think you are?"

"I'm the lawman who's going to take you down if you don't get on the floor." There was plenty of anger in Owen's voice, too.

Emerson made a sound of outrage and moved as if he might charge right at them. He didn't get a chance to do that, though, before someone reached out from the side of the stairs and latched onto the man.

Then the person put a gun to Emerson's head.

FROM THE MOMENT Emerson staggered through the door, Owen had figured that things were about to go from bad to worse. He'd thought that maybe Emerson would just start shooting.

Or order his goons to shoot.

And maybe he would still do that, but for now it appeared that one of those hired guns had taken him hostage. *Appeared*, Owen mentally repeated. There was no way he was going to take this at face value.

Owen immediately grasped Laney's arm and pulled her to the side of arched opening that served as an entrance to the family room. As cover went, it wasn't much, so he made sure he was in front of Laney.

"Do anything stupid—*anything*—and the DA dies," the man behind Emerson growled.

Owen didn't recognize the husky voice and, even though it was hard to see the man in the dark shadows, he got a glimpse of part of his face. Owen didn't recognize him, either.

"Let go of me," Emerson yelled and tried to ram his elbow into the gunman's stomach.

The gunman dodged the blow, bashed the butt of his gun against Emerson's head and curved his arm around his neck. Emerson continued to struggle as the man tightened his choke-hold grip.

"What's going on down there?" Eli shouted. "I texted you to tell you that Emerson charged past the hands. Did he make it all the way to the house?"

"Yeah. I'm handling it," Owen answered. "Stay put," he added to his brother when he heard a sound he didn't want to hear.

Addie crying.

"She's okay," Eli quickly said. "The noise just woke her, that's all."

Owen released the breath that had caused the vise-like pressure in his chest. His baby was safe. For now. He needed to make sure she stayed that way.

"Are you working for Emerson?" Owen asked the gunman.

The guy snorted out a laugh. "Does it look like he's my boss?"

A desperate person out to kill them could make this look like anything he wanted. That included setting up a fake hostage situation. But it didn't look fake. Didn't *feel* that way, either. Emerson's head was bleeding, and he was gasping for air. Plus, there was that panicked look in his brother-in-law's eyes, which looked like the real deal.

"Things obviously didn't go as planned," the man said. "My partner's missing. Maybe your sheriff brother took him out, but he's not answering."

That was possibly Kellan's doing or one of the hands'. Either way, Owen was thankful there was only one of them. But that did make him wonder.

When had it happened?

He'd heard two sets of footsteps—Owen was certain of that—so did that mean Kellan was in the house?

"Because things got screwed up, I need to get out of here, and I'm going to use the DA here to do that," the gunman insisted. "Since it appears he's messed up his car by running it into your porch, I'll be taking that truck parked out front. If you don't have the keys, I'll start shooting, and that woman you're trying to protect just might be the one who takes the bullet."

That sent a shot of anger spearing through Owen. Laney had already been through too much to have this piece of slime threaten her.

"It's okay," Laney whispered to Owen. "Better me than Addie."

He hated that she would even have to consider that. But he was also thankful for it. She was putting his daughter first.

"Give him the keys," Emerson insisted when the man eased up on the choke hold. He sputtered out a cough. "If not, he'll just kill us and take the keys."

Owen stared at him. "You seem pretty cooperative for someone who's being used as a human shield."

Emerson looked Owen straight in the eyes. "I don't want to die. I don't know who's doing this, but we need to get this would-be killer out of the house. My niece is upstairs."

It twisted at Owen to hear Emerson say that. He didn't know if Emerson had genuine concern for Addie the way Laney did or if this was part of the act. Either way, if Emerson left, it would get the gunman away from Addie.

"The truck keys are on the foyer table," Owen told the gunman.

Owen saw the man's gaze immediately go in that direction. The keys were indeed there, and Owen was going to let him take them. Let him go outside, too. And then he would do what he could to stop him so that ambulance could get onto the grounds for Jeremy.

The thug got Emerson moving and he was careful to keep Emerson in front of him. "Take the keys," he growled at Emerson when they reached the foyer table.

Emerson did. His hand closed around the keys just as a shot rang out. For one heart-stopping moment, Owen thought the thug had shot Emerson, but the gunfire had come from the back of the house.

Hell.

The other gunman.

Maybe Kellan hadn't disabled him, after all.

The gunman jerked back, snapping Emerson even closer to him as he put the gun to Emerson's head. Obviously he didn't think the shot had come from his partner.

"I said I'll kill him, and I sure as hell mean it," the gunman yelled, but he wasn't speaking to Owen. "Stay back or the DA dies."

There was another blast of gunfire.

Then another.

Owen cursed and glanced around, trying to figure out who was doing this. Not Kellan. No. His brother would have called out to them to stop from being shot by friendly fire.

"I think the shooter's near the back stairs," Laney whispered.

That was Owen's guess, too, and it sent his heart to his knees. Because the gunman could be heading up to get to Addie.

"Eli, watch the back stairs," Owen called out to his brother. He knew Eli already doing that, but he wanted him to have a heads-up.

"Eli won't let a gunman get into the bathroom," Laney reminded him.

Owen believed that. Eli would do whatever it took to protect the little girl, but that didn't mean a gunman couldn't get off a lucky shot.

"I swear I'll kill him," the gunman repeated. With his choke hold still in place, he maneuvered Emerson into the doorway.

Just as there was another shot. This one hadn't come from the back stairs, though. From the sound of it, the gunman had fired from the living room. That meant he was coming closer.

But something wasn't right.

If this was the second gunman, why did the one holding Emerson suddenly look so concerned? Maybe because he thought it was Kellan.

No. It was something else.

"Move," the gunman ordered Emerson. The thug got him onto the porch as another shot came their way. This one slammed into the door frame right next to the gunman's head.

"Stop or I'll kill you," someone said, the voice coming from the living room.

Owen immediately saw the gun the person was holding. Aimed not at Laney and him but rather at the gunman who had Emerson.

And that someone was Nettie.

LANEY INSTANTLY RECOGNIZED Nettie's voice. At first, she thought the woman was there only because she'd followed Emerson. But then she saw Nettie lean out from the arched entry of the living room. One look at her from over Owen's shoulder and Laney knew that Nettie was responsible for the attacks.

Nettie was the person who'd been trying to kill them.

And had maybe murdered Hadley, too.

Emerson shook his head, his expression registering a mix of shock and relief. Then fear. "Nettie, you need to run. This man will kill you."

Nettie definitely didn't run, but she did stay partly behind the cover of the wall. A wall she'd easily be able to duck behind if anyone started shooting.

"Boss," the gunman said, confirming what everyone had already figured out. Everyone but Emerson, that was.

"Boss?" Emerson snapped. "You idiot. That's my wife, and she didn't hire you." He fired some wild-eyed glances at Laney and Owen before his attention settled on Nettie.

Laney saw the realization register on Emerson's face. He groaned. "No. Nettie, not you."

Nettie didn't deny it. "Let go of him, Stan," she ordered the gunman.

Stan was making some wild-eyed glances of his own,

and there was fear all over his face. "I don't think that's a good idea. It wasn't my fault he came running in here. He crashed his car into to the porch and just bolted in."

"You should have taken care of the situation before that." Nettie's words were arctic cold and so was the look in her eyes. "Let him go."

So, Nettie was going to save her husband. Maybe. But certainly she didn't think that Emerson and she could just walk out and resume their lives.

"Nettie," Emerson said, his voice cracking. "What have you done? What are you doing?"

"I'm cleaning up your mess. You weren't supposed to be here. I told the housekeeper to sneak you a sedative, that you were going off half-cocked and would do something stupid to ruin your career. Your life."

So that was why Emerson had looked drugged. Because he had been.

"I'm trying to fix things," Emerson pled. The gunman tightened his choke hold when Emerson tried to go to Nettie.

"No, I'm fixing things," Nettie argued. "*Again.* First, with that bimbo you were seeing and now with the mess from those pictures."

"Hadley?" Emerson said. "You knew about Hadley?"

"Of course I did," Nettie snapped. "She called me crying, and said you'd broken off things with her, but she wanted me to know all about your relationship. That's what she called it. A *relationship.* Well, I showed her the price she had to pay for sleeping with my husband. I ended her miserable life."

Oh, mercy. Laney felt as if she'd just been punched in the stomach. Nettie had been the one to murder Hadley. It didn't make it easier, but at least now she knew.

"Damn it, I'm your wife," Nettie snapped, aiming a glare at Emerson, "and you cheated on me."

"I'm so sorry." Emerson's eyes shimmered with tears. "God, I'm so sorry."

Nettie dragged in a breath. "I know, and that's the reason you'll live through this." She looked at Owen now. "But not you. Not Laney. You were smart to tell Eli to stay put, because that means he'll live, too. Or rather, he will, if you cooperate."

"Cooperate how?" Owen's voice was just as cold as hers, and while Laney couldn't see his face, she suspected he matched Nettie glare for glare. "You came here, firing shots, ordering your hired goon to fire shots, and each one of those bullets put my daughter in danger. And why? Because you got your feelings hurt when your husband slept with another woman?"

No more coolness for Nettie. The rage tightened her face and, for the first time, Laney saw the hot emotion that had spurred Nettie to not only kill but to plot to kill again.

"Hadley didn't just sleep with my husband," Nettie growled. She didn't shout, but there was a low, dangerous edge to her voice now. "She tried to blackmail me. Blackmail! I wasn't going to let her get away with that."

"So, you murdered her," Owen said. "And then you killed Joe and Nancy."

Nettie didn't deny that, either. "Cleaning up messes— again." Her mouth went into a flat line. "I didn't know that Nancy had put the pictures on a server."

"How'd Nancy even get the key for the box?" Laney asked.

"From me. I took it that night from Hadley, but I didn't know which bank. It took me a while to find that.

But none of this matters. People will forgive Emerson when they learn of the affair."

Laney nearly laughed, and it wasn't from humor. "Do you honestly think that Emerson and you are just going to walk away from this?"

"Yes, because Terrance will get the blame. I've set all of that up." Nettie shifted her attention to Stan, her hired gun. "Let go of my husband."

Stan shook his head. "If I do that, what's to stop you from killing me? You might think of me as part of this mess you want to clean up."

Smart man, because that was no doubt exactly what Nettie was thinking. She could kill Stan, Owen and Laney, and walk out. In Nettie's delusional mind, she might actually believe that everything would be fine.

"Let go of my husband," Nettie repeated and took aim at Stan.

"Nettie," Emerson said, the plea in his voice. "Just please put down your gun. Everyone, put down your guns."

Laney knew that wasn't going to happen. Judging from their expression, so did Stan and Nettie.

"Owen?" Eli called out. "Everything okay down there?"

"Tell him yes," Nettie insisted, her eyes narrowing again. "If you want to save your daughter and him, tell him yes."

Laney could practically feel the debate going on inside Owen. No way did he want to do anything that would risk more gunfire, but even if he did as the woman asked, there were no guarantees that Nettie wouldn't just kill Owen, Stan and her and then go upstairs to do the same.

"Tell Eli yes," Nettie repeated, "or the next shot I fire will go into the ceiling. Maybe into the very room where you're hiding Addie."

Emerson frantically shook his head. "No. You can't do that. Nettie, you can't."

Her expression said otherwise, that she would indeed do the unthinkable.

There were at least fifteen feet of distance between Nettie, Owen and Laney with the foyer and the base of the stairs between them. Emerson and Stan were half that distance. Emerson must have realized he was the one who could get to her first because he rammed his elbow into Stan's stomach. This time, it connected, and the gunman staggered onto the porch before he took off running.

Emerson didn't run.

He launched himself at Nettie.

And the shot blasted through the foyer.

Chapter Sixteen

Owen cursed when he saw what Emerson was about to do, but there had been no time to stop the man. No time, either, to stop the shot that Nettie fired when Emerson lunged toward her.

His brother-in-law made a sharp groan of pain and dropped down right in front of Nettie.

Owen immediately saw the blood spreading across Emerson's chest, and the heard the feral scream that Nettie made. A scream that would almost certainly send Eli running down the stairs if Owen didn't do something about that fast. No way did he want his brother rushing to help. Nettie was still armed and might shoot him.

"Stay put," Owen yelled up to Eli.

Nettie was still screaming, but the sound of Owen's voice must have snagged her attention. She looked at him, her eyes dazed. Maybe in shock. But it didn't last. She took aim at Owen and fired.

Owen shoved Laney back behind the arched opening. It wasn't good cover since the bullet went straight through a chunk of the drywall, but it was better than nothing.

"This wasn't supposed to happen," Nettie said, her

voice a sob now. She was obviously crying. "Oh, God. Emerson wasn't supposed to get shot."

"He needs an ambulance," Owen insisted. "There's one waiting outside. All you have to do is put down your gun and I'll have Kellan send in the EMTs."

"Please," Emerson begged, "do as he says, Nettie. I need help. I'm bleeding out."

Owen glanced over and saw that Nettie, too, was still behind cover, volleying glances between Emerson and him. Emerson was clutching his stomach, moaning in pain, and yes, he was bleeding out.

Nettie shook her head, obviously trying to decide what to do. If she saved her husband, the man she supposedly loved enough to kill for, then she would be arrested for multiple murders and the attacks.

"I love you, Nettie," Emerson added. Maybe he did. Or maybe Emerson was just trying to do the right thing and calm Nettie enough to get her to put down that gun.

"I can't go to jail," Nettie said. Owen could hear the panic in her voice. "I can't live without you."

Emerson tried to speak but his eyelids fluttered down.

"No!" Nettie yelled and fired a shot at Owen. "He's dead. He can't be dead."

"He's not," Owen assured her while he glanced out from behind cover. He kept his attention nailed to Nettie. "Look at his chest. You can see he's still breathing."

Owen had no idea if that was true. Emerson could indeed be dead, but if so, there was nothing Owen could do about it. However, he could do something about Nettie. He got that chance when the woman hurried to her husband. That was all Owen needed.

"Put down your gun, Nettie," Owen warned a split second before he stepped out and took aim at her.

Nettie shrieked, bringing up her own gun, and he saw the madness and rage in her eyes. She was going to kill him. Or rather, she would try. And that was why Owen made sure he pulled the trigger first.

He sent two shots slamming into Nettie's chest.

Laney stepped out to Owen's side and pointed her gun at Nettie. But the woman wasn't down. Despite the bullets Owen had put in her, Nettie might have gotten off another shot—at Owen—but Emerson caught Nettie's leg and dragged her down to the floor with him.

Owen rushed toward them, ripping Nettie's gun from her hand and passing it back to Laney. He didn't want to give Nettie another chance to kill them. But the woman had maybe given up on that. Sobbing, bleeding, she pulled Emerson into her arms.

Despite his heartbeat pounding in his ears, Owen still heard the footsteps and automatically pivoted in their direction at the top of the stairs. It was Eli, who cursed when he looked at the bloodbath in the foyer.

"The gunman ran," Owen relayed to his brother. "He could still be somewhere on the grounds."

"I'll go up and stand guard outside Addie's door," Laney offered.

Owen hated to put her in the position where she might have to defend herself, and his child, but he preferred that to sending her out to look for a hired gun. He nodded, wishing he could say more to her, but he would save that for later. Later, when he was certain there was no chance of another attack.

Eli and Laney passed each other on the stairs as his

brother came down. Eli took out his phone. To call Kellan, Owen quickly realized.

"I'll look for the gunman and check on Jeremy," Eli offered. "But I won't go far," his brother added as he hurried out the front door.

Owen didn't put his gun away in case Stan returned, but he went closer to Emerson and Nettie and tried to figure out what to do to save them. Not that he especially wanted to save Nettie, but he would try. There was no way, though, that he could tamp down the hatred he felt for her. She'd not only tried to kill him, Nettie had endangered plenty of people who he loved.

Including Laney.

That realization came out of the blue and hit him damn hard. But he shoved it away and used his left hand to apply some pressure to the wound on Emerson's chest. There wasn't much he could do for Nettie. The gravelly rale coming from her throat let him know that she was on her last breath.

"I'm sorry," Emerson said. "I swear I didn't know she was behind this. I didn't know she had planned all of this or I would have stopped her." He grimaced, groaning in pain. "I thought it was Terrance."

So had Owen. Or at least, Terrance had been one of their suspects but so had Emerson and Nettie. And Nettie had planned to use Terrance's suspect status to frame him for the murders and attacks.

Owen whirled around at the sound of yet more approaching footsteps—these coming from the front yard.

"It's me," Kellan called out to him.

Owen didn't allow himself to relax because there were still too many things that could go wrong. But he was glad when his brother came rushing in.

Kellan glanced around, as Eli had done, clearly assessing the situation before his attention settled on Emerson and Nettie.

"Nettie did this," Emerson said and started crying when he looked at Nettie, realizing that she was gone.

"Nettie did all of this," Owen added. "She confessed to killing Hadley, Joe and Nancy. She hired the gunmen. And she was going to set up Terrance."

Kellan nodded. "Eli just cuffed one of her guys. Said his name was Stan Martin. He's talking in case we need any more info."

Good. But Owen figured they wouldn't need more. Not with Nettie dead.

"How's Jeremy?" Owen asked.

"He's not hurt too bad. He'll need to go to the hospital, but it can wait for a little while."

Kellan motioned to someone outside and several moments later two EMTs came rushing in. Owen stepped back so they could start to work on Emerson. He was still bleeding, but he was very much alive, and that was more than Owen could say for Nettie.

"If you've got this, I need to check on Addie and the others. Laney," Owen said under his breath. "I need to check on her."

Kellan gave him the go-ahead while he stooped down to talk to Emerson. Owen heard Kellan read him his rights. A necessity because even though it didn't appear Emerson had anything to do with the murders, he'd still obstructed justice and lied during an interview. It might not land him in jail, but it was almost certainly going to cost him his legal license and his job.

It seemed to take forever for Owen to make his way up the stairs. His legs, and heart, felt heavy, and there was still way too much adrenaline pumping through him. That lightened a little when he spotted Laney. She was exactly where he'd expected to find her, standing guard outside the bedroom door.

She looked at him, their gazes immediately connecting, and he saw the relief in her eyes when she ran to him. "Addie's okay," she said. "They're all okay. I just checked on them, and Addie's fallen back asleep."

Owen pulled her into his arms and another layer of that heaviness vanished. With all the shots that had been fired, it was somewhat of a miracle they hadn't been killed.

"Nettie?" she asked, easing back.

"Dead."

He paused to let her absorb that and everything else that went along with it. The woman who'd made their lives a living hell was gone. Now they had to deal with the aftermath and the nightmares.

Laney shook her head. "I'm sorry I didn't see sooner that Nettie was the one. I was looking too hard at Emerson to realize the truth."

Owen sighed. Leave it to Laney to apologize for not recognizing a jealous woman hell-bent on covering up her husband's affair. Because he didn't want her apology, or for Laney to feel regretful in any way for this, he brushed a kiss on her mouth.

She definitely didn't melt against him, didn't give him one of those smoldering looks. Her reaction was that tears sprang to her eyes. So Owen kissed her again. This time he heard that slight hitch in her throat and thought maybe there was a little melting going on. This time when she pulled back, he definitely saw some.

Felt some, too.

Laney gave him a small smile, one he figured took a lot of effort on her part. "I'll be okay. I'll just wait out here while you see Addie."

A few days ago, he would have taken her up on that offer. But since this was now, tonight, he slipped his arm around her and opened the bedroom door.

"It's me," Owen called out. "You can unlock the bathroom door."

Seconds later, he heard someone do just that. He also heard mutterings of relief. Saw relief, too, on Gemma's and Francine's faces when Gemma opened the door. The face that he didn't see was Addie's. But he soon spotted his little girl asleep on a quilt inside the tub.

"Don't go downstairs. Not yet," Owen instructed the women. "Kellan's down there, and he's fine," he added to Gemma.

Clearly relieved, Gemma gave him a hard hug and went into the bedroom to look out the door and into the hall. He was betting she would wait right there until Kellan came up for her.

"The gunman is dead?" Francine whispered and then checked over her shoulder to make sure Addie hadn't heard. She hadn't.

"Arrested." Owen had to pause again. "Nettie's dead, though. She's the one who did this."

Owen figured in the next few hours, Francine would learn a lot more about what had gone on. Everyone in Longview Ridge would. But, for now, that was enough information.

Francine went to the bed and sank onto the foot of it. She didn't come out and say it, but Owen figured she'd done that to give him some alone time with Addie. He wanted that, but he took Laney's hand to make sure that "alone time" included her, too.

Owen sat on the floor next to the tub, easing Laney down with him. He didn't want to wake Addie, but he had to brush his fingers over her cheek and hair. She stirred a little but settled right back down.

"I hope she won't remember any of this," Laney whispered.

That was his hope, too, but he would certainly remember it in crystal clear detail. Both the bad and the good. Because plenty of good had come out of this, too—including what had happened between him and Laney just a couple of hours earlier in the room across the hall.

Owen wanted to hang on to that, but when he looked at Laney, he saw yet another apology in her eyes. Tears, too. This time he didn't sigh. He huffed and hauled Laney onto his lap.

"This wasn't your fault. There's no reason for you to be sorry." With that, he kissed her again. This time it wasn't just to hush her but because he needed to feel her in his arms. Needed his mouth on hers.

And that was what he got.

He felt it. Not just the heat, though, but also the feelings that went deeper than just the lust. He felt everything for her that he hadn't been sure he could ever feel again. Yet, here it was. Here she was, right on his lap and kissing him back.

This time when he pulled back, he didn't see a trace of an apology. Thankfully, didn't see any tears, either, so that meant the kiss had done its job. Now he wanted to carry it one step further.

"I love you," Laney blurted before he could say anything. "I know, you'll probably think it's too soon, that you're not ready for it, but I can't change what I feel for you. For Addie," she added, glancing at the baby. "I love you both, and even if that sends you running, I wanted you to know."

Owen opened his mouth but still didn't get a chance to say anything.

"Please don't run," she whispered, pressing her forehead to his. "Just give it a chance and see where it goes."

"No," he said. This time he saw the flash of surprise and hurt in her eyes, and that was why he continued—quickly, "I don't need to give it a chance. Don't need to see where it's going, because it's going exactly where I want."

Laney blinked, shifted back enough so she could study his face. She smiled a little. "To bed?"

"Absolutely. The bed...and other places."

Her smile widened and she kissed him. It went on a lot longer and became a lot deeper than Owen had planned because he hadn't finished what he'd wanted to say. That was why he broke away.

"Other places like my house," he said. "That I hope you can think of as your house, too."

Laney's smile faded. "You're asking me to move in with you?"

"I'm asking for a whole lot more than that. I'm in love with you, Laney."

She froze, her eyes widening, and for one heart-stopping moment, he thought she was going to say that she didn't believe him. But then she threw herself back into his arms and gave him an amazing kiss. One that told him that this was exactly what she wanted, too.

Now it was Owen who smiled. For a few seconds

anyway, but the movement in the tub had both of them looking at Addie. She was no longer asleep. She sat up, looked at them. And grinned.

"Da-da," she said, reaching for him.

Laney and he reached over and pulled her from the tub. Holding both Laney and his daughter, Owen knew that he had exactly what he wanted in his arms.

* * * * *

I want to thank Delilah Devlin and my daughter, Paige Yancey, for being there when I need some serious help brainstorming.

And thank you to Denise Zaza, who has been with me from the day she bought my first book for Harlequin Intrigue.

A big thank-you to my readers, who continue to buy my books. You make it possible for me to follow my dream of being a full-time author. Thank you!

Chapter One

Anne Bellamy finished editing the document her boss had given her just before he'd left for the gym at exactly four thirty that afternoon. She'd stayed two hours past the end of the usual day in the office of the national security advisor located in the West Wing of the White House to clean up, fact-check and finish the job. The last one out of the office, she gathered her purse and checked her cell phone.

A text message had come through during the time she'd logged off her computer and collected her purse.

Unknown caller.

Curious as to who had her phone number and was texting her so late in the evening, Anne brought up her text messages and frowned down at the cryptic message.

TRINITY LIVES.

Her heart skipped several beats before settling into the swift pace of one who was running for her life. Anne hadn't heard anything about Trinity since the man who'd recruited her to spy on government officials had been murdered.

Her gut clenched and she felt like she might throw up as she returned the text.

Sorry, you must have the wrong number.

She waited, her breath caught in her throat, her pulse hammering against her eardrums.

John Halverson died because he'd got too close.

Anne gasped and glanced around her office, wondering if anyone was watching or could see the texts she was receiving. Wondering if she was doing the right thing, or revealing herself to the wrong persons, she responded to the text again.

Halverson is dead.

Again, Anne waited, afraid of the response, but afraid not to reply.

Halverson was on the right track.

Anne's heart squeezed hard in her chest. John Halverson had been a good man, with a heart as big as they came. He cared about his country and what was happening to tear it apart.

When he'd come to her, he'd caught her at a vulnerable point in her career. A point at which she'd considered leaving the political nightmare to take a position as a secretary or receptionist for a doctor's office. Anything to get out of the demoralizing, disheartening work she did with men and women who didn't always have the best interests of the nation at heart, whose careers and post-government jobs in media and lobbying meant more to them than the country's future.

Anne had kept her head down and her thoughts to herself since Halverson's death, afraid that whoever had murdered the man would come after her. If they knew her association with Halverson, and her involvement in uncovering the graft and corruption inside the office of the National Security Council, she'd be the next target.

She knew Trinity had a firm foothold in the government, and they weren't afraid to pounce on those who dared to cross them or squeal on their activities. The problem was that they were so well entrenched you couldn't tell a friend from a terrorist.

She stared at her phone screen. Was someone trying to warn her? Or flush her out into the open?

Either way, someone knew her secret. She could be the next casualty, courtesy of Trinity.

Anne quickly keyed in her message, not feeling terribly confident she was putting an end to the communication.

I don't know what you're talking about. Leave me alone.

A moment later came a response.

Can't. They're planning an attack. A lot of people could be hurt. I need your help to stop it.

Anne pressed a hand to her breast to still her pounding heart.

No. No. No.

She wasn't the kind of person who could easily lie or pretend. Anne had always been an open book. Anyone could read any emotion on her face. She'd argued this with Halverson, but he'd insisted she could help him. She was in a strategic position, one that touched on a number of key players in politics.

If Trinity had sleeper cells in those positions, she could spot them before anyone else. *Theoretically.*

Anne hated that Halverson had paid the ultimate price. At the same time, she no longer had to report things she saw or heard, which meant she didn't have to worry that she was being watched or targeted.

Until now. Until the text warning her about Trinity.

Shooting a glance around the office and the four corners of the room, she wondered if anyone had a webcam recording her every move. She'd gotten good at discovering small audio and video recording devices stashed in telephone receiver units, lights, ceiling tiles, potted plants and office furniture.

She made a habit of scouring the room at least once a day. She'd found a small audio device once, early on, when Halverson had still been alive. They'd met at a bookstore in Arlington, where Halverson had identified the device and told her about others she should be on the lookout for.

Since Halverson's death, she'd continued looking over her shoulder. As time passed, she'd become lax. No one appeared to be following her or watching her.

How wrong had she been? And why had this person come to her now?

Instead of answering the previous text, she shoved

her phone into her purse and left her office. Her heart hammered against her ribs and her breathing came in shallow pants. She was overreacting. That was all there was to it.

But who had given out her phone number? And how did they know she'd once been involved with Halverson? She'd kept that part of her life as clandestine as possible. Trying to ensure her trysts with Halverson were in as out-of-the-way a venue as she could, she'd usually met him in a public library, where running into people she worked with was highly unlikely. It wasn't a bar, and it wasn't a coffee shop. She'd thought it was the best cover of all. How many terrorists did she know who made good use of a public library?

She'd never been to Halverson's mansion, and she'd always worn a disguise when she'd met with him at the library, never driving her own car, but taking public transportation.

Once out in the open, she inhaled fresh night air. Anne had been so busy working she hadn't realized it had rained earlier. The ground was still wet, and light reflected off the standing puddles. Her phone vibrated inside her purse, causing her heart to skip a beat. She ignored it and strode toward the Metro station, wishing she'd left while there was still some daylight chasing away the shadows. Though night had settled in, people still moved around the city. Men and women dressed in business suits, dress shoes and trench coats hurried home from office buildings, after a long day at work. Still, the number of people headed toward the train station was significantly less than during the regular rush hours.

Anne wished she'd worn her tennis shoes to work rather than the tight, medium-heeled pumps that had been pinching her feet since five o'clock that morning.

Again, the phone vibrated in her purse. She could feel the movement where her purse rested against her side. Ignoring the insistent pulsation, she moved quickly, determined to make the next Metro train headed toward Arlington, where she lived in a modest apartment.

Footsteps sounded behind her.

Anne shot a glance over her shoulder. A man wearing a black jacket and jeans strode behind her, less than half a block away. He also wore a dark baseball cap, shading his face and eyes from the streetlights he passed beneath.

Alarm bells rang in Anne's head. She increased her pace.

The man behind her sped up, as well.

Still a couple of blocks away from the train station, Anne realized the streets had become deserted. The people she'd passed earlier must have hopped into taxis or found their cars in the paid parking lots.

Alone and on the street with a man following too closely behind her, Anne couldn't move fast enough. Then she remembered there was a restaurant at the corner of the next street, which now became her new, short-range goal. Clutching her purse to her side, she sprinted for the door, her feet moving as fast as they could in heels. She didn't slow to see if the man following her was running, too. She only knew she had to get to that restaurant.

When she reached the restaurant door, she almost

sobbed. It was closed—the lights were turned out and no one moved inside.

A quick glance behind her assured her the man had kept up. Whether he'd had to run or not wasn't important. He was still there. Striding toward her, his feet eating the distance between them.

Anne's gaze darted around her, searching for a pub, a convenience store or pharmacy. Anything that stayed open late and had people inside. The block consisted of still more office buildings, closed for the night. She had no choice but to continue on toward the train station and pray she reached it before him.

Starting out with a purposeful stride, she walked fast toward the Metro stop, watching the reflections in the glass windows of the office buildings beside her for the image of the man tailing her. When he appeared in the reflection, Anne shot forward, running all out.

Her breath came in ragged gasps, and her pulse pounded so hard against her eardrums she could barely hear. Rounding a corner, she spied a pub, its sign lit up over the door. With the Metro station still too far to make, she set her sights on the pub and raced toward the door.

Just as she was reaching out, a hand descended on her shoulder and jerked her back. Oh, sweet heaven, he'd caught her. She braced herself for the fight of her life.

At that moment, the pub door opened, and a group of men exited, laughing and talking to each other.

The hand on Anne's shoulder fell away.

With renewed hope, Anne dove through the men and into the pub. Once inside, she went straight to the bar.

"What can I get you?"

"Someone tried to grab me outside the bar," she gushed, her breathing catching in her throat.

The bartender leaned toward her. "You okay?" He glanced past her to a large man standing near the exit.

The man, probably a bouncer, came forward.

"This lady said a man tried to grab her," the bartender told him.

"What was he wearing?" the bouncer asked.

She shook her head. "Dark clothes and a baseball cap, I think. I don't know. I was running too fast to notice."

The bouncer nodded and left the pub. He was back a minute later, shaking his head. "No one out there fitting your description. In fact, there was no one out there at all. I walked a block in both directions."

Anne let go of the breath she'd been holding. Even if the man wasn't within a block either direction, he might be lying in wait for her to continue her progress to the Metro stop. Anne couldn't bring herself to step outside the pub.

"We're closing early tonight for kitchen renovations, lady. You got about thirty minutes until we lock up. Is there anyone I could call for you?" the bartender asked, his expression worried.

Anne shook her head. She didn't have any close friends. She had acquaintances from work. That was it. They had their own lives and she had her solitary existence. Then she remembered John Halverson giving her his phone number and telling her if ever she needed anything, she should call that number.

But he was dead.

Would anyone answer at the number? Did he still

have a staff of people working for the same things he had?

Anne pulled her phone out of her purse and stared down at the icon for her text messages. She didn't want to look at them. Everything had been fine until she'd started receiving the texts.

She pulled up her contacts list and dialed the number Halverson had given her, not knowing if anyone would actually answer.

The line rang several times.

Anne was about to give up when the ringing stopped and a woman answered, "Hello?"

Not knowing what to say, Anne blurted, "I know John Halverson is dead, but I need help. He gave me this number and said to call if I ever needed anything. Please tell me you can help." She stopped and waited for a response, her heart thudding, her gut clenched.

"This is John's wife. Are you in a safe place?"

Anne nodded and then said, "For the moment, but this place closes in thirty minutes. I was being followed and I'm afraid to leave."

"Stay there. I'll have someone come to collect you."

"But you don't even know me."

"You're a human being in need of assistance. I don't care who you are. I'll have someone see you to your home or the police station. Wherever you need to go."

"Thank you," Anne said, sagging with relief. "I'm sorry for what happened to your husband. He was a good man."

"Me, too. If he gave you his number, he would have wanted me to help you. Rest assured, I'm sending someone. Give me the address."

Anne had to ask the bartender for the address. Once she'd relayed it to Mrs. Halverson, the widow insisted she stay on the phone until the person she sent arrived.

"That won't be necessary. As long as I can remain in the pub, I'll be all right," Anne said.

"Then I'll get right on it," Mrs. Halverson said. "I'll text with an expected time of arrival as soon as I have one."

"Thank you, Mrs. Halverson."

"Don't call me Mrs. Halverson. I go by Charlie," the woman said.

"Thank you, Charlie," Anne said, correcting herself, and rang off.

A moment later, a text came across.

Jack will be there in twenty minutes.

That was a text Anne could live with, though she wondered who Jack was, what he looked like and what he'd be driving.

JACK SNOW HAD left his apartment in Arlington an hour earlier, too wound up to sit in front of a television and watch mindless shows or even more mindless news reports.

Much too jittery to find a bar and drink away the anxious feeling he got all too often since returning from deployment and exiting his Marine Force Recon unit, he climbed onto his Harley and went for a ride around the cities. He ended up in the Capitol Hill area near the war memorials. After the sun set, the crowds thinned and the lights illuminating the Lincoln Memorial made the white marble stand out against the backdrop of the black, starless night.

He'd ridden to the Korean War Memorial, parked his bike and stood near the nineteen steel statues of soldiers in full combat gear and waterproof ponchos. They appeared as ghosts, emerging from the shadows. Haunting.

They reminded him of so many operations he and his team had conducted at night, moving silently across rough terrain, like the ghosts of the men the statues had been modeled after.

His heart pinched tightly in his chest. It was as if he were looking at the friends he'd lost in battle, the men he'd carried out only to send home in body bags.

No matter how long he'd been separated from active duty, the images of his friends never faded. Often they appeared in his dreams, waking him from a dead sleep in cold sweat as he relived the operations that had claimed their lives.

He'd get out of his bed, dress and go for a ride on his motorcycle in the stillness of night, letting the wind in his face blow the cobwebs from his memories.

Tonight was different. He'd dreaded even going to bed. Tonight was the anniversary of the death of his high school sweetheart. Yet another reason to lose sleep.

He'd met Kylie in the eighth grade. They'd been together throughout high school and had big plans to go to the same college after graduation.

Though Jack had made it to graduation, Kylie had not. The weekend before the big event, they'd gone to the local mall. Kylie wanted a special dress to wear beneath her cap and gown. Jack had gone with her to help her choose.

That day, a man who'd been dumped by his fiancée days before their wedding had entered the mall, bearing an AR-15 semiautomatic rifle with a thirty-round magazine locked and loaded. Tucked into his jacket pocket was a .45 caliber pistol with a ten-round magazine. He'd come to take out his anger on his ex-fiancée working in a department store. But he didn't end there. Once he started firing, he didn't stop until he ran out of bullets in the rifle's magazine.

Jack and Kylie had just left an upscale dress shop when the bullets started flying. Before they could duck back into the shop or even drop to the ground, the gunman turned the barrel of his AR-15 on them, firing indiscriminatingly.

Jack grabbed Kylie and shoved her to the ground, covering her body with his.

When the first volley of bullets slowed to silence, he looked up.

The rifleman fumbled with another magazine for the AR-15, dropped it and bent to retrieve it.

Jack didn't stop to think about what he was doing. He lunged to his feet and charged the man before he could reload, hitting him with his best linebacker tackle, knocking him to the ground. The rifle flew from the gunman's hands, skittering to a stop several yards away.

The man tried to reach for the handgun in his jacket pocket but couldn't get to it with Jack lying on top of him, pinning him to the hard tile floor.

The mall security cop had dashed to the scene but

hadn't wanted Jack to move for fear the shooter would manage to get to his feet and regain control of his weapon.

The police had arrived shortly after, taking over from Jack.

That was when he'd turned to find Kylie still lying where he'd left her, facedown and unmoving.

She'd taken a bullet straight to her heart and died instantly.

Jack had been devastated.

Her death was the main reason he'd chosen to join the Marines rather than go on to college like many of his classmates. He needed the physical challenge to burn away his anger and the feeling he should have gotten her to safety sooner. He should have done more to save her.

Those deployment nightmares, combined with the traumatic one from his school days, had kept him moving, afraid to stand still for a moment. If he did, the memories overwhelmed him.

He stared at the shadowy figures of the steel soldiers. They were so lifelike Jack felt as if he could fall in step with them and complete the mission.

His heartbeat quickened. As he took a step forward, a vibration against his side brought him back to reality, making him stop.

He reached into his jacket and pulled out his cell phone. The name on the screen read Declan O'Neill.

Jack didn't hesitate. He pressed the talk button and pressed the phone to his ear. "Yeah."

"Dude, where are you?" Declan asked, his tone crisp.

"Downtown DC near the war memorials. What's up?"

"Got a mission for you."

"Give it to me." He needed action. Anything to take his mind off the anniversary of Kylie's death and the loss of his friends in battle. Declan's call was a lifeline thrown to him in troubled waters. A reminder that he was still among the living, and he had a team of friends to work with.

Declan gave him the address of a pub not far from where he was. "There's a female there who's afraid to leave. Someone tried to grab her on her way to the Metro station."

"What does she look like?" Jack asked.

"Long, straight black hair, blue eyes. Wearing a business suit. Tell her Mrs. Halverson sent you."

"Got it. I can be there in less than ten minutes."

"Make it five. The pub is closing. Let us know when you get her to safety." Declan ended the call.

Slipping his helmet over his head, Jack left the steel soldiers to their mission, mounted his motorcycle and commenced with his own mission. He'd hoped for something more than escorting a damsel in distress home for the evening, but at least it gave him a purpose and something else to think about besides Kylie and dead comrades.

Ignoring the speed limit signs and only slowing for the occasional light, Jack made it to the pub in four minutes. A few men straggled through the door, laughing and shaking hands.

Jack scanned the surrounding area for anyone lurking in the shadows, waiting for a lone woman to step out of the pub and into his path. When he didn't see anyone or any movement in the shadows, he parked his bike on the curb and entered the pub, passing by a large man standing near the door.

"Sorry, we're closed," someone called out from the bar.

"I'm not here for a drink. I'm here to pick up a lady."

The bartender snorted. "Sorry, we're closed for that, too. Always. Unless the lady wishes to be picked up." The man chuckled at his own humor.

A black-haired woman in a dark blazer and skirt slid off a bar stool and faced Jack. Her blue eyes narrowed, and her lips pressed into a thin line. She stood stiff, and silently maintained her distance, looking as if she'd bolt if he made a move toward her.

This had to be the woman he'd been tasked to collect. "Mrs. Halverson sent me," Jack said.

The woman drew in a deep breath and the stiffness seemed to melt from her frame. "Oh, thank God." She slung her purse over her shoulder and nodded. "Let's go."

"Hey, lady," the bartender called out. "You gonna be okay?"

She turned toward the man. "I think so." She smiled. "Thanks."

Before they left the building, the woman stopped and frowned. "I guess I should know your full name."

With a half smile, Jack held out his hand. "Jack Snow."

She took his hand in her smaller, softer one and said quietly, "Anne Bellamy."

"You want to tell me what happened?"

She handed him her cell phone with an image of a map with the directions painted in a bright blue line.

"Not here. Not now. I just want to go home. That map will get you there."

He shrugged. "Have it your way. My ride is outside."

When she started to go through the door, he placed his hand on her arm. "Me first."

Anne nodded and let him go through the door ahead of her.

He stopped on the other side and glanced in both directions, taking his time to be thorough in his perusal of the buildings, alleys and every shadow. When he was fairly certain they were alone, he held out his hand.

Anne placed hers in his and let him guide her to the curb, where his motorcycle was parked.

The big guy who'd been lurking near the entrance followed them outside.

Jack shot a narrowed glance his way as he fitted Anne's cell phone into a holder on his handle bar. "Is this the guy who tried to grab you?"

"No. That's the bar's bouncer. He's just making sure we aren't attacked," Anne said. She faced the motorcycle, a frown drawing her eyebrows together. "This is your ride?" The frown deepened. "I've never been on a motorcycle before."

"Well, tonight must be your lucky night. Unless you want to wait another thirty minutes to an hour for one of my buddies to come get you, you'll have to take your chances." He swung his leg over the bike and patted the cushioned seat behind him. "Don't wait too long. You'll only be giving your attacker the opportunity to make another attempt to grab you."

Chapter Two

"How…" Anne tried to swing her leg over the bike, but her A-line skirt hampered her maneuver. Finally, she pulled the skirt up high enough to allow her to mount the cycle and settle behind him. "No judging," she mumbled.

He grinned. "Great legs. Sorry, couldn't help it." Jack handed her a helmet and helped her to adjust the strap beneath her chin. Then he pulled his own helmet over his head and cinched the strap. "Hold on around my waist."

She placed her hands on his hips, barely squeezing, amazed at how firm they were. A rush of awareness rocked through her.

"Seriously?" He took her hands and pulled them around his middle. "Now hold on tight. This beast has a powerful takeoff."

As if to prove his point, Jack cranked the engine and twisted the throttle. The motorcycle sprang forward.

Anne clenched her arms around him in a death grip so tight she was certain Jack could barely breathe. He slowed the bike a little and drove down the street at a more sedate pace.

He looked back with a grin.

Most likely, he was happy to have startled her.

The grin disappeared and a frown replaced it in that split second he'd turned to look back at her.

Anne swiveled her helmet-heavy head and took note of headlights glaring at them. A dark sedan raced toward them at a high speed. Her heart leaped into her throat. "Go!" she yelled.

"Hold on!" Jack shouted. He made an abrupt turn, leaning hard into it.

Anne leaned the opposite direction.

Jack seemed to struggle with navigating the corner and he slowed.

"Lean with me!" he yelled, twisting his right hand on the handle. The motorcycle shot forward, putting distance between them and the vehicle turning at the corner behind them.

If Anne had any doubts they were being followed, she was certain now that the car behind them wasn't on a sightseeing trip in the night.

With the bike being more agile and maneuverable, Jack managed to weave in and out of streets, down back alleys and eventually onto the main road leading out of the city.

Anne held on, leaning when Jack leaned and in the same direction as him, making turns easier.

When she was sure they'd lost the dark sedan. Anne released a sigh of relief.

Jack settled into a smooth drive, following the altered directions on Anne's cell phone.

When they were only a block away from her apartment complex, he slowed almost to a crawl.

"Third building on the left," Anne called out as he neared the parking lot.

He drove to the location and brought the bike to a rolling stop.

Anne clambered off, her legs shaking. She smoothed her skirt down and hiked her purse strap onto her shoulder. "Thank you for getting me to my apartment. Tell Mrs. Halv—"

Jack adjusted the kickstand and dismounted.

"Where are you going?" Anne asked, her brow furrowing.

"To see you to your door and make sure you get inside safely." He cupped her elbow and walked her toward the entrance. "And to find out what this is all about."

She ground to a halt and pulled her elbow free. "I'll be fine." Already hyperaware of the man after holding him around his middle for the past thirty minutes, Anne just wanted to be free of him, and settle in with a cup of her favorite tea to soothe her fractured nerves. "Be sure to thank Mrs. Halverson for me."

"She likes to be called Charlie."

"Thank Charlie for me," Anne said and turned to walk into the building.

Jack's footsteps sounded behind her.

Anne spun to face him. "Seriously, you don't have to go up with me. I can manage on my own now."

"I've been given a mission to see you safely somewhere." He shrugged. "Although the somewhere was vague." He gave a nod toward the building. "I'll assume it was to your apartment."

"I'm here. You can go." She waved her hand as if shooing a pesky animal or child away.

"I'm not leaving until I know you're safely inside your apartment. Remember, we were followed not all that long ago."

"Yes, but you lost the trailing vehicle quite efficiently, though you scared the bejesus out of me in the process." She tipped her head toward his motorcycle. "And you quite convinced me that I don't like riding motorcycles. But thank you for delivering me to my apartment in one piece." With that parting comment, she turned and strode toward the door.

Again, Jack followed.

Anne gritted her teeth and kept going. If he wanted to follow her all the way up to her apartment...fine. As long as he didn't cup her elbow, sending crazy bursts of electrical current all the way through her body.

At her door, she fumbled for the key in her purse. Finally wrapping her fingers around it, she started to fit it into the doorknob.

Before she could, Jack grabbed her arm again.

And like before, that jolt of electricity traveled up her arm and down to her belly. She started to turn to tell him not to touch her when he gently pushed her to one side of the door and pressed a finger to his lips. He wasn't even looking at her, but at her door.

Then he released her arm and gave her door a slight nudge.

It opened without resistance. The doorjamb appeared splintered, as if someone had forced his way into her apartment.

Her heart thudding against her chest, Anne started to step inside.

Jack put out his arm and shook his head, mouthing the word *Stay.*

Too shocked to argue, Anne remained rooted to the floor outside her apartment, while Jack slipped inside.

She counted to ten, her stomach knotting and her breathing unsteady. How long could it take to look for bad guys? Just when Anne had decided she couldn't wait another moment, Jack appeared in the entryway, his mouth set in a grim line. He opened the door wider, flipped the light switch on and stood back. "I take it you didn't leave your place like this when you left for work this morning?"

Anne stepped across the threshold and gasped. "What the h—?"

Her home looked like something from a warzone. The sofa had been flipped on its back. The seat cushions had been flung across the room after they'd been ripped open and the stuffing pulled out. The artwork she'd painstakingly chosen and positioned on the walls had been slashed or painted over with a garish red spray paint.

Every drawer in her kitchen had been dumped on the floor. Knives stuck into the walls as if they'd been thrown one by one.

The photo frame containing a picture of Anne, her mother and her father had been destroyed, the picture pulled out and torn up into tiny pieces.

Tears welled in Anne's eyes as she continued through the little apartment to the bedroom. How much worse could it get? They'd destroyed practically everything she owned.

It got worse. The bedroom, like the living room, was a shambles, with the mattress dragged off the bed frame, a long gash drawn down the center. The pillows were in tatters, the filling scattered across the room. But the message on the wall was what made Anne press a hand to her chest and reel from shock.

Words written in bright red spray paint covered the wall over her headboard.

CONSIDER THIS A WARNING

Beside the words was a symbol Anne was all too familiar with. The crisscrossing Trinity symbol that might mean nothing to most but struck fear in the hearts of those familiar with the organization's history.

Anne staggered backward until her back hit the wall. Then she slid down and gathered her knees to her chest. "This. Can't. Be. Happening."

Jack dropped to his haunches beside her and took her hands in his. "I'm sorry, but it is. And you can't stay here. They know where you live and might come back."

She shook her head, her eyes glazed, her hands shaking in his. "I haven't done anything. Why would they come after me?"

"I don't know." Jack gently pulled her to her feet. "Grab the clothes you can, or better yet, leave it all here and buy new." He slipped an arm around her waist and pressed her body against his. "The main thing is to get you out of here as soon as possible."

She shook her head. "But this is all I own… My things."

"They're just things. At least you weren't here when they came in." He flung open the closet door.

Whoever had trashed her apartment had used the same red paint, spraying a thick swath across the clothes hanging in her closet.

Jack grabbed a gym bag from the floor. "They didn't get this," he said.

He unzipped it and held it open. "Find whatever you can that's undamaged, enough to get you by, and let's get the heck out of here. I don't want them to come back while we're here."

Anne couldn't seem to make her feet move. A crippling lethargy settled over her, making it impossible to think or motivate herself.

Jack dropped the bag and gripped her arms. "Anne." He tipped her chin up and stared into her eyes. "These are just things. We have to leave. I need you to be with me." He gave her a gentle shake. "Now."

Though she knew she needed to comply, she just couldn't.

"I'm not getting through to you," Jack said with a sigh. "Maybe this will work." He bent his head and pressed his lips to hers in a hard, persistent kiss.

The shock of it forced Anne's mind off the destruction and centered it on the feel of his lips against hers. She raised her hands to wrap around the back of his neck and pulled him closer. As if by kissing him, she could block out all the horror of her apartment.

When he finally set her away, he stared down into her eyes. "Are you with me now?" he asked, his tone deep, his voice gravelly.

She nodded. "I am."

He released her arms. "Then pack. You have one minute to get all the undamaged items you can into that bag. If it's nothing, so be it. You're coming with me." He left her alone in the room.

Anne shook out of her stunned haze and scrambled through her clothing, searching for panties, bras, jeans, shirts and skirts she could salvage from the items the intruders had permanently destroyed. She changed out of her skirt and heels into a pair of jeans and loafers.

She jammed what few undamaged things she could find into the gym bag and hurried to find Jack, wanting to be with him at all times. Though he was a stranger, he made her feel safer than she'd felt alone.

He stood by the open door of her apartment, looking up and down the hallway. When he heard her behind him, he shot a glance over his shoulder. "Ready?"

Anne nodded, closed the door and handed him her cell phone. "I think this has to do with the text messages I received before I left work this evening."

Jack took the phone from her and read through the messages, his face growing tighter, a muscle ticking in his jaw by the time he finished. "I take it you didn't read the last two messages."

Anne frowned. "I had other things on my mind, and I'd hoped by ignoring the texts, whoever had sent them would just go away." She snorted. "Obviously, that didn't happen."

"Read them." Jack pushed the cell phone beneath her nose.

Anne focused on the words.

Destroy your phone.

They will track you with it.

"If whoever did this to your apartment can track you using your phone, you need to ditch that phone. The sooner the better." Jack pulled his own cell phone from his back pocket and snapped pictures of the messages on Anne's cell phone. He glanced up at her. "Sorry, but it must be done." He dismantled the phone, pulled the SIM card from it, dropped the card into the kitchen's garbage disposal and ground it into oblivion. Then he placed the phone on the floor and stomped his heel into the screen.

"I need to get pictures of the message on the wall. Wait here," he said and disappeared into her bedroom. When he returned to the living room, he sent the pictures to someone and placed a call.

"We're headed your way. We could be bringing a tail... Good. See you in a few."

"What was that all about?" Anne asked.

"I sent the images to my boss. We've got a couple of computer wizzes who can do some poking around to see what they can find." He took the gym bag from her hand and led the way down the stairs toward the parking lot. He made her wait in the stairwell until he was certain the parking lot was safe.

Jack strapped the bag onto the back of the bike and went back to collect Anne. Slipping an arm around her, he shielded her body with his and walked her to the motorcycle.

Once they'd both mounted the bike, Anne leaned

over Jack's shoulder. "Are you taking me to a hotel? I have nowhere else to go," she said, her heart flipping in her chest and the tears rushing to fill her eyes. She couldn't go to a friend's house. Not with Trinity looking for her.

Jack shook his head. "We're going to Charlie's."

Anne wondered whether everything would have gone on as usual if she'd ignored the first text message. Had she set the course of events by responding? And now that her phone was destroyed, the mysterious texter wouldn't have a way to contact her. Somehow, that didn't give her any sense of relief. Quite the opposite.

JACK DROVE OUT the other end of the apartment complex, choosing a circuitous route to Charlie's estate.

He kept an eye on the small rearview mirror mounted on his handlebar, searching for headlights and praying he didn't find any.

Avoiding the main roads, he wove his way through suburbs and backroads until he finally found himself on the road to the Halverson estate.

If anything was going to happen, it would happen here. It stood to reason that if they had hacked into her phone and knew she'd received messages from someone trying to stop Trinity, they would know she'd place a call to Charlie Halverson.

Since a prior attempt to break into the estate, Charlie had beefed up security and built a stronger wall to keep people out and protect those on the inside. That would be the best place to take Anne.

Getting there unscathed was the plan.

Someone else had other plans for them.

Jack turned onto the quiet country highway leading to the Halverson estate. With eight miles of curvy roads ahead, he couldn't let his guard down for a moment.

As he rounded a sharp bend in the road, a delivery truck darted out of a side road and stopped in the middle of the road, effectively blocking both lanes of traffic.

Warning bells went off in Jack's head. "Hang on," he called out.

Instead of slowing, Jack sped up, aiming straight for the truck.

As he neared, he noted men climbing out of the cab, AR-15s in their hands.

Damn. They'd brought serious weapons to the party.

He swerved at the last moment, taking the motorcycle off the road and down into the shallow ditch, praying Anne could hold on long enough to make it out on the other side.

Her arms tightened around him as they bumped over the rough terrain. At one point he thought the bike might turn over, and then it would be all over for them. Somehow, he managed to right the front tire, gunned the accelerator and sent them popping up over the shoulder and back onto the road. A couple sets of headlights headed toward him, but there was no going back.

Jack powered forward, ready to take to the ditches again if necessary.

The trucks remained on the correct side of the road. As they approached, they slowed.

Jack's hand squeezed tighter on the throttle, preparing to twist it to make the bike go faster.

Then he saw that the lead truck was Declan's black four-wheel drive and the one following belonged to

Mack Balkman. Declan passed him and turned his truck sideways, blocking one lane of the rural road, using the big vehicle as a shield to protect the two people on the motorcycle.

Mack did the same, blocking the other lane.

Jack noted there was a passenger in each vehicle. Probably Gus Walsh and Frank "Mustang" Ford. Cole was probably helping Charlie's computer guy, Jonah Spradlin, look into the texts from Anne's phone history.

A guard stood at the electric gate to the Halverson estate, armed with his own AR-15 rifle and a powerful spotlight.

When Jack rode up to the closed gate, the guard shined the light into his face.

"It's me," Jack said. "Jack Snow. And I have Anne Bellamy with me."

The guard shifted the light to the woman on the back of the motorcycle. A moment later, the gate opened and Jack drove through.

He'd never been quite so content to drive the winding road to the sprawling house at the end, knowing his team had his back, and the fence, gate and guards would see to their safety.

As he pulled up to a stop in front of the massive entrance, the door opened and Cole McCastlain emerged. Charlie Halverson stepped out behind him, followed by her assistant, Grace Lawrence, and her butler, Roger Arnold.

"I understand you've had a little excitement tonight." Cole grinned and held out a hand to help Anne from the back of the motorcycle.

She nodded and half fell against Cole. "Sorry, I'm a

little wobbly after going cross-country on the back of Mr. Snow's motorcycle."

Cole chuckled. "I don't blame you. I'm always a little wobbly after riding a motorcycle. You have to ride often to build up the muscles needed to be comfortable on one."

"Good to know," Anne said. "Not that I plan on riding one ever again, if I can help it."

"Oh, honey," Grace said, moving forward with a smile. "We never say never around here." She held out her hand. "I'm Grace Lawrence, Charlie's assistant." She turned to the older woman. "This is Charlie Halverson. John Halverson's widow."

"Mrs. Halverson, words are not enough to thank you for coming to my rescue. I don't know what I would have done if you hadn't."

"Please, call me Charlie. Mrs. Halverson was my husband's mother." She smiled and took both of Anne's hands in hers. "I'm glad Jack could help. I don't know what's going on, but you're safe now. Please, come inside."

Anne glanced back at Jack. "Thank you."

He nodded, flipped the kickstand down on his bike and joined Cole on the stairs.

Charlie led Anne and Grace into the house.

Arnold joined Cole and Jack. "Declan and the others are on their way in. They sustained some gunfire."

"Are they okay?" Jack asked.

The butler nodded. "There was some damage to their vehicles, but they're fine."

Jack shook his head. If they'd been a little slower on the motorcycle, they would have taken those bullets.

Anne had been on the back of the bike. She'd have been hit first. His heart raced, and he broke out in a sweat. Anne could have died. Just like Kylie. He'd have to rethink his motorcycle if he was tasked to protect Ms. Bellamy.

With that thought came another. Did he want to protect the woman? His history with women went deeper and more tragic than with Kylie. He'd lost his mother to cancer when he was only twelve. And just when he thought he was getting over Kylie and found someone else to love, Jennifer, the nurse deployed to the same base as he was in Afghanistan, had been killed when her vehicle rolled over an IED.

No. He was bad luck to the women in his life.

Women he loved. He could protect Anne Bellamy as long as he didn't make the mistake of jinxing her by falling in love with her. The right thing to do would be to let someone else take over the woman's protection. After saving her from being run down in DC and being shot at on the road to the Halverson estate, he felt he had a vested interest in her well-being.

He couldn't get ahead of himself. If Anne stayed at the Halverson estate, she wouldn't need a personal protector. Jack wouldn't have to worry about her safety or jinxing her.

"What's wrong?" Cole asked him.

"Why do you ask?"

Cole shrugged. "You were frowning."

Jack shook his head, clearing his rampant thoughts. "I was thinking about the mess they made of her apartment and the message on the wall," he lied. Now that he did think about it, he wondered who had put it there and why they thought she was a problem.

"Halverson must have been onto something big with Trinity for them to target him for assassination."

"If they knew about Ms. Bellamy all along, why did they wait until now to go after her?"

"I assume it has to do with the person who texted her," Cole said. "Using the phone number Anne gave Snow, Jonah hacked into the phone system and is going through her call and text history as we speak. We should go to the war room and see if he's found anything."

Jack followed Cole through the house and into Halverson's study, where the trapdoor was hidden. It led into a basement painted white and set up with a conference room and a computer room with an array of monitors, CPUs and keyboards lining the walls.

Jonah Spradlin, Charlie Halverson's young computer guru, sat at a keyboard, looking up at a setup of six monitors. His fingers flew across the keys, then he'd pause and study the screen. He repeated the process several times, shaking his head, his lips pressing together each time.

"Find anything?" Cole asked, taking the seat beside Jonah. Cole pressed several keys on the keyboard in front of him and brought up a screen.

"I traced the call back to a burner phone purchased at a store in Arlington," Jonah said. "I hacked into their computer system, but the name the phone was registered to was Linda Radcliff, a woman who died five years ago."

"Did they have video surveillance at the store?"

"Yes, but I haven't hacked into that system yet. I'm working on it."

"If the phone was registered to a Linda, the person had to be female," Cole surmised. "Surely, the clerk or store owner would have denied the sale if the ID didn't match the person presenting it."

"So, we're looking for a female texter." Jack paced the length of the room and back. "What will that buy us? There are hundreds of thousands of females in this area. We have to narrow it down a little more than that."

"We're working on it. We don't have a lot to go on and now your lady doesn't have a phone for our mystery texter to send messages to."

"She figured out Ms. Bellamy was associated with John Halverson," Jack pointed out. "She's smart. She'll come up with a way to communicate with Ms. Bellamy again."

Cole glanced up. "What's your girl's plan from here?"

Jack frowned. "She's not my girl. And I have no idea. I just got her here."

"I'm going to work tomorrow, as usual." A female voice sounded behind them.

Anne descended the steps into the war room, followed by Grace and Charlie.

Jack faced her, his feet spread, his arms crossing over his chest. "The hell you are."

Anne's eyebrows rose up her forehead. "I have a big meeting to prepare for on Friday. I need to be in my office every day this week. Besides, the person who texted me wanted me to help stop Trinity from doing something. I can't help if I'm locked behind the walls of this estate."

"You're a walking target," Jack said. "It would be suicide for you to step past the gates."

Anne lifted her chin. "I can't hide away forever."

"You can until we figure out what's going on," Jack insisted.

"We can figure it out a lot faster from inside the government offices. I assume since the person texted me, I'm probably in a position to find out something. Otherwise, why would he ask me for help?"

"She," Jack corrected.

Anne cocked an eyebrow. "See? You already know more than when we started."

"Okay, she's female—" Jack threw his hand in the air "—so is half the population of the Metro area."

"I'm going to work tomorrow," Anne said. "I just need a ride in to a Metro station, and I'll take it from there."

"You can't go alone," Charlie said.

"Charlie's right," Jack said. "It's too dangerous. You're not equipped to handle armed assassins."

Again, Anne stared at him with a cocked eyebrow. "And you are?"

"More so than you," Jack shot back.

Charlie clapped her hands together. "Then it's settled."

Jack glared at the woman whose money funded Declan's Defenders. "What's settled?"

"The fact that Anne can't go to work alone." Charlie smiled as if everything was perfectly obvious. "You'll go with her."

Chapter Three

Anne frowned. "Jack can't go with me. You have to have a badge and a security clearance to get inside the office where I work."

Charlie nodded toward her computer guy. "Jonah, can you make it happen before morning?"

He nodded. "I'll do my best." He held out his hand to Anne. "Could I borrow your badge?"

Anne shrank back, her hand on the purse she still carried over her shoulder. "You most certainly cannot. I swore an oath. I could get fired."

"You could die," Jack reminded her.

Anne chewed on her lip, her gut knotting. She'd spent her entire career trying to do right by the people of her country. She prided herself on always taking the high road. Helping someone into the inner sanctum of the West Wing was almost like committing treason.

Charlie touched her arm. "Based on your informer, others could die if Trinity isn't stopped. But you have to do what you think is right."

"If it helps," Declan said. "As a Marine Force Recon team, we all had top secret clearances."

"Had?" Anne questioned. She knew what Marine

Force Recon meant. They were the best of the best of the Marines.

Declan glanced at the other members of his team. "Until we were discharged from the Marine Corps."

"Discharged?" Anne tilted her head, her gaze going to Jack. "Honorably?"

Jack's lips thinned. "No. We were dishonorably discharged."

Anne reeled, shaking her head, her hand tightening on her purse. "Why?"

"For doing what we thought was the right thing," Declan said, his face grim. "Unfortunately, the powers that be didn't agree."

"Did you…kill someone?" Anne asked. "Is that why you were discharged?"

Jack snorted. "No. We didn't kill someone we were ordered to kill. If we had, a lot of innocent people would have been collateral damage. We made the decision to abort."

"I don't understand," Anne said. "I thought, as a country, we weren't in the business of killing innocent people, if we could help it."

"Someone had to take the fall for not taking out a high-powered terrorist." Declan pushed back his shoulders and lifted his chin. "My team took that fall." He spread his arms wide. "And now, because of Charlie, we're fighting the good fight, helping people when the government can't." He stared directly into Anne's eyes. "We understand if you don't feel comfortable giving us your badge. We'll find another way to create one for Jack. He will be with you tomorrow, one way or another."

Anne chewed on the information Jack and Declan had imparted. If what they were saying was true, they'd been booted from the military because they hadn't wanted to kill innocent people. Their government had let them down.

If the informant who'd texted Anne was correct, Trinity had somehow infiltrated the government and was planning on doing something catastrophic. She couldn't let it happen. But how could she, a single mid-level analyst, stop anything from happening? It wasn't as if she could spot a Trinity operative by looking at him.

She didn't know who they were. But they knew who she was, and they didn't want her to tip off anyone as to their intentions.

By going to work, she was putting herself at risk. If she died, no one would know that Trinity was planning something big.

She might not be anyone or know anything, but she did know something was about to go down. Since the informer had contacted her, she had to be close to either the entrenched Trinity operatives or close to the people who would be targeted. Either way, she had to find out what was going down and stop it before anyone got hurt.

Anne dug in her purse, pulled out her employee badge and handed it to Jack. "I'm trusting you to do the right thing, as I hope I am by handing you my badge."

Jack took the card, holding her hand in his for a long moment. "I promise we'll do the right thing. When it comes right down to it, we love this country, despite what some individuals in powerful positions have done to us. We want what's right for the country we swore to honor and protect."

Her fingers curled around his for a moment, then he let go and handed the card to Jonah.

Jonah nodded. "I'll have that badge and your clearance entered into the system before morning."

"I don't want to know how you'll make that possible."

Jonah grinned. "It's best you don't know. Ignorance is bliss."

Anne eyed Jack. "If you're coming to work with me, we'll have to have a good cover story."

Jack grinned. "Look at you going all covert on us."

She frowned. "I'm serious. I can pass you off as the new hire coming to train in my office. I've been interviewing people for the position of my assistant for a couple of weeks but hadn't found anyone I thought could handle the workload or the stress." She gave him a wry smile. "Guess you'll be my selection. If your clearance has come through by morning, we'll have to tell people your security clearance is in process, in case anyone noses around."

"Just what do you do?" Jack asked.

"I'm an analyst for the national security advisor who sits on the National Security Council."

Jack frowned. "That's more than a mouthful. How am I supposed to keep up with all of that?"

Her smile twisted. "Oh, man, you haven't seen anything yet. It's alphabet soup at the White House." Anne's smile turned south. "Do you have a business suit?"

Jack's frown deepened. "I haven't worn a suit since my mother passed away. And that was so long ago I don't own that suit anymore."

Declan eyed Jack. "I have a suit that might fit. We will have to take out the length on the trousers, since you're taller than me."

"My butler, besides being former military, an expert in martial arts and having amazing taste in vehicles, has been known to sew when necessary," Charlie said. "We can get that done tonight, assuming there's enough material in the hem of Declan's trousers to let them out."

Anne wanted to laugh at the deepening frown on Jack's face. "If you don't want to wear a suit, perhaps one of your teammates would prefer to accompany me to work as my assistant."

Cole looked up. "I'll do it." He grinned. "I own a suit. It's dusty, but I'm sure it will do."

Jack rose to his feet. "I'm going. Cole, we need you to help Jonah get me added to the employee database with the correct level of clearance so whatever badge you come up with works when I scan in at the door tomorrow." Jack nodded toward the leader of their team of former marines. "Declan, show me what you have, so I can get Arnold started on the alterations. We don't have much time to get things done by morning."

"Follow me. I have the suit in my closet upstairs."

Anne released a sigh of relief. She hadn't wanted another man to accompany her as her protector. Jack had proven himself twice that night. She trusted him with her life. Her niggle of doubt came because of her body's reaction to the man's touch.

Well, she'd just have to keep her distance from him and avoid bodily contact.

"It's a good thing you and Grace live here at the estate," Jack said to Declan as the two left the war room and climbed up to the study. "When did you invest in a suit?" Their voices faded as they moved through the house.

Anne turned to Charlie. "What did they mean by thanks to you, they're doing the right thing?"

Charlie glanced at the remainder of the men in the room. "I've employed Declan and his team to perform missions to right wrongs, help people and do things the FBI, CIA, state and local police won't or can't get involved in. We call the team Declan's Defenders."

"A kind of vigilante group?"

Charlie shrugged. "Some would say that."

"They're more than that," Grace said. "They saved my life and my roommate's life. I wouldn't be alive today if they hadn't come to my aid." She gave Anne a gentle smile. "You're one lucky woman to have them covering your six."

"Covering my six?"

"We'll have your back," Cole said. "Jack will be there with you at all times. If he needs additional help, we'll be there, as well. You can count on us."

Anne drew in a deep breath and let it go. "Good. This is all new to me. I'm not a spy, soldier or marine. I've never been trained in combat. I studied tae kwon do when I was a teen, but I haven't used it since I graduated high school a few too many years ago to remember how."

Grace chuckled. "I'm just now learning how to fire a handgun. Declan got me my own .40 caliber pistol. It scares me to death to think of using it against another human being." Her face hardened. "But if it's a choice between my life or the life of someone about to attack me, you bet I will pull the trigger. I refuse to be a victim, ever again. And that goes for anyone threatening someone I love."

Anne heard the conviction in Grace's voice and wondered what her story was. What had made her so determined to protect herself and those she cared most about.

"If you knew my husband, you know he was murdered for what he knew about Trinity," Charlie said. "I might not ever find the people who killed John, but I hope I can keep others from suffering from Trinity's machinations."

Anne squared her shoulders. "John contacted me a while back, asking me to report anything out of the ordinary in the National Security Council. I wasn't sure what he was looking for, or what appeared to be out of the ordinary, but I promised I'd help him if I could. He convinced me he only wanted to expose the people who were bent on destroying our government from within. I'm still uncertain how I can help, but if this informant is on the up-and-up, and gives me some clues, perhaps we can bring Trinity down before they have a chance to attack."

"I hope we can. But we can't do it without our own people on the inside," Charlie said. "We might have to get more of Declan's Defenders inside. We'll work more on that tomorrow. Tonight, our goal is to position Jack as your protector. You can't focus on anything if you're afraid for your life."

"Thank you," Anne said. "For taking me in when I didn't know where else to go. Your husband was a good man and you're doing a great job carrying on his legacy."

Charlie's eyes filled with moisture. "He was good and kind and gentle. I miss him." She closed her eyes briefly and opened them again. "In the meantime, you need a place to stay."

"I'll show her to a room," Grace said. "Were you able to salvage any of your clothing? I saw the pictures of the destruction to your apartment. I'm so sorry."

"At least I wasn't there when they broke in," Anne said.

"I might have some clothes you can use until you can replace what you've lost." Grace led the way up the stairs to the study above.

Anne followed. "How long have you been with Charlie and Declan's Defenders?"

Grace grinned. "Since the beginning. I presented them with their first mission."

Anne shot a glance toward the pretty young woman. "Were you being targeted by Trinity?"

She shook her head. "No, but my roommate had disappeared. Declan helped me put the pieces together, and ultimately, we found my roommate. Declan saved my life in the process."

"They're as good as Charlie claims they are?" Anne asked.

Grace nodded. "The best."

Anne felt a little better about handing over her badge to the team. And she felt better knowing she didn't have to ferret out Trinity and their plan of attack on her own. With Jack watching her back and Cole and Jonah scouring the internet for clues, they might have a chance of discovering what was going to happen before it actually occurred.

She hoped she was right.

JACK ENTERED THE suite assigned to Declan and Grace. They'd been together since Charlie first hired him. It was because of the work Declan had done helping Grace stay alive while searching for her roommate that Charlie had come up with the brilliant idea to establish a team of trained combatants to handle situations outside of the police and federal agencies' hands.

Declan had never been happier than he was with Grace. After being separated from the military for doing the right thing, he deserved to be happy.

Declan crossed the sitting room and entered the bedroom he shared with Grace, opening a closet at the far end. He sorted through the shirts hanging there and dug deep into the back of the closet, eventually pulling out a white dress shirt and charcoal gray suit. "The suit was tailored to fit me, but I think we're about the same across the chest." He handed the shirt and blazer to Jack.

Jack tried on the shirt over his black T-shirt. It appeared to fit just fine. The sleeves were a tad short, but they would work. He slipped his arms into the suit jacket and pulled it over his shoulders. It fit his chest and waist, but the sleeves would need lengthening.

"Try the trousers," Declan said.

Jack kicked off his shoes, shucked his jeans and slipped his legs into the trousers. "They're a little loose around the waist and hips. A belt will keep them in place."

Declan patted his flat belly. "Guess I'm putting on a little weight. I might need to step up my exercise routine."

"We're just built differently." Jack looked at himself in the mirror. "If we can let out the pant legs two

inches and the sleeves at least an inch, this will work."
He removed the suit, dressed in his jeans and shoes and
faced Declan.

His team leader handed him the hangers with the
shirt and suit. "Are you up for playing the part of Anne's
assistant tomorrow?"

He nodded. "I suppose so. Although I'm not quite
certain what exactly all the people who support the National Security Council actually do."

"Let's see if Cole and Jonah have made any progress
on that badge. While we're in the war room, we can do
some research on the NSC. Since you'll be a new hire,
you won't be expected to know much."

"I'll need to know how things work in order to look
for potential moles or covert terrorists hiding among
the people working around Anne."

"Good point. It's not like having an enemy pointing
a gun in your face."

Jack's jaw tightened. "No, it's more like having an
enemy smile to your face and then shoot you in the back
as soon as you turn around."

"True." Declan led the way down the stairs to the
kitchen, where they found Roger Arnold, the butler.

He listened to Jack's instructions and nodded. Then
he took the suit and shirt. "I'll have them ready within
an hour." Arnold left the kitchen.

"Let's see what Cole and Jonah have come up with."
Declan motioned toward the study and descended into
the war room via the trapdoor.

Cole and Jonah stood beside a printer/laminator
in the corner of the room. When it spit out a badge,
Jonah held it up. "Cross your fingers," Jonah said. He

slid Anne's card through a reader that quickly blinked green. Then Jonah slid the new card through the machine.

Jack held his breath. When it blinked green, he let go of the breath he'd been holding. "It works here, but will it work to get me into the West Wing?"

"It should." Jonah handed him the card and shut down the machines. "I've set it up just like Anne's, with all the security access codes embedded in their database."

"You were able to access their database that quickly?" Jack shook his head, amazed at what Jonah and Cole were capable of.

"Of course. It's a government system. The Russians and Chinese aren't the only people capable of hacking into it." Jonah snorted. "It has so many back doors that anyone with a little knowledge can get in."

"I'm glad you're on our team," Jack said. "I'd hate it if you went over to the other side."

Jonah held up his hand. "Been there, done that. John Halverson recruited me out of that nightmare. I can still access the dark web, but I'm not selling secrets, and hopefully, I'm not someone's target."

Jack exchanged a glance with Cole.

John Halverson had collected a strange group of operators to staff his team. For that matter, Charlie was continuing his legacy by hiring a Marine Force Recon team that had been dishonorably discharged. Jack couldn't judge anyone, not after how their careers in the military had ended.

Cole motioned for Jack to join him in front of the monitor. "You'll need to know a little about the offices and people you'll be coming into contact with who support the National Security Council."

"Just what is the National Security Council besides the president and all of his security advisors?" Jack asked.

"Just that. The council is headed by the president of the United States. The most prominent people on the council are the vice president, secretary of state, secretary of defense, secretary of treasury, national security advisor and director of national intelligence."

For the next hour, Cole and Jack went over the names and faces of the people involved in setting foreign policy for the US government. By the time they finished, Jack's head was spinning.

"If the informant thinks Ms. Bellamy is the closest person to the sleeper agent, you need to stick with her. Pay attention to them. There are a lot of government officials, committees, directors and more in Washington. We can't begin to monitor all of them."

"That's what's scary," Jack said. "I'll send you the names of the people Anne works with most."

"We'll run background checks on them," Cole said.

"They wouldn't be in the positions they are without having been through background checks," Jack pointed out.

Jonah nodded. "True, but we'll go a step further. The dark web is a great place to go if you want the dirt on just about anyone."

Feeling a little better about the task ahead, Jack stepped outside to grab a breath of fresh air. All the talk about government positions, councils, offices and more had left him wondering how anything got done with so many people involved.

Jack left the study through the French doors leading out onto an expansive porch that wrapped around the side of the house. A garden stretched out before him, luring him away from the house. The sky had cleared, the stars shining bright and the metropolitan area glowing to the northeast.

Scents of roses and honeysuckle filled the air, calming him. He wondered if Anne was having any trouble falling asleep after the eventful day she'd had. Having been chased several times and nearly killed, she was probably lying awake, afraid to close her eyes.

As if his thoughts had conjured the woman, he saw her ahead of him, sitting on a bench in an arbor. Though her face was in the shadows, he knew it was her.

His pulse quickened and his feet carried him forward several steps before his mind kicked in, reminding him that he couldn't get involved with the woman. She didn't need him jinxing her. If this tasking was to work, he had to keep a level head and a safe distance, emotionally.

With that in mind, he didn't have to ignore the woman.

Jack announced his presence by clearing his throat softly.

Anne jumped to her feet and spun to face him, her eyes wide and white in the semidarkness.

"Oh," she said, her body sagging. "It's you."

"Sorry, were you expecting someone else?"

"No. Not at all. I'm just a little spooked." She

wrapped her arms around her middle. "Aren't you? After all we've been through today?"

He shrugged. "I've been through my share of danger."

"How do you cope? I can't even close my eyes without seeing men jumping out of trucks with scary military-grade rifles." She shivered.

"You never get used to it, but if you dwell on it, you never get any rest."

She rubbed her arms. "Well, I can't turn it off that easily. Frankly, I'm scared."

"Then call in sick tomorrow."

She shook her head. "I can't. I'm helping the national security advisor prepare the agenda for the council meeting to be conducted a few short days. I have to be there."

"What if you'd died today? Isn't there someone else to take over?"

Anne frowned. "That's supposed to be my new hire. I've been too busy to find and train someone to help out."

"The national security advisor couldn't prepare for the meeting himself?"

Anne shrugged. "He's a very busy man. He meets with many of the other directors and committees so that he's fully familiarized with the important items that will be on the agenda. That wouldn't leave him enough time to pull it all together."

"Sounds like you're what we call key personnel."

She laughed. "I guess. Though I'm sure if push came to shove, Mr. Louis could find someone to help. I like to think I'm irreplaceable, but no one really is." She lifted her chin to the sky and drew in a deep breath, letting it out on a sigh. "Why did it have to be me? I'm not the right person to spy on others. I keep my nose down and do my job."

"I'm sure you do more than that, or your informant wouldn't have tagged you."

"I'm beginning to think the informant might just be flushing out anyone who had anything to do with John Halverson. That way they can get rid of them and have open season on anything they have planned in the government."

Jack nodded. "In that case, it wouldn't hurt to find your informant. Cole and Jonah are still working on that. Tomorrow, we need to get you a new phone. We'll take a page from your texter's book and buy a burner phone that can't be traced as easily."

"If the person who sent the texts is on the up-and-up, how will she get word to me?"

"I don't know, but I'm assuming she has her methods and will find a way."

Anne nodded. "Well, I'll do my best to introduce you to the people I work with most. Then I have to get some work done. You might have to do some sleuthing on your own. I can have you deliver stuff to different departments to get you in."

"Sounds good. Does the office building have a map?"

She smiled. "Actually, I have one you can borrow. I created it when I started working for the NSA. I got lost one too many times trying to find my way around."

"It's getting late," Jack said. "Shouldn't you be hitting the sack?"

"I don't know that it will do much good. I'm too wired."

"Have you considered taking a long, hot shower?" he asked and immediately imagined her naked beneath the spray. No, this wasn't a good direction for his thoughts to drift.

"I will." Anne inhaled deeply and blew it out. "But for now, I'm trying to absorb the zen of this garden. I'm hoping between the roses and the honeysuckle, I'll calm down."

"How's it working for you?"

She laughed. "Not so great until you came out."

"Does that mean talking to me is helping?"

She tilted her head. "Surprisingly, yes."

"Why is it so surprising?"

"You're not someone I'd consider calming."

Jack chuckled. He knew he shouldn't encourage her, but he couldn't help it. "How so?"

"Well, for one, you ride a motorcycle. That screams bad boy all over the place."

"A lot of people ride motorcycles," he pointed out.

"True. Maybe I'm stereotyping, but I think of motorcycle riders as rebels." Her gaze swept over him. "And you look like a rebel. Or someone with something to hide or someone who doesn't like to get too close to anyone."

Her comment took the wind out of his sails. "It doesn't always pay to get close," he admitted softly.

"If you don't get close to people, you miss out on some of the best life has to offer, even if it's only for a short time." Anne turned away, leaving her face in profile, half bathed in starlight, the other half hidden.

"You talk like someone with experience in loss."

She nodded. "I lost my husband to cancer when I was thirty. We had four years together." She turned toward him. "I wouldn't trade those four years for anything. Who did you lose?"

Her question was so unexpected and blunt Jack reeled backward. "I don't want to talk about it." He'd lost so many. His mother, Kylie, Jennifer, Razor, Kemp, Matheson—the list went on. Getting close to someone led to pain. The faces of all those he'd lost scrolled through his mind like a movie reel.

Her hand on his arm startled him, bringing him back to the garden and the scent of roses and honeysuckle.

"Of the people you've lost, would you have avoided them had you known you were going to lose them?"

He didn't answer, his chest so tight he could barely breathe.

"Your life has been that much richer for having known and loved those people," Anne said.

Jack gripped her arms. "It hurts too much to lose someone you care about." He shook his head. "I don't ever want to feel that kind of pain again."

Her eyes rounded as she looked up into his, her lips lush and kissable. "But you miss out on the love and joy, the laughter and happiness if you're afraid to open yourself to the pain."

"I can't," he said, through gritted teeth. "I can't."

"Yes, you can." Then she did something surprising. She lifted her lips to his, and before he knew what he was doing, he'd pulled her to him, his mouth crashing down over hers.

Her body melted against his. Her hands against his chest rose to circle around his neck, drawing him closer. She opened to him, her tongue meeting his in a dance so erotic it set his blood on fire.

Jack tangled one hand in her hair, the other smoothing down her back to press her closer, the hardness of his erection pressing into her soft belly.

When he had to come up for air, he drew in a ragged breath. "That…shouldn't…have happened," he said like a runner gasping for air at the finish line. He leaned his forehead against hers. "I'll ask Declan to get someone else to go with you tomorrow. I'm not fit to be your protector."

Anne shook her head and leaned back to stare up into his eyes. "It's been an insane day. Our emotions are high. This could have happened to anyone." She stepped out of his arms and smoothed her hands over her shirt, her gaze anywhere but at him. "I still want you." Her eyes widened and she shot a look toward him. "I mean, I still want you to come with me. You've saved my life twice. I trust you to keep doing it."

He raised his hand as if swearing on a stack of Bibles. "I promise not to do that again."

She held up her hand to stop him. "Don't. Just don't. I'm not mad. In case you didn't notice, you weren't the only one kissing in that scenario." She pushed her fingers through her hair. "Let's call it a night and reboot this relationship in the morning."

He nodded and waved a hand toward the house. "Go ahead. I think I'll stay out here for a few more minutes."

Anne hesitated for a moment, then turned and entered the house.

Jack remained out in the garden, mentally kicking himself for having kissed the woman. He couldn't take it back, and he couldn't erase the feeling her lips had left on his. He wanted to kiss her again.

And again.

But that just couldn't happen.

Anne's life depended on it.

Chapter Four

Anne didn't sleep at all that night. As if being accosted outside a pub, chased on the back of a motorcycle and nearly shot wasn't bad enough, kissing Jack had completely thrown her off balance. Her mouth and core tingled well into the night. She could still feel his lips against hers and the hard ridge of his desire pressed to her belly.

Hell, the kiss took center stage in her mind, wiping out the fear of being chased and shot at. What was wrong with her? No kiss should do that.

Except the one from the man who saved her from all the bad stuff that happened that day. And he would be working closely with her until the ordeal was over.

How would she manage to function when all she'd be able to do was think about the sexy former marine on the motorcycle, storming in to save her? She had real work to finish in preparation for the next meeting of the National Security Council. Shaun Louis, her boss, the national security advisor, wouldn't be happy if she came to work distracted. He relied on her to keep everything straight, from the agenda to the types of drinks they stocked in the conference room and much more. The president didn't suffer fools. He had little patience for underlings wasting time or woolgathering about sexy marines. Shaun made certain all was in order before the president arrived.

By the time the sun came up, Anne had dressed, brushed her hair and secured it into a messy bun at the crown of her head and applied her makeup. She ventured out of her room to explore the house and maybe find a much-needed cup of coffee.

Downstairs she located the kitchen by following the sounds of clattering pans and voices.

When she entered, butterflies erupted in her stomach and her pulse leaped.

Jack stood with his back to her, talking to Declan.

For a brief moment, Anne allowed herself to study the tall, sandy-blond-haired man with shoulders so broad they made her pulse quicken. He wore jeans and a white T-shirt, and his feet were bare. He could have just rolled out of bed, but damn, he was sexy.

"Ah, there you are," Declan said, straightening away from the counter he leaned against. "Looking for coffee?"

Jack turned his gray-eyed gaze toward Anne and gave her a deep, penetrating look she could swear went all the way through her soul, rattling her normal, clear thoughts.

What had Declan asked? Anne dragged her gaze away from Jack. "Yes. Coffee would be lovely."

Declan pulled a mug from an upper cabinet, poured a steaming cup of fragrant brew and handed it to Anne. "Sleep okay?"

"Yes, thank you," Anne lied, watching Jack out of

the corner of her eye. Had he lost any sleep after kissing her? Probably not. The man looked awake and ready to go.

"Charlie instructed Arnold to drive you two into DC and drop you off a couple blocks from your office building. You can walk from there."

"That's not necessary," Anne said. "If we could just get a ride to the Metro station, we can get ourselves to work."

Declan nodded. "That might be better, anyway. The fewer folks who see you in one of Charlie's limos the better."

"Right." Anne spooned sugar into her mug and followed it with cream, wondering when Jack was going to open his mouth to add to the conversation. Would he say anything about that kiss? She hoped he wasn't someone who kissed and told. He didn't strike her as someone who shared any more than he had to about his personal life.

"How soon do you want to leave?" Declan asked.

She glanced at her watch. "Fifteen minutes okay? Is it too early?"

Declan shook his head. "Arnold's been up and out in the garage for over an hour already. Any time you want to leave would be good with him."

"Then fifteen it is," she said, looking over the rim of her mug at Jack. "Can you be ready by then?"

He tipped his mug, downing the remainder of his coffee. Then he ran his hand across the sexy stubble on his chin. "I'll be ready." Jack left her drinking her coffee and disappeared into the hallway.

A man emerged from a door against the far wall of

the kitchen, carrying a box of pancake mix. "Ah, Ms. Bellamy, I'm Carl, Charlie's chef. Can I interest you in a hearty breakfast?"

She smiled. "Thank you, but I won't have time."

"How about a pastry or a blueberry muffin?" he offered.

"I wouldn't mind half of a blueberry muffin," she admitted.

"Perfect. I just cut one in half for Snow."

"Snow?" she questioned and then remembered. "Oh, yes. Jack." Her face flushed with heat. "I forgot. I think of him as simply Jack."

Declan laughed. "I'm sure he'd love to know you call him simple Jack."

"That's not what I meant." She frowned. "He's smart and thinks fast on his feet. Or on his motorcycle, in my case. Was he that way in the Marine Corps, too?"

Declan glanced down at the coffee in his mug. "He was our slack man. The youngest man on the team. The guy everyone dumped on. He carried all the heavy equipment and never complained." Declan looked up. "He had our backs and we had his. You can trust Snow to protect you with his life."

The intensity of Declan's words struck Anne straight to the heart. "Knowing he will be with me today is a relief."

Carl brought her half of a blueberry muffin on a white plate with a dribble of blueberry sauce on the side and a fork.

"Thank you." Anne carried it to the table with her mug of coffee. The muffin was so moist it melted in her mouth, the blueberries so sweet they made her want to groan. Before she realized it, the muffin was gone, and she'd finished her coffee. Carrying her dishes to the sink, she passed the chef. "That was amazing."

He smiled. "Glad you liked the muffin. It's a recipe I learned in the navy."

Anne's brow twisted. "Is everyone around here prior military?"

Declan laughed. "No. Grace and Charlie aren't."

"The Halversons have a special place in their hearts for our military men and women," Carl said. "And we have a special place in our hearts for them. God rest Mr. Halverson's soul."

"Arnold will have the car out front waiting for you when you're ready," Declan said. "If you and Jack need backup, all you have to do is call."

"Assuming I get a new phone," Anne said. The thought of receiving additional texts from her secret informer gave her chills. But she felt lost without a phone and knew she'd have to get another soon. If for no other reason than her boss liked to have a direct line to her if he needed anything.

Anne left the kitchen and waited in the entryway at the base of the stairs for Jack to join her.

The sound of a door opening and closing brought her attention to the top of the stairs.

Jack appeared, dressed in the borrowed suit, his sandy-blond hair slicked back, his face cleanly shaved. He was so handsome.

Anne's breath caught and held in her chest.

The man could have been a model on a magazine cover.

Anne had to admit she liked the blue-jean-clad, barefoot man she'd seen minutes before in the kitchen better than the man in the business suit. He was the kind of man a woman would love to wake up to in the morning.

Getting a firm grip on her thoughts would prove to be a challenge that day. Anne squared her shoulders. "The suit fits," was all she could manage to say.

"Arnold is a magician with a needle and thread." Jack tugged at the red necktie. "Haven't worn a tie in a while. Now I remember why."

"You'll live," she said and started for the door before she actually drooled on the man.

As Declan had predicted, the butler had one of Charlie's vehicles waiting at the bottom of the stairs outside the grand entrance.

Jack reached the door handle before Anne could and opened the door for her.

She moved past him, her shoulder brushing against his arm.

A flash of electricity rippled through her shoulder and south to the pit of her belly. She dove into the car and slid across the seat as far over as she could. The man had an effect on her that she couldn't fathom or control. She hadn't felt this kind of attraction since she'd fallen in love with Mason.

Jack folded his long body into the back seat beside her and closed the door.

Arnold glanced into the rearview mirror before pulling away from the house and driving down the long, winding road to the front gate.

By the time they passed through the gate to the highway, Anne was twitchy. "Are you nervous about your first day on the job?" she asked to fill the silence.

Jack shrugged. "Should I be?"

"I was." Anne stared out the window.

"How long have you been with the national security advisor?" Jack asked.

"Two years," she said.

He glanced her way. "And before that?"

"I was a staffer with the director for Europe and Russia."

"What made you go into politics?"

Anne thought back. "I guess I was a young, idealistic student in college. It bothered me that people couldn't get along. Everyone was completely polarized on the issues. I wanted to bring a level head to the table. Perhaps I could make a difference." She gave him a lopsided grin.

"How's that going for you?"

She shook her head. "Not much has changed. You either are for or against the issues, and people will either love or hate you for your beliefs."

"Sounds pretty cynical."

She sighed. "It is. But it's the direction this country has been going for quite some time."

"If you don't like it, why don't you quit?"

"I've thought about it."

"What would you do if you quit?"

She stared out the window. "I don't know. Maybe I'd join the Peace Corps and help people of underdeveloped countries pull themselves out of poverty."

"Sounds noble."

She turned to him. "What about you? Is being a part of Declan's Defenders enough for you?"

Jack turned away and looked out the window on

his side of the vehicle. What he didn't know was that his expressions were clearly reflected in the window. "I never pictured myself in any other career but the military. I trained hard to hone my combat skills." He snorted softly. "When we were booted out, there weren't any jobs available that could use the skills I'd worked so hard to excel at."

"Until Charlie?"

He nodded.

"What was it you liked about being a marine?" she asked.

His chin lifted and his shoulders moved back as if instinctively. "I was part of something bigger than just me. We thought what we did meant something. We were fighting to protect our way of life, the people of our nation and the innocent people in the way of terrorists. We thought what we were doing was right."

"And now?"

His lip curled. "I still think the marines are doing what they think is right. I'm not so sure the politicians and leadership have the best interests of the nation at heart."

"Sadly," Anne said. "I agree."

"Yet, you still work with them."

"I hope that in some small way, I can influence decisions by providing the most up-to-date facts about the issues." Anne had had lofty goals when she'd gone to work for the national security advisor. The day-to-day grind had taken the steam out of them.

"In the meantime, you have a potential terrorist hiding among the politicians and staffers. That should make things interesting."

Anne chewed on her lower lip. "How do I identify someone like that? I have no idea where to begin. And I don't have the phone I did for my informant to give me clues."

"*If* your informant has your best interests at heart. What if she is setting you up to take a fall?"

"If she was, why would she have me destroy my phone?" Anne drew in a deep breath. "I'm going to take this a day at a time. I have my work to do for the meeting coming up. I need to focus on that."

Jack nodded. "I'll help you where I can. Meanwhile, I'll get to know the other players in your universe as part of my initiation into the job."

Anne hoped he could find some clue as to who might be planning an attack before the attack occurred. She didn't know at what point she should alert others of the potential. They'd been through so many drills anytime a bomb threat came across.

She just hoped she didn't wait too long.

ARNOLD DROPPED THEM off at the closest Metro station.

Jack sat beside Anne as they rode the train into downtown DC and got off at the Farragut West Metro Station close to the White House.

As they walked toward one of the most recognizable and historical buildings in the United States of America, Jack studied the streets, buildings and alleys along the way. During the day, they didn't seem sinister, but at night, they could take on an entirely different vibe. The Metro station was a few blocks from the White House, giving a predator multiple places and opportunities to stage an attack.

Having conducted combat operations in the urban terrain of cities in Afghanistan and Iraq, Jack had a good idea of where the danger zones were.

But their first obstacle to overcome was the Secret Service guards and the ID reader they'd have to pass to gain access to the West Wing.

As they neared the building, Anne spoke in a low tone. "You aren't carrying any knives, guns or any other kind of weapons, are you?"

"You ask me now?" Jack stared at her as if she'd lost her mind.

She looked up at him, her eyes rounding. "You aren't, are you?"

He laughed. "No. Cole went over the rules of entering the White House. I'm clean of any weapons."

Anne let out a nervous sigh. "Thank God. The last thing I want is for you to be hauled off to jail for trying to bring a weapon into the building connected to the one where our president lives."

"We'll be okay," he said, in what he hoped was a soothing tone. "Just act normal."

"How?" she muttered. "This is an insane situation. I'm beginning to wonder what normal is."

He touched her elbow and led her up the steps as they entered the building and passed through a metal detector. He was glad he'd worn antiperspirant, since it was a grueling three tries before he got his card to work in the reader. But then they were on their way to Anne's office, passing men and women in business attire as they went.

He'd read that there were around four hundred employees working in the West Wing of the White House.

The task would be daunting to investigate all of them for the person or persons who could be the sleepers among them.

Anne opened the door to a suite of offices. "This is where you'll be working," she said.

The first person they encountered was a staffer, a young woman with light blond hair, sitting at a desk directly in front of the door. "Good morning, Ms. Bellamy." The woman smiled up at her. Her eyes widened when Jack stepped up beside Anne.

"Gina Galinsky, this is Jack Snow. He's my new assistant. Please see that the desk in my office is set up for him. He'll need supplies, computer access and a desk phone."

"I'll get right on that." Gina jumped to her feet. "Welcome, Mr. Snow."

Jack held out his hand. "Nice to meet you, Gina." He gave her the grin he used when he used to go out carousing with the guys.

Gina's cheeks flushed a light pink and she batted her eyes. "I'll just see to your desk. Anything you might need, just ask. You'll like working with Ms. Bellamy. She's super smart and nice."

"I'm sure I will." Jack followed Anne into the office to the right of the staffer's desk. Another office door led to the left.

Once Anne was inside her office, she closed the door and pointed to a desk with papers stacked in a neat pile and a photo frame leaning on one corner. "That's my desk." She turned to an empty one on the other side of the room. "That will be yours, though I'm not sure what you will do with it."

"I'll work like I am your assistant. The more I appear to be the real thing, the less likely anyone will think otherwise."

"Good point. I'll be sure to give you assignments that will take you around to the people I interact with most." She settled behind her desk. "For now, you'll have to work with tech support to get access to the computer system and databases."

Jack sat at the other desk, pulled the keyboard forward and keyed in the log-on ID and password Cole had set up for him the night before. The computer screen came to life.

Anne left her chair and crossed the room to look over his shoulder. "How did you do that?"

He grinned. "Cole and Jonah set me up."

She shook her head. "It took my last assistant a good week to get full access." She pinched the bridge of her nose. "I don't want to know how he did it, but I want to fire all the guys in tech support and hire Charlie's team." She returned to her desk and fired up her computer. Within minutes, she was typing away, her fingers tapping the keyboard furiously.

Jack asked a few questions about the organization of the files and database and then he poked around on his own, not sure what he was looking for, but careful not to pry too hard into places that required special access or passwords.

Within a few minutes, Anne printed out a document and asked Jack to deliver it to the homeland security advisor in a room down the hallway. "Hand it directly to him and tell him I need his input by end of day."

"Yes, ma'am." Jack gave her a mock salute and left the office.

He took his time getting there, smiling and introducing himself to the staffers inside that office.

The woman at the desk blocking entry into the next suite of offices smiled up at him. "May I help you?"

She had shoulder-length dark hair, brown eyes and dark framed glasses.

"I have a document I need to deliver to the advisor for homeland security."

The woman held out her hand. "I can take it and make certain he gets it."

"Ms. Bellamy asked me to deliver it into his hands, even if I had to wait." He smiled at the woman who had to be in her midthirties, wearing a cream, black and tan plaid skirt. "I can wait." He glanced at the nameplate on her desk. "Dr. Saunders."

She blushed, pushed her glasses up her nose and straightened the papers on her desk that were already straight. "You can call me Millicent." She waved to a chair beside her desk. "Please, have a seat. Mr. Carpenter should be here momentarily. He had a meeting over an hour ago and should be on his way back soon."

As if on cue, a balding man with a wrinkled suit and a bit of a paunch hurried into the office, his face ruddy and a sheen of perspiration breaking out on his forehead. "Millie, send a note to the national security advisor's office to add the border wall as a discussion item on the agenda."

"Mr. Carpenter, you know POTUS doesn't want it on the agenda if you don't have solutions to the problem."

"He needs to know what's happening and which political action committees are in an uproar."

Millicent shrugged. "Yes, sir." She typed on her keyboard, her fingers flying over the keys. "Done." Then she pushed back from her desk and stood. "Mr. Carpenter, Ms. Bellamy's assistant has a note for you." She waved a hand toward Jack. "If you two will excuse me, I wanted to touch base with Anthony Schuster about a matter that cropped up today." She left the office without looking back.

"Anthony Schuster?" Jack pushed to his feet.

"Director for Europe and Russia." Carpenter tipped his head toward the door Millicent had gone through. "Millie has a PhD in foreign policy, speaks fluent German, Russian and Greek. I think she would prefer to work with Schuster, but the position as his assistant was already full when we hired her on. My gain, his loss. She's brilliant. Now, if you'll excuse me, I have work to do. The NSC meets soon, and everyone is scrambling."

As Carpenter started for his office, Jack stepped forward, towering over the shorter man. "Mr. Carpenter, I have a document from Ms. Bellamy in the national security advisor's office."

"I know who Anne is," Carpenter said with a frown. He jerked the document out of Jack's hand. "The question is who are you?" He looked over the rim of his glasses at Jack.

"Jack Snow, Ms. Bellamy's new assistant."

The man shook Jack's hand. "Nice to meet you," Carpenter said. "I'm surprised she was able to get an assistant in so quickly. It can be like passing a bill through

Congress to get help around here." He smirked when Jack didn't react. "That was a joke."

Jack chuckled. "Sorry. First day on the job. I guess I'm a little nervous."

"No need to be. We're all in this together and help where we can."

"Thanks," Jack said. "How long have you worked here?"

"Six months. I came in after the last guy left. I think the president fired him. But he claimed he left for medical reasons. The job can be stressful."

"I get that."

"I hope you're up for it," the homeland security advisor said. "Not everyone can handle it."

"I've been in stressful situations," Jack said, thinking back to some of the missions he'd been on, when he'd had to make life-and-death kinds of decisions. "I think I'll manage."

"Thank Ms. Bellamy for me. She's been here over a couple of presidencies. People like her are like the glue that holds us together. I'm not sure what any of us would do without her."

"Hopefully, we won't have to find out." He nodded toward the document in Carpenter's hand. "Ms. Bellamy asked that you provide your feedback before the end of day."

"I'll do that," Carpenter promised.

Jack left the office and returned to Anne's.

Gina had been in and stocked his desk with pens, pads of paper, a leather notebook and a Rolodex. He hated to see her go to that much trouble when he wasn't going to be around any longer than it took to find the mole in the West Wing.

Having only met a handful of the over four hundred people who worked there, he had to admit he was a bit overwhelmed with the task in front of them.

Before he realized it, hours had passed, and his stomach rumbled loudly.

"I take it you're hungry," Anne said from across the room.

"I can wait," he said. "I've gone longer without food."

"I don't normally take lunch, but I could use a walk and some fresh air." She stood, stretched and looped her purse over her shoulder. "Come on. I'll take you to my favorite sandwich shop."

As they left the building, Anne made sure to introduce him to people she ran into in the hallway. No one questioned his sudden hire, nor did they ask for details about his background. Everyone appeared to be in a hurry to get work done.

Outside, Jack was almost surprised the sun was still out. He felt he'd been inside for a very long time.

"Sometimes I don't see the sun at all," Anne said, as if reading his mind. "I get to work in the dark and leave in the dark."

"That doesn't leave much time for a life."

She shrugged. "Since my husband died, my work has been my life," she said, quietly.

"How long has that been?" Jack asked.

"Three years."

"You must have loved him very much," he commented.

"I did."

Jack felt a tightening in his chest. If he'd been back in high school, he might have mistaken the feeling for jealousy. But how could he be jealous of a dead man? He'd just met Anne. She was someone way out of his league mentally and professionally. She was brilliant and admired by her colleagues. The only thing Anne and Jack had in common was the mission to discover someone who might be planning an attack.

Oh, and a couple shared kisses. But those didn't count. They couldn't.

Chapter Five

Anne didn't really have time to take a lunch, but trying to work in her office while Jack was at the desk nearby was tantamount to impossible. She couldn't get past the fact they'd kissed the night before. And today, he acted as if nothing had happened.

How could he be so cool and unaffected when she was fidgeting in her chair, having a difficult time focusing on the monitor in front of her?

By noon, she had to get up and move or climb the walls.

The air outside was heavy, with clouds hovering over the city. She wished she'd thought to bring an umbrella. Hopefully, the rain would hold off until they returned to the West Wing.

The sandwich shop was a couple of blocks from the White House, giving her time to regroup her thoughts and get a grip on her emotions. She should be more worried about the person who'd texted her and the one who'd subsequently tried to kill her.

The shop was crowded inside, with no seats available.

"We can go somewhere else, or sit outside and risk getting rained on," Anne said.

Jack glanced up at the clouds. "I won't melt," he said. "But you might not want to get wet."

"We can always leave if it starts to rain." Anne settled into a seat at one of the bistro tables and studied the menu.

Jack took the seat beside her, instead of across. He glanced around as if searching for enemy personnel.

Anne set her menu on the table and shook her head. "I really don't think anyone will try to attack during broad daylight."

"The last time I thought that, I lost a buddy of mine. The time before that, a truckload of nurses rolled across an improvised explosive device. None of them lived. And before that someone opened fire in a shopping mall in the middle of the day, killing my ex-girlfriend, a father of three children, a pregnant woman and a teenage girl." He gave her a hard stare. "Forgive me if I don't trust the daylight to keep the bad guys at bay."

He'd spoken in a low tone that only she could hear, but the intensity of his stare and the urgency of his words hit her hard. This was a man who'd seen more death and sorrow than even she had experienced through the loss of her husband.

"I'm sorry," she murmured. "You're right to be cautious."

He sat back in his chair and finally looked down at the menu, but only briefly before he laid it aside.

The waitress took their orders and disappeared.

While they waited for their sandwiches, Anne gave Jack insights on some of the people he'd met that morning.

"Gina has been with Shaun and me for the past year

and a half. Her ex-husband is a lobbyist for one of the car manufacturers. She divorced him when she found out he'd cheated on her while she was attending school at Georgetown University. She's smart, reads fast and catches a lot of my editing errors. And she's a Washington Redskins fan. I can't imagine her being a sleeper spy with Trinity."

"I hadn't met anyone who worked directly with Trinity until a few weeks ago, when a woman tried to kidnap Charlie from a charity ball."

Anne leaned forward, her pulse picking up. "Seriously? You've met a Trinity agent?"

He nodded. "She'd suffered a head injury and lost her memory for a while. But she'd already left Trinity and had started to work with John Halverson before the head injury." Jack frowned. "If she's an example of the assassins Trinity puts out…"

"What?"

"Let's just say, they're highly skilled in martial arts and weapons. And they aren't afraid of much."

Anne shivered. "If the person who texted me knows all this, why did she choose me? I don't know any of that. The most violent thing I've ever done is throw my keyboard across the room when it quit being effective."

Jack chuckled and then frowned. "You had to have been chosen because of your position and your involvement with Halverson."

Their sandwiches were delivered at that moment, forestalling further discussion about Trinity or Halverson.

Once they'd finished their meal, a different waitress appeared with a dessert menu.

Anne wondered why they had a different waitress but didn't mention it. "I don't want dessert." She held up her hands, refusing to take the menu.

"I'll just leave the menu here, if you change your mind." The waitress laid the menu on the table and disappeared before Anne could say anything else.

When she glanced down at the menu, she noticed it didn't close all the way. She didn't want dessert, but she didn't like leaving the menu at an odd angle.

Anne opened the menu and stared down at what was keeping it from closing, and gasped.

Inside the menu was a cell phone. A second later, it vibrated against the menu.

Anne looked up at Jack.

He turned the phone toward him and read the text. "It's your texter."

Take the phone.
It can't be traced or tagged with a GPS tracker.

Anne stared at the phone as if it was a snake coiling to bite.

TAKE IT.
We don't have much time. Targets are being assigned.

Jack looked left and right, his gaze scanning the immediate area. "Did you get a good look at the waitress who left the menu?" he asked.

Anne shook her head. "She was a brunette. I think. But that's about all I remember."

The original waitress showed up with their check.

"Can I get you anything else?" she asked as she laid the bill on the table.

"The waitress who brought our dessert menu, is she in the back?" Jack asked. "We'd like to talk to her."

The woman's brow creased. "Dessert menu?"

"Yes, this one," Jack held up the menu.

She opened it, studied it and shook her head. "That's not from here. It's from a restaurant a couple blocks from here."

Jack pulled out his wallet, gave the waitress enough to cover their meal and a tip and stood.

"What about the cell phone?" Anne asked.

"Leave it. I'd be afraid to take anything into the White House that hasn't been thoroughly checked out." Jack jumped.

"What?" Anne asked, startled by his movement.

"Nothing. Just my cell phone vibrating in my pocket." He pulled it out and studied the message before handing it over to Anne. "It's for you."

Anne's stomach clenched as she read the message.

Very well. I'll communicate through Snow's phone.

A LIGHT DRIZZLE started as they made their way back to the West Wing of the White House.

Jack had insisted on walking around the area near the sandwich shop, hoping to find the woman who'd pretended to be a waitress and had left the phone on the table.

He couldn't believe he'd been so nonchalant about her. She could have been carrying a gun or a knife and killed either one of them, had she really wanted to.

"I don't know about you, but I'm not feeling very comfortable about any of this," Anne said as she hurried to keep up with him.

Jack hadn't realized he was walking so fast. He slowed his pace to match Anne's. "I'm sorry. That was my fault. No excuses. I shouldn't have let her get that close to you."

"You couldn't have known she would walk right up to us."

"No, but I should have been ready for anything." He cupped her elbow and drew her closer. "I promised to protect you. I've failed."

"You did a great job last night. I'm not ready to consider you as having failed," Anne argued. "Apparently, my contact wants to continue the conversation about the pending attack. I should take this information to my superiors. I'm afraid that if what she's said is true, it would only warn the attacker and he'd continue to hide until another opportunity came up. But I feel like I need to let someone know."

"You already have. You've let Declan's Defenders know. We'll work this out. Cole and Jonah have to come up with something soon."

"In the meantime, she's going to contact us through your phone." Anne moved closer. "I hate that she's so vague at this point. *Targets are being assigned?* What does that mean? We have no idea where to start looking. Did she say anything else?"

Jack pulled his phone out of his pocket. "No. You saw for yourself."

Anne read the words again as if hoping to read more into them than she had before. "She said she would communicate, but so far, she hasn't given us anything substantial to go on." Anne glanced back at the sandwich shop in the distance. She shook her head. "Leaving the phone was the right thing to do, wasn't it?"

He nodded. "I wouldn't have trusted it."

"Yeah. You never know if someone could load it with some explosive device. Or it could be set up as a listening device."

"I don't like that she so easily tapped into my phone. Where did she get the number? I wonder if she's hacked into Charlie's computer or phone."

"Cole and Jonah have managed to hack into the White House security system," Anne pointed out. "Why not this woman who insists she's trying to stop an attack?"

Jack's thoughts had already gone down that path. Whoever this woman was, she had some skills in hacking into phones and making herself semi-invisible. Why hadn't she done what Jack had and infiltrated the White House herself?

He glanced at Anne. Why would she when Anne was well known by everyone in the West Wing? She was the perfect person to snoop around right under everyone's noses. A stranger, like the woman texting them, or even Jack, would be more noticeable if they were caught in the wrong places.

A siren sounded nearby. Then another. A fire truck raced past, followed by an ambulance, heading toward the White House.

Jack shot a glance toward Anne. "Do you think the target has already been acquired?"

Anne's eyes widened. "I hope not." She turned with Jack and hurried toward her office building.

A block ahead, the ambulance and fire truck had pulled to a stop, blocking traffic on the usually busy road.

"What's happening?" Anne asked, craning her neck to see over the gathering crowd of emergency personnel and rubbernecking tourists, who were snapping photos of the first responder vehicles.

Jack stood on the tips of his toes to see over the heads of others. "They're performing CPR on someone. A woman, I think." Then he noticed the cream, black and tan plaid fabric of the person's skirt and his heart slid to a stop. "Millicent?"

"What did you say?"

Jack gripped her hand and pushed through the throng to get a closer look.

The police had arrived and were holding the people back to give the emergency personnel room to work. A couple of them were asking questions.

"Anyone here see what happened?" an officer asked loudly.

A woman covered her hand with her mouth, stifling a sob, before she said, "I s-saw it all."

The officer pulled a notepad and a pen out of his pocket and stopped in front of the woman. "Can you tell me what happened?"

"The car. It came out of nowhere." A sob made her body tremble. "The driver didn't even swerve. He sped up and hit her as if he was actually aiming for her." The woman buried her face in her hands. "It was horrible. She slid up over the hood of the vehicle and fell to the side."

"Could you describe the car?"

She shook her head. "It all happened so fast. The car was a dark sedan. Maybe a four-door." She wrung her hands as tears spilled from her eyes. "I don't know. It all happened so fast."

"Did you happen to see the license plate?" the policeman asked.

"No. I didn't. I wish I had."

A hand on Jack's arm made him look down at Anne's face.

"Can you see the woman?" Anne asked.

He nodded, his jaw tight. "I recognize her skirt."

"You recognize her skirt?" Anne's brow furrowed. "I didn't know you had friends in DC. You knew her?"

He shook his head. "No, I met her this morning in the West Wing."

Anne pressed her hand to her lips. "One of our own?"

He nodded.

"Who?" Anne asked, her voice not much more than a whisper.

"Dr. Millicent Saunders."

"Millie?" Anne started to push forward. "I just had lunch with her the other day. We promised to get together to go to a museum. Can you tell if she's all right?" She clung to his arm. "Please tell me she's all right."

"They're loading her into the ambulance right now. They have an IV hooked up and they've strapped her to a backboard." Jack dropped down from his toes. "The ambulance is leaving." He stared at the buildings on the corners, the street signs and the names of the businesses. "Let's get back to the West Wing."

"But what about Millie?"

"The EMTs will do their best." Jack fished his phone from his pocket and called Declan. "One of the staffers from the West Wing was a victim of a hit-and-run. Millicent Saunders."

"You think it had anything to do with our mystery woman's warning?" Declan asked.

"I don't know, but it wouldn't hurt to investigate." He gave Declan the address of where the incident had occurred and names of some of the businesses nearby. "A witness reported it appeared as if the driver deliberately hit the woman."

"I'll see if Cole and Jonah can pull video recordings from the businesses or street cameras," Declan said.

"Anything to report on the technical front?" Jack continued talking in a low tone that wouldn't carry far as he walked alongside Anne, his gaze scanning the street, the sidewalks and the vehicles coming and going.

"Nothing so far," Declan said. "Jonah's tapping into the dark web for any message traffic involving Trinity."

"Good luck."

"Same to you and Ms. Bellamy," Declan paused. "If that woman was targeted because she works in the West Wing, you will definitely need to watch your backs."

Jack ended the call and slipped his cell phone into his pocket. He cupped Anne's elbow as they crossed the street, his body tense, ready to run if someone drove a car at the two of them. He didn't relax until they were on the other side and headed toward the West Wing.

The Secret Service agents were all abuzz about Dr.

Saunders's accident. Word had traveled fast from the street to the White House. Even though they passed through the metal detectors with no problem, Jack and Anne were stopped to be scanned with wands.

"Have there been any threats to the White House?" Anne asked.

The agent waving the wand over her arms and down her torso shook his head. "No, but when one of our employees is run down in the street, we take a few extra precautions. Tours of the White House have been suspended for today until the incident can be investigated."

Jack was glad that the security had gotten a little tighter, but not completely reassured, since he suspected the threat might also come from inside the walls of the nation's capitol building.

With all the Secret Service personnel, how did someone from one of the most dangerous covert organizations get inside the West Wing?

Jack studied every person he passed in the hallway, wondering if he or she was a Trinity-trained assassin. Was it the guy in the glasses whose pants were two inches too short, wearing white socks with his black suit? Or the woman with her hair pulled back into a tight ponytail, wearing a sleek black pantsuit, looking like she could throw a side kick and render him unconscious in the blink of an eye?

More than four hundred people worked in the West Wing of the White House. What if the Trinity mole was one of the Secret Service agents with access to every room? If that were the case, why hadn't he made the move yet? What was he waiting for?

If Millicent Saunders had been targeted for some

reason, what was the reason? What had Carpenter said about Dr. Saunders? She was fluent in Russian, German and Greek and would have been a better fit for a position with the director for Europe and Russia. She'd left her desk that morning to pay a visit to that office. Had she stumbled upon something that could have revealed the mole?

Hopefully, Declan and his crew would find something that would give them a place to start. Jack felt like he was striking out and, based on the texts, they were running out of time to locate and neutralize the Trinity assassin.

When they reached Anne's office, she waited until he'd entered and closed the door to the outer office and leaned against it. "I'm not cut out to do this," she said. "I'm not trained for this kind of thing."

Jack went to her, placed a finger over her lips and leaned close to whisper in her ear. "We don't know if this place is bugged. We should probably limit our conversations to your work."

She stared at him, wide-eyed, and nodded. "You're right. We should keep it…professional." Her voice faded and her gaze shifted from his eyes to his lips.

Jack should have moved away at that point, but he was so close now he could feel the heat of her body and smell the herbal scent of her hair.

Her tongue swept out to slide across her bottom lip. "We should get back to work," she whispered.

"Yes, ma'am." Still, he didn't move but leaned closer, his lips hovering over hers. "What is it about you that makes me want—"

A knock sounded on the door. "Ms. Bellamy, you have a visitor," Gina called out.

Jack backed away, cursing himself for losing control, yet again.

Anne's hand fluttered against her throat and then smoothed her hand over her jacket and skirt. "I'll—" she said, her voice coming out in a squeak. Clearing her throat, she tried again. "I'll be right out." Then she turned, yanked open the door and smiled at the visitor. "Dr. Browne, what brings you to see me?"

Remembering his duty to protect, Jack hurriedly stepped up beside Anne. "Dr. Browne, is it?"

The older man nodded, his brow puckering. "And you are?"

"Jack Snow, Ms. Bellamy's new assistant."

"My apologies, I should have introduced you two. Mr. Browne is our Russian special advisor. Please, come in." Anne stepped to the side, allowing Dr. Browne to proceed into the room. "It's a pleasure to see you."

Dr. Browne entered the office and paced across the room before he turned. "I came as soon as I heard about Dr. Saunders."

Anne nodded. "We heard, as well, and we're hoping she has a full recovery."

"As am I," the older gentleman said. "But I'm here because she was on her way to see me when she was struck down."

"Dr. Browne, you can't blame yourself for what happened to Dr. Saunders." Anne took the older man's hands.

He shook his head. "I'm not blaming myself. I'm concerned. She contacted me just before lunch. She said she had something she wanted me to look at, something that could have a direct impact on the upcoming NSC meeting."

Jack stiffened. "Did she say what it was?"

"No. She wouldn't tell me unless we could meet in person." Dr. Browne scrubbed his hand over his face. "I had scheduled another meeting for lunch. I was to meet her immediately following that, at the same restaurant." He hung his head. "She never made it. When I called her office, I heard what had happened and came immediately."

Chapter Six

Anne promised Dr. Browne she'd do her best to find out what Dr. Saunders had wanted to discuss with him. The man was so distraught he left the building, heading for his home in Arlington.

"What would Dr. Saunders have wanted to discuss with Dr. Browne?" Anne paced across her office and back.

"She was just leaving her office when I delivered the document to Carpenter," Jack said. "But she didn't say anything about meeting with Dr. Browne. If I recall correctly, she was heading to the director for Europe and Russia's office."

"I used to work in that office." Anne ran her finger down a list on her desk, lifted the phone and punched several keys. "I'd like to speak to Dr. Schuster."

Jack stood in front of her desk, waiting to hear her one-sided conversation.

"Dr. Schuster…"

"Oh, Anne, did you hear about what happened to Millicent?"

Anne nodded. "Yes, I heard. That's what I'm calling about. I understand she paid you a visit before lunch."

"Yes, yes, she did," Schuster said. "I asked her to come by. I had a message from the American ambassador to Russia that I'd hoped she could help me decipher."

"And what was that message, if you are at liberty to share?" Anne asked, looking up at Jack as she spoke. She met his gaze, holding her breath while she waited for the other man to speak.

"It was a short message the ambassador received from a Russian aid worker. But it didn't make much sense."

"Why didn't the ambassador clarify with the Russian aid worker?" Anne asked.

"He said he got the message via a social media photo. It was in Russian and cryptic. He said he normally didn't respond to social media, but the photo concerned him."

"Did you get the photo and the message?"

"We did, but that's what has us stumped. We had it, then it disappeared out of our emails."

"But Millie saw it before it disappeared?"

"Yes, she did. Then we heard about her accident. When we looked back at the email, it was gone. As if it never existed."

"Did you happen to print a copy of it?"

"We did, but Dr. Saunders took it with her. She couldn't make heads or tails of it, either, and wanted to meet with someone else who was an expert in Russian to see if they could figure it out."

"Do you remember what the message said?" Anne asked.

"Sure. Millicent translated it to *XC-16 Bringer of Death*."

"And can you tell us what the image was of?"

"The Russian aid worker took a photo of himself and a village behind him." Schuster paused. "It appeared as if there were bodies lying on the ground. The aid worker's eyes were bloodshot, and he was bleeding from his nose. I'm not sure what it was all about, but he didn't look well at all."

Anne shivered. "Did the ambassador know where the photo was taken?"

"He did not."

"Did the Russian aid worker identify himself?"

"No, he did not. He had a social media name, but it wasn't a typical name. He might have used it to disguise his identity. Posting the wrong thing on social media can get you in trouble in the US, but it can get you killed in Russia."

"If you hear anything else from the ambassador, or you think of anything else Dr. Saunders might have said about the message, will you let me know immediately?"

"Sure. You don't think the message had anything to do with Dr. Saunders's hit-and-run, do you?" Schuster asked.

"I really don't know. But it doesn't hurt to check into this message." She ended the call and went over the information with Jack. Then she called the office of Chris Carpenter, the homeland security advisor. "Chris, Anne Bellamy here. What hospital did they take Dr. Saunders to? I'd like to send her some flowers."

He gave her the name of the hospital. "We haven't heard anything about her condition. I've asked the nurse in ICU to notify us of any change."

"Let me know what you find out. And thanks." She placed the phone in the cradle, pushed to her feet, looped her purse strap over her shoulder and headed for the door.

Jack fell in step beside Anne as they left her office and walked down the long hallway to the exit. "Let me guess, we're going to the hospital to see Dr. Saunders, aren't we?"

She nodded. "I hope she's okay. If she's conscious, we need to ask her a few questions."

"If she's not?" Jack asked.

"We need to go through her belongings and see if we can find that printout."

Jack's lips twisted into a wry grin. "Now you're getting the hang of investigations."

"I don't like sneaking around, but I also don't like my friends being targeted by assassins." She stepped out smartly. "We have to determine what's so important people have to die to keep the secrets."

At a street corner, Anne raised her hand to hail a cab.

Jack slipped an arm around her waist and pulled her away from the street. "Let me. I don't want anyone aiming two tons of steel at you."

"What about you?" she asked.

"I can move a little faster." He tipped his gaze toward her feet. "I'm not wearing heels."

Anne liked the playful wink he gave her before he turned to wave down a taxi.

The taxi drove them to the hospital where Millie had been taken.

Once inside, they learned she'd just come out of surgery and was in a room in ICU.

Anne and Jack rode the elevator up to the ICU floor

and stopped at the nurses' station. "We're looking for Millicent Saunders."

The nurse glanced at the computer monitor in front of her without looking up. "She just got out of surgery and hasn't woken yet. Only relatives can visit. Are you relatives of hers?" At that point, she looked up, her eyes narrowing slightly.

Anne opened her mouth, but Jack jumped in before she could say anything.

"Yes, we are. Actually, Anne is Millie's first cousin, and I'm Anne's husband. The rest of Millie's family is in Georgia. They asked us to come check on her. They're arranging transportation to get here as soon as possible."

The nurse's brow lifted, and she smiled. "You're welcome to sit with her in her room. She won't wake any time soon. She suffered a concussion as well as internal injuries. They're keeping her under to give her a chance to heal." The nurse gave them the room number.

"What did they do with her personal effects?" Anne asked. "We might need to take her clothing home and have them cleaned or bring in fresh items. Did they bring her purse up with her?"

"All of her things are stored in a cubby in her room." A beep sounded behind the counter. "If you'll excuse me, I need to check on another patient." The nurse left her station and hurried to the room with a light blinking over the door.

Jack took Anne's hand and led her to the room the nurse had indicated.

Millicent Saunders lay comatose in a hospital bed covered in crisp white sheets and a blanket, with wires and tubes running from her arm and chest. The machine beside her bed emitted a steady beeping sound to the rhythm of her heart.

Millie's face and arms were scraped and bruised. As Anne stared down at her friend, her chest tightened and her fists clenched. "Whoever did this needs to pay."

"Agreed." Jack slipped his arm around Anne's waist, bent and pressed a kiss to the top of her head. Then he stepped away and searched the cubby where personal items were stored. "Here's her purse. Do you want to go through it?"

"Sorry to be digging into your things, Millie, but we have to find out who's responsible for what happened to you." Anne dragged her gaze away from the woman on the bed and joined Jack at the cubby.

After a few minutes of going through Millie's purse, they couldn't find anything suspicious or even interesting. Despite the purse having been flung with Millie across a road, it was still neat and organized. "Nothing."

Jack was searching through her pants pockets and then her trench coat. He pulled out a folded sheet of paper and smoothed it flat. "Bingo."

Anne looked over his arm at the grainy image of a man with red-rimmed, bloodshot eyes. In the background were bodies lying on the ground.

At the sound of wheels rolling to a stop in the hallway, Jack quickly slipped the printout into his pants pocket and Anne shoved the purse and clothes back into the narrow closet and closed it.

A nurse entered the room and smiled. "Are you relatives of Ms. Saunders?"

Anne's first instinct was to tell the truth, but she bit down hard on her lip and her cheeks filled with heat.

"Y-yes, ma'am," Jack answered.

"I'm just checking her vitals and IV. Can I get you two anything? Afraid all I can offer is a cup of ice water. There is a coffee machine in the lounge area down the hall."

"Thank you," Jack said. "We have to leave for a few hours, but we hope to be back soon. If she wakes, tell her that her loved ones were here."

"I probably won't be here." The nurse checked the IV drip, updated the chart on her laptop and looked up. "My shift ends in an hour."

"Will she be okay?" Anne asked.

"I'm not the doctor," the nurse said. "You'll have to ask him when he makes his rounds in the morning." She touched Anne's arm. "All I can say is that time will tell."

Anne and Jack left the hospital and flagged a taxi that took them back to the White House. By the time they entered her office, many of the West Wing employees were already on their way out, heading home.

"I need to check my emails and gather a few things, and I'll be ready to go."

"Take your time. I'll get our team moving on locating the guy." He unfolded the paper and spread it out on his desk. Then he took a photo image of the picture and texted it to Declan.

Anne logged into her computer and checked her email. She might as well have been gone a week, if the number of emails in her box was any indication. She stared at dozens of unread messages, most of them about the traffic accident involving Dr. Saunders, with a reminder to look both ways before crossing busy intersections. Anne quickly deleted those and searched for a message from Chris Carpenter. Though Millicent belonged to his department, he had promised in an email to get back to her with his input for the NSC agenda by the end of the day.

After a thorough search of her inbox, she sighed, finding nothing from Chris. Anne turned to the telephone on her desk, keyed Chris's number and waited for a response, hoping he was working late and that was why he hadn't gotten back to her.

His voice mail picked up after five rings.

"Chris, this is Anne Bellamy, I still need your input for the agenda. We finalize in the morning. Have a good evening." She ended her call, brought up the agenda, checked it against the messages that had come in, made minor changes and saved. Then she logged off the computer, looped her purse over her shoulder and turned to Jack. "I'm ready to leave when you are."

Once they were outside the building, Anne squared her shoulders. "I need to do something about my apartment. I can't just leave it like it is."

"Charlie has a lot of connections. Let's talk to her when we get back to the estate."

"We should have called the police and filed a report last night. I was just too shocked to think straight."

"After being chased and shot at, we couldn't stick around and wait for someone to pick you off." He gripped her elbow. "As it is, we're way too out in the open for my liking."

"I'm glad we left the office while there's still daylight."

"Daylight didn't help Dr. Saunders. It just made it easier for her attacker to hit her."

Anne's gaze darted left then right as they approached a crosswalk that would lead them through a busy intersection. They waited with a dozen other people. When the walking man sign lit up, everyone shuffled forward.

Anne hesitated.

Jack leaned close to her. "Just move quickly and be aware." With his hand at the small of her back, he hurried her through the intersection to the sidewalk on the other side. "Are you okay with the subway? We can stop at a café and wait for Arnold to collect us."

"No. The Metro makes more sense. I don't wish the traffic on anyone." With Jack at her side, Anne felt more confident they would make it back to the Metro station close to the estate unscathed. As many people as were riding the train heading out of the city, an attacker wouldn't have a chance to get to them or get away.

At least, that was what Anne hoped.

JACK STAYED ALERT throughout their walk to the Metro station, his gaze sweeping the crowd surging toward the mass transit. He watched for anyone who might be carrying a gun, a knife or any other kind of weapon. If someone stared too long at Anne, Jack was sure to block their access to her as they passed.

The Metro station posed more of a challenge as people crowded onto the platform and waited for the next train headed in their direction. As the crush move forward, Jack kept Anne in the curve of his arm, using his body as a shield as much as he could. He liked how she fitted perfectly in his arms, not too tall or short, but just right. With her forehead level with his mouth, he could easily have pressed a kiss to her temple.

Thoughts like that would get him killed. Not because Anne would hurt him for taking advantage of their nearness, but because it meant he wasn't paying close enough attention to his surroundings and the people populating it.

After all that had occurred the night before and what had happened to Dr. Saunders, Jack was surprised they made it into the train with no problems.

For the first several stops they stood, holding on to overhead straps. As people exited the train, they were able to find seats.

Jack pulled his cell phone from his pocket and texted Arnold the approximate time they'd be at the Metro station for him to collect them.

As he sent the message, another came in from an unknown caller.

Saunders was no accident.

Anne leaned over his arm and read the message. "It's her, isn't it?"

Jack nodded.

You're being followed.

Anne drew in a sharp breath.

Jack's glance shot up and he scanned the train car.

For the most part, the people appeared to be tired commuters on their way home.

The only people who stood out as different were the

guy wearing a headset with a hooded sweatshirt pulled up over his head and an old man with a scraggly beard, wearing a Fedora hat and carrying a cane. A woman with shoulder-length blond hair, wearing a classy gray suit, stood by the door, her head down as she thumbed the screen on her cell phone, probably catching up on her texts, email or social media. Another woman sat close to the exit door, her purse clutched beneath her arm, her gaze looking out of the train, her face reflected in the window. The rest of the people on the train wore business suits or business casual clothing and carried briefcases or satchels.

Jack leaned close to Anne and took her hand. "Be ready to move."

She nodded, her fingers squeezing his gently.

Keeping a close watch on the people in the train car, Jack rose to his feet, bringing Anne with him. He positioned Anne in front of him and they headed toward the car next to them, crossing through the connection.

As the train pulled into the station, Jack waited while everyone who was getting off did. Then, as others climbed aboard, he nudged Anne. "Get off."

She did and Jack followed right behind her. They walked alongside the train for several yards as if heading for the exit.

The man with the headset and hoodie had exited the train, as well as the old man with the cane and a dozen businessmen and women.

The signal that the train was about to leave the station sounded.

He leaned close to Anne's ear. "Ready to jump?"

She nodded.

"Go," he whispered. With his hand tight around hers, he stepped onto the train with Anne. The doors closed immediately behind them.

As the train pulled out of the station, Jack took note of the old man with the cane moving toward the exit. The young guy with the hooded sweatshirt stood next to the train, his narrowed gaze on the windows as they passed out of the station.

Anne held on to a metal pole, staring out the window until they'd left the station. Then she turned her gaze to the people in the car. "Do you think we shook him?" Just then, Jack's phone buzzed with a text.

Jack and Anne leaned over Jack's phone to read the text.

Good. You lost your tail.

Jack glanced around the train car and through to the next car.

Some of the same people were still on the train, including the blonde by the door and the woman clutching her purse.

Jack responded to the message.

Headset and hoodie or old man?

He watched the blonde staring at her cell phone. Her fingers didn't move.

The train pulled into another station and the blonde left the train. The reply came.

Neither. Man in dark suit, black running shoes.

"I didn't see him," Anne said, shaking her head.

Are you still with us? Jack typed.

For another long moment, she didn't answer.

Jack assumed she had been the blonde who'd gotten off the train and she was busy walking home, or to her next stop.

Still with you, but not for long.

Jack and Anne both looked up as the train slowed at their stop. They scanned the few remaining people going on to the next station along the line. But they didn't have time to study everyone to make a determination.

They had to get off.

Jack slipped an arm around Anne's waist and guided her off the train and to the exit.

Arnold was there with the car to collect them.

As he sat in the back seat, Jack closed his eyes, trying to recall the faces of the people on the train.

"Could she have been the woman sitting by the door with her purse clutched to her chest?" Anne asked, her thoughts running along the same lines as Jack's.

"Maybe she was the bearded man with the tweed jacket and thick glasses," Jack said. "She could have worn a disguise."

"Hiding in plain sight," Anne concurred.

"I'm not doing such a good job of protecting you if I can't figure out who the good guys are, much less the bad ones." He sighed. "We might have to switch this up and put one of the other members of my team with you."

Anne curled her arm through his. "I don't want

someone else. I'm just starting to get used to having you around."

"Yeah, but I can't risk losing focus. I should have seen the man following us before our anonymous spy pointed him out."

"How could we have known?" Anne asked. "A man in a black suit is like so many other men in black suits walking the streets of DC."

They pulled into the Halverson estate and wound through the trees to the sprawling mansion.

Declan met them on the stairs. "Charlie had a function to attend tonight. But you might want to see what we've found."

Jack was tired and would have liked something to eat, but the excitement in Declan's voice was hard to ignore. "Show us."

Declan led him through the foyer into the study and down the steps into the basement war room.

The rest of the team and Grace were gathered around Cole and Jonah, staring at the array of monitors. They glanced up when Declan, Jack and Anne entered the room.

"Look what we found on social media from a couple of days ago," Cole said, his face grim. He tipped his head toward the six monitors.

In one image, a woman wearing a dark headscarf held her lifeless child in her arms, her face contorted in grief.

In another photo, several bodies were laid out side by side on the ground.

At the same time as Jack saw the man in the third image, Anne gasped. "Isn't that the man in the photo

Millicent was carrying?" She pointed to the screen with the picture of a man wearing an aid worker's shirt, giving a child a shot in the arm. A line of men, women and children waited their turn behind the child.

"It looks like him," Jack said. He pulled the folded paper from his pocket and held it up to the screen.

Declan nodded. "We did a facial scan of the image you sent and found this man's photo taken in a small Syrian village a couple days ago. The time stamps on the others are a day or two after the image of him giving shots to the villagers."

Anne shook her head as she stared at the last three monitors. "Are all of those people dead?" she asked.

Declan nodded. "It appears so. And I don't see any sign of a bombing."

"Do you think the aid worker poisoned them?" Jack asked, studying the people in line for the shot. "He appears to be vaccinating them."

"We have a name for the man—Aleksandr Orlov. He's a Russian aid worker. We traced him to the village in Syria. We also found a report by the World Health Organization that they quarantined the village until they can determine why every person in the village died."

"An epidemic?" Anne asked.

"I spoke with a WHO rep late this afternoon," Declan said. "They don't know, and they're not taking any chances."

"We found something else." Cole touched a few keys and an article appeared. "We searched for Aleksandr Orlov and found a connection between him and this article about a new cancer vaccine being codeveloped between a Russian pharmaceutical company and one here in the US."

Cole moved his mouse and highlighted the US company's name—Waylon Pharmaceuticals.

"And get this," Jonah said. He clicked on his mouse and a city map overlaid the dead bodies. "Waylon Pharm is here in the metro area."

"Isn't it a stretch to think Orlov was testing a cancer vaccination on a Syrian village?" Jack asked.

"Probably," Declan said. "But if it's true, that's a good reason to stop Dr. Saunders from sharing the information with the NCS, which is due to meet in two days—if someone from the drug company wants to influence Russian sanctions, that is."

"That doesn't explain why someone was after Anne—Ms. Bellamy," Jack said. "She didn't know anything about the deaths in Syria until today. She was attacked yesterday."

Declan tapped his chin and stared at a far corner. "True. The two incidents seem unconnected. Ms. Bellamy's getting texts from someone who knows something about Trinity. That in itself is enough to trigger Trinity. They don't like it when they're outed. From what Jasmine says, they kill people who leak information. There are no second chances in their organization."

"Who's Jasmine?" Anne asked.

Jack nodded toward one of his teammates. "Gus Walsh's significant other. She's had some dealings with Trinity."

Anne frowned. "And lived to tell about it?"

Gus's lips twisted. "Sort of."

Anne's frown deepened. "What do you mean *sort of*?"

Jack shook his head. "It's a long story and one that can wait until we figure out what happened to Dr. Saunders, and the reason behind someone going after you." He turned back to the monitors. "What do the Saunders and Bellamy incidents have to do with each other?"

Declan sighed. "At this point, we don't know."

"Why would a Trinity dissident contact Ms. Bellamy?" Cole asked softly, as if to himself.

"Remember, the original message was her reaching out because Trinity was planning an attack that could impact a lot of people," Jack pointed out.

"Who are they attacking?" Declan asked.

"I assume since the message came to me," Anne said, "the attack has something to do with the national security advisor, the National Security Council, which includes the president and vice president, or anyone in the White House."

Gus snorted. "That narrows it down."

Jack tipped his head. "Now we're dealing with a hit-and-run of one of the people working with the Department of Homeland Security."

"Who was, by the way, chasing down something outside her area's responsibility," Anne reminded them.

"She was working with the director for Europe & Russia," Jack said.

Anne's lips twisted. "And she had scheduled to meet with a subject matter expert on Russia."

"About an incident that occurred in Syria," Declan added.

Cole tapped the monitor with Orlov's image. "An incident involving a Russian aid worker."

Jonah pointed to the article on the monitor. "And a potential cancer vaccination."

"And a whole lotta dead people," Jack finished, his tone flat. "Sounds like a lot of loose dots that may or may not be connected."

"I say we contact the pharmaceutical company and find out what their part is in the cancer vaccination," Anne said.

"I'm betting they won't tell you anything," Declan said. "Especially if their drug has caused the deaths of an entire village in Syria."

"Doesn't hurt to ask," Anne said. "What have we got to lose?"

"It'll have to wait until morning." Jack glanced at his watch. "They won't be open for business at this hour." He stepped away from the monitors. "Might as well have dinner and call it a night."

Cole and Jonah remained seated. "We'll dig into Waylon Pharmaceuticals and look for more about the XC-16 vaccine."

With the information they'd just received roiling around in his mind, Jack turned toward the exit to find Charlie descending into the basement war room.

"What did I miss?" she asked.

Chapter Seven

Anne stood back and listened as Declan's Defenders explained to their benefactor, Charlie, what they'd found and their plan for continuing their search through the internet and a proposed trip to Waylon Pharmaceuticals the following day. Her mind and heart felt bruised as she contemplated what they'd learned. Unscrupulous people were willing to test an anticancer vaccine on innocents. Cancer—it had killed her husband. She knew more than most the tantalizing hope a vaccine or cure could bring to millions. To have that hope twisted into this perversion was more than wrong. It was evil.

Charlie nodded. "Chef Carl has dinner prepared for you all. Please, come eat."

Anne's belly rumbled. The food they'd eaten at lunch had long since been converted into fuel and burned.

As they started up the stairs, Charlie waited for Anne to catch up to her. "What's on the agenda for the National Security Council this week?"

Anne stiffened. "I don't normally discuss the agenda with people outside work."

"Then answer this…is there an issue that could be directly impacted by recent events?"

Anne shrugged. "Almost anything can be directly impacted by the recent events. But I'll review the agenda once more to see if there is anything that is so controversial it warrants trying to kill a staffer in the West Wing."

"Good." Charlie said with a firm nod. "Politics can get downright bloody if you let them get out of hand."

Anne hid a smile. Charlie was opinionated, but she really cared about people, and wanted the best outcome for them.

"How did Mr. Halverson get involved with Trinity?" Anne asked.

Charlie shook her head. "I don't know. He wanted the best for the people who worked for him and he got involved with the political arena in Washington, DC. I think he was frustrated with the corruption and the fact politicians could be bought. I'm sure that when he discovered Trinity played a part in our country's leadership, he probably took it as a personal challenge to expose and eliminate their influence."

"I don't know why he asked me to keep an eye out for people who might be involved with Trinity." Anne laughed, though she saw no humor in the situation. "I work hard at my job and try to do things right for our leadership. I want what's best for our country."

Charlie draped an arm over Anne's shoulder. "That's why John chose you to help him. Your heart is in the right place. That's not always true for other members of our government."

"Why would this person who's texting me think I can help stop something horrible from happening? I'm not a trained military person. I don't know martial arts and I don't carry any kind of weapon."

"You're smart and you notice things. My husband obviously trusted you, and this person knows it. And you have the right people around you now who can have your back and provide that support you need when things go south." Charlie tilted her head back toward the war room. "Declan's Defenders are all good men. They fought for the country as Marine Force Reconnaissance and now as private citizens concerned for the well-being of their nation."

Anne nodded. "I don't know what I'd do if I didn't have Jack and his team helping me with this situation. Thank you for that."

Charlie hugged Anne briefly. "My husband would have wanted me to carry on his legacy. I only wish he'd involved me before his death. I'm playing this by ear. I have no idea how deeply he dug into Trinity. I assume it was deep enough to get him killed. Which leads me to think he struck a nerve. Someone in a position of power might have connections with Trinity and my husband was getting too close to the truth." Her lips formed a tight line. "I want to find the one responsible for putting a hit out on my husband. And when I do, I'm bringing him and his entire organization down."

Anne could feel the determination in the older woman's hold on her shoulders. If anyone could find the leader of Trinity, Charlie Halverson was the woman for the job. She had the right people working for her. It could be nothing more than a matter of timing, hard work and a little luck.

The entire team gathered around the enormous table

in the formal dining room of the Halverson mansion, along with Grace. Three other women joined them.

"Anne, you haven't met some of the other members of our little family here," Charlie said. "Riley Lansing is Grace's former roommate."

A petite woman with black hair and hazel eyes held out her hand to Anne. "I understand Snow is working with you to figure out who is texting you about a potential attack. I assume the target is the White House or the West Wing, since that's where you work." She shook her hand. "If there's anything I can do, let me know."

"Riley works at Quest Aerospace," Charlie said. "And she was trained to be a sleeper agent for the Russians."

Anne's eyes widened. "A sleeper agent?" She wondered if being in the same room with the woman compromised her own job.

Riley smiled. "My parents raised me that way, but I was a lost cause because I grew up in America. This is my country. Not Russia. I'm raising my brother here and want only the best for this place I call home."

"And you might not have been formally introduced to Mack Balkman." Charlie continued. "He's one of the Declan's Defenders who helped Riley recover her brother when he'd been kidnapped."

"Hi, I'm Emily Chastain." A pretty young woman with strawberry blond hair and blue eyes held out her hand. "I'm with Mustang. I teach Russian at the university. Mustang helped me when there was an incident at the Russian embassy. I wouldn't be alive today if he hadn't come to my rescue." She smiled up at the former marine with brown hair and brown eyes.

Mustang held out his free hand. "Frank Ford. But you can call me Mustang."

"I'm Gus." A black-haired man with deep brown eyes stepped up to her. He brought with him a woman with equally black hair and brown eyes. "This is Jasmine. Can we eat now?" He winked.

Jasmine held out her hand. "He's only this rude when he's hungry."

Anne shook the woman's hand, taken aback by how firm her grip was and how strong she seemed. "Are you the one who had dealings with Trinity?"

Jasmine shot a glance toward Gus, who held out a chair for her to sit.

He nodded silently and tipped his head toward the seat.

Jasmine shrugged and sank onto the chair. "Yeah."

The rest of the group took their seats.

Anne sat next to Jack, across from Jasmine and Gus. She unfolded her napkin and spread it across her lap before she looked directly at Jasmine, curiosity pushing her to speak. "Jasmine, would you have any idea why this woman who is texting me won't just come out and meet me face-to-face?"

The other woman's lips thinned. "If she's a former member of Trinity, her life is on the line. Usually, the only former members are dead members."

A chill rippled down Anne's spine. She reached for Jack's hand beneath the table and held on to it. No wonder her texting woman remained out of sight or in disguise. "How would she know what's going to happen at the White House if she's left Trinity?"

"From what Gus has told me, she doesn't know exactly what's happening, or if what was planned has changed," Jasmine said. "She could have been the one assigned for the attack and decided she didn't want to be a part of it. In which case, she knows they're going to make a move, but they would have changed when, where, how and who, based on her defection."

Anne nodded. "That makes sense. But why would someone come after me? I don't know anything."

"You're receiving texts from someone who might be a former Trinity assassin." Jasmine stared across the table at Anne. "They have a vested interest in finding your informant. They're probably hoping you can lead them to her."

Anne shivered.

Jack's hand tightened around hers.

Carl, the chef, brought out tray after tray laden with food. He'd prepared roast beef, potatoes and carrots along with freshly baked yeast rolls, asparagus and a pasta salad.

Talk about what had happened to Millicent and the close call on the Metro filtered around the room until everyone had a chance to fill their plates. Silence fell over the table as they ate the delicious meal.

When Carl returned to the table with crème brûlée, a collective groan sounded from the people gathered around.

When Jack passed her the dish, Anne stared at the dessert longingly but held up her hand. "I wish I could, but I can't. I'm completely full. I need to walk off what I've already eaten."

"Me, too." Jack's glance swept the gathering. "Please

excuse us. We're going to get some air and then call it a night."

Declan nodded. "I don't blame you. It's been an eventful day."

Jack stood and helped Anne to her feet, his hand settling at the small of her back.

She had to admit she liked how warm and comforting it felt. Even more, it caused a spark of desire to grow deep inside. A spark she hadn't thought she was capable of since her husband's death. Jack had changed that in just the day she'd known him.

As they started out of the room, Declan called out, "Gus and I will visit the pharmaceutical company tomorrow and let you know what they have to say as soon as we're done."

"Thanks," Jack said. "Good night."

Jack led the way to the study where a French door led out into a rose garden.

As soon as she stepped out of the house, Anne drew in a deep breath and let it out slowly. "Wow, Charlie has a great chef." She patted her belly. "I'll have to work out twice a day for the next month to make up for that."

"You don't have to make up for anything. You look like you need to put some meat on your bones."

She snorted softly. "Most women on Capitol Hill think you have to be model thin."

"You already are, and most people are wrong."

She laughed, the sound catching in her throat as a sob escaped. Anne pressed a hand to her chest. "Why is this happening to me? And poor Millicent…she didn't do anything."

He turned her to face him. "Did you think that it might be that you were meant for this mission?"

"But I'm not like you. I've never hit anyone in my life. I don't even like to squish bugs."

"If you didn't care, you'd have quit before we got started."

"How do you know? These people who are after my informant might have come after me anyway." She shook her head. "I can't help but feel I'm the wrong person for this job."

"I wish you weren't in this position." He cupped her cheeks in his palms and tipped her chin up. "Because it's so dangerous, not because I don't think you can handle anything thrown your way. I think you've held up remarkably well under the circumstances. No one knows how they will react when things go wrong, until those things go wrong. You're amazing. Taking it one step at a time…one breath at a time." He bent and pressed a kiss to her forehead. "I'm impressed."

She covered his hands with hers and turned her face into his palm, pressing her lips to his skin and loving the heat and strength of him. "I couldn't do it without you."

WHETHER IT WAS her soft cheek against his palm or the starlight shining down on them, Jack couldn't say which was more potent. Either or both had him lowering his face to hers, touching his lips to her soft mouth.

And he drank in her essence, filling his soul with her in his arms. He'd tried to resist, but he couldn't. She didn't realize just how strong she was. To every curve ball thrown her way, she'd reacted with speed and agility. This woman might not think she could handle what was happening, but she'd already proven she could. She was smart, pretty and determined.

Jack skimmed the seam of her lips with his tongue. When she opened to him, he swept in, took her in a long, sensuous caress.

Anne's hands slipped up his chest and into the hair at the back of his neck, pulling him closer.

She felt so warm and soft against him he could barely breathe.

He explored her mouth, then her cheek and the long line of her neck down to where it connected to her shoulder.

Jack wanted more, but they were out in the open. Anyone could look out the window and see them standing in the garden. This wasn't right. He shouldn't be kissing her. He was supposed to protect her, not take her to bed. But that was where he wanted her. In bed, naked and moaning his name.

Finally, he broke away and stepped back until his arms fell to his sides. "We should call it a night," he said, his voice husky, his heart pounding against the wall of his chest as if it was trying to escape.

She pushed her hair back from her face, her blouse stretching over her chest as she moved. Then she nodded. "You're right. We should." She turned toward the house.

Jack didn't move. He knew he should let her go to her room alone. That was the right thing to do.

When she turned back to him, she asked, "Aren't you coming?"

"I'm going to check on something before I hit the sack."

She nodded, her gaze lingering on him. Then she left him standing there in the starlight. Alone.

Jack waited until she was inside and safe before he turned his back to the house and closed his eyes. What was he thinking, kissing her? Didn't he know how this would end? If he got involved, she'd end up like the other women in his life he'd ever cared for. He could not let that happen to Anne.

Giving her a good ten-minute lead, he entered the house and retreated up the stairs to his bedroom, grabbed a pair of shorts and crossed the hallway to the bathroom.

After a cool shower that did nothing to quell his desire, he gave up and left the bathroom to return to his room.

As he reached for the door handle, the door beside his opened.

Anne stood in the doorway wearing an oversize T-shirt that came down to the middle of her thighs. Her eyes flared as she took in the fact he was only wearing shorts and carrying the clothes he'd changed out of.

She drew in a deep breath, stepped out of the doorframe and came to him. "Jack, I have no right to ask this… We've only known each other for a short time…" She stared down at her hands twisting together and then looked up into his eyes, her kiss-swollen lips parting. "What I'm trying to say is—"

Footsteps sounded on the stairs below.

Anne's eyes widened. She reached out, grabbed his hand and dragged him through the doorway into her room. Once they were both inside, she closed the door and leaned against it, staring up at him. "I really don't want to be alone tonight."

She stood before him, in that damned T-shirt, looking so vulnerable and sexy Jack couldn't think straight. If he had a functioning brain cell, he'd step past her and leave.

But he didn't…have a brain cell…he didn't leave.

He couldn't pull his gaze away from her long legs peeking out from under that T-shirt. "You don't know what you're asking," he said, his voice choked with desire.

A smile curled the corners of her lips. "Oh, I think I do." She held up her hands. "I'm not asking for forever. I don't expect commitment. I just don't want to be alone."

"You could ask one of the ladies to stay with you for the night," he suggested, though he really didn't want her to choose that option.

"I don't want one of the ladies to stay with me." She stepped toward him. "I feel safest when I'm with you." She took the clothes from his hands and dropped them on a chair. Then she laid a hand on his bare chest, her gaze following her fingers as she curled them into his skin. Her voice lowered. "But that's not all I feel." Then she lifted up on the tips of her toes and pressed her lips to his. "I feel warm…no…hot." She laced her fingers behind his head and pulled him down to her. "I can't unfeel that heat. It won't go away with a cool shower. I tried." She shook her head. "I can only think of one thing that will help."

His groin was so tight. His shaft pressed against her soft belly. He clenched his fists by his sides, afraid if he placed his hands on her, he'd be a goner. There would be no going back. "What will help?" he murmured against her hair.

She took his hands and wrapped them around her waist, shifting them lower to cup her bottom. "Just say you don't want me, and I'll leave you alone."

He chuckled. "Isn't that what I'm supposed to say?" Jack dug his hands into her flesh. She was so soft, but firm. As if of their own volition, his arms tightened around her, pulling her closer, crushing her slowly against his body.

"You…me…whatever feels right." She pressed her lips to the pulse beating wildly at his throat. "This feels right." She kissed his throat and traveled lower to press her lips to his collarbone. "And this."

Jack moaned. "You're killing me, Bellamy."

"As long as you let me, I'm going to do a whole lot more," she murmured against his skin.

"And I thought you were a proper businesswoman, all stiff and starched." He slid his hands lower, cupped the backs of her thighs and lifted her.

Anne wrapped her legs around his waist and rested her arms across his shoulders. "I'll take this as a yes."

"Yes, I'll stay with you. No, you don't have to commit. And maybe I'm interested in the whole lot more you alluded to." He kissed her lips, her eyelids and her cheeks as he walked her toward the bed. Then he leaned over, depositing her on the mattress, her legs draping over the side. Then he stared down into her eyes. "How far are we going?"

Anne pushed up on her elbows, a half smile lifting one side of her mouth. "All the way?"

He straightened.

Her brows dipped. "Am I being too forward? It's been a long time since I seduced a man."

"Let me guess…since you were with your husband?" He shook his head, turned away and reached for his pants. He prayed he had protection stored in his wallet. He hadn't been with a woman since he'd left the military. Hell, he hadn't wanted to be with a woman until now.

He fumbled with his wallet, flipped it open and let out a sigh of relief when he found the little packet tucked into one of the hidden pockets.

Hands circled him from behind.

He hadn't heard her move from the bed, but Anne stood behind him her front pressed to his back, and if he wasn't mistaken, she'd removed the T-shirt.

With a groan rising up his throat, he turned in her arms and held up his find. "We might be heading into wild and crazy territory, but not without firm roots in reality."

"Whew," she said on a sigh. "And I thought I'd blown my chances."

"I thought I was blowing mine, if I couldn't find one." He tossed the packet onto the bed and angled her chin upward. "Now, where were we?"

"You're overdressed," she whispered, her fingers sliding beneath the elastic of his waistband, pushing the shorts over his hips.

Jack took over and stepped out of his shorts, his shaft jutting forward.

Anne stood before him, wearing only a pair of lacy pink panties.

He raised an eyebrow. "Now who's overdressed?"

Anne slid her fingers beneath the elastic of her panties and dragged them very slowly over her hips and down her thighs. Then she kicked them to the side, lifting her chin at the same time.

With a beautiful, naked woman standing before him like a gift, all of Jack's patience flew out the window. He scooped her up in his arms and carried her to the bed. Depositing her on the mattress, he crawled up her body and leaned on his arms over her. "Who'd have thought you were a beast beneath that straitlaced suit?"

He bent to nibble on her earlobe.

"You should never judge a woman by the clothes she wears," she said, her hands sliding up over his shoulders to weave into his hair.

He claimed her sassy mouth with his and kissed her until he was senseless and eager to move on to tastier parts of her body. Starting with the long, slim line of her neck. He kissed a path over her collarbone and down to the swell of her right breast. For a long moment, he paid homage to the nipple, flicking it with his tongue and then rolling it between his teeth.

Anne arched her back off the bed. Her fingernails dug into his scalp every time he touched his tongue to the tight little bud of her nipple.

His shaft hardened, throbbing with his own need. But he wanted her to lose herself first. With that goal in mind, he moved to the other breast and treated it to equal torture and pleasure until Anne moaned softly beneath him.

With Anne thrashing against the comforter, Jack moved down her body, tonguing each rib and leaving a trail of kisses down to the tuft of hair at the juncture of her thighs.

As he cupped her sex, her fingers curled into the blanket and she drew her knees up, digging her heels into the mattress.

Jack loved that she gave herself with such abandon, her soft moans making him even hotter and eager to consummate their first time together. Parting her folds, he thumbed the strip of flesh between.

Anne sucked in a sharp breath, her body rocking with each stroke of his hand.

Replacing his thumb with his tongue, he swept across that nubbin of nerves and then flicked and swirled until she writhed beneath his mouth.

Her body grew rigid and she remained steady, her breath held and her fingers digging hard into his shoulders.

Then she was dragging him up her body, her hands sliding over his backside, feverishly stroking him. "Don't make me wait another minute," she growled. Her hand reached out to her side, slapping at the mattress until she found what she was searching for. She grabbed the little packet, tore it open and pulled out the little piece of protection.

Without missing a beat, she slid it over his staff and down to the base. "Now," she said. "Do it. Now."

Jack chuckled, though it cost him. He was so hard he could barely draw in a breath. He settled himself between her legs and nudged her with the tip of him. "Are you sure about this?"

"Oh for Pete's sake." She gripped his hips and pressed him into her, not slowing to accommodate his size, or to give herself a chance to get used to him. She slammed him all the way in, and held him there, her hands tight on his buttocks.

"Is that how you like it?" Jack bent to kiss her forehead as he pulled back.

Again, she brought him home. Then she settled into a rhythm, pushing him back and pulling him in.

Jack let her for a short time, holding back his own release. Then he took control, pumping in and out, loving the feel of her channel constricting around him. He made love to her until he pitched over the edge, his body stiffening, sensations rocking him in waves until he collapsed on top of her and rolled to the side.

For a long moment, he lay with her in his arms, his hand smoothing over the soft skin of her hip. "Wow," he said when he could get his vocal cords to respond.

"Wow," she echoed.

Then he laughed and she joined in, snuggling close to him, their connection unsevered.

Jack held her close, ignoring the nagging thought in the back of his head. He cared for her. And by caring for her, he'd doomed her, just as he had the other women he'd dared to love.

Chapter Eight

Anne slept soundly through the night, held close in Jack's arms, her body sated from the most incredible lovemaking she'd experienced in many years. Maybe ever. When her husband had fallen ill, their sex life had faded to nothing as he battled fatigue and worse. She hadn't realized how much she'd missed the passion, the heat. Not a single bad dream disturbed her slumber, and she didn't have to fight off any bad guys invading the room. When morning came, she opened her eyes, a smile on her face.

As she stretched, she realized that the body that had been spooned around her throughout the night was no longer there.

All grogginess disappeared, and she sat up, pulling the sheet up over her naked breasts. "Jack?" she whispered.

There weren't any places to hide in the room. It didn't have a connecting bathroom or a huge walk-in closet. Still, Anne rose from the bed, wrapped the sheet around her body and padded over to open the closet and look inside. He wasn't there.

Jack was gone.

Irritation warred with disappointment and a hint of fear.

Why had he left before she'd awakened? She would have loved snuggling a little before getting up for the day. Or, worse…had he been dissatisfied with her performance in the bed?

Anne found the T-shirt she'd tossed to the floor the night before and slipped it over her head. She gathered clothes and toiletries and hurried across the hallway to the bathroom. After a quick shower and even quicker work with the blow-dryer, she felt more like her stodgy self, dressed in a boring business suit, ready to go to the White House and get the rest of the agenda pulled together for the national security advisor to review and approve.

When she had that done, she'd meet with the police at her apartment and get that report filed. She couldn't live in Charlie's house forever. Eventually, she'd have to go home.

Home.

Her apartment had never felt less like home than at that moment. She wished Jack was there to wrap his arms around her shoulders and make her feel better instantly.

Convinced Jack had ducked out to avoid the awkwardness of the morning after, Anne left the bedroom where she'd had the most blissful sex she could remember. She cast one last glance at the neatly made-up bed that had been so beautifully used the night before.

With a sigh, she descended the sweeping staircase to the foyer and followed the sound of voices into the kitchen.

There she found Declan, Grace, Charlie and the chef, Carl. But no Jack.

"Jack went out for a run earlier. He should be back soon," Declan said. "We promised to keep an eye out for you."

"Thanks." Anne went directly to the coffeepot and poured a cup.

"It's Carl's day off, so we're fending for ourselves for breakfast," Charlie explained as she put two pieces of bread in the toaster. "I've been known to cook an egg or two. Can I interest you in an omelet?"

Anne shook her head, amazed that her billionaire hostess would offer to cook eggs for her. "I'll stick to coffee."

"Gus and I will go to the pharmaceutical company around ten this morning," Declan said. "We'll let you know what we learn when we do."

Anne nodded. "I need to file a police report about my apartment. I should have done it the day I found it. But better late than never."

"I'll call my contact in the police department and have them help you out," Charlie offered. "What time can you be there?"

"A little before noon. I want to be back at my desk after lunch. We have the council meeting tomorrow, and I need to be sure I've tied up all the loose ends."

"Are you at liberty to say what you'll be discussing?" Grace asked.

Anne shook her head. "The council can disclose that information if they choose in a news conference. It's not up to me."

Grace smiled. "I understand. I just thought maybe

whatever will be decided in the meeting might have something to do with why Trinity feels the need to cause trouble."

Anne stared at Grace, wondering if what she'd just said held the key to what had been happening with the texter who'd tried to warn her there would be trouble. If the agenda was the reason for the attack, what did Trinity hope to gain?

She'd have another look at the schedule and try to read between the lines of what would be under discussion. How could something on the slate make Trinity desperate enough to stage an attack? But then she hadn't received all the agenda items as of the end of yesterday.

Anne checked her watch. They needed to get going if they wanted to catch the Metro into the city.

"Arnold has the car out front," Charlie said. "He's ready to go whenever you and Jack are."

"Thank you." Anne set her coffee mug in the sink. "I just need Jack, and we'll be on our way."

"It's nice to be needed," a man with a deep voice said behind her.

Anne spun to face Jack, neatly dressed in his suit and tie, his hair damp from a shower and slicked back from his forehead.

Her heart beat hard in her chest and heat rushed up her neck into her cheeks.

His gaze met hers without mercy, a smile quirking one corner of his mouth.

Anne dropped her gaze first and looped her purse over her shoulder. She turned to Charlie with a smile pasted on her face. "Thank you for all you've done. I'll do my best to get my apartment in order. I can't keep taking advantage of your hospitality."

Charlie waved a hand in her direction. "Don't be silly. You're welcome to stay as long as you like or need. After all the damage that was done, your apartment won't be livable for a while. Speaking of which, I can have my handyman help you out."

"Thank you. That would be great. And I'll pay him to do the work. Again, I can't let you do everything for me."

"Humor this old gal." Charlie hugged Anne. "I'm being selfish. I get to have people around. It beats an empty house."

"You're not old." Anne smiled at the woman, grateful beyond words for what she'd done for her. "Thank you." She left the room ahead of Jack, headed for the front entrance, with purpose in her steps.

Jack caught up with her at the door and opened it for her. "In case you didn't hear me while you were sleeping, good morning, beautiful," he said, his tone rich, deep and sexy as hell.

Anne wanted to hang on to her irritation at being alone in the bed when she'd awakened.

As she passed him, he leaned closer, speaking in a tone only she could hear, "I had to go for a run. I get stiff if I don't exercise at least every other day." He tapped his thigh. "This old war injury gives me fits. And you were sleeping so well I didn't have the heart to wake you."

And like that, he wiped away her irritation. All she had left to cling to was her fear she'd somehow not measured up. After all, he'd left the bed before she'd known it, even if it was to go for a therapeutic run.

Anne didn't comment. What would she say? *Was I any good? Have you had better? What could I do different...assuming we were to make love again?*

She'd been the one to guarantee he'd have no obligation following that night. No commitment. Jack had been quick to agree.

Oh, hell, she didn't have time to worry about what a man thought about her sexual prowess. She had a life-and-death situation to contend with. If she lost her focus, she could end up run over by a vehicle like Millicent had been. Or have her neck snapped in a back alley by a Trinity assassin.

That thought shook her enough to bring her focus back to where it belonged. On the job ahead, not the man behind her.

As promised, Arnold was waiting at the bottom of the steps with Charlie's SUV.

Jack opened the back door for Anne and waited while she got in. Then he rounded the vehicle and climbed in beside her.

Arnold pulled away from the curb and started down the long, twisting driveway to the highway beyond.

Anne sat on her side of the vehicle, her hands in her lap, her gaze out the side window, trying to ignore how incredibly turned on she was by the man sitting beside her. And how nervous she felt about seeing him again after their incredible lovemaking. Well, it had been incredible for her.

She was so intent on looking out the window that she didn't actually see anything.

A hand closed over hers and squeezed gently. "Did I say something to make you mad?"

She started and would have pulled her hand free, but he held on. "No," she murmured.

He turned her hand over and traced the lines in her palm. "If I did, I'm sorry. You have no idea how hard it was to leave you in bed. I wanted to wake you up and make love to you all over again. But you were sleeping so well I couldn't do it."

Anne's heart swelled. "I wouldn't have minded missing a few minutes of sleep," she said softly, finally looking at him.

He sighed. "You had me worried. I thought you were going to hold me to the no-commitment, no-obligation theory when all I want to do is find the nearest hotel room and get naked with you."

Anne shot a glance toward Arnold.

Charlie's butler never glanced back in the rearview mirror. His gaze remained on the road ahead as they passed through the estate's gate and turned onto the highway.

For the rest of the ride to the Metro station, Anne clutched Jack's hand, her thoughts along the same lines as Jack's. Heat burned through her, coiling around her core. If she didn't get her act together, she'd end up in the hospital or the morgue.

But she couldn't bring herself to let go of Jack's hand until they arrived at the station.

Jack emerged from the vehicle first and looked around before he opened the door for Anne.

After being followed on their Metro ride the day before, Anne made a concentrated effort to study everyone standing at the platform waiting for the train.

When the train arrived, Jack held Anne's hand as they boarded the car and found a place to sit for the ride into the city. They exited at the Farragut West station and walked the rest of the way to the White House. Thankfully, though the clouds hung heavily over the city, the rain held off, allowing them to arrive dry at the West Wing of the White House.

Anne made it a habit to arrive thirty minutes to an hour early for work. The extra hour gave her time to determine where she'd left off and make her list of tasks to accomplish that day. By the time the majority of the White House staff arrived, she had her head on straight and was ready to tackle any problem that might crop up during the day.

She checked her computer inbox for Chris Carpenter's input for the NSC agenda. As he'd promised, his email was waiting for her. She opened it and transferred his changes to the official agenda. When she'd adjusted it to the correct format, she spent a few minutes going over the outline of what was to be discussed with the president, vice president, secretary of state, secretary of defense, secretary of treasury, national security advisor and director of national intelligence.

The usual border control issues, upcoming foreign dignitary visits and military deployment decisions were listed along with discussions concerning various nations that might impact national security. They would hear from the director for Asia on the changes to trade agreements. The director for Europe and Russia would speak on imposing sanctions on Russia for human rights violations in Crimea, Syria and other countries Russia had a presence in.

The agenda didn't appear much different from the last time the NSC had met. Some problems never seemed to go away or get resolved.

After going over the document three more times, Anne printed a copy and carried it to the office next to hers, where Shaun Louis, the national security advisor, worked. She glanced at Gina, the staffer seated at the desk in front of the NSA's office. She was the first line of defense to keep people from interrupting Shaun. "Is he in?"

She nodded and held her fingers up to her ear, indicating he was on the phone.

Knowing he wanted the slate as soon as it was ready, Anne tapped softly on the door and poked her head through.

Shaun was still on the phone.

Anne held up the document and waited for him to acknowledge her.

He waved for her to enter.

She handed off the paper and left the room. Barring any major changes, the slate was ready for the next day's meeting of the National Security Council.

Anne hurried back to her office, closed the door and went to work. It wasn't until later she remembered to call the police.

When she did, they put her on hold.

"I take it you're ready to deal with your apartment?" Jack asked quietly. He'd removed his jacket and rolled up his sleeves to work at the computer, digging through whatever files he could tap into.

She nodded. "I have to get started on the cleanup. I don't like relying on others as much as I have with Mrs. Halverson."

"Ms. Bellamy? This is Detective Hutcheson. Mrs. Halverson gave us the heads-up that you'd be calling. I've been assigned to your case. What time would you like to meet?"

"Within the next thirty minutes if at all possible," Anne glanced at her watch, surprised at fast the morning had flown. "I'll take a long lunch, but I need to get back to work."

"That's perfect. I was going that direction for a meeting after lunch. I can be there in thirty minutes."

"Thank you." Anne ended the call and stared at Jack. "We'll need to get moving if we want to catch a train that direction."

Jack had already rolled down his sleeves and buttoned them. He shrugged into his jacket and smoothed a hand over his hair. "Let's go."

Anne led the way from the office down the hallway to the exit.

They didn't take long getting to the Metro station and a train happened along at that moment, going in the direction they needed.

Once on board, Anne stood near a door, her hand on a pole to keep her balance. She leaned close to Jack. "See anyone suspicious?"

He smiled. "I'm not even sure I could pick out the bad guys at this point."

Anne snorted. "Me, either."

Fortunately, they weren't accosted, and they arrived

at the station close to her apartment complex. Once off the train, Anne hurried along the sidewalk.

As they reached the building, an unmarked dark sedan pulled into the parking lot. A man stepped out, wearing a charcoal gray blazer, black polo shirt and trousers. He pulled a notepad out of his pocket and looked down at it before glancing up at the building.

"Detective Hutcheson?" Anne asked, closing the distance between them.

The man turned and held out a hand. "That's me. You must be Ms. Bellamy."

She shook his hand. "This is Jack Snow, my…"

"Boyfriend," Jack interjected and shook the detective's hand. "Thank you for coming on such short notice."

"It's not a problem," Hutcheson said. "Mrs. Halverson has been such a help to the department I'm only happy to return the favor." He nodded toward the building. "I understand the break-in happened two nights ago?"

Anne nodded. "It did. I haven't had time to do anything about it. Work has taken up most of my time."

"Understandable. But the longer you delay the investigation, the harder it is to find the culprit," the detective said. "Show me."

Anne led the way to her door and unlocked it. Then she stood back and let the detective enter. The place was as she'd left it two nights ago. And she had the same reaction to the destruction as she had the first time she'd seen it. She rested a hand over her belly, feeling as if she'd been sucker punched. Her place of solace was now chaotic and destroyed. She began to think she would never feel safe there again.

Jack slipped an arm around her waist and pulled her against him.

They spent the next half hour answering questions for the detective. Anne told him about the man who'd followed her from work that night and how she'd ducked into the pub and waited for Jack to come get her. She didn't mention the text she'd received that day or the ones she'd received since.

After the detective left, Jack took her key from her and locked the door to her apartment. "Why didn't you tell him about the texts?"

"If our informant doesn't want to be identified, I'm not going to bring her up. She was there for us on the train last night. I could be wrong, but I feel like she's a bit of a guardian angel looking out for us."

"What if she's the one causing all the trouble?" Jack asked.

Anne shook her head. "I don't think she is. Call it intuition, or stupidity. I don't think she's the one who tried to grab me the other night, nor was she the one to destroy my apartment. I think whoever has been bothering me might want to get to her."

Jack took her hand and squeezed it gently. "I really hope you're right."

Anne prayed she was, too. She didn't want either one of them to be hurt because she'd trusted someone she had never seen or met.

Chapter Nine

Just as they reached the Metro station, Jack's phone buzzed in his pocket. He pulled it out to read Declan's name in the caller ID screen. He hit the talk button. "What did you find?"

"It took some finagling, but we finally got in to talk with the director of research and development who is overseeing the cancer vaccination project."

Jack came to a stop inside the station, his gaze searching the platform and the people standing there waiting for the next train. "And?"

"He said he couldn't go into too much detail about the XC-16 vaccine. They'd been working on it for the past two years, getting closer than they've ever gotten before. The vaccine triggers the immune system to kill cancer cells, which was a great step forward. But experimenting on mice proved to be deadly for the mice. Even at extremely low doses, the mice died within hours of receiving the vaccination."

"So the serum killed cancer, but killed the patients, too?"

"Exactly. The drug was deemed too dangerous to experiment with on human subjects. They made some changes to the formula and they had some better results. The mice didn't die as suddenly. They lived at least a week before they started showing signs of decline. Ultimately, the experiments were thought to be a failure, as the mice died anyway."

"What did they say about the man in the picture? Do they think the man in the photo might be using one of their vaccines?" Jack asked.

Declan snorted. "The director said no one had authority to test the XC-16 vaccine on humans. They're using nanotechnology to deliver the vaccine into the patient's system and it's considered unstable at this time. In fact, the program had been put on hold until they could figure out what was killing the mice they'd used as test subjects. The researcher in charge of the program was laid off until further notice."

"Did you get the name of the researcher?" Jack asked. "Maybe we can learn more from him. He might be more likely to spill information since he's been laid off."

Declan chuckled. "We did. His name is Leon Metzger." He texted the man's address to Jack. "We planned on going there next."

"Hang on while I look at the location." Jack pulled the phone away from his ear, put it on speaker and stared down at the text. The address came up and he clicked on it, bringing up the map on his phone.

Anne leaned over his shoulder. "That's not far from here. It's close to the next stop. I almost rented a condo in that area."

Jack glanced at his watch. "Do you have time to swing by there?"

Anne nodded. "As long as we get back to my office before two o'clock."

"I think we can make it. Did you hear that, Declan? We're only about a five-minute train ride to that location. We'll swing by."

"Good, because it'll take us at least thirty minutes fighting traffic. Let us know if he's there and we can meet you there."

"Roger," Jack said and ended the call.

The train rolled into the station and they boarded.

When they got off at the next stop, Jack used the GPS directions on his phone to get them to the row of condominiums where Metzger lived.

"Fourth door on the left," Jack said.

Anne pressed the doorbell.

Jack could hear the echo of the bell inside the hallway. No one came to see who was there.

Anne pressed it again.

Jack heard another sound coming from the garage attached to the condo. He stepped close to the garage and pressed his ear to the overhead door. The hum of an engine sounded inside. Why would someone have his car engine running with the garage door closed? As soon as the thought entered his head, he knew something wasn't right.

Jack tried the front door, but it was locked. He ran around to the back of the building and counted to the fourth back door and tried it. Not wanting to leave Anne alone for too long, he hurried back around to find her standing on her toes, looking into the window of the condo.

"I don't see anyone moving around inside."

"I think it's because whoever lives here is in the garage, with the car running," Jack said, his face grim.

"That would be stupid. He could die of carbon monoxide poison—" Anne's eyes widened. "Oh, dear."

"Call 911. I'm going to break a window to get inside."

"Calling," Anne said. "Hurry."

Jack grabbed a landscaping brick and threw it into a window on the first floor. The glass shattered, leaving a large hole.

Using a stick, Jack broke away the remaining shards of glass, ducked through the window and ran through the kitchen to the door leading into the garage.

He could smell the sulfurous smoke before he opened the door. A white sedan stood where the owner parked it, the engine running. Inside, slumped over the wheel was a man in a gray T-shirt, his face pale and waxy.

Jack pulled his shirt up over his nose, slammed his hand onto the garage door opener and yanked open the car door.

The man behind the wheel slumped sideways. If Jack hadn't been there to catch him, he would have fallen out of the car.

Grabbing beneath the man's shoulders, Jack dragged him from the car and out of the fume-filled garage into the open air and laid him on the grass.

"The fire department is on the way," Anne said, slipping her phone back into her purse. Her brow pinched. "Is he…"

Jack felt for a pulse at the base of the man's throat. "I don't feel a pulse and he's already cold. I'd say he's dead."

SIRENS SOUNDED IN the distance, getting louder as they moved closer. A red truck pulled into the condo driveway, red lights blinking from its roof. Emergency medical technicians jumped down from the truck, grabbed their gear and ran toward where Jack and Anne stood. The first one there dropped to his knees, felt for a pulse and frowned. He pulled out a stethoscope and pressed it to the man's chest. He shook his head, folded his stethoscope and stuffed it into his pocket.

Anne held her breath, wishing the man would find a pulse, knowing he wouldn't.

A police cruiser pulled to a stop beside the fire truck and, a minute later, an ambulance arrived.

For the next thirty minutes, Jack and Anne answered the questions they could, and waited for the police to clear them to leave. Eventually, Leon Metzger's body was loaded into the ambulance and carried away to the morgue.

Anne had her own set of questions, but Jack had stepped away while the techs worked on Metzger and called Declan, who assured him they'd look into this incident immediately. For the time being, they had to be patient.

Anne and Jack walked to the Metro station and caught the train back to the Farragut West station. They found seats near the back of the car and sank into them.

"You think it was suicide?" Anne asked softly.

"We won't know until they do the autopsy."

Anne wasn't sure, but her gut was telling her it wasn't suicide. "He didn't look like someone who was going to commit suicide. He looked like he was going for a date or something."

Jack nodded in agreement. "Metzger didn't look like he was ready to die. He was dressed in his best, with the scent of cologne lingering on his skin, like he was trying to impress someone." He lowered his voice. "And I noticed something on his kitchen calendar when I ran through there. He had a vacation coming up. Bermuda in big capital letters. He was looking forward to the future."

"Why would someone want to kill a research scientist?" Anne asked.

"Better question is—" Jack glanced toward her "—who had something to lose if he talked about his research with the cancer vaccine?"

Anne's eyes narrowed. "The company developing it?"

"You heard what the program director said," Jack said. "They put the project on hold until they could figure out what was killing the mice. They went as far as laying off some scientists."

"You think he took his research elsewhere?" Anne asked.

"It's possible. But he'd have to take it a lot farther than in the same country where the scientific community speaks the same language." Jack's brow furrowed. "You have to know they talk to each other."

Anne stared at the back of the seat in front of her. "Some place like Russia? And they used the vaccine on the people in that Syrian village, because they would trust anyone to help them when they needed help most." She shook her head, her stomach roiling at the senseless murders. "They experimented on those people." She pressed her knuckles to her lips. "They killed everyone in that village, including the children."

"We don't know that for certain. This is all circumstantial at this point. Until the World Health Organization can get in there and test some of the bodies, we won't know anything."

Anne nodded. "You're right. At this point, all we can do is guess at what's happening. In the meantime, I have tomorrow's NSC meeting to prepare for. I should be getting the finalized agenda back from the national security advisor. Then I need to update the briefing slides and stage them for tomorrow morning. The president hates to be kept waiting on technical glitches."

"Then we just have to make sure there are no glitches. Are you in charge of the audiovisual equipment?"

"No, but I help the guy who is. Terrence Tully is our conference room facilitator. He makes certain the conference room is in perfect order, there are seats for everyone invited to speak and drinks for everyone. He sets up the audiovisual connections and loads the briefings. I'll be there to make sure all the images come across correctly."

"That means we have to be at the office early tomorrow." He didn't ask the question. He stated a fact.

Anne was always extra early on NSC meeting day. "Right. I'll want to be even earlier than we were this morning."

"I can do early," Jack said.

The train came to a stop at the Farragut West. Jack took Anne's arm and helped her out of the train and through the exit into the late afternoon sunshine. "We missed your two o'clock deadline," Jack said as they entered the West Wing.

"I'm not sweating it. I only set the hour as something to aim for. I can stay as late as I need to. We'll see how many changes Shaun came up with. That will determine how late I'll be here."

"Anything I can do to help...let me."

She gave him a weak smile. "I will." Anne paused outside the door to the NSA office suite, hesitating before diving in. "I admit I've never seen a dead body up close and personal like that."

"You never get used to it," Jack said. "It's hardest when you knew the guy."

Anne shot him a glance but didn't question him. He didn't need her forcing him to relive something as catastrophic as losing a friend in battle.

As soon as she stepped through the door, Anne was hit by one request after another.

Shaun had her in his office going over the last-minute fixes to the agenda and the images he expected to use for his portion of the briefing.

"Who put the question of Russian sanctions on the agenda?" he asked.

"Chris Carpenter."

"We settled that a couple months ago. Why does he insist on rehashing it?"

Anne didn't speculate. Chris had his reasons. It wasn't her place to question them. The council would decide what was important and assign taskings to different government bodies to accomplish what they wanted done. She sat in the meetings on rare occasions if they wanted someone to clarify an issue. Normally, she was simply moral support. But sometimes she provided valuable background information if members had questions.

Anne checked the entire slate and researched all the issues in order to advise the NSA so that he might brief the president. Shaun didn't necessarily need her advice, but he liked to bounce ideas off her. She figured it was one of her job duties to listen to her boss's thoughts and ideas. He was the one who had to present to the president, vice president, the chief of staff, and other members of the council.

Once she had all the changes incorporated on the slide presentation, she saved a copy to her desktop as backup and moved another copy into a file they used specifically for the council meetings. Terrence would know where to go to get the presentation and Anne would be there to double-check the right document was loaded.

Once she'd completed setting up the agenda and the supporting documents that Shaun might need, she poked her head back into her boss's office. "Do you need anything else?"

He was on his feet, slipping into his suit jacket. "No, thank you. I have another meeting to attend tonight. I'll be in early tomorrow morning."

"Have a good evening, Mr. Louis," she said.

"And you." He paused as he passed her. "Anne, is there anything else going on with you?"

She looked at him in surprise. She'd been working hard every day to get this meeting arranged. Anne prided herself on keeping her emotions to herself. She didn't like weak or whiny women, and in keeping with that, she refused to be one of them. "No, sir. Why do you ask?"

"You seem to be distracted. I hope you aren't experiencing any problems outside of work."

Anne bit down hard on her tongue to keep from telling her boss everything that had gone wrong over the past few days. But she stopped herself in time. Shaun didn't need to know her life was getting more complicated by the minute and that she had an assassin after her. "No, sir. Everything is perfect." A perfect mess. She pasted a smile on her face. "Have a good evening."

"You'd tell me if something isn't right in your world, wouldn't you?" he persisted.

"Yes, sir," she said, holding up her hand as if swearing an oath, though she was lying through her teeth. She didn't like telling untruths, but sometimes a person didn't need to share even a small portion of her life with her colleagues. Her boss had much bigger issues to concern him. The safety of the nation was far more important.

The text messages she'd been receiving could be hoaxes, for all she knew. She had yet to identify the person who'd sent them. Not one of the Secret Service staff had received anything indicating a threat to the president, vice president or any other member of the council. If they had, the meeting would have been postponed and everyone in the White House would have been warned.

Should she have raised an alarm when she'd received the first volley of messages?

Her boss continued on toward the door.

"Mr. Louis," Anne blurted out.

"Yes, Anne?" he said and turned to face her, his eyebrows cocked.

The words she knew she should say lodged in her throat. Finally, she forced air past her vocal cords. "Have a nice evening, sir."

Shaun's eyes narrowed slightly, and for a moment, he looked like he wanted to say something, but he didn't. "Thank you," he said and left.

Anne let go of the breath she hadn't realized she'd been holding and walked back into her office. Once she shut her door, she paced the length of the room.

Jack rose from where he'd been seated and crossed the room to stand in front of her. "What's wrong?"

She shook her head. "I'm not cut out to be a spy."

"You don't have to be." He held open his arms.

Anne sucked in a deep breath, fighting the urge to take advantage of his offer to comfort her. She had been at this job long enough to know right from wrong. At that moment, she was almost convinced she'd been wrong to keep a potential threat from the others working in the West Wing. "I should tell someone that something bad might happen soon."

He dropped his arms to his sides. "Do you know for certain when and where?"

"No." She huffed out a frustrated breath and held out her hand. "Give me your phone. It's about time we got some answers from our text woman."

JACK HANDED OVER his cell phone and waited while Anne keyed in a text to the mysterious woman who'd been less than helpful in their search for answers.

Anne hit the send button and looked up. "Now we

wait and see if she actually responds. Telling someone there's going to be trouble without giving any specifics is almost worse than letting them be surprised."

"I disagree. At least we're not blind sheep being herded over a cliff. We are aware and watching." Jack wished he'd found more information through his search of the West Wing database he had access to. Nothing had seemed to stand out.

Cole and Jonah were in a better position to cybersnoop. With the ability to hack into many different government and corporate databases, they could get in and get out without being detected.

As the new White House staffer, Jack would be easily detected. He suspected that anyone in the White House with connections to Trinity would be extra careful about contact with them. They wouldn't use their government computers or the cell phones they used for work. That kind of sloppiness could get someone killed.

He looked over Anne's shoulder at the words she'd typed to the woman who'd been texting.

Tomorrow is a big day, lots of targets in the NSC meeting. Need help. Can you give us any more specifics?

After a minute passed, Jack began to think their texter wasn't online. After three minutes, he shook his head. "We might as well call it a night. Tomorrow will be an early day."

Anne nodded and stepped close to Jack. She reached around him and turned on a small desk fan before she spoke, creating noise to drown out her words. "She might not contact us while we're here. We don't know what kind of surveillance equipment is employed within these walls."

Jack nodded, inhaling the fragrance Anne used. Or was it the fresh scent of her shampoo? Whatever it was, it was intoxicating.

She stepped away and gathered her purse.

Jack slipped into his jacket and they left the office and the West Wing of the White House.

The evening crush of people hurried toward the Metro in their mad rush to get home.

Jack kept a close watch on Anne, afraid someone would make a move while she was buried in a sea of humanity. If someone was to attack, now would be the time. It was too dangerous. He gripped her arm and pulled her into one of the cafés along the way.

She looked up at him, a questioning expression on her face.

"I couldn't protect you from everyone," he whispered. "We'll wait until the crowd thins out before continuing on."

Anne nodded and looked around at the little restaurant. "We could go ahead and have dinner here. By the time we get back to the estate, it will be late."

"I'm all for it." He grinned. "We were so busy at lunch we never stopped to eat."

Anne pressed a hand to her belly. "That must be why I'm so hungry."

They waited to be seated by the hostess and looked at the menu.

Jack studied Anne across the table. He could imagine this as a real date. They sat in companionable silence, comfortable in each other's company. He wouldn't consider her unconventionally beautiful with her straight black hair and blue eyes. But her true beauty came from her intelligence, compassion and life experiences. This was a woman who, despite the trying circumstances, forged ahead and went to work, instead of cowering in a corner, afraid to live because someone was after her.

As they waited for the waitress to return, Jack reached across the table and captured Anne's hand. "You amaze me."

She appeared clearly startled by his touch and words. A smile quirked upward on one side of her mouth. "Why do you say that?"

"You've been nothing but a trouper through this whole ordeal."

She snorted softly. "I'm only as strong as the man who's been by my side practically from the start." Anne squeezed his hand. "I couldn't do this without you."

He shook his head. "I believe you could."

"Well, I'm glad I don't have to." For a long moment, they held hands across the table.

Like a couple.

For the first time in a long time, even though he knew it put Anne in jeopardy, Jack wished this relationship would continue after they resolved the danger.

His phone vibrated in his pocket, jerking him back to reality. He dug it out and stared down at the text from their informer.

Be at the movie theater on 6th and H Street for the 7:35 showing.

Along with the text was an attachment with two tickets to *Godzilla*.

Chapter Ten

They didn't have a moment to digest the information before the waitress arrived with their order. Having barely touched her salad, Anne felt bad that she'd left so much of the delicious meal on her plate. The thought of meeting with their informer face-to-face for the first time had her stomach knotted and her anxiety level at a fever pitch.

Jack leaned toward Anne. "I have to admit I'm worried."

"You're worried?" She laughed, the sound fading off. "Me, too."

"All the what-ifs are going through my mind." He pulled his phone out of his pocket and hit a button.

"Who are you calling?" she asked.

"Declan." He waited for the connection. "Hey. We have a situation." He gave his team lead the information they'd been given and the location of the theater, speaking in a soft tone that wouldn't be overheard. "No, it's the first time she's offered to meet with us. We need more information than what we're going on. We're going." He nodded.

Anne wished she could hear what Declan was saying. If they weren't in a public place where someone could eavesdrop on their conversation, she'd have Jack put the phone on speaker. But there were still too many people around. People who could be waiting for the opportunity to catch their informer. She stared at the man sitting alone at a table in the corner, reading a newspaper. Anne's eyes narrowed. Or was he?

"Thank you," Jack was saying into his phone. "We'd appreciate the ride." He ended the call. "Declan's coming with Arnold to give us a ride back to the estate after our rendezvous. They'll be here in forty-five minutes or less and wait for us to signal for them to come."

Anne let out a long breath. "It's good to know they'll be here as backup."

He looked at her through troubled eyes, his brow creased.

"What?" she asked, knowing something was bothering him.

"I want Arnold to take you back to the estate. I'll handle this with the team."

She stiffened. "No!" Her heart beat fast at the possibility that Jack might be going into harm's way, and she wouldn't be there with him. "The informer expects to see me with you. If I'm not there, it could go wrong."

"It could go wrong regardless. And I won't let you get hurt," he said, his voice tense.

She touched his arm. "I know you won't. I know you'll protect me. But if we don't do this right, I could be in danger for a lot longer." She squeezed his arm. "Let's just get this over with and see what happens."

"I don't like it," he said.

"I'm sure you don't," Anne said, her jaw firming. "But I'm going. With or without you."

THEY STAYED AT the café until just before time for the designated movie showing. Thankfully, the theater wasn't far from where they were. They could walk the few blocks and arrive in time for the movie.

Jack walked alongside her, his hand protective at the small of her back. Darkness settled in around them. The streetlights flickered on, one by one. "Is this what it would feel like to go on a date with you?" Jack asked. She suspected he was trying to ease her tension.

Anne laughed, the effort helping to calm her nerves only slightly. "I hope not. I'd like to think going on a date with me wouldn't include the threat of being mugged, shot, or run over by a vehicle." She glanced around, looking for any of the threats mentioned. "Why? Are you going to ask me out on a date?"

"The thought crossed my mind," he said, his tone light, his gaze scanning the street, sidewalk and alleys all around them.

Warmth filled Anne's chest. In all the craziness, this man was thinking about asking her out. "If you did ask, I might say yes." She slipped her hand through his arm. It almost felt like they were going on that date. Except for the nagging fear of someone watching them, possibly lining them up in their crosshairs.

A shiver rippled down the back of Anne's neck. That feeling of being watched increased until she felt as if she needed to spin around, run or throw herself on the ground, out of whatever line of fire.

But nothing happened. No one jumped out to nab or

stab her. Bullets didn't fly out of the darkness and they arrived in time for the movie at the designated theater.

Using the digital tickets that had been sent to them via text, they entered the theater and Jack walked her past the theater room listed on the ticket.

"Why aren't we going in?" Anne asked in a hushed tone.

"I wanted to make sure no one was following us." He entered the next door, paused just inside and waited.

When no one followed, Jack took Anne's hand. "Okay, let's meet our text girl." He left the wrong theater and entered the correct one. Once inside, he glanced up at the seats. The lights had already been dimmed for the advertisements. There was enough of a glow from the screen to see which seats were filled and which were empty.

"Let's sit in the seats near the top." Anne liked the idea of having her back to the wall, from where she could see everyone entering and leaving the theater.

"Though I like the idea of having my back to the wall, I'd feel better if we sat near the exit, closer to the middle."

Anne agreed with his logic and they chose a couple of seats on the end of a row, near the exit. As she walked up to her seat, she counted the number of people in the theater. Since it was a weeknight, there weren't many. Most of them were probably tourists who didn't have to go to work the next day. A family of six sat near the back of the room, while several older couples sat in a group near the front. A young couple sat close together, holding hands and sharing a bucket of popcorn. There were more people, who appeared equally innocuous.

Where was their texter girl?

Once Anne took her seat, she couldn't watch the people behind her, which made her feel exposed.

Jack sat a little sideways in his seat, as if looking at her. Anne did the same, looking at him. That way they could see a little to the side and back of them and cover each other's blind spots.

As the time for the movie grew closer, more people drifted in. Some climbed to the top, while others took seats in the middle and lower rows.

A family of five entered the theater and chose the row directly in front of Jack and Anne. They all moved to the center, except the teenager wearing a baseball cap, his shoulders slumped. He sat a couple seats away from the rest and hunkered down. It put him directly in front of Anne.

Anne glanced around. Why had the teen chosen that particular seat? Their informer might come in, see someone too close and move on, afraid of being overheard.

She couldn't do much about it and it was too late to move. The film credits rolled onto the screen and the movie started. The teen chose that moment to stand and walk to the back of the theater, probably to get even farther away from his family, as teens were like to do.

Anne breathed a sigh and relaxed, or tried to, beside Jack, her attention on the people in the room as the giant monster proceeded to crush and destroy everything in its path.

Twenty minutes into the movie, Anne had begun to give up hope that her informer had actually shown up.

Then the images on the screen turned dark until

the theater was almost pitch-black. The moviegoers all seemed to be holding their breath, waiting for the monster to jump out and scare them. When it did, people in the theater screamed and laughed at their own jitteriness. The monster roared, and noise filled the auditorium.

"Anne." A soft voice sounded next to Anne's right ear. When she started to turn to see who it was, the voice continued. "Don't look. I don't have much time. They followed me into the theater. It's only a matter of time before they find me."

"Who followed you?" Anne asked.

"Trinity."

A cold shudder shook Anne's body.

"Why are they after you?" she whispered between the roars of the monster.

"I was one of them. But I'm not anymore."

"I thought they didn't let anyone leave," Jack said, keeping his gaze forward on the screen.

"They don't. You're in for life. I'm trying to avoid the other alternative." She touched Anne's shoulder. "I'm sorry I got you into this. They're after you two now because of me."

"What does finding you have to do with what's happening at the White House?" Anne asked.

"I caught wind of some of their plans."

"What plans? Who are we dealing with? Should I shut down the White House until it's cleared?"

"No," the woman said. "They want the White House closed. We need to let things happen so we can identify the sleepers. If you shut down the White House, we won't find them before it's too late."

"But if we just let things happen, it might be too late for some," Jack said.

"We can't let Trinity call the shots. Not anymore. They have to be stopped. The security of our nation is at risk."

"Why me? Why us?" Anne asked. "I need to let the Secret Service know what's going on so they can be prepared."

"I know something is going to happen, but I don't know what."

"Can you identify the Trinity agents inside?" Jack asked.

"No. After a certain stage in our training, we aren't allowed to mix and mingle with the others. Knowing other agents allows you to see them when they're coming after you. Trinity doesn't want us to know when the target is one of its own."

"You've given us this warning. What can we do with it? We don't know who we're up against or what their plan is. It's an impossible situation. And the NSC meeting is tomorrow."

"I know. The attack will be after the meeting begins."

"With what?"

"I don't know. But be ready to get out when it goes down."

"Where will you be?" Anne asked.

"Nearby."

"How do we know you aren't one of them?"

"If I was, you'd be dead by now."

Movement behind her made Anne turn. "Wait." She managed to snag the woman's arm.

"Why meet? Why not text us?" Anne couldn't help it. She was suspicious of everyone now and didn't trust the woman who wouldn't show her face.

"Too much texting can be captured. I've endangered you as it is," she whispered before shaking free and rushing away.

In a flash, the woman was halfway down the steps on the other side of the theater, heading for the exit door on that side. She was dressed as the teen with the baseball cap and a hoodie pulled up over the hat.

A couple of dark figures entered from the door close to Jack and Anne.

Anne slid lower in her seat.

The men spotted their informer across the auditorium and ran after her.

The woman slipped through the exit. A few moments later, the two dark figures followed.

"Shouldn't we help her?" Anne asked.

"She's a trained assassin. You're not." Jack texted Declan, then rose, gripped her arm and helped her to her feet. "Come on, we're getting out of here." Then he grabbed Anne's hand and led her out the way they'd come in. Once out in the lobby of the theater, Jack pulled Anne against the wall, sank his hands into her hair and kissed her long and hard.

A man in dark clothing ran past them and entered the theater they'd just left.

Anne barely noticed. With Jack's mouth crushing hers, all thoughts flew out of her head. She gripped his shirt collar and returned the kiss.

When Jack finally raised his head, he took her hand again and hurried out the door.

Arnold had the car waiting at the curb, with Declan in the passenger seat.

Anne slid in and scooted to the far side of the seat to make room for Jack.

He bent his long frame and dropped into the seat beside her. "Go, Arnold. The sooner, the better."

Arnold jabbed the accelerator. The car lurched forward.

Anne slammed back against the seat and immediately buckled her seat belt.

"What just happened?"

"We had a narrow escape," Jack said.

"Don't speak too soon," Declan said. "We have a tail."

Arnold stepped on the accelerator and made a sharp right turn. The car fishtailed, the rear end sliding across the pavement until the tires engaged and the vehicle straightened.

"We still have them," Declan called out.

Something crashed through the rear window of the SUV, shattering the glass.

"Get down! They're shooting at us." Jack called out. He shoved Anne's head down in his lap and leaned over her with his body.

Arnold picked up speed and then rounded another corner, taking it fast, slinging them sideways.

Anne couldn't see anything but Jack's legs. The safety restraint and Jack's arms kept her from being flung out of her seat. After several more turns, Arnold slowed.

Jack sat up and looked out the window. "I think we lost them."

Anne sat up and pushed her hair out of her face. She glanced back at the hole in the rear window and shivered. Had the bullet hit a few more inches to the left or right, someone in the SUV could have been killed.

Arnold drove them back to the estate, choosing a more circuitous route. It took longer, but they didn't pick up another vehicle with people shooting at them.

When they arrived at the front steps of the Halverson mansion, Charlie, Grace, and the rest of the team came out to greet them.

Anne was glad to have their support. Mostly, she was glad to have Jack at her side throughout the ordeal. She couldn't begin to repay him. She probably wouldn't be alive if not for him.

Jack emerged from the vehicle and helped Anne to her feet. "Guys, we have to come up with a plan. I have a feeling tomorrow is going to be a rough day."

THE TEAM MET in the war room.

Cole and Jonah had their computer screens up with a variety of images displayed, including a street image of the men getting out of a dark van and entering the theater a few minutes before Jack and Anne left.

"That was close," Cole said. "We had just brought up the theater's webcam when the van pulled up."

"Did you get a license plate on that van?" Declan asked.

"We gave it our best shot. It had what appeared to be a temporary tag on it," Jonah said. "We tried to trace it, but it was a tag from over two years ago."

"What did you get from your informer lady?" Declan asked.

"Not enough." Jack's lips pressed together tightly. "She confirmed our suspicions that she was a trained agent for Trinity."

"Which means they're out to kill her," Gus said. "You know the only way out—"

"—is in a box." Jack nodded. "We know."

"That's why she hasn't come out in the open to meet with us face-to-face up until now," Anne said. "I kind of forced her to do it. I asked for more specifics on what Trinity is planning. I hope she made it out of the theater safely."

"She thinks whatever's going to happen will take place tomorrow," Jack said. "That's the only new info she passed along."

"And tomorrow is the National Security Council meeting," Anne added. "I think we should warn the president and Secret Service."

Jack's brow furrowed. "As our informer said, it will just postpone the inevitable and the sleeper Trinity agents will still be working there until the next attempt is made."

"By holding back the information, we put our president and the people in the White House at risk," Charlie said. "How can we even consider not alerting them?"

Anne nodded. "Security will be extra high during the council meeting. I can't imagine anyone getting into the session who hasn't been thoroughly screened."

"What about the rest of the building?" Jack asked. "What if they create a diversion?"

"There will a full contingent of Secret Service personnel on hand for tomorrow's meeting," Anne said.

"One of which could be a Trinity plant," Declan pointed out.

"We need to have the team inside the White House." Declan turned to Charlie. "Are you okay with us getting past security and inside however we can?"

She held up her hands. "I'm all for the team being there. Whatever methods you deem necessary, short of killing. Although, if it's a Trinity operative, you know what to do." She nodded toward Jonah. "Can you make it happen?"

"I'll do the best I can." Jonah turned to his computer and started keying furiously.

Cole settled in the seat beside him. "We'll need someone with the Secret Service. Some of us can come in as tourists visiting the White House. Tours have resumed since Millicent's incident." He waved a hand in the air. "We've got this. We'll have what we need in place by morning. Get Arnold in here. We might need help getting uniforms and equipment."

"What can I do to help?" Anne asked.

"Get a good night's sleep," Charlie said. "You might be in for a helluva day tomorrow." She took Anne's arm and led her up the stairs. Over her shoulder, she called out, "Let me know if you need anything from me. I'm afraid I'm only good for contacts."

"Thanks, Charlie," Declan called out.

Jack's gaze followed Anne up the stairs. He wanted to go with her but needed to be in on the planning for the day ahead.

Jack turned back to the operation planning. "Bring up a schematic of the White House. This operation

could even be more dangerous than some we've conducted in the Middle East. We won't be able to take
weapons inside."

Chapter Eleven

Anne lay awake well past midnight, listening for the sound of Jack's footsteps. She'd purposely left her door unlocked, hoping he'd come up and check on her. Maybe she was selfish, but she wanted a repeat of the night before. If things went south the next day, she wanted to have the memory of making love with Jack to be with her no matter what happened.

She must have fallen asleep because the next thing she knew, something was tickling her lips. She opened her eyes to find Jack leaning over her, a smile curving his lips.

"Hey," he said.

She blinked open her eyes.

He wore a pair of running shorts and nothing else.

Anne moved over in the bed, making room for him.

He slipped beneath the sheets and pulled her into his arms. "Go back to sleep. I just wanted to hold you."

"Mmm," she murmured, pressing her lips to his bare chest. He smelled of aftershave and man musk. Anne committed that scent to memory. She felt tomorrow would be a turning point. Whatever happened could set the course for her career, her life and perhaps her relationship with this man. "Promise me," she whispered.

"Promise you what?" he asked, smoothing her hair off her cheeks, tucking a strand behind her ear.

"You won't get hurt." She slipped her arm over his chest and held on tight. "I don't know if I can go through that again."

"Go through what, darlin'?" He kissed her temple and the tip of her nose.

"Losing someone I care about." There, she'd admitted to something she'd tried hard not to do since her husband's death. Care about someone so much it hurt. And a man who was a stranger mere days before. Was she insane? She scooted closer, until her body was flush with his. Yes, she was insane, but she didn't care. For the first time since Mason's death, she wanted someone else in her life and was willing to risk losing her heart again. To a man who risked his life in the work he performed.

His arms tightened around her. "You know, you were supposed to be the job. Nothing more."

"What do you mean, the job?"

"I wasn't supposed to get involved." He tipped her chin up so that he could stare into her eyes. "But I'm failing at that miserably."

"Miserably?" Her lips twisted. "That doesn't sound good." She tilted her head and pressed a kiss to his chin.

Jack turned his head and captured her lips in a soul-defining kiss that left her breathless and wanting so much more.

"I promised myself I wouldn't love another woman," he said. "But I'm afraid I might be falling for you."

Her heart pounded hard in her chest. "And that's a bad thing?"

"Yes. I'm bad luck to the women in my life."

"How so?" She shook her head. "You've been nothing but good luck for me. I could have been dead twice over if you hadn't come along and scooped me up on the back of your motorcycle."

He held her close, crushing her to his chest. "I'm afraid for you, Anne."

"I'm willing to take the risk," she said.

Jack rolled her onto her back, pressing her into the mattress with the weight of his body. "I'm not sure I'm willing to risk your life, because I want you so badly."

"It's my life. Doesn't that make it my decision?" she said staring up into his eyes. She wrapped her arms around his neck and pulled him down to her. "Make love to me, marine. Whatever this is we're feeling can't be all bad, and we can figure it all out after tomorrow. Let's make the most out of what's left of tonight."

"Tonight, then," he said and proceeded to fulfill all the fantasies she'd had about him before she'd fallen asleep.

They didn't get much sleep, but they made memories into the wee hours of the morning. By the time her alarm went off, Anne was already awake, staring at Jack as he caught a few minutes of sleep. She wanted to remember him so relaxed and sexy, lying naked in the bed beside her. If all went well that day, they might have more nights like this. If not, she'd have her memories to hold close.

The alarm blared. Anne turned it off and pressed a kiss to Jack's lips.

He opened his eyes and smiled. "Is it that time?"

"I'd rather not go to work today at all," Anne said.

He pulled her into his embrace. "If only we could stay here and forget the world outside."

Anne kissed him again and leaned up on her arm. "It's like a bandage that needs to be removed. Let's rip it off and get it over with."

"Then we can pick up where we left off here?"

Anne nodded. "That's the plan." She rose from the bed and padded naked to retrieve her T-shirt from where it had been tossed in the night. After she pulled it over her head, she grabbed her toiletries and paused with her hand on the doorknob.

Jack had risen from the bed and stood looking out the window.

His body was magnificent, all muscle and sinew.

Her core heated again with desire. If only they didn't have to go to work. If only they didn't have to save the world…

With a sigh, she left the room, crossed to the bathroom and got into the shower.

A few moments later, the shower curtain shifted to the side and her handsome former marine stepped into the shower with her. He held out his hand. "Soap."

She gave him the bar and watched in shivery anticipation as he worked up a lather and then spread it over her shoulders and downward to cup each breast and tweak the nipples with his sudsy fingers.

By the time he cupped her sex, she was past ready. When he lifted her by the backs of her thighs, she swallowed the moan rising up her throat and lowered herself over his shaft.

They made love until the water cooled.

Then they dried each other off and dressed quickly, aware of the hour and the fact they had to get to the station in time to catch the early train into the city.

Combed and dressed, they made their way down to the kitchen where the rest of the team had gathered.

"Arnold is driving you two into the city this morning, so you won't have to catch the train."

Anne glanced at the clock. They were still early enough they would miss the worst of rush hour. "Thank you. At least we won't have to worry that there might be bad guys on the train in."

Jack nodded. "Right. Let's save the confrontations for later."

"We can hope there won't be a confrontation at all," Charlie said.

"Then we wouldn't smoke out the Trinity assassins entrenched in the White House," Declan said.

"True," Charlie conceded. "I hate to be a downer, but we'll only be scratching the surface of the organization by identifying and eliminating some of the pawns in their game. Until we find the leader and take him out, we won't hear the end of Trinity."

"You have a point," Declan said. "We'll work on that. Hopefully, we'll recruit Anne's texter to join our team. Between her and Jasmine's help we might have a shot at finding their leader and bringing him down."

Carl had breakfast cooked and laid out on the table. They all took their seats and dug in, not knowing what the day would have in store for them.

Anne could imagine the marines eating like it might be their last meal for a long time. In the desert, they probably went for long stretches without decent meals as they prepared for and conducted battles.

Today would be like that, only in a falsely civilized theater of operations. Even though they'd be in the heart of the city, they would be up against some of the most ruthless opponents they'd ever contended with.

Anne prayed they all came out of it alive.

IF JACK HAD his way, he'd leave Anne at the Halverson estate where she'd be safe. Knowing her like he did, he didn't even suggest it. She wouldn't stand by and let things happen to the people she worked with. If there was any way she could help, she would. Staying home from work wasn't an option, and if he insisted, he worried she'd find a way in, no matter what, without his protection.

With that in mind, Jack held open the door to the SUV Charlie had provided for her to climb into, glad she'd chosen to wear a pantsuit and sensible shoes. If there was any running involved with the day's events, she'd have a better chance in flat shoes than the heels she normally wore with her skirts.

Declan, Mack and Cole were getting into the White House as tourists and would be close by if needed. Arnold and Charlie had pulled some strings and secured a Secret Service uniform for Gus. Jonah had hacked in and had Gus added to the Secret Service roster for the day. Gus had already reported to the Secret Service Office in the West Wing of the White House. Hopefully, he hadn't had any difficulties assimilating. Mustang would enter the West Wing as a new staffer assigned to fill in for Dr. Saunders in the national homeland security advisor's office during Saunders's recovery.

Declan's Defenders would be in or near the West Wing during the National Security Council meeting. They would be able to monitor for anything unusual and be there to help out if something bad were to happen.

Not knowing who would initiate the event or what would transpire had Jack on edge. After spending time in the West Wing, he found it unsettling that some in the building might be Trinity assassins planted over time. He might have passed them in the hallways.

He handed an earbud to Anne.

"What is this?" she asked.

"Radio communications."

She shook her head. "Not that I even know how to use them, but how would we get them past security?"

"Put it with your cell phone when you go through the scanner. If they ask, it's a Bluetooth earbud for your cell phone. The worst they can do is set it aside and hold it until you leave for the day. The best would be if they let it pass and you have it in case you get in a tight situation and you need to communicate with one of us."

She stared at the device as if it might bite her.

Jack chuckled. "It won't hurt you."

Arnold dropped them off a block away from the West Wing. He would find a place to park and remain close by throughout the day. As a prior military man himself, he could provide backup in case they needed him. If nothing else, he would be there to provide transportation should they need to get somewhere quickly.

With a practiced eye, Jack surveyed the surroundings, searching for anyone who seemed out of place or looked as if they might initiate an attack. He kept Anne close to him as they walked to the West Wing and entered. As usual, they passed through the metal detectors, dropped their cell phones and earbuds into a dish to go through an X-ray machine and scanned their IDs. They reached Anne's office without any undue delays. Since it was early, there weren't as many people in the building yet, although there were more than Jack expected.

"Is this usual for this many people to be this early?" he asked.

Anne laughed. "The NSC meeting is a big deal. We like it to go smoothly. Most areas have someone come in early to make sure there are no loose ends remaining to be tied."

"Dedication."

"Some major decisions come out of these meetings," Anne said.

He moved closer and lowered his voice. "Anything dealing with the major pharmaceutical companies?" Jack asked.

"I don't think so," Anne responded. "Why do you ask?"

"I'm trying to connect the dots between the Russian aid worker in the dead Syrian village, the pharmaceutical company experimenting with cancer vaccinations and the potential attack on the National Security Council. None of it's adding up."

"I know what you mean."

"Would the NSC be interested in a pharmaceutical company performing unsanctioned drug testing on humans in Syria?"

Her brow puckered. "That might be something that

would be discussed. And the word *sanction* brings up another thought. Imposing sanctions on a country known to conduct biological warfare on populations." Her eyes widened. "Do you think Trinity is working with the Russians and the big pharmaceuticals? Maybe they don't want the NSC to shut down trade between the US and Russia. It might cut into their profits."

Jack pulled his cell phone from his pocket and called Jonah. "I need you to check into members of the NSC and who might have connections to Waylon Pharmaceuticals. Text me with anything you might find as soon as you get it. Thanks."

A knock sounded on the door to Anne's office.

Jack, being closest, opened the door.

Gina poked her head inside. "Mr. Louis wants to see you, Anne."

"Thank you, Gina. I'll be right there."

Gina left, closing the door behind her.

Anne glanced at Jack. "Be careful today."

"Same to you." He winked. "I'm counting on seeing a lot more of you."

She crossed to where he stood, leaned up on her toes and pressed a kiss to his lips. "Me, too."

Jack pulled her into his arms and kissed her hard, his tongue pushing through to slide along hers in a long, sexy caress. Then he set her away from him. "Do you still have your earbud?"

She patted the pocket of her suit jacket and nodded.

"Don't forget to use it."

"I won't." She gave him one last glance before he opened the door and stood back.

"Have a good day, Ms. Bellamy," Jack said. He prayed she would have that good day.

Anne left the office and went to the one next door.

While Anne met with her boss, Jack fitted his earbud in his ear and switched it on. "Testing," he said quietly. "Snow here."

"Gus here. Stationed outside the NSC room as sentry."

"Declan here with Cole and Mack, waiting to get into the White House tour. Close by, if you need us."

"Mustang at Dr. Saunders's desk, awaiting computer access. Deliver me from boredom."

"We can only pray for boredom," Jack said softly.

"Amen," Declan responded.

"Arnold?"

"On a park bench, feeding the pigeons. Here if you need me."

"Is Ms. Bellamy wired?" Declan asked.

"She has the gear," Jack said. "Whether she chooses to use it is up to her."

"Gotcha. Stay cool," Declan said. "And call if you need us."

"T minus two hours and counting." Jack said. "See you at close of business."

Unable to sit still for long, Jack paced the length of the office, turned and paced back. The NSC meeting wasn't for another two hours. What would he do until then? He sat at the computer and thumbed through what little data he could tap into. As a new staffer, he still didn't have access to much. Not that there would be anything on the White House database that could incriminate any of the president's advisors. They'd have to be completely stupid to put anything on the shared databases that could compromise their careers.

He did find a draft copy of the NSC agenda Anne had worked on until it was finalized.

Jack glanced through the topics and yawned, until he got to the line listing the scheduled address by the director for Europe and Russia. He was to speak on Russia's most recent involvement in the Middle East and move for sanctions.

Had he been close when he'd speculated that some folks on the council would not want sanctions imposed against Russia? Would some people do anything to stop the sanctions from being invoked?

Leaving the office, Jack strode through the halls of the West Wing, too wound up to stay in one place. He was back in his own hallway when Anne emerged from the national security advisor's office.

She smiled as she walked toward him, a stack of paper in her hand. "Can't stop. Have to get to the conference room to help with setup," she said as she passed him.

"Can I help?" he asked.

Anne shook her head. "Sorry. Just me and the conference room facilitator, Terrence Tully."

He tapped his ear with a pointed look as a reminder that she had an earbud for communications, should she need it.

She gave a brief nod and continued down the corridor toward the conference room.

Jack's gaze followed her until she disappeared around a corner. He wanted to go after her and be with her every second of the day but knew he couldn't. She had a job to do, and he couldn't follow her everywhere.

It didn't make it any easier knowing someone might make a move that day.

The wait was excruciating. But the longer they waited, the longer the people in the building remained unharmed.

Chapter Twelve

Anne hurried to the conference room where the NSC meeting would take place. A Secret Service agent was in the room with a K-9.

The dog had its nose to the floor, sniffing. After a complete circuit of the room, the Secret Service guy nodded toward Terrence Tully, the conference room facilitator, who stood in the corner. "It's all yours." And the agent left.

"Hey, Terrence." Anne smiled. "How've you been?"

He moved about the room straightening chairs and setting out water glasses for the attendees. "Good. You?"

"Great," she answered, lying through her teeth. Anne laid a paper copy of the agenda on the conference table in front of each chair.

"Long agenda today?" Terrence asked.

"The usual," Anne responded. "Missed you at the last meeting."

He shrugged. "I've been traveling a little. Had to burn some use-or-lose vacation."

She nodded, familiar with the life of a staffer at the White House. Too often they lost vacation time because they couldn't take the time off. Or, in her case, had no reason to take the time off.

Alone since her husband's death, she had no desire to travel. Without someone to share the beauty of the places visited, there didn't seem to be a point.

Her thoughts drifted to Jack. Traveling with him could be fun. She could imagine lazing on a beach beside him, soaking up the sun. Or hiking a mountain trail in Colorado.

Shaun stuck his head in the door. "It's almost time. POTUS is on his way."

Her heart skipped several beats and she stepped to the door where Shaun stood. "Let me know if you need anything. I'll be in my office."

Shaun's eyes narrowed. "No, you won't."

Anne frowned. "What do you mean?"

"You're staying here. I want you here. You'll stand in the back of the room in case I need you to answer any questions."

"Are you sure?" Anne asked.

"Absolutely. Unless you had other plans."

If anything was going to happen that day, the target had to be the National Security Council meeting, where all the key players were present. Again, she worried that she should have warned the Secret Service of the potential attack. At the very least, she would be in attendance, watching for any preemptive signs from any of the staff or supporting staff. She could be there to help get people out, if things went south.

Anne squared her shoulders. "I'd be honored to attend."

"Good, because it's time."

The vice president arrived, followed by the secretary of state, secretary of defense, secretary of treasury, director of national intelligence, director for Europe and Russia, the director for Asia, director of foreign policy and others.

Anne moved to the back of the room, out of the way, as the advisors to the president assembled in the room and stood behind a chair, waiting for the president. Each person wore his best suit, and was clean-shaven and perfectly coifed.

A Secret Service agent entered the room first.

The vice president stood at attention and announced, "Ladies and gentlemen, the president of the United States."

Everyone stood at attention as the chief executive walked in and took his position at the head of the conference table. "Please, take a seat," he said.

The meeting began with reports from the various advisors as they worked their way down the agenda. When they reached Chris Carpenter's agenda item on Russian sanctions, Anne tensed.

Chris cleared his throat and plunged in. "As you are aware, the Russian bombing of a base in Syria was investigated and found to be deliberate and catastrophic, with over three hundred civilian casualties and twice that many injuries. The Russian president has no comment. We stood by while Russia waged war on Crimea without lifting a finger. I move that we, as a nation, impose sanctions on Russia until they cease waging war on civilians."

Immediately, the other members of the National Security Council jumped in, everyone talking at once.

"One bombing is not sufficient grounds to impose sanctions," Anne's boss said.

"Maybe not, but how about Russia allowing one of its largest state-owned pharmaceutical companies to secretly test drugs on human subjects in Syria?" Chris's comment was met with stunned silence.

Anne held her breath, wanting to jump in with what she knew. She waited for Chris to explain his statement.

"As you all are aware, a member of my staff was injured by a hit-and-run driver in the street right outside this compound. You could put it down to an accident, but I say it was deliberate. She had just met with Dr. Schuster, who I've asked to join us today." He waved a hand toward the director for Europe and Russia. "Dr. Schuster, what did you share with Dr. Saunders?"

Dr. Schuster nodded toward the screen on the wall. "If you could bring up the image…"

The screen flickered and the grainy image of the Russian aid worker came into focus. "Our ambassador in Russia received a communication from this man, whom we later identified as Aleksandr Orlov, a Russian aid worker deployed to a small Syrian village, where he was supposedly giving regular vaccines to the local population. The World Health Organization has since found that the vaccine administered was a drug called XC-16, designed to eliminate cancer."

Anne held her breath. This was exactly what they'd discovered.

"The drug had only been tested on mice and found to be unstable and potentially dangerous. If released, it could decimate a population." He waved toward the image on the screen. "That entire village and the Russian aid workers are dead. Given the company that sent the drug to Syria is owned by the Russian government, we contend the Russians knew the potential harm and still tested it on humans, without getting their consent or informing them of what they were getting into. The vaccines were probably passed off as something innocuous, like the ones for measles, mumps and rubella. We can't know, since the entire population of that village is unable to answer questions."

"That, Mr. President," Chris said, "along with the bombing and the crimes against Crimea, are sufficient justification to impose sanctions on Russia."

The president glanced around the room at his advisors. "Although I agree the charges are egregious, imposing sanctions against Russia is a big step with lingering ramifications." He looked around the room at his other advisors. "How many of you agree with Mr. Carpenter's proposal?"

Anne looked at the faces of those present, trying to read into their expressions.

"Sanctions could disrupt the balance of power throughout Europe," the secretary of state said. "Many Europeans rely on the Russians for many of their products and there are many US corporations that would suffer if they were unable to do business with Russia."

Out of the corner of her eye, she saw Terrence back into a corner, close his eyes and cover his ears.

Alarmed, Anne turned to face him when an explosion rocked the building and sent her crashing to her knees.

People yelled, women screamed, chaos ensued.

The president's bodyguards scooped him out of his chair and rushed him from the room.

The remaining members of the council scrambled from their chairs and ran for the door.

A Secret Service agent grabbed the vice president's arms and hurried him toward the exit.

"Ms. Bellamy, come with me." Terrence Tully gripped her arm and helped her to her feet. "We have to get to somewhere safe."

Shaken and disoriented, her ears ringing from the concussion caused by the explosion, Anne let him guide her toward the door, following the vice president and his bodyguard.

They ran down the hallway and entered another door that led to another, and finally ended up at a side door marked Emergency Exit Only.

They burst through, out into the open, near a street.

Sirens wailed, emergency vehicles screamed around corners in the distance and people ran from the building.

Once outside, Anne slowed, digging her feet into the soft ground. "Wait. We have to help the others out of the building."

"No, we don't." Tully bent, slung her over his shoulder in a fireman's carry and ran toward a white van.

Anne, her ears still ringing and her world turned upside down, fought to free herself of his hold. "Let me down!" she yelled.

Her cries could barely be heard over the wailing sirens converging on the White House. Anne screamed louder when she caught a glimpse of a Secret Service man angling toward the van, with a gun held to the vice president's head.

The man shoved the vice president alongside Terrence.

"Let us go!" Anne shouted. "You can't get away with this. That's the vice president of the United States."

Tully didn't answer, just carried her to the van.

The door opened before they reached it and a man jumped out.

As Tully stood her upright, the man from the van slung a large gunnysack over her head, trapping her arms inside.

Anne jerked free of his hands and ran. Unable to see, she tripped and fell,

Someone landed on her back, knocking the air from her lungs.

She fought, kicked and yelled for help, but no one came.

Again, she was lifted off her feet, then deposited on the floor of the van. The sound of the door sliding made Anne twist and struggle against the sack. She rolled to the side and ran into something hard and unmoving. The door slammed closed and she had no way to escape.

JACK HAD BEEN pacing in Anne's office when the explosion sent him sprawling against the tile floor. He rolled to his feet and ran toward the offices, touching a finger to his earbud. "Declan, did you hear that?"

"Roger. Tourists are being ushered out. I tried to dodge the security staff, but there's no getting by. We're heading out on the White House lawn."

"Mustang?" Jack queried as he pushed through the rush of people running for the exit.

"Still in the West Wing," Mustang said in Jack's ear. "Secret Service is herding people out. I've managed to duck them by hiding in a closet."

"Gus?" Jack murmured as he passed several of the men and women that were scheduled to be in the NSC meeting.

For a long moment, Gus didn't answer.

Jack listened for Gus's response, worry eating at him when he didn't see Anne among those rushing down the corridor from the conference room where the meeting was to be held.

"Gus?" Declan queried.

"Sorry," Gus said, the sound of heavy breathing coming through the connection. "I'm sitting on the guy who set off the explosion. Caught him with his hand on the detonator, dressed as Secret Service personnel."

"Jack," Declan said into Jack's ear. "What about Ms. Bellamy?"

Jack arrived at the door to the designated conference room. Everyone had made it out. The room was empty. "I'm here. In the room they were supposed to meet. No president. No vice president…" His stomach sank as he made a clean sweep of the room. "No Anne."

"Did you give her the earbud?"

Jack exited the conference room and ran in the opposite direction from where he'd come. "I did. Bringing up the GPS on my phone now." Thank God, the earbuds were also equipped with a GPS tracking device. As long as she didn't lose it, they could find her.

Still dashing down the corridor, searching every

room along the way, Jack brought up the application on his cell phone and held his breath, waiting for the reassuring green dot to appear on the map grid.

When it did, he stopped running. "Damn." His pulse pounded so hard he couldn't hear himself think and his knees grew weak.

"What?" Declan's voice came through as if in a tunnel.

"She's not even in the building."

"Not in the building?"

"No." Jack performed an about-face and ran back through the corridors of the West Wing. "She must be in a vehicle, because she's moving quickly through the streets, heading for the highway."

"We're almost to the exit of the West Wing," Declan said. "Meet you there."

"Arnold?" Jack said. "Can you make it to the street with all the emergency personnel in the way?"

Arnold gave them a location a couple of blocks away.

Jack caught up with Mustang on his way out of the building. They were delayed briefly by the Secret Service staff but made it out to find Declan, Cole and Mack waiting for them.

"Gus is staying to make sure his guy doesn't get lost in the shuffle. Needless to say, the man isn't talking. Gus said he had the Trinity tattoo on the inside of his wrist, beneath the watch he wore. He's definitely one of the sleepers."

Jack didn't wait around to ask or answer questions; he took off at a sprint, pushing past people who stood on the streets, staring at the White House, wondering what had happened. He didn't have time to stop and fill them in. Anne was moving farther away by the second. If they didn't catch up with her soon…

He couldn't think what would happen to her if they discovered she had a tracker on her. Hell, even if they didn't, what were their plans for the White House staffer?

Jack was first to arrive at the corner where Arnold was just pulling to a stop.

He jumped into the front passenger seat.

Declan, Mack, Cole and Mustang dove into the back seats of the big SUV.

"Go! Go! Go!" Jack urged. He held his phone in front of him, watching as the green light crossed the Potomac into Arlington. "They're getting away."

Declan leaned over the back of Jack's seat and touched a hand to his shoulder. "Not as long as she has that tracker on her."

Jack's heartbeat slammed against his chest. He willed the SUV to move faster, but the traffic held them at nearly a standstill. They inched forward, crawling through downtown toward the 14th Street bridge. Once they reached the major highway, they would gain some speed. In the meantime, Anne's signal showed them blowing through Arlington, heading west.

A call came through on his phone from their informer.

Though he didn't want to switch applications, Jack had to.

"Go ahead," Declan said. "I've got Anne's tracker up on my phone now."

Jack answered the call.

"Did everyone make it out?" The voice he recognized from the movie theater sounded in Jack's ear.

"No," Jack gritted out. "Someone has Anne. We have them on a tracker, but we don't know how long it will be before they figure out she has one. They're heading into Virginia."

"On my way," she said.

Jack gave her the route they'd taken and the direction the tracker was headed.

"I'll catch up," she said. "Let me know if things change. You can reach me at this number for now."

Jack wanted to throw the phone out the window, he was so mad at the woman for putting Anne at risk.

Anne didn't have a cell phone on her. She wouldn't be able to call them. If they were going to use her to negotiate a trade for their informant, how were they going to get in touch? And would their defector agree to the trade to save Anne's life?

She by God better. The Trinity-trained woman was in a much better position to defend herself than Anne. Anne didn't have any skills in self-defense, a situation Jack promised he would remedy as soon as he got her back.

Assuming they got her back alive…

He couldn't think that way. Anne was a fighter, even if she didn't have combat skills. She was smart and could figure out a way to survive. She was strong and determined.

Jack brought up the tracking application and held his breath until the green light appeared again. They had to get to her before anything bad happened. And when they did save her, it was all on for bringing down Trinity. No organization should be able to pick off some-one like Anne, just because she'd had contact with one of their defectors. And no covert organization should be able to infiltrate the US government so thoroughly. Trinity had to be stopped.

Arnold proved to be an excellent driver, weaving his way in and out of traffic, slowly closing the gap between them and Anne's location. At the rate they were gain-ing, they might actually catch up to them before they pulled off the main road. As it was, the goons were only ten miles ahead of them.

As long as the police didn't try to pull Arnold over for exceeding the speed limit by thirty miles an hour, they had a chance.

Jack leaned forward in his seat, willing the SUV to go faster. At some points, they were flying down the interstate at over one hundred miles per hour. Already, they were a danger to other vehicles on the road.

Arnold handled the vehicle like a professional race car driver, cool, calm and collected. It was just as well he was doing the driving. Jack was anything but calm and composed.

Five miles between them. Five miles away from Anne. They had to catch up to them before they turned off onto smaller roads. That would slow their speed significantly and make it harder for them to catch up.

If anything horrible happened to Anne…

No, he couldn't think that way. He couldn't allow his past to shape his future with Anne. For her sake, he had to let those thoughts go or he wouldn't be effec-tive. And she needed him at the top of his game, not dragged down by memories. He was more than capable of finding her and helping her. And meting out justice to her abductors.

Jack shook his head. The black cloud that hung over him could not affect her. She would not be the fourth victim of his bad luck.

His mother's death had been because of the cancer. Not him.

Kylie had been a victim of a shooter.

Not Jack's bad luck.

And Jennifer, the nurse he'd met while deployed, had died because of an IED explosion.

None of those had anything to do with the fact he'd loved them. None. Of. Those.

Then why did he feel he was responsible for their deaths? He was the one factor in common with those three women. He'd loved them. And he was falling in love with Anne. Holy hell. He was falling in love with her.

His chest was so tight he could barely breathe.

The vehicle they were following was now only three miles ahead of them. Then two.

"Go, go, go," Jack murmured. Slowly, the distance reduced until only one mile of road stood between him and Anne.

Jack stared ahead, his gaze searching the vehicles in the distance. Which one was Anne in? Then he saw it.

A white van hogging the left lane swerved right and left, trapped between the vehicle in front of him and the one in the right-hand lane.

"There." Jack pointed. "That has to be them." He looked down at his phone.

The car in the right lane exited the highway.

The white van whipped into the right lane and sped past a truck that had been blocking the left lane.

Arnold increased his speed.

As they approached the truck, it moved to the right lane.

Arnold passed it and caught up to the white van.

"That's them," Jack said, his lips pressing into a thin line. "Now what?"

Chapter Thirteen

Once she was bagged and dumped into the van, Anne had been secured by being wrapped in what she imagined was duct tape. They'd sat her up and circled her body, gunnysack and all, several times with tape, making it impossible for her to move her arms. Thankfully, the sack was made of a loosely woven material. She could breathe and even see shadowy forms through the gaps between the threads.

Once they were out of the city, the driver increased their speed, weaving in and out of traffic. Every time he swerved, Anne rolled across the floor of the van and bumped into someone she assumed was the vice president.

The entire time, she wiggled and shifted, trying to work the sack and the tape up her body. It was a slow process and she didn't know if she was being watched, but she couldn't do nothing. She thought about the earbud she'd put in her pocket. By now, they were well out of range of the two-way radio. And it didn't matter because she couldn't see where they were going.

If she was going to get out of the situation, she had to do it on her own. And she had to do something. She couldn't stand by and let these people hurt the vice president of the United States.

After a while, a voice sounded from the front of the van. "We're being followed."

More promising words could not have been spoken. Hope swelled in Anne's heart.

"How did they find us?" someone else said. "Check them. One of them might have a phone or tracking device on them."

While the van driver increased his speed and swerved between vehicles, the other two men in the vehicle worked over the other captive first.

"You won't get away with this," Anne heard the vice president say. "By now they will have launched helicopters. Every law enforcement agency will be on the lookout for you. They'll set up roadblocks."

"Shut up." A loud smack sounded, followed by a grunt.

Anne bunched her legs up and kicked hard at one of the shadows she could see squatting in front of her.

The man fell over, cursed, righted himself and punched her in the side of the head.

Pain knifed through her temple and she saw stars.

"VP's clean," a man said.

"Check the woman."

Something sharp nicked Anne's arm and the tape around her was cut loose.

With her arms somewhat free, Anne scrambled to shove the gunnysack off her head.

When she managed to free herself, hands reached out and grabbed her from behind. The man wearing the dark suit of a Secret Service agent knelt before her and ran his hands over her body.

Anne kicked at him, landing a heel in his gut.

He grunted, grabbed her ankles and yanked her hard, laying her flat out on the floor of the van, and threw his body over hers. He straddled her hips and continued his search.

The man holding her arms gripped her wrists and pulled them up over her head.

She thrashed and twisted her body, but she was pinned by the weight and strength of her captors.

He found the earbud in her pocket and held it up. "What's this?"

"It's my earbud. I use it to listen to music," she said, praying he wouldn't take it. If by some slim chance the vehicle following them contained Jack or any member of his team, she could use the communication device to contact them.

"Give it to me." Terrence Tully, the driver, held out his hand.

The man sitting on her slapped it into the man's palm.

A moment later, the earbud flew out the window.

Anne's heart sank, but she refused to give up hope.

"That's all the electronics I found."

"Cufflinks?" Tully asked.

"None."

"Ditch their shoes," the man holding her wrists said.

The man sitting on her twisted around, yanked off her shoes and handed them to Tully. They flew out the window, as well.

"Lose the tail," commanded the man sitting on her.

The driver turned sharply, sending the van off the nearest exit.

Anne couldn't see where they were headed, but the vehicle slowed.

Good. Slow was good. The people following them might have a chance of catching up.

The man sitting on her reached for a roll of duct tape and wrapped it around her ankles.

Though she fought, struggled, bit, kicked and cursed, they sat her up and secured her wrists behind her back. She tried her best to leave a gap between them to give her a chance to work her way out. Alas, they cinched them tightly and shoved her onto the floor.

One of the men sat near the rear of the van, looking out the back window; the other two looked out the front. Rain started falling, slowing them down as they wound through curvy back roads, hydroplaning as puddles built on the road.

"Turn here," the man who'd moved to the passenger seat said.

The driver cut sharply to the right, slinging Anne over onto her side again.

"I think we lost them," the man in the back called out.

After another short burst of speed, Tully turned to the left. The new road was bumpier, and water splashed up against the side of the vehicle. Had they turned onto a dirt road?

Again, Anne tried to sit up and look out the window. The rutted road made it difficult. When she finally managed to sit up, she braced her back against the side of the van and stared out at what she could see from the floor of the van.

Tree limbs drooped over the road, brushing against the sides of the vehicle. The rain and the tunnel of greenery blocked out the sun, making it appear dusky outside.

If they'd lost whoever was tailing them, they'd never find them out in the backwoods.

Anne glanced over at the vice president. "Are you okay?" she whispered.

He lay on his side, his wrists and ankles bound much like hers. He nodded. "They will mobilize the military and deploy all the law enforcement agencies."

The man peering out the back window snorted. "By then, it'll be too late."

"What is it you want?" the VP asked.

The dude looking out the back threw a glance toward Anne. "Ask her."

She frowned. "I'm nobody. What do I have that you could possibly want?" She knew, but she wanted to hear them say it.

The man in the passenger seat turned and snarled at Anna. "A connection to her, the woman who betrayed us."

"Who are you talking about?" the VP asked.

Passenger-seat guy jerked his head toward Anne. "Ms. Bellamy knows. She's known all along. If she hadn't hired someone to look out for her, we'd wouldn't have had to go to so much trouble."

Anne dropped all pretense. "For one, I don't even know who she is. All I know is you are all part of Trinity. And she wanted out. I've never even seen her face."

Passenger-seat man's hand snaked out and slapped her hard across the cheek. "You lie."

Anne flinched, her chin going up. "It's true. She only talks to me via text."

"You met with her in the movie theater. We almost had her then."

"You saw more of her than I did," Anne said. "She was behind me."

"Doesn't matter. You are our bargaining chip."

"Do you really think she'll hand herself over to you in trade for me?" Anne snorted.

"If not you—" passenger-seat guy tipped his head toward the vice president "—then the VP."

"Trinity trained her to be ruthless," Anne argued. "She's probably halfway across the country by now."

"That's not her style," Tully said. "She's hung around the DC area for over a year. We just couldn't catch up to her. She's a master of disguise and an expert at technology. She wouldn't have involved you if she didn't feel like she could save the world."

"Well, her plan backfired. She didn't save anyone," Anne said. "She'll be long gone."

"If you hope to live," the guy in the passenger seat snarled at her, "you better hope she's not."

The van lurched to a stop.

"Everyone out," Tully said.

The two not driving exited the van. One reached in and pulled the VP out, bent forward and threw him over his shoulder. The other man waited until they were out of the way, then reached in for Anne.

She scooted across the van floor, trying to get away. He grabbed her ankle and yanked her to the edge of the floor and then flung her over his shoulder and marched toward a little white farmhouse that had seen better days. The windows had been boarded up and the front porch drooped as if the posts it was built on had rotted through.

Tully parked the van as far beneath a tree as he could, got out and hurried to the house.

He tried the door handle. When it didn't open, he cocked his leg and kicked the door hard. It flew open, crashing against the wall inside. The roof over the porch shuddered.

Anne twisted and struggled. With her wrists and ankles bound, she couldn't do much.

The man carrying her entered the house and dropped her on the floor.

She hit feetfirst but couldn't get her balance and crumpled to the floor, hitting her hip and then her shoulder. "That's going to leave a bruise," she muttered. Bruises were the least of her worries, though. Trinity recruits were trained assassins. From what she'd learned from John Halverson, they were very secretive and didn't like anyone knowing who they were.

The fact Anne and the VP had seen their faces could be bad news. They didn't let people live who could recognize them. Another reason to kill their defector.

Even if they got Anne's informant to agree to trade herself for the release of Anne and the VP, they wouldn't be good on their word. They'd kill the defector, Anne and the VP, too.

Anne had to find a way out of this mess and get the VP out, as well. She wasn't ready to die.

She glanced around the room, searching for anything she could use to cut through the tape around her wrists.

Whoever had abandoned the house had left little in the way of furniture. But there was an old wooden crate in one corner and a stack of yellowed newspapers.

After the Trinity assassins dumped their captives, they stepped out onto the porch.

Through the open door, Anne strained to hear what they were saying.

From what she could tell, they were checking for cell phone reception.

"It should be enough to get through to him," Tully said. He entered the house and stood in front of Anne. "What's the phone number of your boyfriend?" he demanded.

"I don't have a boyfriend," she said, her chin rising. She wished Jack was her boyfriend, but they barely knew each other. Hadn't she insisted they weren't obligated to a commitment just because they'd slept together?

Tully pulled a gun from his jacket pocket and pointed it at the VP's head. "What's your boyfriend's phone number?"

Anne struggled to remember, her heart slamming hard against her chest. She told him what she thought it was and held her breath, praying it was correct.

He dialed the number, hit the call button and touched the screen again to put it on speaker. The phone rang once.

"This is Snow."

Tully smirked at Anne. "Got your girlfriend and the VP. We want to make a deal with you."

"Are they alive?"

"Yes."

"I want proof."

Tully nodded toward the man closest to Anne.

He reached down, grabbed Anne by her hair and yanked her head back.

Tully shoved the phone close to her face. "Say hello to your lover."

JACK HELD HIS breath, waiting for the sound of Anne's voice.

"Jack." Anne sounded scared but strong.

He let go of the breath lodged in his throat. "Anne, are you okay?"

"We're fine," she said. "For now."

"We'll find you." Jack's free hand clenched into a fist. "And when we do, we'll kill every last one of the bastards."

A man laughed on the other end of the connection. "Won't do you much good to find them, if they're already dead. Keep your shirt on and get in touch with our traitor. Tell her it's her for these two. You have one hour before I start shooting. I don't care who goes first." His tone grew sharper. "Maybe you do." Then he ended the call.

"We have to find them," Jack said.

"They can't be far. We had them up to the last turn."

Jack knew they'd found and ditched the tracking device when they'd passed the location of the green dot and the van they'd been following was still way ahead of them.

Then the van had veered off the highway onto an

exit and taken to back roads. They'd managed to keep up for several miles. Then the van seemed to disappear.

The fact that it had started raining didn't help. And the deeper they went into the backwoods, the narrower the roads became and the denser the vegetation. The van could have gone off the road and been swallowed up by trees and bushes.

Arnold had pulled off the highway onto a dirt road and stopped the vehicle.

Jack had nearly come apart. "We can't stop now. They might be right around the next curve."

"Or we could have passed them already," Arnold argued. He got out of the SUV.

"Where are you going?" Jack asked, preparing to take the driver's seat if Arnold wasn't willing. "You can't quit now."

"I'm not quitting. I'm getting something that will help us get a better view."

That was when the call had come through.

While Jack had been on the phone with Anne's captors, Arnold carried what appeared to be a remote-control drone to the front of the SUV. The others had gotten out, as well. Arnold laid the drone in the middle of a dirt road and reached into the back of the SUV for the controls. In less than a minute, he had the drone rising into the air, the images it recorded showing up on the video display.

After the assassin ended the call, Jack leaped out of the SUV and ran to Arnold, who stood staring at the monitor while maneuvering the joystick on the controls.

"See anything yet?" Jack asked.

"Not yet," Arnold said, his head down, concentrating on the screen in front of him.

"You'd better contact your Trinity informer," Declan said.

Jack redialed the number of the woman who'd gotten Anne into this mess in the first place, anger and frustration making him want to hit someone. Preferably the people holding Anne hostage.

"Sitrep," their informer said as she answered.

"They want to make a trade."

She sighed. "I was afraid it would come down to that. Current location?"

"I don't know where they are but hang on." He texted her a pin drop of their location and then got back on the phone. "How soon can you be here?"

"Three minutes, tops. I'd almost caught up with you when you left the highway. Then I lost you."

"Sounds familiar. We lost the white van we were following, but our guy is looking for it with a drone."

"Good thinking."

Two minutes later, a motorcycle pulled up behind the SUV and a woman climbed off, pulled off her helmet and shook out long, auburn hair.

She walked straight up to him and held out her hand. "Jack Snow, I'm CJ Grainger."

He recognized her voice, even if he didn't recognize her face. "You got her into this, what are you going to do to get her out of it alive?"

"I don't know yet."

"We have less than an hour to figure it out," Jack said.

"There," Arnold said. "Do you see that?"

Declan, Mustang, Cole and Mack crowded around the monitor.

"I don't see anything but treetops and a tin roof," Declan said.

Arnold pointed to the right of the tin roof at the top of a tree. "See the white angles making corners on the edges of the green tree?"

Jack shoved his way through the men gathered around and stared at what Arnold pointed at. "That could be the van."

A movement beside the house caught their attention. A man stepped out from beneath the porch and walked to the tree, where he opened what was clearly the door of a vehicle.

"That's it," Jack said. "Where are they from here?"

Arnold pulled his phone from his pocket and touched an icon. A map opened up, with a blue dot and a green dot. "We're the green dot. The blue dot is the location of the drone." Arnold glanced at Declan. "Drive the SUV. I'll fly the drone."

"We can't go storming in. The Trinity operatives will kill their captives and disappear into the woods," CJ said.

"We'll get close and go the rest of the way in by foot," Jack said.

With that plan in mind, the men piled back into the SUV and followed the directions on Arnold's phone app.

CJ brought up the rear on her motorcycle.

When they were within half a mile of the location, they pulled the SUV off the road and hid it in the brush. Declan's Defenders got out. Arnold opened the rear of the SUV and handed them a variety of weapons, including three AR-15 semiautomatic assault rifles with scopes, two 9 mm Glocks, a couple of smoke grenades, a small brick of C-4 plastic explosives and two detonators.

"Are we going to war?" CJ asked.

"We don't know how many there are of them," Jack said, as he fitted a full magazine into the pistol he held. "And you're damn straight we're going to war. They infiltrated the White House, set off an explosion, and they're holding Anne and the vice president of the United States hostage. I consider what they've done an attack on this country."

CJ nodded. "Point made."

Declan stepped forward. "Secret Service, FBI, other agents are aware the VP has been taken. They'll be searching soon, following leads. My guess is this battle will be joined soon enough by more forces."

"Are you armed?" Jack asked CJ.

She nodded. "I have what I need. But I thought you would want me to offer myself up in exchange before you go storming in and risk getting them killed."

Jack shook his head. "Everything we've learned about Trinity is that they don't negotiate, and they don't let anyone live who might be able to identify them."

"You've got it right," CJ said. "I'm letting you know now, though, I would willingly let you trade me for the hostages if I thought it would do any good."

"It won't," Declan said and slammed his magazine into the Glock he'd chosen to carry. "Let's go. We're wasting time."

They moved out, slipping through the woods, paralleling the road in to the small farmhouse.

As they neared the house, they stopped and assessed the situation.

Two men stood on the porch.

From what Jack could see, someone was moving around inside. He couldn't see Anne or the vice president. He assumed the man moving around inside was guarding the two hostages.

Declan held up three fingers.

Jack nodded.

Declan gestured to Mack, who carried one of the AR-15 rifles. He motioned for Mack to cover them.

Mack moved to a better position, dropped to the ground and pointed his rifle at the men on the porch.

Cole held up the C-4 explosives and indicated the van.

Declan nodded and pointed to his watch, then held up five fingers, giving Cole five minutes to set the charges and give them time to get in position.

Which left Mack, Mustang, Declan, CJ and Jack to get in, take down the bad guys and rescue Anne and the vice president.

They circled the house and came at it from the back, where the trees and brush grew closer to the structure.

Jack prayed they were doing the right thing by going on the offensive versus attempting a trade. Either way, someone was going to die that day. And he hoped it wasn't going to be Anne or the vice president of the United States.

Chapter Fourteen

Anne slowly worked her way into the corner with the old wooden crate. Two of her three captors had stepped out of the house, leaving only one to watch over her and the vice president.

The man inside was the guy who'd been watching the rear of the van as they raced out of DC. Now, he looked like he was bored, and paced the floor.

Every time he turned away from her, Anne pushed herself backward, sliding on her bottom toward the crate. When he spun and paced back in her direction, she froze.

Finally, she made it to the crate. She rubbed the tape across the rough corner of the wooden crate. One by one, she could feel she was tearing through the layers of tape until the last piece ripped and she was able to pull her wrists free.

Her captor spun and walked toward her.

Anne held her breath, afraid the man had noticed she'd moved and was coming to ask her why.

But then, he seemed to change his mind, as if he was too preoccupied by something else, and he stepped out the door.

Quickly, while he was out of the house, she peeled the tape off her ankles, leaving a piece across the top to fool the assassins into thinking she was still bound.

The three men all entered the house together.

"Time's running out," Tully said. He hit Redial on his cell phone and punched the speaker button.

The phone rang and rang, finally going to Jack's voice mail.

Tully growled low in his chest. "I've decided. I'm shooting the girl first." He punched the end button and glared at Anne. "Guess he wasn't that interested if he's willing to let you go first." He raised his pistol and aimed it at Anne's head.

"I'm going outside." The man who'd been pacing stepped out of the house. The other shrugged and joined him.

Which left Terrence with his gun still pointing at Anne's head.

"Why do you suppose your boyfriend didn't answer his phone?"

"How do I know?" Anne said. "He might be in a dead zone."

"I can tell you who is going to be in a dead zone."

"Don't." The vice president spoke up. "Don't shoot her. If someone has to go first, let it be me."

"Sorry, dude," Tully said with an evil smile. "You're our ticket out of here alive. Once we have our defector, we'll need leverage. You're a big-ticket item that will buy us a chopper out of this." His smile turned to a sneer. "No, the lady is expendable. You're not."

Anne bunched her muscles. With Tully staring at her, she didn't stand much of a chance of getting away, but she'd be damned if she sat still and waited for a bullet to blow through her head.

Just as she was about to throw herself at him, an explosion shook the little house. Sheetrock crumbled and fell from the ceiling. Part of the tin roof flew off, exposing the inside of the building to laden skies.

Tully dropped to the floor, cursing. "What the hell was that?"

As he staggered to his feet, Anne took the opportunity she needed and threw herself into him, hitting him like a football linebacker. Since he didn't have his balance, yet, he fell backward, landing hard on his back. His gun hit the ground and slid across the floor.

The sound of shots being fired outside made Anne duck automatically.

When her captor reached for his weapon, Anne beat him to it and kicked it out of range. He grabbed her ankle and pulled hard.

Anne twisted but fell to her knees. She kicked and kicked again, but his grip was too strong. Then she turned and aimed her kicks at his face, catching him in the nose. He yelped, let go of her ankle and pressed his hand to his face.

Anne crawled across the floor and reached for the gun.

"Drop it or I'll shoot the vice president," someone said behind her.

Anne rolled to her back, the gun in her hand aimed at the door.

The man who'd been in the van's passenger seat during their ride stood leaning heavily on the doorframe, blood dripping from a wound to his left shoulder. He held a pistol in his right hand, aimed at the vice president.

"Don't shoot him. I'll drop it," she called out, setting the gun on the floor beside her.

The wounded man shifted his aim to her. "I should have killed you first."

Anne refused to close her eyes. Refused to show her fear. If the man was going to shoot her, he would have to look her in the eye, knowing he was a bastard.

The sharp report of gunfire sounded.

Anne waited for the impact, the pain and the bleeding.

When none of that came to pass, she touched a hand to her chest and watched as the man holding the gun on her dropped to the floor.

Jack stepped into the doorframe, a handgun gripped in his fist. His gaze swept the room. When it landed on Anne, the tension seemed to melt from his body. "Anne."

A movement out of the corner of her eye made Anne turn away from the best thing that ever happened to her.

Tully was scrambling across the floor, toward the gun the dead man had dropped.

Anne swept the weapon she'd dropped from the floor, sat up and pulled the trigger. The kick surprised her. But her aim was true.

Tully dropped where he was and lay still.

Jack collected the guns from the floor and stuck them into his pockets. Then he went to Anne and drew her to her feet and into his arms. "I didn't know what I would find. I'm so glad I found you alive."

She captured his face between her palms and kissed him hard. "Hold that thought." Then she broke free of his embrace and dropped to her knees beside the vice president. "Sir, are you all right?" She removed the tape from around his wrists while Jack freed his ankles.

"Yes." The VP laughed, the sound cracking. "I am now." He sat up and rubbed the raw skin on his wrist. "And I have you to thank for that."

At that moment, Declan entered the little house. "We took care of the guy out front." He and Jack helped the vice president to his feet and out onto the porch.

Arnold drove the SUV up to the house and ushered the vice president into the front passenger seat as Anne and Jack walked down off the porch, hand in hand.

"You don't know glad I was to see you," Anne said. "How in the world did you find us?"

"Your earbud had a GPS tracker in it."

"But the driver tossed it from the van back on the main highway."

Jack grinned. "And they lost us. But we have our secret weapon." He tipped his head toward Arnold. "Charlie's butler is a man of many talents. He had a drone and an arsenal in the back of the SUV. The drone we used to locate the white van, and the weapons…well you know the outcome of that."

A woman wearing a black leather jacket and matching pants approached them. Her long auburn hair fell down around her shoulders like a fiery curtain. "Anne Bellamy," she said and held out her hand.

Anne stared at the hand. "I know that voice."

"I'm CJ Grainger, former Trinity operative."

Anne took the hand and pulled the woman close, frowning. "You show up now? After all we've been through?"

CJ nodded. "I'm sorry. Had I shown up earlier, I'd be dead, and these guys would still be active in the White House. Trinity is down three operatives."

"Make that four," Declan corrected. "Gus caught the one who set off the explosives in the West Wing."

Anne let go of CJ's hand, the frown easing. "Forgive me if I'm not so grateful. It's been a tough day."

CJ smiled and touched Anne's arm. "I'm sorry I brought you into it, but I had to have someone on the inside to look out for the others." She nodded toward the vice president. "If I thought you would have survived a trade, I would have done it in a heartbeat. But I know how Trinity works. They don't leave witnesses."

"What are you going to do, now that we know who you are and what you look like?" Jack asked.

CJ shrugged. "I guess I'm going to have to reengage. I can't disappear completely. Trinity will never leave me alone as long as it's still in existence."

"Then you'll help us bring Trinity down?" Declan asked.

CJ nodded. "It's good to know I won't have to do it alone."

"Come on," Declan said. "We need to get the VP back to DC before they mobilize the military."

Two F-35 fighter planes flew overhead.

Mack laughed. "Too late."

"I'm sure they scrambled as soon as the explosion went off in the West Wing," Cole said. "And I'll bet the president was hustled out of the White House onto the Marine One helicopter and taken to Andrews and Air Force One."

A larger airplane flew overhead.

All eyes turned to the sky.

Jack chuckled. "Good call, Cole. That's Air Force One." He handed his cell phone to Anne. "You better call your boss and let him know you're all right and you have the vice president with you."

Anne did just that, thankful that she was able to report the good news. Things could have turned out a lot different had Jack not given her that earbud and if Arnold hadn't brought along a drone. She hadn't known how lucky she was going to be when that man on a motorcycle appeared outside a bar in DC to whisk her away to safety.

When she was done with the call, she reported to Declan. "They're sending a helicopter out to pick up the vice president. We're about to be bombarded with federal investigators, county sheriff, state police and every other law enforcement agency in the area." She turned to CJ. "Now would be a good time to disappear."

CJ nodded. "I'll meet up with you soon."

"Come to the Halverson estate," Declan said. "Charlie will want to meet you."

CJ smiled. "I look forward to it. She's filling a big pair of shoes her husband left behind. John Halverson was a good man with good intentions. I'm glad to see she's carrying on with his legacy." She drew in a deep breath. "Thank you all for helping me smoke out the trouble in the White House." CJ gave a mock salute, turned on her black bootheels and vanished into the woods.

Anne slipped her arm around her hero and leaned into him. "I guess we can't leave yet, can we?" She sighed. "It's been a long day."

"And it will be a lot longer before we get back to Charlie's." He hugged her close. "But I'm okay with that. As long as you're here with me."

"Same."

The day slipped into evening. A helicopter arrived, landing in a field near the small farmhouse. The president had armed the helicopter with a press secretary. A slew of law enforcement personnel came, questioned and went. And the reporters…they swarmed to the location almost as quickly as the agents.

The press secretary fielded all the questions and reassured the country that the president and vice president were well, and on their way back to DC. It would be business as usual in the White House come Monday morning. No, it wasn't a foreign terrorist attack, but a homegrown terrorist strike. No mention was made of Trinity.

Anne was okay with that. She didn't want the bad guys to get all the attention. And with Declan's Defenders on to them, it was only a matter of time before they were neutralized.

When they got back to the Halverson estate, it was close to midnight.

Charlie met them at the front entrance and hugged every one of them. Carl had food prepared in the kitchen. Everyone ate in silence, promising to debrief in the morning.

Anne ducked into the shower, rinsing off the dust and grime from the explosion and the abandoned farmhouse. Standing in front of the mirror, she tallied the new bruises and counted herself lucky that bruises were all she'd acquired.

She entered her bedroom and stood at the door in the T-shirt she'd been using as a nightgown. How many days had it been since she'd first met Jack? It hadn't been many, but it seemed like a lifetime.

And though she'd spent the past eight hours with him, she couldn't wait to see him again. Leaving her room, she went to the one next door and knocked lightly.

The door opened immediately. Jack took her hand and drew her through. He'd had his shower before her, and his hair was still wet. He looked so good and strong it made her heart swell.

"I wish I'd known all I had to do was get attacked to meet a man like you, Jack Snow. I would have done it years ago."

"Years ago, it might not have been me."

"Good point. I'm glad I wasn't attacked until recently. And I'm even more grateful my hero turned out to be you."

He tipped her chin up and stared down into her eyes. "If I recall correctly, you're my hero. Seems you shot a man to save my life."

She shrugged. "If I hadn't shot him, you would have."

"I don't know. I was so glad to see you I didn't see him going for that gun."

"We make a good team." She leaned up on her toes and linked her hands behind his head, bringing his face down to hers. "Enough talk about heroes. I'm more interest in making love with you."

"Yes, ma'am. That's a much better use of our time."

Epilogue

Jack sat at the conference table in the war room below John Halverson's study, having slept in until eight o'clock. Anne sat beside him, holding his hand beneath the table. All was better with the world, but not quite good enough.

Yes, he had the woman of his dreams beside him. She was well and alive after a frightening attempt by Trinity to kill her. Which brought him to the conclusion something had to be done about Trinity.

Declan stood at the end of the conference table, a cup of coffee in his hand. He looked tired, like all of them felt. "I've been trying to figure out what the vaccination deaths in Syria had to do with the explosion in the West Wing," he said. "We learned this morning that Waylon Pharmaceuticals completed a sale of one of its divisions this morning. It happens to be the one doing the research on the nanotechnology-based cancer vaccination. If sanctions had been voted in, that sale would not have taken place. Maybe it's adding one plus one and coming up with three, but we think the explosion delayed implementing sanctions long enough to complete the sale. We think they only wanted to delay a decision on imposing Russian sanctions. At the same time it gave Trinity the cover they needed to kidnap the vice president and Anne so they could lure CJ out of hiding."

"Seems like a lot of trouble for those two goals," Jack said.

"The sale netted close to a billion dollars," Declan said.

Mustang and Gus emitted low whistles.

"That might be worth disrupting an NSC meeting," Jack admitted.

"That brings us to why we're all here this morning." Declan took a deep breath and continued, "Though I never had the pleasure of meeting John Halverson, I feel as though I've gotten to know him through the people whose lives he touched and the work he was doing to bring down a mafia-like organization that has the potential to rot our great country from the inside out."

Jack nodded, his lips pressing together.

"You all know Jasmine, aka Jane Doe, a former member of Trinity." He nodded toward Jasmine, who sat beside Gus at the conference table. "And most of you got to meet the latest addition to our little team yesterday at a little farmhouse in the Virginia countryside." He waved a hand toward the auburn-haired woman who stood near the door.

She had politely refused to take a seat, as if being in an enclosed room made her nervous.

"CJ is with us because she wants the same thing we do. The destruction of Trinity. We've managed to eliminate some of the operatives, but there will always be more where they came from, as long as the organization remains intact."

"We need to cut off the head of the snake," Jack said.

Declan nodded. "In order to effect change, we have to neutralize their leadership. We hope that between CJ and Jasmine we can learn more about the inner workings of Trinity so that we can find the leader of the organization and take him down."

Charlie sat at the other end of the table, her hands folded together on the surface. "My husband died trying to do what you all are about to undertake. I hope you succeed where he did not. And I pray you all survive the effort. If anyone feels they've done enough and want out, now's the time to go. No hard feelings. I will understand and stand by your decision."

Declan raised his eyebrows. "Anyone want out?"

As one, the men of Declan's Defenders responded with a resounding, "Hell no."

"Okay then," Declan clapped his hands together. "Let's make it happen."

He turned to CJ. "You've put yourself at risk by joining forces with us. You need someone to have your back and look out for you."

CJ shook her head. "I don't need a bodyguard, if that's what you're suggesting."

"I'm not suggesting that," Declan said. "Cole is more like the eyes in the back of your head, an extension of your abilities."

CJ frowned. "Cole?" She looked around the room at the men. "Which one of you is Cole?"

Cole lifted a hand.

She snorted. "Again, I don't need a babysitter or bodyguard. I've managed to survive on my own for over a year since I left Trinity. If I have someone following me around, that leaves me even more exposed."

Cole lifted his shoulders. "It's your choice. But it helps to have another set of eyes watching your back. We've been a team for a long time. Each man on this team has saved my life at least once, and I've saved theirs."

"I'll think about it," CJ said. "And if I agree to this arrangement, it will be on my terms. For now, I've got work to do to figure out who the leader is of Trinity. Thank you for inviting me to come here today. It is nice to know I'm not alone." She turned and started for the stairs leading out of the basement. She'd only gone three steps when she turned back. "Cole, I'll be in touch."

"Do you need my phone number?" he asked.

"No need. I'll find you," she said confidently and left.

Jack chuckled at the look of irritation on Cole's face. "Cole, I suspect you will have your hands full with that one."

Cole's brow creased. "I suspect you're correct in that assumption." He drew in a deep breath and let it out. "Well, let's get this party started.

* * * * *

COMING SOON!

We really hope you enjoyed reading this book. If you're looking for more romance, be sure to head to the shops when new books are available on

Thursday 9th January

To see which titles are coming soon, please visit

millsandboon.co.uk/nextmonth

JOIN US ON SOCIAL MEDIA!

Stay up to date with our latest releases, author news and gossip, special offers and discounts, and all the behind-the-scenes action from Mills & Boon...

 millsandboon

 millsandboonuk

 millsandboon

It might just be true love...

MILLS & BOON

THE HEART OF ROMANCE

A ROMANCE FOR EVERY KIND OF READER

MODERN

Prepare to be swept off your feet by sophisticated, sexy and seductive heroes, in some of the world's most glamourous and romantic locations, where power and passion collide.
8 stories per month.

HISTORICAL

Escape with historical heroes from time gone by. Whether your passion is for wicked Regency Rakes, muscled Vikings or rugged Highlanders, awaken the romance of the past.
6 stories per month.

MEDICAL

Set your pulse racing with dedicated, delectable doctors in the high-pressure world of medicine, where emotions run high and passion, comfort and love are the best medicine.
6 stories per month.

True Love

Celebrate true love with tender stories of heartfelt romance, from the rush of falling in love to the joy a new baby can bring, and a focus on the emotional heart of a relationship.
8 stories per month.

Desire

Indulge in secrets and scandal, intense drama and plenty of sizzling hot action with powerful and passionate heroes who have it all: wealth, status, good looks…everything but the right woman.
6 stories per month.

HEROES

Experience all the excitement of a gripping thriller, with an intense romance at its heart. Resourceful, true-to-life women and strong, fearless men face danger and desire - a killer combination!
8 stories per month.

DARE

Sensual love stories featuring smart, sassy heroines you'd want as a best friend, and compelling intense heroes who are worthy of them.
4 stories per month.

To see which titles are coming soon, please visit

millsandboon.co.uk/nextmonth

MILLS & BOON
MEDICAL
Pulse-Racing Passion

Set your pulse racing with dedicated, delectable doctors in the high-pressure world of medicine, where emotions run high and passion, comfort and love are the best medicine.

MILLS & BOON
True Love
Romance from the Heart

Celebrate true love with tender stories of
heartfelt romance, from the rush of falling
in love to the joy a new baby can bring,
and a focus on the emotional
heart of a relationship.

MILLS & BOON
Desire

Indulge in secrets and scandal, intense drama and plenty of sizzling hot action with powerful and passionate heroes who have it all: wealth, status, good looks… everything but the right woman.

MILLS & BOON

HISTORICAL

Awaken the romance of the past

Escape with historical heroes from time gone by. Whether your passion is for wicked Regency Rakes, muscled Viking warriors or rugged Highlanders, indulge your fantasies and awaken the romance of the past.

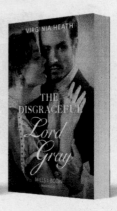

LET'S TALK
Romance

For exclusive extracts, competitions
and special offers, find us online:

- [f] facebook.com/millsandboon
- [twitter] @MillsandBoon
- [instagram] @MillsandBoonUK

Get in touch on 01413 063232

For all the latest titles coming soon, visit
millsandboon.co.uk/nextmonth